SISTERS OF THE REVOLUTION

A FEMINIST SPECULATIVE FICTION ANTHOLOGY

EDITED BY
ANN AND JEFF VANDERMEER

Sisters of the Revolution: A Feminist Speculative Fiction Anthology
edited by Ann and Jeff VanderMeer
editorial assistants: Tessa Kum and Dominik Parisien

ISBN: 9781629630359
Library of Congress Control Number: 2014908072

Sisters of the Revolution: A Feminist Speculative Fiction Anthology © PM Press 2015
Collection, introduction and story notes ©2015 by VanderMeer Creative

This is a work of collected fiction. All events portrayed in this book are fictitious, and any resemblance to real people or events is purely coincidental.
All rights reserved, including the right to reproduce this book or portions thereof in any form without the express permission of the publisher.

PM Press
P.O. Box 23912
Oakland, CA 94623
www.pmpress.org

Cover: Josh MacPhee/AntumbraDesign.org
Interior Design: Adam Jury

10 9 8 7 6 5

"The Forbidden Words of Margaret A." by L. Timmel Duchamp. © 1980. First published in *Pulphouse: The Hardback Magazine No.8*. Reprinted by permission of the author.

"My Flannel Knickers" by Leonora Carrington. © 1988. First published in *The Seventh Horse and Other Tales* (Dutton Adult). Reprinted by permission of the author's estate.

"The Mothers of Shark Island" by Kit Reed. © 1998. First published in *Weird Women, Wired Women* (Wesleyan). Reprinted by permission of the author.

"The Palm Tree Bandit" by Nnedi Okorafor. © 2000. First published in *Strange Horizons*. Reprinted by permission of the author.

"The Grammarian's Five Daughters" by Eleanor Arnason. © 1999. First published in *Realms of Fantasy*. Reprinted by permission of the author.

"And Salome Danced" by Kelley Eskridge. © 1994. First published in *Little Deaths* (Dell). Reprinted by permission of the author.

"The Perfect Married Woman" by Angélica Gorodischer. © 1992. First published in *Secret Weavers*. Reprinted by permission of the author.

"The Glass Bottle Trick" by Nalo Hopkinson. © 2000. First published in *Whispers from the Cotton Tree Root: Caribbean Fabulist Fiction* (Invisible Cities Press). Reprinted by permission of the author.

"Their Mother's Tears: The Fourth Letter" by Leena Krohn. © 2004. First published in *Tainaron* (Prime Books). Reprinted by permission of the author.

"The Screwfly Solution" by James Tiptree, Jr. © 1977. First published in *Analog*. Reprinted by permission of the author's estate.

"Seven Losses of *na Re*" by Rose Lemberg. © 2012. First published in *Daily Science Fiction*. Reprinted by permission of the author.

"The Evening the Morning and the Night" by Octavia E. Butler. © 1987. First published in *Omni Magazine*. Reprinted by permission of the author's estate.

"The Sleep of Plants" by Anne Richter. © 1967. Originally published in *Tenants*, 1967. Translated by Edward Gauvin. Reprinted by permission of the translator.

"The Men Who Live in Trees" by Kelly Barnhill. © 2008. First published in *Postscripts 15*. Reprinted by permission of the author.

"Tales from the Breast" by Hiromi Goto. © 1995. First published in *absinthe* (Winter 1995). Reprinted by permission of the author.

"The Fall River Axe Murders" by Angela Carter. © 1981. Reproduced by permission of The Estate of Angela Carter c/o Rogers, Coleridge & White Ltd., 20 Powis Mews, London W11 1JN.

"Love and Sex Among the Invertebrates" by Pat Murphy. © 1990. First published in *Alien Sex*. Reprinted by permission of the author.

"When It Changed" by Joanna Russ. © 1972. First published in *Again, Dangerous Visions*, ed. Harlan Ellison. Reprinted by permission of the author's estate.

"The Woman Who Thought She Was a Planet" by Vandana Singh. © 2003. First published in *Trampoline* (Small Beer Press). Reprinted by permission of the author.

"Gestella" by Susan Palwick. © 2001. First published in *Starlight 3* (2001) Tor Books. Reprinted by permission of the author.

"Boys" by Carol Emshwiller. © 2003. First published in *SCIFICTION*. Reprinted by permission of the author.

"Stable Strategies for Middle Management" by Eileen Gunn. © 1988. First published in *Asimov's June 1988*. Reprinted by permission of the author.

"Northern Chess" by Tanith Lee. © 1979. First published in *Women as Demons*. Reprinted by permission of the author.

"Aunts" by Karin Tidbeck. © 2011. First published in *ODD 2011* and reprinted in Karin Tidbeck's *Jagannath* (Cheeky Frawg Books). Reprinted by permission of the author.

"Sur" by Ursula K. Le Guin. © 1982. First published in *The New Yorker*. Reprinted by permission of the author.

"Fears" by Pamela Sargent. © 1984. First published in *Light Years and Dark* (Berkely Books). Reprinted by permission of the author.

"Detours on the Way to Nothing" by Rachel Swirsky. © 2008. First published in *Weird Tales*. Reprinted by permission of the author.

"Thirteen Ways of Looking at Space/Time" by Catherynne M. Valente. © 2010. First published in *Clarkesworld, Issue #47, August 2010*. Reprinted by permission of the author.

"Home by the Sea" by Élisabeth Vonarburg. © 1985. First published in *Tesseracts 1*. Reprinted by permission of the author.

Contents

Acknowledgments

The editors would like to thank Jef Smith for the vision to conceive of this project. Also thanks to Jef for coming to us with this project, for overseeing it, and for skillfully handing the story permissions. Thanks to all the good people at PM Press for publishing it. Special and heartfelt thanks to all the contributors to the Kickstarter project, especially the writer Marcus Ewert who was right there with us in the online trenches drumming up support and additional monies during the final hours of the Kickstarter deadline.

Additional thanks to Tessa Kum and Dominik Parisien who joined us on this adventure as editorial assistants, who continue to assist us in navigating the oceans of various slush piles, offer suggestions and opinions, and act as sounding boards for our outlandish ideas.

A book like this cannot exist without the writers and their wonderful stories. We thank not only those writers whose work you find in these pages, but all the writers who continue to write despite daunting obstacles and an ever-changing and sometimes unwelcoming publishing landscape. Thanks as well to all the people who support the work: agents, estates, family, partners, friends, readers, and fans. Thanks for giving feminist writers not just a room of their own but an entire world.

Introduction

Some anthologies are canon-defining. Others are treasuries or compendiums, baggy and vast. Still others, like *Sisters of the Revolution*, serve as a contribution to an ongoing conversation. For decades, editors have put forward anthologies that capture the pulse of feminist speculative fiction. Each time, the task becomes more difficult, as more material comes to light that was underappreciated when published and more enters the English language through translation—a kind of time travel occurs whereby suddenly the full outlines of an impulse or a prior period become clearer.

Our contribution to the conversation includes the great flowering of feminist speculative fiction in the late 1960s through the 1970s, which created the foundation for the wonderful wealth and diversity of such fiction in the present day. The entry into the field of so many amazing writers at once transformed science fiction and fantasy forever. The ways in which these women—Sheldon, Russ, and many others—entered into a conversation with the science fiction community also changed reader perceptions. They helped to usher in a creative space that allowed more women to consider writing science fiction. It is no surprise that this period of flowering coincided roughly with the flourishing of the New Wave literary movement because the New Wave created its own unique space by championing experimentation and literary values. Feminist speculative fiction and New Wave science fiction often shared similar interests and curiosities, and in the subset of their convergence represented something truly new and different.

The two decades thereafter represent a period in which competing impulses sought to push differing views of what science fiction could be: a kind of retrenchment and conservativism measured against an attempt to build on the triumphs of the 1970s. The rise of a predominantly U.S.-based humanism was perhaps too moderate to be considered particularly progressive or conservative, while the infusion of cyberpunk allowed some women writers additional freedom but otherwise, at least initially, could not be considered a space for creation of feminist fiction. These are all interesting contradictions that exist in a time period prior to both the rise of third-wave feminism in the SF community and what seems to us a current renaissance in feminist speculative fiction.

Usually, as anthologists, we keep a distance of at least a decade when acquiring reprinted stories. In this case, too, a robust trilogy of Tiptree Award anthologies, web-based publications, and other sources have contributed to a sense of the present being well-charted. For this reason, although we have included a sampling of interesting stories from the aughts, we have not conducted a formal and rigorous review of that period—nor, frankly, could an anthology of this size accommodate the results of such a review. Adding to our caution is the sense of how feminist speculative fiction, in addition to speaking to the world, often constitutes a conversation within its own ranks—a reevaluation and repositioning that acknowledges what went before, sometimes to lift up and sometimes to repudiate.

Indeed, this phenomenon—this discussion—goes beyond the world of speculative fiction. A perfect anthology of feminist fiction would probably consist of over a million words pulled from both the ranks of science fiction & fantasy and mainstream realism. Not only would such an anthology fully recognize and document the true complexity of influence and kinship but also result in further intersectionality—what is invisible to one side of the divide would suddenly be not just visible but in focus. (Some sense of what we mean can be gleaned from the anthology *Surrealist Women*, which exists in the transitional space between genre and mainstream and collects a radical subset of surrealism that speaks to direct political activism.)

For all of these reasons, we present this anthology as a kind of primer that adds as its unique element a partial reconciliation of "genre" and "mainstream" writers while also adding some writers not typically present in prior anthologies of this type. We have also arranged the contents of *Sisters of the Revolution* with an eye toward how the stories speak to one another rather than chronological order.

We think of this anthology—the research, the thought behind it, and the actual publication—as a journey of discovery not complete within these pages. Every reader, we hope, will find some writer or story with which they were not previously familiar—*and* feel deeply some lack that needs to be remedied in the future, by some other anthology. We welcome discussion and criticism of *Sisters of the Revolution* as a means of further rendering visible what is invisible—just as we will continue to use our general anthologies as a means of further cataloguing the wealth of feminist fiction published in the past and in the present day.

This anthology, then, is really the first in a series of new explorations— the beginning volume of something bigger and even more diverse and rich. In a perfect world, *Sisters of the Revolution* would be followed by several more volumes, each edited by someone different, with a profoundly different perspective, and thus each time reflect a different take on issues of literary quality, approach, and point of view.

Here, however, is our current contribution to the conversation, which we hope will delight, challenge, and interest you. It has already opened new horizons for us as editors.

—*Ann and Jeff VanderMeer, January 2015*

L. TIMMEL DUCHAMP

The Forbidden Words of Margaret A.

L. Timmel Duchamp is an American writer, editor, and publisher. Her short fiction has been published in *Asimov's Science Fiction*, *Pulphouse*, and a variety of anthologies such as *Full Spectrum*. In addition to her own writing of both fiction and essays, she runs Aqueduct Press, providing a platform for the voices of others. "The Forbidden Words of Margaret A." tells the story of a woman imprisoned for speaking out. Her words are considered so dangerous that the government adopted a constitutional amendment limiting free speech, specifically the words of Margaret A. The story was first published in *Pulphouse: The Hardback Magazine* in 1980.

[N.B.: The following report was prepared exclusively for the use of the National Journalists' Association for the Recovery of Freedom of the Press by a journalist who visited Margaret A. sometime within the last two years. JATROF requests that this report not be duplicated in any form or removed from JATROF offices and that the information provided herein be used with care and discretion.]

Introduction

Despite the once-monthly photo-ops the Bureau of Prisons allows, firsthand uncensored accounts of contact with Margaret A. are rare. The following, though it falls short of providing a verbatim transcript of Margaret A.'s words, attempts to offer a fuller, more faithful rendition of one journalist's contact with Margaret A. than has ever been publicly available. This reporter's awareness of the importance to her colleagues of such an account, as well as of the danger disseminating it to a broader audience would entail for all involved in such an effort, has prompted the deposit of this document with JATROF.

Before describing my contact with Margaret A., I wish to emphasize the constraints that circumscribed my meeting with Margaret A. Members of JATROF will necessarily be familiar with the techniques the government uses to manipulate public perception of data. Certainly I, going into the photo-op, considered myself well up on the government's tricks for controlling the contextualization of issues it cares about. Yet I personally can vouch for the insidious danger of momentarily forgetting the obvious: where Margaret A. is concerned, much slips our attention, keeping us from thinking clearly and objectively about the concrete facts before our eyes. I'm not sure *how* this happens, only that it does. The information we have about Margaret A. somehow does not get added up correctly. I urge readers, then, not to skip over details already known to you, but to take my iteration of them as a caveat, as a reminder, as an aid to thought about an issue that for all its publicity remains remarkably murky. I thus ask my readers' indulgence for excursions into what may seem unnecessary political analysis and speculation. I know of no other way to wrest the framing of my own contact with Margaret A. out of the murk and mire that tends to obscure any objective recounting of facts relating to the Margaret A. situation.

To start with the most obvious: Margaret A. permits only one photo-op a month. The Bureau of Prisons (naturally pleased to make known to the public that the government can't be held responsible for thwarting the public's desire for "news" of her) doesn't allow Margaret A. to choose from among those who apply, and in this way effectively controls media access to her. The Justice Department of course would prefer to dispense with these sessions altogether, but when at the beginning of Margaret A.'s imprisonment they denied all media access to her, their attempt to sink Margaret A.'s existence into oblivion instead provoked a constant stream of speculation and protest that threatened them with not only the repeal of the Margaret A. Amendment,[1] but even worse a resurgence of the massive civil disorder that

---

1 The amendment is officially titled "The Limited Censorship for the Preservation of National Security Act," but since the only object the amendment sets out to accomplish is the total obliteration of Margaret A.'s words, surely calling it "The Margaret A. Amendment" places the emphasis where it belongs. And though their name for it is better than the anti–free speech activists' calling it the "Save America Amendment," I don't particularly hold with the free speech activists calling it the "Anti–Free Speech Amendment," either. The amendment wouldn't exist if it weren't for Margaret A. herself. And both the anti–free speech and free speech activists seem to forget that.

had prompted her incarceration and silencing in the first place. Beyond obliterating Margaret A.'s words, I would argue that the government places the next highest priority on preventing the public from perceiving Margaret A. as a martyr. That consideration alone can explain why the conditions of her special detention in a quonset hut within the confines of the Vandenberg Air Force Base is such that no person or organization—not even the ACLU or Amnesty International, organizations which deplore the fact of her confinement—can reasonably fault them. The responsible journalist undertaking coverage of Margaret A. must bear these points in mind.

Selection for and Constraints upon the Photo-op

I've been fascinated by Margaret A. my entire adult life. I entered journalism precisely so that I'd have a shot at firsthand contact with Margaret A. and have systematically pursued that goal with every career step I've taken. (I realize that to most members of JATROF it is the implications of the Margaret A. Amendment and not Margaret A. herself that matter most. The words of Margaret A., however, for a brief time radically changed the way I looked at the world. Since losing it, I've never ceased to yearn for another glimpse of that perspective. Surely of all people, JATROF members can most appreciate that such a goal does not belie the ideals of the profession?) Accordingly, I studied the Bureau of Prison's selection preferences, worked my way into suitable employment, then patiently and quietly waited. I lived carefully. I kept myself as clean of suspect contacts as any working journalist can. When finally I was selected for one of Margaret A.'s photo-ops, *Circumspection has been rewarded*, I congratulated myself. Reading and rereading the official notification I felt as though I had just been granted a visa to the promised land.

   An invitation to meet Simon Bartkey had been attached to the visa, however. Naturally this disconcerted me: an in-person screening by a Justice Department official is quite a bit different from scrutiny of one's record. But I told myself that I'd been "good" for so long that my professionalism would see me over this last hurdle. Thus one month before I was due to meet Margaret A., my producer and I flew to Washington and met this Justice Department official assigned to what they call "the Margaret A. Desk"—an "expert" who cheerfully admitted to me that he had never heard or read any of Margaret A.'s words himself. I couldn't help but be impressed with the show they run, for the BOP has it down to a fine procedure designed to ensure that everything flows with the smoothness and predictability of a high-precision robotics assembly. Besides providing an opportunity for one last intense scrutiny of the journalists they've selected, to their way of thinking, a visit to

Simon Bartkey sets both the context journalists are supposed to use as well as the ground rules.

Let me note in reminder here that Simon Bartkey has survived three different administrations precisely because he's accounted an "expert" on "the Margaret A. situation." Since the early days of the Margaret A. phenomenon, each administration has fretted about the public's continuing fascination with her. Bartkey expressed it to me in these words: "This ongoing interest in her defies all logic. Her words—except for a few hoarded tapes, newspapers, and *samizdat*—have been completely obliterated, and the general public has no access to them, and certainly no memory of them. The American public has never been known to have such a long attention span, especially with regard to someone not continually providing ever new and more exciting grist to the media's mill. Why then do people still want to *see* her? Why haven't they forgotten about her?" (How it must gall politicians that Margaret A. has for the last fifteen years enjoyed higher name recognition than each sitting U.S. president during the same period.)

Though it was the most important event in my life (I was nineteen when it happened), I can't remember any of her words. I was too young and naive at the time to hold onto newspapers and the ad hoc ephemera figures like Margaret A. invariably generate, and certainly never dreamed that her words could be expunged from the internet. And like most people I never dreamed a person's *words* could become illegal. One hears rumors, of course, of old tapes and newspapers carefully hoarded—yet though I've faithfully tracked every such rumor I've caught wind of, none has ever panned out.

For perhaps twenty of the fifty-five minutes I spent being briefed by him, Bartkey took great pleasure in explaining to me how the passage of time will ultimately eclipse Margaret A.'s public visibility. Leaning back in his padded red leather chair, he announced that the generational gap more than anything will finally isolate those who persist in "worshiping at the altar of her memory." His fingers stroking his mandala-embossed bottle green silk tie, he insisted that Margaret A. can mean nothing to college kids since they were only infants at the time of the Margaret A. phenomenon. He might conceivably prove to be correct, but I don't think so. The kids I've talked to find the Margaret A. Amendment so irrational and egregious an offense against the spirit of the First Amendment that they're suspicious of everything they've been told about it. If no records of Margaret A.'s words still exist, neither do reports of the massive civil disorder their civics textbooks use to justify the passage of the amendment. The *fact* of the Margaret A. Amendment, I think, has got to fill them with suspicions of a cover-up. Consider: the only images they connect with Margaret A. now are the videos and photos taken of this U.S. citizen living in internal exile, a small middle-aged woman dwarfed by the deadly array of missiles and radar installations and armed guards surrounding her. I doubt that young people are capable of understanding that anyone's particular use of language in and of itself could have threatened the dissolution of every form of government in this country (much less provoked the unprecedented, draconian measure of a constitutional amendment to silence it). I've seen the cynical skepticism in their faces when older people talk about those days. How could any arrangement of words on paper, any speech recorded on tape be as dangerous as government authorities say? And why ban no one else's speech, not even that of her most persistent followers (except of course when quoting her)? Young people don't believe it was that simple. When I listen to their questions I've no trouble deducing that they believe the government is covering up the past existence of a powerful, armed, revolutionary force. They consider the amendment not only a cover-up but also a gratuitous measure designed to curtail speech and establish a precedent for future curtailments.

Needless to say I didn't share such observations with Bartkey any more than I offered him my theory that the new generation is not only suspicious of a cover-up but also dying for a taste of forbidden fruit. While doubting its vaunted potency (or toxicity, depending on one's point of view), they long to know what it is they're being denied. This sounds paradoxical, I admit, yet I've heard a note of resentment in their expressions of skepticism. The dangers of Margaret A.'s words may not be apparent to them, but by labeling the fruit forbidden—fruit their *elders* had been privileged enough to taste— the amendment—which they consider a cover-up to start with—is provoking resentment in this new generation coming of age. Rather than developing amnesia about Margaret A., the new generation may well become obsessed with her. I wouldn't be at all surprised if new, bizarrely conceived cults didn't spring up around the Margaret A. phenomenon.

I don't mean to imply that I'd approve of bizarre cults and obsession with forbidden fruit. The fascination I and others like me feel for Margaret A. is probably as incomprehensible to the young people as the government's fear of her words. (Our diverse reactions to Margaret A. seem to mark a Great Divide for most people in this country.) But something about the very *idea* of her—regardless of whether *her* ideas are ever remembered—the very *idea* of this woman shut up in the middle of a high-security military base because her words are so potent . . . well, that *idea* does something to almost everyone in this country, including those who find the Margaret A. phenomenon frightening (excepting, of course, the anti-free speech activists). If I were Bartkey I'd be worried: it's only a matter of time before the Margaret A. Amendment is repealed. And if Margaret A. is still alive then, things could *explode*.

Margaret A.'s "Security"

All we ever saw of Vandenberg proper was its perimeter fence and gate. Even before we'd handed our documents to the guard three people wearing nonmilitary uniforms converged on us and ordered us out onto the tarmac. One of them then climbed into the van and turned it around and drove it somewhere away from the base; the other two ordered us into a tiny quonset hut off to the right. This confused me, and I wondered whether there had been a foul-up of some sort, or whether the background checks had turned up something about one of us the Justice Department didn't like. (I even wondered—fleetingly—whether for some convoluted tangle of reasoning they kept her there in *that* quonset hut, outside the base's perimeter fence).

What followed in the hut rendered my speculations absurd. Bartkey had of course made us sign an agreement that we be subject to strip searches, that we use *their* equipment, that all materials be edited by them, and that we submit to an extensive debriefing afterwards. I bore with the strip and body cavity search without protest, of course, since journalists are commonly obliged to endure such ordeals when entering prisons to interview inmates. (I'm sure colleagues reading this know well how one attempts in such circumstances to put the best face on an awkward, uncomfortable situation.) Nor did I protest the condition that the Bureau of Prisons be granted total editorial power, for obviously the Margaret A. Amendment might otherwise be flouted. But their insistence that we use their equipment—*that* bothered me for some elusive, hard-to-define reason. Bartkey had explained that their equipment ran without an audio track, and since no one by the terms of the Margaret A. Amendment could legally tape her speech, my conscious reaction focused on that obvious point. But as I was putting my thoroughly searched clothing back on I learned that I could not take my shoulder bag in with me and realized that not only would there be no audio tape, there would also be no pen and paper, no laptop computer, no note-taking beyond what I could force into my own, ill-trained mental memory. Naturally I protested. (I am, after all, the woman who relies on her computer to tell her such things as when to have her hair cut, what time to eat lunch, and how long it has been since she's written to her mother.) It made no difference, of course. I was told that if I didn't choose to abide by the rules they'd take the producer and crew in without me.

After hitting us with another review of all the ground rules, they herded us into the windowless back of a Bureau of Prisons van and drove us an undisclosed turn-filled and occasionally bumpy distance. The van stopped for at least a minute three separate times before pausing briefly—as at a stop sign, or to allow the opening of a gate (I deduce the latter to have been the case)—and then moved for only two or three seconds before coming to a final halt. When the engine cut it only then came to me in a breathless rush that what I had been waiting for nearly half my life was actually about to happen. Margaret A.'s words are forbidden. Yet for a few minutes *I* would have the privilege of hearing her speak. Only "trivialities," granted, they would allow nothing else—guards with radio receivers in their ears would be on hand to see to that: but still the words would be Margaret A.'s, and even her "trivial" speech, I felt certain, would be potent, perhaps electrifying. And I believed that on hearing Margaret A. speak I would remember all that I had forgotten about those days and would understand all that had eluded me throughout my adult life.

This pre-contact assumption derived not from romantic dreams cherished from adolescence, but from what I had (discreetly) gleaned about the conditions of Margaret A.'s life of exile. I had learned, for instance, from a highly reliable source formerly employed by the Justice Department, that the Bureau of Prisons had run through more than five hundred guards on the Margaret A. assignment, all of whom had quit the BOP subsequent to their removal from duty at Vandenberg.[2] What continues to strike me as extraordinary about this is that the guards assigned to Margaret A. have always been—and continue to be—taken exclusively from a pool of guards experienced in working in high security federal facilities. Each guard previous to meeting Margaret A. is warned that all speech uttered within the confines of the prisoner's quarters will be recorded and examined. Before starting duty at Vandenberg each newly assigned guard undergoes rigorous orientation sessions and while on duty at Vandenberg reports for debriefing after each personal contact with Margaret A. Yet no guard has ever gone on to a new assignment following contact with Margaret A. Another curious statistic: those assigned to audio surveillance of the words spoken in Margaret A's quarters inevitably "burn out" during their second year of monitoring Margaret A.[3] Consider: Margaret A. is forbidden ever to speak about anything remotely "political." How then can she so consistently corrupt every guard who has had contact with her and disturb every monitor who has

---

2 Though the Margaret A. Amendment does not prevent the press from reporting on publicly available facts on the conditions of Margaret A.'s internment, the major U.S. media have never addressed the startling data about the high turnover in personnel assigned to Margaret A.'s "security." Considering how fascinated the public would be by such details, what then keeps the media from openly reporting such facts? Surely the entire industry cannot share the reason I had for hiding my interest in Margaret A.!

3 It is a matter of public record that in one case a monitor incurred a felony charge for attempting to smuggle a Margaret A. surveillance tape out of the listening post at Vandenberg.

been assigned to listen to her (non-political: "trivial") conversation?[4] It never occurred to me to wonder what Bartkey meant when he said that all conversation with Margaret A. must be confined to "trivial, non-political smalltalk." He and other officials outlined for me the sorts of questions I must avoid raising—ranging from the subject of her confinement, the Margaret A. Amendment, and the public's continuing interest in her to the specific points upon which, according to rumor (since documents no longer exist, one can refer only to rumors or fuzzy nodes of memory), she had spoken during the brief initial period of the Margaret A. phenomenon. I think I assumed that the corruption of her guards had more to do with Margaret A.'s personality than with the "smalltalk" she exchanged with them (never mind that this did not address the monitors' eventual termination by the Justice Department). Thus as our escort opened the back door of the van I told myself I would now be meeting not only the most remarkable woman in history, but probably the most charismatic, charming, and possibly lovable person I would ever have the pleasure of knowing.

Contact with Margaret A.

While my producer and crew unloaded the BOP's equipment from the van, I—the one who would later be asked on camera for my observations and impressions of Margaret A. and the conditions of her confinement— strolled around the tiny compound surrounding the quonset hut I presumed to be Margaret A's. At first I noticed little beyond the intimidating array of surveillance and security equipment and personnel. The twenty-foot steel fence reinforced with coils of razor wire and topped by a glass-enclosed, visibly armed guard post cut off view of everything outside the compound but the hot dry sky. (The southern California sun in that environment seemed stiflingly oppressive.) Several hard-eyed uniformed men carried automatic rifles. Was it possible they thought we might attempt to spring Margaret A.? My consciousness of the eyes of such heavily armed men watching, waiting, anticipating shook me, making me feel like a jeweler opening a safe for robbers, fearful that with one "false" (i.e., misunderstood) move I would be a dead woman. Because Margaret A. is not a "criminal," one forgets how dangerous the government has decreed her to be.

Yet the weight of this official presence exerted a subtle impression on me I became aware of only when speaking with Margaret A. The uniforms, the

---

4 Informed readers may recall that the Bureau of Prisons initially eliminated all verbal communication between Margaret A. and all other human beings until the Supreme Court ruled that such treatment would virtually amount to perpetual solitary confinement, a condition they judged unnecessary for obtaining reasonable observance of the Margaret A. Amendment.

guard post, the overdetermined regulation of our every movement and intention conspired to make me forget that Margaret A. has never been arraigned
before a judge much less stood trial before a jury.[5] Thus when I spotted the
scraggly little plants growing in a corner of the compound's coarse dry sand,
I instantly perceived an "extra privilege" generously bestowed upon her by
the BOP, and so rather than enter Margaret A's quarters with a sense of how
intolerably oppressive it would be to live immured within that steel fence
and guard post with its glaring mirrored windows and menacing weaponry
permanently looming over one, I thought how fortunate Margaret A. was to
be able to walk around outside in her compound and "garden."

I make this confession in order to illustrate how subtly perception can be
influenced. It strikes me as counterintuitive that the heavy presence of surveillance and security would contribute to a perception of the legitimacy of
Margaret A.'s incarceration, yet apparently the Justice Department's experts
believe this, for that oppressive presence is never censored out of videos and
stills, while a variety of small concessions that Margaret A. has won for herself have *never* survived the BOP's editing.[6]

Thus when I entered Margaret A.'s quarters accompanied by three guards
and a crew grumbling over the antiquation of the BOP's equipment, I looked
at all I saw through peculiarly biased eyes. It's *not so bad*, I thought as I sur-
veyed the first of Margaret A.'s two rooms. I noted the cushions softening
the pair of wooden chairs with arms and was astonished at the beautifully
executed woven tapestry covering a large part of the ugly toothpaste-green
wall. *It's not as bad as most jail cells, and is certainly far better than the
underground dungeons in which most political prisoners are kept*, I reminded
myself. It occurs to me in retrospect that probably I wanted to believe that
Margaret A. lived in tolerable circumstances so that the chances of her hanging on as long as it took to achieve her release would be reasonably high. And
so before Margaret A. came into the room, my eyes fixed on the small computer sitting on a table near the outer door while I mused on how because of
that computer Margaret A.'s way with words (and perhaps even her words

---

5 Technically speaking, Margaret A. is considered to be held in preventive detention—since
   even one word spoken by her would legally constitute a violation of the Margaret A. Amendment. Though constitutional scholars have argued that the amendment itself violates the letter
   and spirit of the Constitution, its solidly reactionary composition ensures the U.S. Supreme
   Court's ongoing adherence to its earlier ruling against judicial interference in security measures undertaken jointly by the Executive and Legislative branches. For a brief summary of
   the legal peculiarities of Margaret A.'s incarceration, see the ACLU's pamphlet *When the Rule
   of Law Breaks Down: The Executive, Judicial and Legislative Conspiracy Against Margaret A.*
6 Anxious to preserve a clean profile that would stand up to Justice Department scrutiny, I did
   not make the inquiries that would have informed me of these concessions before observing
   them with my own eyes. For a complete log of Margaret A.'s battles for these concessions,
   contact Elissa Muntemba, her principle attorney, through the California branch of the ACLU.

themselves) might have a chance to survive, and rejoiced that in spite of the Margaret A. Amendment the BOP weren't sitting as heavily and oppressively on her as they do on most political prisoners.

But then Margaret A. appeared and for a few crazy, breath-stopped instants time seemed to halt. After greeting the guards (whose faces, I mechanically noted, were suddenly suffused with wariness and unease) she simply stood there, a small stout figure in gray cotton shirt and pants, looking us over—as though we were there for her inspection rather than the other way around. I struggled a few agonized seconds with frog in my throat and glanced at the guards in expectation of an introduction. But looking back at Margaret A. I realized the absurdity of my expectation and scorned myself for taking the guards as hosts at an arranged soiree. Though I had no idea of it at the time (and I still don't quite understand how it worked), that moment marked the loss of a professional persona that had hitherto sustained me throughout my career in journalism.

My producer finally took the initiative: "Allow me to introduce myself," she began as, holding out her hand, she advanced towards Margaret A. Margaret A., however, shattered this moment of returned normalcy, for she ignored the proffered hand and commented that creating a facade of social conventions would cost more than she herself could afford—even if we felt ourselves able to afford it.[7]

Margaret A.'s pointed refusal to shake hands opened another edge to an already tense situation and jolted me into a more sharply critical attitude towards everyone and everything around us. It was at that moment, for instance, that I understood to the marrow of my bones a bit of what this detention must mean to Margaret A. Previously I had felt an abstract outrage at her silencing and detention. But at that moment when Margaret A. mentioned the cost of social pretense, I *felt* the reality of her situation, I dimly sensed how apparently small things could exert enormous pressure on even a psyche strong enough to withstand the weight of official oppression such as that so constantly forced upon Margaret A.'s senses.

Having learned from my producer's embarrassment, I merely smiled and nodded at Margaret A. when my producer introduced me to her. Still Margaret A. rebuffed me, for the slight twitch of her lip (not amusement, for

---

7 My reconstruction of our conversation with Margaret A. is, unfortunately, not verbatim. Neither my producer, myself, nor the crew have eidetic memories (and if any of us had it is likely the Justice Department would have discovered such a fact and consequently disqualified us from contact with Margaret A.), and thus all recollections of Margaret A.'s words have come through a concerted effort by the group to remember, though even this was hampered by our separation from one another for the first forty-eight hours following contact with Margaret A. in accordance with the Justice Department's debriefing procedures.

her ancient, frozen eyes remained just as wintry and distant) made me feel foolish enough to blush (thus making me feel even more foolish). The rebuff and my reaction to the rebuff in turn provoked first resentment in me—for a moment I felt indignant at her lack of manners—and then, seconds later, abashment as it occurred to me that Margaret A. must take me for a lackey of the system that had specially targeted her.[8]

The crew did not bother with introductions, they simply set up shop and began taping with the equipment they despised. The producer reminded them to shoot without regard to our conversation, to scan everything in the two rooms of the hut and to be sure to get a shot of Margaret A.'s "garden." And then she nodded at me, as though to remind me that I should be getting on with my part of the affair, too. I looked back at Margaret A. and frantically tried to recall the first question I had planned to ask her. But nothing came, my mind had gone blank. Panicking, I blurted out the first question that popped into my head: "Who cuts your hair for you?"

Margaret A. flicked her eyebrows at me and snapped something to the effect that that was the sort of information the BOP would gladly provide me with. My entire body went hot with embarrassment; glancing around me I caught my producer frowning and the guards rolling their eyes. It was at that moment that it hit me: though Margaret A. is black, all the guards I had seen at Vandenberg were, to a person, white. (I suspect it was a combination of my noticing Margaret A.'s closely clipped woolly hair and my thinking that I could not imagine any of the guards whom I had seen—male or female—ever cutting it.) I wished then I could ask her if her guards had always been exclusively white and if so how she felt about it. But apart from worrying about such a question getting me into trouble with the BOP, I felt uneasy about what *she* might make of it. I had no idea whether the racial identity of one's guards would be relevant to someone to whom the imposition of any guards at all was an outrage . . . Fortunately, I recalled one of the questions I had prepared, a question I thought could pass as personal (and thus "trivial"). "Has incarceration and the prospect of a lifetime of incarceration changed the way you feel about yourself as a human being?" I queried. Margaret A. looked straight into my face, as though to check out where that question was coming from. Uneasily I glanced around at the guards; though they paid no

---

8 For most of the time of my contact with Margaret A. I wondered, disillusioned, how I could have spent so many years yearning after a meeting that was proving to be such a letdown. Margaret A. did not stir me, she did not even warm me toward her, personally: I not only found it impossible to pity her—even though for the entire time I was in her quarters I glimpsed out of the corner of my eye the steel fence confronting the room's single window and constantly snatched covert glances at the rifles the guards carried—but several times felt a flare of resentment toward her. Margaret A. has not a charismatic cell in her body.

special attention to me (thus indicating the question to be acceptable, since if it weren't, the BOP official monitoring the interview would have passed orders to the guards through the receivers I could see in their ears), I felt menaced by their presence as I hadn't before. *This room*, I thought, *is too small for so many bodies and machines.*

I wish I could remember Margaret A.'s exact words, but all I can give you is a paraphrase. She started with a humorous comment to the effect that one thing her incarceration had done for her was to indicate to her how seriously the official world took her, and consequently to make her take herself more seriously than she ever had before. Imagine, she said with a wry not quite sardonic smile, I was a nobody until people I had never met started listening to me. Just imagine if people took every word that came out of your mouth as seriously as they take every bullet fired out of a gun. I don't think I ever took myself particularly seriously until after they threw me into solitary confinement and allowed me no human contact. They told me it was dangerous for anyone to hear anything that came out of my mouth. For several weeks I lived in the kind of quarantine you might dream up for the deadliest most mysteriously contagious of diseases. I was sure I was going to crack up. But can you imagine the ego trip? Can you imagine your own words being considered that potent? This official reaction made me a uniquely powerful person, accorded powers never attributed to any other mortal in history that I've ever heard of. At first I couldn't take it that seriously myself. Later I got a little scared. But how could I go on being scared when there's not a chance in a million I'll ever be allowed to speak freely again?

This reply took me entirely by surprise. I had expected her to talk about her bitterness at the unfairness of the system in denying her due process (which she could have done, I think, without necessarily mentioning the issue overtly), at the wreck her incarceration had made of her life, at the horror of her exile from friends and family. But because of the point of view she presented to me I comprehended afresh how extraordinary the apparatus of her silencing is—that so many resources are being devoted solely to that end, and how much credit, actually, they grant her by finding it necessary to protect themselves against the words of a woman who had been a simple mother and middle school teacher without party affiliation or organization (for the formation of an organization around her came only in the last three months of her freedom). The Margaret A. phenomenon had streaked into brief exhilarating visibility like the first unexpected flash of lightning crackling across a late evening summer sky.

I asked her next about whether she missed her daughter (who it is well known moved to New Zealand subsequent to her mother's incarceration) and other family members. Margaret A. took several minutes in replying to this question, and such was the complexity and unexpectedness of her answer that I'm afraid I cannot vouch for the accuracy of my paraphrase.[9]

The press and other institutions in our world consider privacy to be a privilege, Margaret A. began, a luxury, not something that must be respected of every person. Human society would not be the same were privacy not considered a privilege. Consequently my daughter has paid a price for my frankness, a price exacted by the press and other institutions. I imagine most people would lay that exaction at my door, working on the assumption that my frankness invited disregard of my own—and therefore my daughter's— privacy. But for me the issue with regard to my daughter becomes a matter of whether or not my self-censorship would have been worth the maintenance of the status quo of my daughter's life before my words attracted widespread attention. Could I have afforded to pay the price silence would have exacted from me? It is always a question of determining what lies at stake in what one does or omits to do. Undoubtedly you yourself forfeited your privacy for the sake of taking part in this photo-opportunity. I wonder if you have weighed the price of your presence here today.

It surprised me that the guards did not interrupt this speech. I myself heard some of the subversion in her reply even as she spoke, for I felt certain she was referring not only to the strip and body cavity search I had had to submit to, but to the years of keeping myself "clean" of suspect contact, years of playing the game as primly as Simon Bartkey himself could wish. I suppose her fingering of the press "and other institutions" and her references to "human society" and "our world" sounded vague enough to the monitors that they didn't grasp exactly what she was talking about. But the expression on my producer's face indicated that she had no trouble understanding Margaret A.'s words, and that like me she considered them subversive, too.

We then had only three minutes left of the allotted time. Though the camera crew had been in and out of the other room, Margaret A. and I had so far remained in the one room. I asked her if she would show me her other room while answering my last question or two. She flicked her eyebrows at me as though to deride my asking her permission while my colleagues had been aiming their cameras at whatever caught their fancy, but then gestured me to go before her through the doorless opening in the wall. I had wanted to ask her about her gardening, but when I saw the books piled on the lino- leum floor beside the patchwork quilt-covered mattress I instead asked her if she read much and if so what. She said she read only poetry. I snatched a

---

9 And indeed our joint attempt to reconstitute this answer resulted in such acrimony that in the end we finally agreed not to discuss it at all.

quick look at the book on the top of the pile and caught only the name Audre Lorde. Aware of time ticking away, I glanced at the bath fixtures taking up most of the room and wondered at the water standing in the tub. I asked her about it, and she said she was allowed one bath a day and that her bathwater was all that she had to water her garden with. Frantically, aware that only half a minute remained, I asked her how she spent her time. Instead of answering, she told me that there was no point in her attempting to reply to that question, that she knew the guard would stop her before she had finished since they had done so on the two other occasions she had attempted to answer it.

A guard then told us our time was up. This was a moment I hadn't prepared for, hadn't begun to imagine. My entire adult life had been leading up to this time spent with Margaret A., and suddenly it was over, never to be repeated, and I would never again have a chance to listen to this woman whose words are forbidden.[10] I stood frozen for a few seconds, staring at Margaret A. as though to memorize the moment. Looking at her impassive, aging face I realized that our meeting meant nothing to her, that we were only another media crew come to gape, that after a few months she probably would not even remember me, that surely she considered all the media people to be faceless robots playing the game that mattered not at all to her (except, perhaps, as insurance against excessively abusive treatment by her captors).

During the next few hours I slipped into a dull numbness, mechanically answering questions and listening to the debriefers' comments, hardly caring about what might follow. I had done the only thing I'd ever aspired to, and now it was over. The interview had been a disappointment and the future looked like an anticlimax—gray, dull, pointless.

The Question of Professional Standards

After the debriefing while en route to the L.A. affiliate that had lent us the van, we joked for ten or fifteen minutes about the transparency of the BOP's "deprogramming" techniques. For me at least it had been an ordeal (and I suspect it had been for them, too, since we found it necessary to joke about it). Not only did I need to keep my wits about me in order to give the debriefers the answers they considered correct, but I just as importantly needed to preserve intact (as much as that was possible) the memory of Margaret A.'s words. All of us apparently passed muster without a glitch, for our producer assured us that the official in charge had let her know that he was pleased with our debriefings.

---

10 The BOP has a rule that prohibits media personnel from more than one contact with Margaret A.

When finally the joking had worked some of our unease out of our systems, the crew began complaining about the pointlessness of the whole Margaret A. situation. They said they couldn't see what the big deal with Margaret A. was, they contended that the Margaret A. phenomenon must always have been super media hype since there certainly wasn't anything special about Margaret A herself. They groused, too, about the BOP's deleting their shots of the computer, the "garden," and the partially filled tub and saucepan for bailing: touches that they had hoped would lift our photo-op above the mediocrity of those that had come before (when of course ours would show as almost identical to the others). Those particular cuts perplexed and perturbed them more than the BOP's cutting every shot in which Margaret A's lips were moving. They joked about the BOP's fear of lip-readers, then segued into a discussion of the government's paranoia in making such a big deal of a woman who was, they thought, simply boring.

After several minutes of listening in silence to the discussion, our producer disagreed. "The woman's a destroyer," she declared. "She's so damned sure of herself and her opinions that only the most confident people would be capable of resisting her subversive incursions."

The crew snickered. "What subversion?" they wanted to know. "You mean her refusing to shake your hand?"

The producer ignored this below-the-belt crack. "Those idiots monitoring us were too slow to catch what she was talking about. When she used the word 'institutions,' only an idiot would have missed what she was referring to." That counter-put-down shut them up—and ended the conversation about Margaret A.

No one seemed to notice my silence. And in fact I managed to talk to Elissa Muntemba and even negotiated my own on-camera interview without raising suspicions of myself.[11] The suspicions came later, in other contexts—after I had begun to ask of myself the very questions I believe Margaret A. in my place would insist upon asking. Not surprisingly the producer of the Margaret A. photo-op was the one to suss me out. *She* knew, even if no one else could trace it back to Margaret A.'s "influence." "You're a Margaret A. convert," she accused me. "She really got to you, didn't she?" I so detested the language she used that without considering the consequences I launched into a discussion of our complicity with the BOP. But she cut me off before I'd even finished my second sentence. "Professional journalists can't afford

---

11 It would have been pointless for me to have attempted serious analysis in the interview, for anything "radical" would have been cut, or the interview itself trashed. I consciously chose to toe the invisible line because I considered it important to get out the word that Margaret A. still had juice in her, that far from having been discouraged by her silencing, rather she took it as sign that she was on the right track.

to be susceptible to subversion," she scathed at me. *Does she understand at all what she's saying when she uses the word "afford"?* I wondered. Of course she didn't, for she went on to berate me for being a gullible fool, for betraying professional standards—and then told me I was terminated. "I won't mention this in your file," she said—but later I wondered what such an assurance could mean since she obviously made a point of sabotaging every attempt I made at securing new employment within the mainstream media industry.[12]

This question of professional standards is a troubling one for JATROF members. The position of journalists like my producer amounts to using the government's contextualizations for determining the parameters of objectivity. Any consideration of facts outside of such contextualizations then become acts of subversion. If my contact with Margaret A. has taught me anything, it is that the self-censorship demanded of journalists is too high a price for me to pay. The question then becomes one of how the journalist reconciles the ideals of the profession with the practice my producer insists reflects "professional standards."

Summary

First, for those concerned with Margaret A. herself, I can attest that her incarceration and silencing have not demoralized or disempowered her. On the contrary, the government's efforts to obliterate her words seem to have strengthened rather than weakened the particular, distinctive articulation that characterizes Margaret A.'s speech. Should the day come when the government cannot resist public opposition to the Margaret A. Amendment (for as time passes, more and more people will consider the government's fear of Margaret A. either hysterical paranoia or a cynical excuse for its tight control of the news media), Margaret A. will likely be prepared.

Second, my experience doing a Margaret A. photo-op suggests that as journalists we need to question the conflation of the government's contextualization with the parameters of objectivity and professional standards, especially when such contextualization demands the obliteration not only of words but even of facts. Journalists currently work in an environment in which their asking even so simple a question as "What would the harm be in showing a shot of a bathtub?" can lead to charges of a subversive lack of objectivity. The "limited censorship" of Margaret A.'s words has thus demonstrably altered journalists' definition of objectivity and professional standards. JATROF members, I feel certain, will want to consider the cost to

---

12 Like other journalists who have crossed the invisible line of self-censorship, I now face the
   choice of changing professions or emigrating, and choose the latter.

themselves and the profession of their continued submission to the principle of self-censorship the Margaret A. Amendment has so clearly spawned.

Following the Margaret A. photo-op, I learned at the cost of my career—thinking that since I had achieved my goal of interviewing Margaret A. I need no longer be "careful"—that this censorship process extends beyond the coverage of Margaret A. into other areas. It is perhaps ironic that the initial trajectory of my career was dictated by the determination to achieve one single goal, that of personally interviewing Margaret A., when in fact that very interview has called into question the price I paid to achieve it. That price included not only a loss of personal and professional integrity, but also a blinkering of my ability to see the world I live in. My meeting with Margaret A. woke me into a world I seem never to have really seen before, a world it is my mission as a journalist to expose and explore. It is my belief that Margaret A.'s words were forbidden because of their power to show us the world anew, without blinders. I may never fully share Margaret A.'s vision; I may never have a true record of Margaret A.'s words. But because of Margaret A., I now grope for the blinders that have been narrowing and dimming my vision, that I may tear them from my eyes and see a world far wider and brighter than I'd ever dreamed existed.

LEONORA CARRINGTON

My Flannel Knickers

Leonora Carrington was a famous English-born surrealist painter and writer who lived in Mexico for most of her life. "From a very young age," Carrington has said, "I used to have very strange experiences with all sorts of ghosts [and] visions." Although her art has overshadowed her fiction, Carrington's odd stories have been important to many writers, including Angela Carter. Collections include *The Seventh Horse* and *The Oval Lady*. "My Flannel Knickers" brings to mind how women, creative women in particular, are marginalized and hidden, yet, in another context, put on display at the same time for everyone to see. It was first published in *The Seventh Horse* in 1988.

Thousands of people know my flannel knickers, and though I know this may seem flirtatious, it is not. I am a saint.

The "Sainthood," I may say, was actually forced upon me. If anyone would like to avoid becoming holy, they should immediately read this entire story.

I live on an island. This island was bestowed upon me by the government when I left prison. It is not a desert island, it is a traffic island in the middle of a busy boulevard, and motors thunder past on all sides day and night.

So . . .

The flannel knickers are well known. They are hung at midday on a wire from the red green and yellow automatic lights. I wash them every day, and they have to dry in the sun.

Apart from the flannel knickers, I wear a gentleman's tweed jacket for golfing. It was given to me, and the gym shoes. No socks. Many people recoil from my undistinguished appearance, but if they have been told about me (mainly in the Tourist's Guide), they make a pilgrimage, which is quite easy.

Now I must trace the peculiar events that brought me to this condition. Once I was a great beauty and attended all sorts of cocktail-drinking, prize-giving-and-taking, artistic demonstrations and other casually hazardous gatherings organized for the purpose of people wasting other people's time. I was always in demand and my beautiful face would hang suspended over fashionable garments, smiling continually. An ardent heart, however, beat under the fashionable costumes, and this very ardent heart was like an open tap pouring quantities of hot water over anybody who asked. This wasteful process soon took its toll on my beautiful smiling face. My teeth fell out. The original structure of the face became blurred, and then began to fall away from the bones in small, ever-increasing folds. I sat and watched the process with a mixture of slighted vanity and acute depression. I was, I thought, solidly installed in my lunar plexus, within clouds of sensitive vapour.

If I happened to smile at my face in the mirror, I could objectively observe the fact that I had only three teeth left and these were beginning to decay.

Consequently I went to the dentist. Not only did he cure the three remaining teeth but he also presented me with a set of false teeth, cunningly mounted on a pink plastic chassis. When I had paid a sufficiently large quantity of my diminishing wealth, the teeth were mine and I took them home and put them into my mouth.

The Face seemed to regain some of its absolutely-irresistible-attraction, although the folds were of course still there. From the lunar plexus I arose like a hungry trout and was caught fast on the sharp barbed hook that hangs inside all once-very-beautiful faces.

A thin magnetic mist formed between myself, the face, and clear perception. This is what I saw in the mist. "Well, well. I really was beginning to petrify in that old lunar plexus. This must be me, this beautiful, smiling fully toothed creature. There I was, sitting in the dark bloodstream like a mummified foetus with no love at all. Here I am, back in the rich world, where I can palpitate again, jump up and down in the nice warm swimming pool of outflowing emotion, the more bathers the merrier. I Shall Be Enriched."

All these disastrous thoughts were multiplied and reflected in the magnetic mist. I stepped in, wearing my face, now back in the old enigmatic smile which had always turned sour in the past.

No sooner trapped than done.

Smiling horribly, I returned to the jungle of faces, each ravenously trying to eat each other.

Here I might explain the process that actually takes place in this sort of jungle. Each face is provided with greater or smaller mouths, armed with different kinds of sometimes natural teeth. (Anybody over forty and toothless should be sensible enough to be quietly knitting an original new body, instead of wasting the cosmic wool.) These teeth bar the way to a gaping throat, which disgorges whatever it swallows back into the foetid atmosphere.

The bodies over which these faces are suspended serve as ballast to the faces. As a rule they are carefully covered with colours and shapes in current "Fashion." This "fashion" is a devouring idea launched by another face snapping with insatiable hunger for money and notoriety. The bodies, in constant misery and supplication, are generally ignored and only used for ambulation of the face. As I said, for ballast.

Once, however, that I bared my new teeth I realized that something had gone wrong. For after a very short period of enigmatic smiling, the smile became quite stiff and fixed, while the face slipped away from its bonish mooring, leaving me clutching desperately to a soft grey mask over a barely animated body.

The strange part of the affair now reveals itself. The jungle faces, instead of recoiling in horror from what I already knew to be a sad sight, approached me and started to beg me for something which I thought I had not got.

Puzzled, I consulted my Friend, a Greek.

He said: "They think you have woven a complete face and body and are in constant possession of excess amounts of cosmic wool. Even if this is not so, the very fact that you know about the wool makes them determined to steal it."

"I have wasted practically the entire fleece," I told him. "And if anybody steals from me now I shall die and disintegrate to tally."

"Three-dimensional life," said the Greek, "is formed by attitude. Since by their attitude they expect you to have quantities of wool, you are three-dimensionally forced to 'Sainthood' which means you must spin your body and teach the faces how to spin theirs."

The compassionate words of the Greek filled me with fear. I am a face myself. The quickest way of retiring from social Face-eating competition occurred to me when I attacked a policeman with my strong steel umbrella. I was quickly put into prison, where I spent months of health-giving meditation and compulsive exercise.

My exemplary conduct in prison moved the Head Wardress to an excess of bounty, and that is how the Government presented me with the island, after a small and distinguished ceremony in a remote corner of the Protestant Cemetery.

So here I am on the island with all sizes of mechanical artifacts whizzing by in every conceivable direction, even overhead.

Here I sit.

KIT REED

The Mothers of Shark Island

Kit Reed is an American author of novels and short fiction. She is a resident writer at Wesleyan University. Many of her stories are considered feminist science fiction and have been published in such diverse places such as the *Magazine of Fantasy and Science Fiction*, the *Yale Review* and the *Kenyon Review*. She is a Guggenheim Fellow and her stories have been nominated for the James Tiptree, Jr. Award. "The Mothers of Shark Island" gives a different perspective on motherhood, and the story's publication in *Weird Women, Wired Women* in 1998 was not without controversy.

On Shark Island the prisoners are free to roam the courtyard in the daytime; the walls are high and the cliffs precipitous. Nobody escapes the Chateau D'If. The few mothers who try are never seen again—devoured by the schools of sharks running in the channel or dashed to bits on the rocks at the bottom of the cliff.

By night guards stalk the parapets, but from moment to moment the faces of our captors change. Are we them? Are they us? Sometimes it is we who march in yellow arm bands—slit-eyed trustys, collaborating in our own imprisonment; we patrol with leather billy clubs, grimly keeping the other women in line. Unless we are the prisoners here, watching the guards from the high windows of our cells.

Who are the kept and which are the keepers among us here?

Who decided we had to be interned? When did we start being in the way?

Was it our randy, eager sons who sent us up the river—no remaining witnesses to prove that they are not self-invented?—*Mom, you look tired.* Or was it our images, the new improved version—our daughters with their sweet, judgmental smiles?—*Mom, let me do that.*

Is it in our stars that we are jailed, or is it something we did? Oh God, is it something we said that they can't forgive? This is the terror and the mystery. Why they put us here after everything we did for them.

Years of snowboots and school clothes and lopsided cakes and guitar lessons and tuition and trying not to pressure them—all that effort and now our young run free and use up the earth while we are here.

By day we pace and ponder. By night we tap out messages on the pipes. *Cour—age— Syl—vi—a. Per—se—ver—ence— Maud. Rev—o—lution is near. New— prisoner— in— Block— Nine.*

Unlike pneumonia, motherhood is an irreversible condition.

Like Edmund Dante I am close to the woman in the cell next to mine although I've never seen her face. We whisper through the crevice I have made over months—no. Over years, gouging the stone with my fingernails, swallowing the dust and moving the bed in front of the hole to hide any trace. The unknown mother and I keep each other afloat, although like our guards she is not always the same person.

How many women have come and gone in the cell next to mine? We do not exchange names. But at night we spin stories for comfort and number the details; what we did for them on our way to the Chateau D'If. How cruel it is that we are here.

But our work lives are over. What else would they do with us? The nights are colder than the stones we sleep on and we are lonely here and sad, and if we could go back and change the past so that our children still needed us, we would not do it.

We wouldn't know how. We had to let them grow up. Now they intern us for war crimes.

Friends! We were never the color our children have painted us. We are innocent, I tell you. Innocent!

The prisoners speak.

REBA: I am the Mother Goddess, dammit. What I says goes.

I was a prisoner in my own house, trampled flat by the three of them: Gerard, who made me a mother in the first place. Demanding little Gerry.

Whiny June. All day on the road, you know the story, practice, lessons, car pool, late nights folding wash and when I finally crawled into bed big Gerard's hands on me, yeah fine, but spring up at dawn to unload that dishwasher, drop kids at school on the way to work, where the men in my law firm—men with *wives* at home to do these things for them leapfrogged my spent body on their way to the top.

And Gerard! He said, "Starched shirts wouldn't be such a problem if you'd only quit your job." Said, "This house is a mess!"

After a while you just get tired. Too wasted ever to make partner. I quit my job. At first it was almost nice. Plenty of time to clean and wash and fold and cook and make the house nice and drop the kids at school, art lessons, team practice, plenty of time to lie down with Gerard who said, "That's more like it, you smell so *good*." I liked having his nose in my neck.

But when I got up again I was the one who had to change the bed and iron the sheets and drive the children everywhere while their hair got glossy and their teeth white and strong and they? What did they think of me? They said, "What do you know? You're just a Mom."

Life conceived as endless stovepipe, or is it Mobius strip. He wants less starch in his shirts, more in the collars; kids say cut my sandwiches cut this way, cut them *that way*. All that and when you walk down the street your children hang back so people will think they're walking with somebody else; he puts his nose in your hair and says "I can't understand it, we used to have so much to talk about."

Crying makes you ugly so you drop a hundred bucks on Victoria's Secret but he isn't interested in yours; instead of punching your shoulder and climbing on he rolls away and goes to sleep, smelling of somebody else.

Right, I got depressed, I did Pillsbury Ice Box Cookie rolls straight from the fridge, gnawing while I ironed in front of the soaps. Gerard complained— kids squabbling, trash piling up because the more you do around the house the more there is to do, try perpetual mess machine and here's the man who made you a mother in the first place going, "Is that all you have to do with your time?"

Talk about couldn't go on like that. Talk about couldn't stand another day. Oh I did everything they wanted okay, fixed this, bought the kids clothes for that, but I schemed. A few purchases and I was ready.

One day I was miserable, reviled.

They came down the next morning and I was wearing the cape. "I am the mother goddess, dammit, and you are going to do what I say."

June snarled, "I didn't want cereal, I wanted Pop Tarts."

I pointed my finger and lightning came out.

Gerry whined, "Where's my Exo-skeleton T-shirt?"

Zot! He never whined again.

Gerard came in and sat down in front of his plate without even looking up from the paper. "What's to eat?"

I bopped him with my staff. He was sniveling. "Reba, I love you. What did I ever do to you?"

"Not enough!" I rose up and rumbled down on him like thunder. I gnashed my teeth and lightning struck. My family looked at me and they trembled. "I am the mother goddess, dammit. This is my kingdom now."

They fell down and worshiped me.

Didn't they pay tribute then? Presents for me, sweets; sniveling Gerard begged for my smile. I ran a taut ship: hot breakfast, wash and ironing before Gerard could leave for work, the kids vacuumed and scoured the tub; KP at night, "Nothing thawed or nuked, Gerard, something French." We ate well. When he balked I banished him to the dungeon. He tried to kite out a message to the Battered Men's shelter. I called the cops. Who'd believe a little thing like me could do things like that to a big guy like Gerard? He got ten years.

After that it was peaceable in the kingdom: sweet, smooth, with me in silks and jewels my kids worked two jobs to buy. Sympathy from Gerard's colleagues, "He made your life a living hell."

But where's the joy in ruling when your most abject subject is in jail? I retired to my chamber in a cloud of thought.

When I came out my remaining subjects were all grown up. June, working as a supermarket checker, Gerry at State U. She blamed me for not being around to fix her SATs. He barked, "Get out of the manger, Mom. I'm in love."

They made their lives, I think. They think I did.

While I was sleeping, my grown daughter Junie—*my little Junie*—picked up my staff and—ZOT, I am here.

See your mother come in the door in the green quilted coat that means she's here for another extended stay, see her smile that lovably tentative, tender smile and wonder why when we do love her, we do LOVE her, these encounters are always so hard. Psychic space. A mother who is also a mother-in-law takes up so much psychic space!

Nuclear families are built on privacy. If a nucleus can shatter, our mother's has fragmented, leaving her lost in the stars. We form our own. We are the new family here.

Is it her fault these encounters are so difficult? Ours?

She keeps coming back. We think every time: This time we'll make it different, and discover that in spite of all our best efforts, it never is. Mothers, daughters. What are these patterns that determine our mutual future? When and how were they set? Is this loving estrangement really her fault? Mine? In spite of our best efforts she and I bring all the old freight to these meetings. What she said to us when we were little, what we failed to say to her.

And spoil ourselves wondering about the old patterns that it's too late to change. Why it was always so hard.

Is it in our stars that it is this way, or is it in our genetic encoding? Do our daughters see their own futures coming in the door with the same loving, fearful eyes?

I whisper these questions to the woman in the cell next to mine but she is sick now, too sick to really answer.

When she speaks, it is to the eternal chain of mothers and daughters, leading from forever into eternity. I lay my ear flat against the chink in the wall, holding my breath so I can hear.

All we can do is love them, she says.

The prisoners speak.

MARILYN: You think I asked for this? Dingy cell with flaking stone walls and no comfort at night but the message that come in on toxic pipes? Lead pipes bring water and carry waste out of our cells—lead, when we had all the old paint stripped from our houses just to keep our babies safe. Morse code. *H-E-L-L-).*

I gave my children everything. Vitamins to keep them strong and lessons to make them accomplished and flash cards to get them smart, and if I brooded over their progress, who wouldn't? Who wouldn't be enchanted by the genetic miracle: raw material to perfect. Pliable small people, look a lot like me. Speak the same language, members of the same club. We are them, yes? No.

My fault, for failing to understand the truth.

Mothers, do not be deluded. They may be cute when they're little, follow you anywhere, do anything to please you, laugh at your jokes. You work hard to shape them, to do the right thing, but be aware. No. Be warned.

They are nothing like you.

Your children's adult lives devolve into a litany of reproaches, a dizzying transport of blame.

"You used to make me wear terrible clothes. That green T-shirt. Those hideous pink shoes."

"You asked too many questions. Always getting in my face."

Or is it: "You never listened to me."

"You made me eat mixed-up food."

We used to talk about it when we lived in the world, we daughters who were mothers of small children of our own. We talked about our mothers. We talked about it a lot. We conspired. —Not going to get like that, *we vowed. We colluded with our own daughters.* —Promise to tell us if we start getting like that. *And they vowed,* —We will, we will.

On her mother's seventieth birthday CSB accidentally washed the cake.

Contemplating her mother, EBM said: —There ought to be an island somewhere, *surrounded by sharks.*

Before our eyes, the Chateau D'If sprang into existence. We looked at it and marveled.

Remember, she was still in the world with us; the Chateau D'If was designed with her in mind, not us.

As long as she lived, we could maintain our position.

Now she is gone.

Now we are in the front ranks. And the Chateau D'if? Admit it. It was only ever a matter of time.

The prisoners speak.

ANNE: They're yours, but only for a minute.

They grow up.

You get old. Maybe the worst crime is not the atrocities you committed in the kitchen—the pudding disaster. The casserole nobody would eat.

It's not the wardrobe errors: "The other moms all wear jeans."

Nor is it the social gaffe: "Why did you have to tell them that, Mom?"

I think the unforgivable sin is getting old.

Sooner or later you are the outsider, begging your daughters to suffer your presence in her house. Slip in gratefully and try to be unobtrusive. Hope to earn your keep by doing little things around the place. Pat the sofa pillows and put them *just so.* Scour the sink and while you're at it throw out that dead plant. Do little favors and try not to make too much noise coming into a room.

"Mother, did you move my notebook? I can't find anything!"

"Nobody asked you to straighten my dresser drawers, Mom."

Don't reason with them. Don't argue. "But they're a mess!" And if she and her husband are having a fight, go sit at the top of the cellar stairs.

You become aware that they stop talking when you come into a room. One afternoon you find them waiting for you. "We've loved having you with us, Mother, but it's time to make some plans."

They tried to erase me, but I have left traces. Signs so the world will know what happened here. A hairpin in her stocking drawer. A gift painting she will be afraid to take down. When they took me I put long claw marks in one of their walnut doors.

On Shark Island there is no time off for good behavior. There are only lifers here.

The woman in the cell next to mine has died. In the night I hear feeble tapping on the pipes and I move the cot and put my mouth close to the crevice in the wall. I murmur, What is it? Are you all right in there? The sound of her harsh breathing tells me she will never be all right. She dies with her mouth pressed to the opening in the wall. Only I hear her last lament.
—All I did was love them too much.

AT THE TOMB OF THE UNKNOWN MOTHER
In the Chateau D'If the management declares a day of mourning. Matched pairs of trustys lower the coffin into the fresh place prepared for it while the mothers grieve. We never knew her name but it is clear to the women marshaled here that in her own way, she stands for all of us. She is the past, present and future generations of mothers exiled here.

The unknown mother died without betraying her origins; she died without recanting; *I did the best I could!* She died without regrets and without repenting. She died in a state of invincible ignorance, innocent of the nature of her unknown sin.

The prisoners lament.
Oh.
Oh how.
Oh how much we love her.
Oh how hard we try to keep from going where she has gone
and oh, how we conspire with our own sweet daughters.
How delicately we tread the line!

Your daughter asks. "Is it being a mother that makes you crazy?"
You have spent your life proving that you have always been the same person. Therefore you dissemble. "If I'm crazy, I was born this way."
When you are in a less vulnerable mode you usually say, "You'll be a mother some day. Then you'll see."

The prisoners speak.
SUSANNAH: One tough babe, I am, and she could reduce me to a jelly. *Not going to be like that, never going to be like that.*

Tales brought back by sailors: my daughter has a daughter of her own. In the gift packet allowed prisoners on high holidays, my daughter includes snapshots of her son and her new baby girl. They are beautiful together—my daughter and this small, new woman, her daughter, who bears my name. I look at the children's faces and I see hers. Tears come too fast to swallow. We look alike.

Shark Island is for lifers. So is motherhood.

The prisoners speak.

MELANIE: This place is rough. The stones are cold and I don't like it here. On my cot at night I try to figure out what I did that was so terrible, numbering my crimes.

Okay, I nagged them about their homework, for one. I bought them clothes they hated, which they told me later, and in spades. I made too much mixed-up food. Mushrooms. Onions. Yeugh! I gave them until the big hand reached the six to clean their plates or else.

I always said, "Why don't you go outside and play?"

I loved them, God I loved them, I still do.

I've been saving stuff. Sharp things. One of these nights, I'm going to gouge out the cement from around the bars and pull them loose and I am getting out of here. The going will be slow; I'll climb down the outside wall with bleeding toes and shredded fingertips. When I reach a point where I can swing out and avoid the rocks, I'll jump.

And if I can elude the sharks . . .

SARAH: Not me. I know a better way out. A friend who *never had children* is waiting just beyond the barrier reef. She has a skiff. If I make it, I'm going to find the people who put me here. I'm going to grab my children by the shoulders and look into their eyes . . .

REBA: And I, I am going to feign death. When the guard comes in to hold the mirror to my mouth I'll overpower her . . .

ANNE: And put on her uniform?

MARILYN: Or get work in the laundry room and hide myself in the bottom of a laundry cart!

Sunrise and moonrise race past in quick succession, a brilliant parade of time passing outside our cell windows. I look up and see new stars. I see novas burst and expire.

The future is written in their faces—the pictures my daughter sends on birthdays and holidays. Her daughter grows.

How quickly these things happen. How long our sentence here. How little time we had outside! Past and future, birthdays, Christmases, times of joy—we were only ever here.

The prisoners speak:

VAL: Since we're all, er. Getting down here, I might as well tell you, some of us have been working on a tunnel. At the signal tonight we're going out.

The devil's advocate, I say to her, You may make it because right now you are a trusty, but the rest of us can't. At night we're locked down us in the cells.

VAL: No problem. While the screws were sleeping Peggy stole the keys. She kept them long enough to get impressions; she's made duplicates. My cell. Sarah's. Reba's. Yours. Are you with me?

MELANIE/MARILYN: You bet.

ANNE: Count me in . . . I think.

REBA: Would you believe I'm standing guard tonight?

VAL: Then you can help us!

REBA: I can't help you, but I promise to look the other way.

VAL: Okay, then. Everybody. Are you with us?

God knows I am tempted, but my blood is drumming with the recurring story. There is something I know without knowing how I know.

My heart stutters and my belly trembles. I can't.

VAL: Amazing free offer and you *can't?*

Someone I care about is coming. I know it. How can I explain this without explaining it? The grief and the terror. The sense of the inevitable that gives me such hope? I am polite, but evasive. —I can't afford to leave here now.

REBA: What do you mean, you can't afford to leave? You can't afford to stay!

I tell them, Message I got. Tapped in on the pipes.

MARILYN: What do you mean, message you got?

New— prisoner— in— the— holding— pen.

I tell them because I am afraid not to tell them.

Unless I mark this with words it may disappear. —I heard it tapped out on the pipes. It's the new prisoner.

She was allowed one phone call. Instead she took the silver dollar the children provide the internees for that single phone call, and gave it to the guard, who brought the news to me.

VALERIE: —Twelve hours and we're free women! What's one new prisoner more or less?

ANNE: Twelve hours and we're out of here. What's the matter with you anyway?

MARILYN: Free women! What's the matter with you?

The mothers of shark island are offering me freedom that I can't afford to grasp. I explain as best I can: She's waiting down there, alone and scared because she's new. *They're moving her upstairs tomorrow night. A few favors and I may be able to get her into the Unknown Mother's cell.*

My heart overflows. —We can whisper at night.

REBA: All that for somebody you never met?

I do not exactly lie but I am evasive. —I only said she was a new prisoner. New in a place she vowed never to come. But even with the best of intentions—you know. *I tell them,* I never said we'd never met.

I do not add: She looks like me.

A thief cuts the heart out of his mother to sell to the caliph, who has offered him a fortune for it. He throws her body aside and puts his treasure into a box. Eager to collect the money, the thief runs too fast. He trips on a rock and falls flat. The box slips from his hands and flies open. His mother's heart rolls out. As he sits up the thief hears it crying, *Are you hurt, my son?*

Tonight the mothers of Shark Island make their break. At least they'll try. They may even make it if the island is less secure than we think. If the escaping mothers survive the jump into the deep, treacherous channel . . .

And if they can outswim the voracious sharks . . .

Even if they do make it, nothing much will change.

Motherhood isn't a job description, it's a life sentence.

Let the others dodge the sweeping searchlights and the spray of machine gun fire. Let them struggle through the icy waves and drag themselves up on the shore and let them fan out in the nation like a legion of avengers, intent on . . .

Intent on . . .

She's coming. They know it. She's at the door. Soon she'll ring the bell. Arrested by something they don't know yet, *our children quicken.*

—Lover, did you hear something?

—No, I didn't hear anything.

She goes to the door anyway/he shrugs on his bathrobe and goes to the door. Try not to let their voices sink. —Oh, it's you.

See her come in the front door in the green quilted coat that means she's here for another extended visit; see her smile that tentative, tender, heartbreakingly lovely smile and wonder why when we do love her, we do LOVE her, these encounters are always so hard.

Listen, my darlings, my colleagues, mes sembables, *past and future:*
These visits are hard, but they're all we have of each other, me and you.
And as for the future?
The future was only ever us.

Therefore I let the other escapees go, in hopes of a happy outcome, but as for me? I will spin out my story here.

Listen, there's a new prisoner in the holding chamber, and I have sent down word that there's an empty cell on the other side of mine and yes I can already hear her speak:

"Mom, for the time being can you pretend like you, like, don't know me?"

"Oh love my daughter, my past and my future."

Anything for you.

NNEDI OKORAFOR

The Palm Tree Bandit

Nnedi Okorafor is a novelist of African-based science fiction, fantasy, and magical realism for both children and adults. Born in the United States to two Nigerian immigrant parents, Nnedi is known for weaving her African culture into creative evocative settings and memorable characters. Okorafor's short stories have been published in anthologies and magazines, including *Dark Matter: Reading the Bones*, *Strange Horizons*, and *Writers of the Future Volume XVIII*. A collection of her stories, titled *Kabu Kabu*, was published by Prime Books in 2013. Her novel *Who Fears Death*, won the World Fantasy Award and was a Tiptree Honor book. She is a professor of creative writing and literature at the University of Buffalo. "The Palm Tree Bandit" perfectly encapsulates what it means to subvert often patriarchal myths and folktales. It was first published in *Strange Horizons* in 2000.

Shhh, shhh, concentrate on my voice, not the comb in your hair, okay? Goodness, your hair is so thick, though, child. Now I know you like to hear about your great-grandmother Yaya, and if you stop moving around, I'll tell you. I knew her myself, you know. Yes, I was very young, of course, about seven or eight. She was a crazy woman, bursting with life. I always wanted to be like her so badly. She had puff puff hair like a huge cotton ball and she'd comb it out till it was like a big black halo. And it was so thick that even in the wind it wouldn't move.

Most women back then wore their hair plaited or in thread wraps. You know what those are, right? Wrap bunches of hair in thread and they all stick out like a pincushion. They still wear them like that today, in all these intricate styles. You'll get to see when you visit Nigeria this Christmas. Hmm, I see you've stopped squirming. Good, now listen and listen close. Yaya sometimes wore a cloak and she'd move quieter than smoke.

In Nigeria, in Iboland, the people there lived off yam, and in good times they drank palm tree wine. Women were not allowed to climb palm trees for any reason—not to cut down leaves or to tap the sweet milky wine. You see, palm wine carried power to the first person to touch and drink it. Supposedly women would evaporate into thin air because they weren't capable of withstanding such power. Women were weak creatures and they should not be exposed to such harm. Shh, stop fidgeting. I'm not braiding your hair that tight. I thought you liked to hear a good story. Well then, behave.

Not all of the women evaporated when they climbed a palm tree, but the parents of the offender were cautioned and cleansing rituals were performed to appease the gods for her misdeed. A she-goat and a hen had to be sacrificed, and kola nut, yams, and alligator pepper were placed on shrines. The people of this village did not eat meat, and to sacrifice an animal, one had to find a goat willing to offer itself for sacrifice. You can imagine how hard that must be.

Well, there was a young woman named Yaya, your great-grandmother. Most people dismissed her as an eccentric. She was married to a young conservative man whose job was to talk sense into families who were having internal disputes. He had a respectable reputation. Everyone loved him, since he had saved marriages, friendships, and family relationships. But his woman, well, she was a different story. She wrote for the town newspaper but that wasn't the problem. Her problem was her mouth.

She'd argue with anyone who was game. And as she was smart, and she was beautiful, so all the men in the village liked to engage her in discussion. The problem was she'd mastered the art of arguing and the men would either grow infuriated or stalk away exasperated. Rumor had it that the only argument she lost was with the man she married.

Yaya was a free spirit and when she wasn't arguing, she was laughing loudly and joking with her husband. But one day Yaya was arguing with Old Man Rum Cake, the village chief elder. Cake was over a hundred years old and he liked to watch Yaya flit about the village. She both annoyed and intrigued him.

This was the reason for his comment about the glass of palm wine she was sipping: "You know women aren't even supposed to climb palm trees, let alone drink it when it is sweet," he said.

At the time, Yaya only humphed at his comment, and went on with their argument about whether garri was better than farina with stew. Nevertheless, Yaya's mind filed the comment away, to chew on later. It didn't take much to get Yaya's gears going.

That very evening, she ravished her husband into exhaustion, and while he slept his deepest sleep, she dressed and snuck out of the house. Under the mask of night, she crept toward the three palm trees that grew in the center of town, wrapped a rope around her waist and shimmied up the trunk of one of the trees. She took her knife out of her pocket and carved a circle about a foot in diameter, her people's sign for female: a moon. Then she cut three huge leaves and brought them down with her, setting them at the trunk of the tree.

The next morning was chaos. Men looked confused. Some women wailed. What was to become of their desecrated village? The chief called a town meeting—the culprit had to be located and punished. But who would do such a thing? What woman could survive such an encounter? Yaya almost died with laughter, pinching her nose and feigning several sneezes and coughs. Cake proposed that the woman who did it had most likely evaporated. "And good riddance to bad rubbish," he said.

The next week she struck again, this time tapping palm wine from one of the trees and leaving the jug at the trunk of the tree. Next to the moon she carved a heart, the sign for Erzulie, the village's Mother symbol. This time, it was mostly the men who were in an uproar. The women were quiet, some of them even smiling to themselves. A month later, Yaya struck a third time. This time, however, she almost got caught. Three men had been assigned to walk the village streets at night. For the entire month Yaya had watched them, pretending to enjoy sitting near the window reading. She thought she had adequately memorized their night watch patterns. Still, there she was in the palm tree just as one of the men came strolling up. Yaya froze, her cloak fluttering in the breeze, her hands dripping with tapped wine. Her heart was doing acrobatics. The young man looked up directly at Yaya. Then he looked away and turned around, heading back up the street, reaching into his pocket for a piece of gum. Yaya just sat there, leaning against her rope. He hadn't seen her. He'd looked right through her. She glanced at the heart she had carved in the tree next to the moon. She gasped and then giggled, a mixture of relief and awe. The carving pulsed and Yaya knew if she touched it, it would be pleasantly warm.

When she got home, there was a green jug in front of her bed. She glanced at her snoozing husband and quietly picked it up and brought it to her lips. It was the sweetest palm wine she'd ever tasted, as if only a split second ago it had dripped from the tree. She plopped into bed next to her husband, more inebriated than she'd ever been in her life.

In the morning, her husband smelled the sweetness on her and was reluctant to go to work. Later on people smelled her in the newsroom, too. Many of her coworkers bought chocolates and cakes that day to soothe a mysterious craving. They began calling the mysterious woman who could survived climbing palm trees the Palm Tree Bandit and eventually, as it always happened in villages, a story began to gel around her.

The Palm Tree Bandit was not human. She was a polluting spirit whose only reason for existing was to cause trouble. If there was a night without moon—such nights were thought to be the time of evil—she would strike. The chief, who was also the village priest, burned sacrificial leaves, hoping to appease whatever god was punishing the village with such an evil presence.

However, the women developed another story amongst themselves. The Palm Tree Bandit was a nameless wandering woman with no man or children. And she had powers. And if a woman prayed hard enough to her, she'd answer their call because she understood their problems. Legend had it that she had legs roped with muscle that could walk up a palm tree without using her hands, and her hair grew in the shape of palm leaves. Her skin was shiny from the palm oil she rubbed into it and her clothes were made of palm fibers.

Soon, Yaya realized she didn't have to keep shimmying up palm trees. One moonless night she had contemplated going out to cause some mischief but decided to snuggle against her husband instead. Nevertheless, when she woke up, she found another jug of palm wine wrapped in green fresh palm tree leaves inside her basket full of underwear. There were oily red footprints leading from the basket to the window next to it. Yaya grinned as she quickly ran to get a soapy washcloth to scrub the oil from the floor before her husband saw it. That day, the village was alive with chatter again. And the Palm Tree Bandit's mischievousness spread to other villages, kingdoms away. Instead of an uproar, it became a typical occurrence. And the palm wine tapped was as sweet as ever and the leaves grew wide and tough. Only the chief and his ensemble were upset by it anymore. Otherwise, it was just something more to argue and giggle about.

Eventually, women were allowed to climb palm trees for whatever reason. But they had to offer sacrifices to the Palm Tree Bandit first. Shrines were built honoring her and women often left her bottles of sweet fresh palm wine and coconut meat. No matter where the shrine was, when morning came, these items were always gone. So your great-grandmother was a powerful woman, yes, she was. Just as squirmy as you, girl.

My story is done, and so is your hair. Here you are, Yaya number four. Of this story, there's no more. Run along now.

ELEANOR ARNASON

The Grammarian's Five Daughters

Eleanor Arnason is an American writer. Her short fiction can be found in *New Worlds*,
The Magazine of Fantasy & Science Fiction, and *Asimov's Science Fiction Magazine*,
among others. Her latest collection is *Big Mama Stories*. Because much her work deals
with cultural and societal change, she has often been compared to Ursula K. Le Guin.
Arnason was the recipient of the first James Tiptree, Jr. Award. Her fiction has also won
the Mythopoeic Award, the Spectrum Award, and the HOMer Award. In this original
fairytale, a mother sends her five daughters off to conquer the world in their own ways.
"The Grammarian's Five Daughters" was first published in *Realms of Fantasy* in 1999.

Once there was a grammarian who lived in a great city that no longer exists, so
we don't have to name it. Although she was learned and industrious and had a
house full of books, she did not prosper. To make the situation worse, she had
five daughters. Her husband, a diligent scholar with no head for business, died
soon after the fifth daughter was born, and the grammarian had to raise them
alone. It was a struggle, but she managed to give each an adequate education,
though a dowry—essential in the grammarian's culture—was impossible. There
was no way for her daughters to marry. They would become old maids, eking
(their mother thought) a miserable living as scribes in the city market. The
grammarian fretted and worried, until the oldest daughter was fifteen years old.

Then the girl came to her mother and said, "You can't possibly support
me, along with my sisters. Give me what you can, and I'll go out and seek my
fortune. No matter what happens, you'll have one less mouth to feed."

The mother thought for a while, then produced a bag. "In here are nouns, which I consider the solid core and treasure of language. I give them to you because you're the oldest. Take them and do what you can with them."

The oldest daughter thanked her mother and kissed her sisters and trudged away, the bag of nouns on her back.

Time passed. She traveled as best she could, until she came to a country full of mist. Everything was shadowy and uncertain. The oldest daughter blundered along, never knowing exactly where she was, till she came to a place full of shadows that reminded her of houses.

A thin, distant voice cried out, "Oyez. The king of this land will give his son or daughter to whoever can dispel the mist."

The oldest daughter thought a while, then opened her bag. Out came the nouns, sharp and definite. Sky leaped up and filled the grayness overhead. Sun leaped up and lit the sky. Grass spread over the dim gray ground. Oak and elm and poplar rose from grass. House followed, along with town and castle and king.

Now, in the sunlight, the daughter was able to see people. Singing her praise, they escorted her to the castle, where the grateful king gave his eldest son to her. Of course they married and lived happily, producing many sharp and definite children.

In time they ruled the country, which acquired a new name: Thingnesse. It became famous for bright skies, vivid landscapes, and solid, clear-thinking citizens who loved best what they could touch and hold.

Now the story turns to the second daughter. Like her sister, she went to the grammarian and said, "There is no way you can support the four of us. Give me what you can, and I will go off to seek my fortune. No matter what happens, you will have one less mouth to feed."

The mother thought for a while, then produced a bag. "This contains verbs, which I consider the strength of language. I give them to you because you are my second child and the most fearless and bold. Take them and do what you can with them."

The daughter thanked her mother and kissed her sisters and trudged away, the bag of verbs on her back.

Like her older sister, the second daughter made her way as best she could, coming at last to a country of baking heat. The sun blazed in the middle of a dull blue, dusty sky. Everything she saw seemed overcome with lassitude. Honeybees, usually the busiest of creatures, rested on their hives, too stupefied to fly in search of pollen. Plowmen dozed at their plows. The oxen in front of the plows dozed as well. In the little trading towns, the traders sat in their shops, far too weary to cry their wares.

The second daughter trudged on. The bag on her back grew ever heavier and the sun beat on her head, until she could barely move or think. Finally, in a town square, she came upon a man in the embroidered tunic of a royal herald. He sat on the rim of the village fountain, one hand trailing in water.

When she came up, he stirred a bit, but was too tired to lift his head. "Oy—" he said at last, his voice whispery and slow. "The queen of this country will give—give a child in marriage to whoever can dispel this stupor."

The second daughter thought for a while, then opened her bag. Walk jumped out, then scamper and canter, run and jump and fly. Like bees, the verbs buzzed through the country. The true bees roused themselves in response. So did the country's birds, farmers, oxen, housewives, and merchants. In every town, dogs began to bark. Only the cats stayed curled up, having their own schedule for sleeping and waking.

Blow blew from the bag, then gust. The country's banners flapped. Like a cold wind from the north or an electric storm, the verbs hummed and crackled. The daughter, amazed, held the bag open until the last slow verb had crawled out and away.

Townsfolk danced around her. The country's queen arrived on a milk-white racing camel. "Choose any of my children. You have earned a royal mate."

The royal family lined up in front of her, handsome lads and lovely maidens, all twitching and jittering, due to the influence of the verbs.

All but one, the second daughter realized: a tall maid who held herself still, though with evident effort. While the other royal children had eyes like deer or camels, this one's eyes—though dark—were keen. The grammarian's daughter turned toward her.

The maiden said, "I am the crown princess. Marry me and you will be a queen's consort. If you want children, one of my brothers will bed you. If we're lucky, we'll have a daughter to rule after I am gone. But no matter what happens, I will love you forever, for you have saved my country from inaction."

Of course, the grammarian's daughter chose this princess.

Weary of weariness and made restless by all the verbs, the people of the country became nomads, riding horses and following herds of great-horned cattle over a dusty plain. The grammarian's second daughter bore her children in carts, saw them grow up on horseback, and lived happily to an energetic old age, always side by side with her spouse, the nomad queen. The country they ruled, which had no clear borders and no set capital, became known as Change.

Now the story turns back to the grammarian. By this time her third daughter had reached the age of fifteen.

"The house has been almost roomy since my sisters left," she told her mother. "And we've had almost enough to eat. But that's no reason for me to stay, when they have gone to seek their fortunes. Give me what you can, and I will take to the highway. No matter what happens, you'll have one less mouth to feed."

"You are the loveliest and most elegant of my daughters," said the grammarian. "Therefore I will give you this bag of adjectives. Take them and do what you can with them. May luck and beauty go with you always."

The daughter thanked her mother, kissed her sisters, and trudged away, the bag of adjectives on her back. It was a difficult load to carry. At one end were words like rosy and delicate, which weighed almost nothing and fluttered. At the other end, like stones, lay dark and grim and fearsome. There seemed no way to balance such a collection. The daughter did the best she could, trudging womanfully along until she came to a bleak desert land. Day came suddenly here, a white sun popping into a cloudless sky. The intense light bleached colors from the earth. There was little water. The local people lived in caves and canyons to be safe from the sun.

"Our lives are bare stone," they told the grammarian's third daughter, "and the sudden alternation of blazing day and pitchblack night. We are too poor to have a king or queen, but we will give our most respected person, our shaman, as spouse to anyone who can improve our situation."

The third daughter thought for a while, then unslung her unwieldy bag, placed it on the bone-dry ground, and opened it. Out flew rosy and delicate like butterflies. Dim followed, looking like a moth.

"Our country will no longer be stark," cried the people with joy. "We'll have dawn and dusk, which have always been rumors."

One by one the other adjectives followed: rich, subtle, beautiful, luxuriant. This last resembled a crab covered with shaggy vegetation. As it crept over the hard ground, plants fell off it—or maybe sprang up around it—so it left a trail of greenness.

Finally, the bag was empty except for nasty words. As slimy reached out a tentacle, the third daughter pulled the drawstring tight. Slimy shrieked in pain. Below it in the bag, the worst adjectives rumbled, "Unjust! Unfair!"

The shaman, a tall, handsome person, was nearby, trying on various adjectives. He/she/it was especially interested in masculine, feminine, and androgynous. "I can't make up my mind," the shaman said. "This is the dark side of our new condition. Before, we had clear choices. Now, the new complexity puts all in doubt."

The sound of complaining adjectives attracted the shaman. He, she, or it came over and looked at the bag, which still had a tentacle protruding and wiggling.

"This is wrong. We asked for an end to starkness, which is not the same as asking for prettiness. In there—at the bag's bottom—are words we might need someday: sublime, awesome, terrific, and so on. Open it up and let them out."

"Are you certain?" asked the third daughter.

"Yes," said the shaman.

She opened the bag. Out crawled slimy and other words equally disgusting. The shaman nodded with approval as more and more unpleasant adjectives appeared. Last of all, after grim and gruesome and terrific, came sublime. The word shone like a diamond or a thundercloud in sunlight.

"You see," said the shaman. "Isn't that worth the rest?"

"You are a holy being," said the daughter, "and may know things I don't."

Sublime crawled off toward the mountains. The third daughter rolled up her bag. "All gone," she said. "Entirely empty."

The people looked around. Their land was still a desert, but now clouds moved across the sky, making the sunlight on bluff and mesa change. In response to this, the desert colors turned subtle and various. In the mountains rain fell, misty gray, feeding clear streams that ran in the bottoms of canyons. The vegetation there, spread by the land-crab luxuriant and fed by the streams, was a dozen—two dozen—shades of green.

"Our land is beautiful!" the people cried. "And you shall marry our shaman!"

But the shaman was still trying on adjectives, unable to decide if she, he, or it wanted to be feminine or masculine or androgynous.

"I can't marry someone who can't make up her mind," the third daughter said. "Subtlety is one thing. Uncertainty is another."

"In that case," the people said, "you will become our first queen, and the shaman will become your first minister."

This happened. In time the third daughter married a young hunter, and they had several children, all different in subtle ways.

The land prospered, though it was never fertile, except in the canyon bottoms. But the people were able to get by. They valued the colors of dawn and dusk, moving light on mesas, the glint of water running over stones, the flash of bugs and birds in flight, the slow drift of sheep on a hillside—like clouds under clouds. The name of their country was Subtletie. It lay north of Thingnesse and west of Change.

Back home, in the unnamed city, the grammarian's fourth daughter came of age.

"We each have a room now," she said to her mother, "and there's plenty to eat. But my sister and I still don't have dowries. I don't want to be an old maid in the marketplace. Therefore, I plan to go as my older sisters did. Give me what you can, and I'll do my best with it. And if I make my fortune, I'll send for you."

The mother thought for a while and rummaged in her study, which was almost empty. She had sold her books years before to pay for her daughters' educations, and most of her precious words were gone. At last, she managed to fill a bag with adverbs, though they were frisky little creatures and tried to escape.

But a good grammarian can outwit any word. When the bag was close to bursting, she gave it to her fourth daughter.

"This is what I have left. I hope it will serve."

The daughter thanked her mother and kissed her one remaining sister and took off along the highway, the bag of adverbs bouncing on her back.

Her journey was a long one. She made it womanfully, being the most energetic of the five daughters and the one with the most buoyant spirit. As she walked—quickly, slowly, steadily, unevenly—the bag on her back kept jouncing around and squeaking.

"What's in there?" asked other travelers. "Mice?"

"Adverbs," said the fourth daughter.

"Not much of a market for them," said the other travelers. "You'd be better off with mice."

This was plainly untrue, but the fourth daughter was not one to argue. On she went, until her shoes wore to pieces and fell from her weary feet. She sat on a stone by the highway and rubbed her bare soles, while the bag squeaked next to her.

A handsome lad in many-colored clothes stopped in front of her. "What's in the bag?" he asked.

"Adverbs," said the daughter shortly.

"Then you must, like me, be going to the new language fair."

The daughter looked up with surprise, noticing—as she did so—the lad's rosy cheeks and curling, auburn hair. "What?" she asked intently.

"I'm from the country of Subtletie and have a box of adjectives on my horse, every possible color, arranged in drawers: aquamarine, russet, dun, crimson, puce. I have them all. Your shoes have worn out. Climb up on my animal, and I'll give you a ride to the fair."

The fourth daughter agreed, and the handsome lad—whose name, it turned out, was Russet—led the horse to the fair. There, in booths with bright awnings, wordsmiths and merchants displayed their wares: solid nouns, vigorous verbs, subtle adjectives. But there were no adverbs.

"You have brought just the right product," said Russet enviously. "What do you say we share a booth? I'll get cages for your adverbs, who are clearly frisky little fellows, and you can help me arrange my colors in the most advantageous way."

The fourth daughter agreed; they set up a booth. In front were cages of adverbs, all squeaking and jumping, except for the sluggish ones. The lad's adjectives hung on the awning, flapping in a mild wind. As customers came by, drawn by the adverbs, Russet said, "How can we have sky without blue? How can we have gold without shining? And how much use is a verb if it can't be modified? Is walk enough, without slowly or quickly?

"Come and buy! Come and buy! We have mincingly and angrily, knowingly, lovingly, as well as a fine assortment of adjectives. Ride home happily with half a dozen colors and cage full of adverbs."

The adverbs sold like hotcakes, and the adjectives sold well also. By the fair's end, both Russet and the fourth daughter were rich, and there were still plenty of adverbs left.

"They must have been breeding, though I didn't notice," said Russet. "What are you going to do with them?"

"Let them go," said the daughter.

"Why?" asked Russet sharply.

"I have enough money to provide for myself, my mother, and my younger sister. Greedy is an adjective and not one of my wares." She opened the cages. The adverbs ran free—slowly, quickly, hoppingly, happily. In the brushy land around the fairground, they proliferated. The region became known as Varietie. People moved there to enjoy the brisk, invigorating, varied weather, as well as the fair, which happened every year thereafter.

As for the fourth daughter, she built a fine house on a hill above the fairground. From there she could see for miles. Out back, among the bushes, she put feeding stations for the adverbs, and she sent for her mother and one remaining sister. The three of them lived together contentedly. The fourth daughter did not marry Russet, though she remained always grateful for his help. Instead, she became an old maid. It was a good life, she said, as long as one had money and respect.

In time, the fifth daughter came of age. (She was the youngest by far.) Her sister offered her a dowry, but she said, "I will do no less than the rest of you. Let my mother give me whatever she has left, and I will go to seek my fortune."

The mother went into her study, full of new books now, and looked around. "I have a new collection of nouns," she told the youngest daughter.

"No, for my oldest sister took those and did well with them, from all reports. I don't want to repeat someone else's adventures."

Verbs were too active, she told her mother, and adjectives too varied and subtle. "I'm a plain person who likes order and organization."

"How about adverbs?" asked the mother.

"Is there nothing else?"

"Prepositions," said the mother, and showed them to her daughter. They were dull little words, like something a smith might make from pieces of iron rod. Some were bent into angles. Others were curved into hooks. Still others were circles or helixes. Something about them touched the youngest daughter's heart.

"I'll take them," she said and put them in a bag. Then she thanked her mother, kissed her sister, and set off.

Although they were small, the prepositions were heavy and had sharp corners. The youngest daughter did not enjoy carrying them, but she was a methodical person who did what she set out to do. Tromp, tromp she went along the highway, which wound finally into a broken country, full of fissures and jagged peaks. The local geology was equally chaotic. Igneous rocks intruded into sedimentary layers. New rock lay under old rock. The youngest daughter, who loved order, had never seen such a mess. While neat, she was also rational, and she realized she could not organize an entire mountain range. "Let it be what it is," she said. "My concern is my own life and other people."

The road grew rougher and less maintained. Trails split off from it and sometimes rejoined it or ended nowhere, as the daughter discovered by trial. "This country needs engineers," she muttered peevishly. (A few adverbs had hidden among the prepositions and would pop out now and then. Peevishly was one.)

At length the road became nothing more than a path, zigzagging down a crumbling mountain slope. Below her in a valley was a town of shacks, though town might be the wrong word. The shacks were scattered helter-skelter over the valley bottom and up the valley sides. Nothing was seemly or organized. Pursing her lips—a trick she had learned from her mother, who did it when faced by a sentence that would not parse—the fifth daughter went down the path.

When she reached the valley floor, she saw people running to and fro.

"Madness," said the daughter. The prepositions, in their bag, made a sound of agreement like metal chimes.

In front of her, two women began to argue—over what she could not tell.

"Explain," cried the fifth daughter, while the prepositions went "bong" and "bing."

"Here in the Canton of Chaos nothing is capable of agreement," one woman said. "Is it age before beauty, or beauty before age? What came first, the chicken or the egg? Does might make right, and if so, what is left?"

"This is certainly madness," said the daughter.

"How can we disagree?" said the second woman. "We live topsy-turvy and pell-mell, with no hope of anything better." Saying this, she hit the first woman on the head with a live chicken.

"Egg!" cried the first woman.

"Left!" cried the second.

The chicken squawked, and the grammarian's last daughter opened her bag.

Out came the prepositions—of, to, from, with, at, by, in, under, over, and so on. When she'd put them into the bag, they had seemed like hooks or angles. Now, departing in orderly rows, they reminded her of ants. Granted, they were large ants, each one the size of a woman's hand, their bodies metallic gray, their eyes like cut and polished hematite. A pair of tongs or pincers protruded from their mouths; their thin legs, moving delicately over the ground, seemed made of iron rods or wire.

Somehow—it must have been magic—the things they passed over and around became organized. Shacks turned into tidy cottages. Winding paths became streets. The fields were square now. The trees ran in lines along the streets and roads. Terraces appeared on the mountainsides.

The mountains themselves remained as crazy as ever, strata sideways and upside down. "There is always a limit to order," said the daughter. At her feet, a handful of remaining prepositions chimed their agreement like bells.

In decorous groups, the locals came up to her. "You have saved us from utter confusion. We are a republic, so we can't offer you a throne. But please become our first citizen, and if you want to marry, please accept any of us. Whatever you do, don't go away, unless you leave these ingenious little creatures that have connected us with one another."

"I will stay," said the fifth daughter, "and open a grammar school. As for marriage, let that happen as it will."

The citizens agreed by acclamation to her plan. She settled in a tidy cottage and opened a tidy school, where the canton's children learned grammar.

In time, she married four other schoolteachers. (Due to the presence of the prepositions, which remained in their valley and throughout the mountains, the local people developed a genius for creating complex social groups. Their diagrams of kinship excited the awe of neighbors, and their marriages grew more intricate with each generation.)

The land became known as Relation. In addition to genealogists and marriage brokers, it produced diplomats and merchants. These last two groups, through trade and negotiation, gradually unified the five countries of Thingnesse, Change, Subtletie, Varietie, and Relation. The empire they formed was named Cooperation. No place was more solid, more strong, more complex, more energetic, or better organized.

The flag of the new nation was an ant under a blazing yellow sun. Sometimes the creature held a tool: a pruning hook, scythe, hammer, trowel, or pen. At other times its hands (or feet) were empty. Always below it was the nation's motto: WITH.

KELLEY ESKRIDGE

And Salome Danced

Kelley Eskridge is an American writer, essayist, screenwriter, and editor. Her stories have appeared in magazines and anthologies in the United States, Europe, Australia, and Japan, including *Century* and the *Magazine of Fantasy & Science Fiction*. Her collection *Dangerous Space* was published by Aqueduct Press. "And Salome Danced," a unique gender-bending story of the theater, received the Astraea Prize and was nominated for the James Tiptree, Jr Award in 1995. This story was first published in the anthology *Little Deaths* in 1994.

They're the best part, auditions: the last chance to hold in my mind the play as it should be. The uncast actors are easiest to direct; empty stages offer no barriers. Everything is clear, uncomplicated by living people and their inability to be what is needed.

"What I need," I say to my stage manager, "is a woman who can work on her feet."

"Hmmm," says Lucky helpfully. She won't waste words on anything so obvious. Our play is *Salome*, subtitled *Identity and Desire*. Salome has to dance worth killing for.

The sense I have, in these best, sweet moments, is that I do not so much envision the play as experience it in some sort of multidimensional gestalt. I feel Salome's pride and the terrible control of her body's rhythms; Herod's twitchy groin and his guilt and his unspoken love for John; John's relentless patience, and his fear. The words of the script sometimes seize me as if bypassing vision, burrowing from page into skin, pushing blood and nerve to the bursting limit on the journey to my brain. The best theatre lives inside.

I'll spend weeks trying to feed the sensation and the bloodsurge into the actors, but . . . But I can't do their job. But they can't read my mind. And people wonder why we drink.

Lucky snorts at me when I tell her these things: if it isn't a tech cue or a blocking note, it has nothing to do with the real play as far as she's concerned. She doesn't understand that for me the play is best before it is real, when it is still only mine.

"Nine sharp," she says now. "Time to start. Some of them have already been out there long enough to turn green." She smiles; her private joke.

"Let's go," I say, my part of the ritual; and then I have to do it, have to let go. I sit forward over the script in my usual eighth row seat; Lucky takes her clipboard and her favourite red pen, the one she's had since *Cloud Nine*, up the aisle. She pushes open the lobby door and the sound of voices rolls through, cuts off. All of them out there, wanting in. I feel in my gut their tense waiting silence as Lucky calls the first actor's name.

* * *

They're hard on everyone, auditions. Actors bare their throats. Directors make instinctive leaps of faith about what an actor could or might or must do in this or that role, with this or that partner. It's kaleidoscopic, religious, it's violent and subjective. It's like soldiers fighting each other just to see who gets to go to war. Everyone gets bloody, right from the start.

* * *

Forty minutes before a late lunch break, when my blood sugar is at its lowest point, Lucky comes back with the next resume and headshot and the first raised eyebrow of the day. The eyebrow, the snort, the flared nostril, the slight nod, are Lucky's only comments on actors. They are minimal and emphatic.

Behind her walks John the Baptist. He calls himself Joe Something-or-other, but he's John straight out of my head. Dark red hair. The kind of body that muscles up long and compact, strong and lean. He moves well, confident but controlled. When he's on stage he even stands like a goddamn prophet. And his eyes are John's eyes: deep blue like deep sea. He wears baggy khaki trousers, a loose, untucked white shirt, high top sneakers, a Greek fisherman's cap. His voice is clear, a half-tone lighter than many people expect in a man: perfect.

The monologue is good, too. Lucky shifts in her seat next to me. We exchange a look, and I see that her pupils are wide.

"Is he worth dancing for, then?"

She squirms, all the answer I really need. I look at the resume again. Joe Sand. He stands calmly on stage. Then he moves very slightly, a shifting of weight, a leaning in toward Lucky. While he does it, he looks right at her, watching her eyes for that uncontrollable pupil response. He smiles. Then he tries it with me. *Aha*, I think, *surprise, little actor.*

"Callbacks are Tuesday and Wednesday nights," I say neutrally. "We'll let you know."

He steps off the stage. He is half in shadow when he asks, "Do you have Salome yet?"

"No precasting," Lucky says.

"I know someone you'd like," he says, and even though I can't quite see him I know he is talking to me. Without the visual cue of his face, the voice has become trans-gendered, the body shape ambiguous.

"Any more at home like you, Joe?" *I must really need my lunch.*

"Whatever you need," he says, and moves past me, past Lucky, up the aisle. Suddenly, I'm ravenously hungry. Four more actors between me and the break, and I know already that I won't remember any of them longer than it takes for Lucky to close the doors behind them.

* * *

The next day is better. By late afternoon I have seen quite a few good actors, men and women, and Lucky has started a callback list.

"How many left?" I ask, coming back from the bathroom, rubbing the back of my neck with one hand and my waist with the other. I need a good stretch, some sweaty muscle-heating exercise, a hot bath. I need Salome.

Lucky is frowning at a paper in her hand. "Why is Joe Sand on this list?"

"God, Lucky, I want him for callbacks, that's why."

"No, this sheet is today's auditions."

I read over her shoulder. *Jo Sand.* "Dunno. Let's go on to the next one, maybe we can actually get back on schedule."

When I next hear Lucky's voice, after she has been up to the lobby to bring in the next actor, I know that something is terribly wrong.

"Mars . . . Mars . . ."

By this time I have stood and turned and I can see for myself what she is not able to tell me.

"Jo Sand," I say.

"Hello again," she says. The voice is the same; *she* is the same, and utterly different. She wears the white shirt tucked into the khaki pants this time, pulled softly across her breasts. Soft black shoes, like slippers, that make no noise when she moves. No cap today, that red hair thick, brilliant above the planes of her face. Her eyes are Salome's eyes: deep blue like deep desire. She is as I imagined her. When she leans slightly toward me, she watches my eyes and then smiles. Her smell goes straight up my nose and punches into some ancient place deep in my brain.

We stand like that for a long moment, the three of us. I don't know what to say. I don't have the right words for conversation with the surreal except when it's inside my head. I don't know what to do when it walks down my aisle and shows me its teeth.

"I want you to see that I can be versatile," Jo says.

The air in our small circle has become warm and sticky. My eyes feel slightly crossed, my mind is slipping gears. *I won't ask, I will not ask . . .* It's as if I were trying to bring her into focus through 3-D glasses; trying to make two separate images overlay. It makes me seasick. I wonder if Lucky is having the same trouble, and then I see that she has simply removed herself in some internal way. She doesn't see Jo look at me with those primary eyes.

But I see: and suddenly I feel wild, electric, that direct-brain connection that makes my nerves stand straight under my skin. *Be careful what you ask for, Mars.* "I don't guess you really need to do another monologue," I tell her. Lucky is still slack-jawed with shock.

Jo smiles again.

Someone else is talking with my voice. "Lucky will schedule you for callbacks." Beside me, Lucky jerks at the sound of her name. Jo turns to her. Her focus is complete. Her whole body says, *I am waiting.* I want her on stage. I want to see her like that, waiting for John's head on a platter.

"Mars, what . . ." Lucky swallows, tries again. She speaks without looking at the woman standing next to her. "Do you want . . . oh, shit. What part are you reading this person for in callbacks, goddamnit anyway." I haven't seen her this confused since her mother's boyfriend made a pass at her years ago, one Thanksgiving, his hand hidden behind the turkey platter at the buffet. Confusion makes Lucky fragile and brings her close to tears.

Jo looks at me, still waiting. Yesterday I saw John the Baptist: I remember how he made Lucky's eyebrow quirk and I can imagine the rehearsals; how he might sit close to her, bring her coffee, volunteer to help her set props. She'd be a wreck in one week and useless in two. And today how easy it is to see Salome, who waits so well and moves with such purpose. I should send this Jo away, but I won't: I need a predator for Salome; I can't do a play about desire without someone who knows about the taste of blood.

"Wear a skirt," I say to Jo. "I'll need to see you dance." Lucky closes her eyes.

＊ ＊ ＊

Somehow we manage the rest of the auditions, make the first cut, organize the callback list. There are very few actors I want to see again. When we meet for callbacks, I bring them all in and sit them in a clump at the rear of the house, where I can see them when I want to and ignore them otherwise. But always I am conscious of Jo. I read her with the actors that I think will work best in other roles. She is flexible, adapting herself to their different styles, giving them what they need to make the scene work. She's responsive to direction. She listens well. I can't find anything wrong with her.

Then it is time for the dance. There are three women that I want to see, and I put them all on stage together. "Salome's dance is the most important scene in the play. It's a crisis point for every character. Everyone has something essential invested in it. It has to carry a lot of weight."

"What are you looking for?" one of the women asks. She has long dark hair and good arms.

"Power," I answer, and beside her Jo's head comes up like a pointing dog's, her nostrils flared with some rich scent. I pretend not to see. "Her dance is about power over feelings and lives. There's more, but power's the foundation, and that's what I need to see."

The woman who asked nods her head and looks down, chewing the skin off her upper lip. I turn away to give them a moment for this new information to sink in; looking out into the house, I see the other actors sitting forward in their seats, and I know they are wondering who it will be, and whether they could work with her, and what they would do in her place.

I turn back. "I want you all to dance together up here. Use the space any way you like. Take a minute to warm up and start whenever you're ready."

I can see the moment that they realize, *ohmigod no music, how can we dance without . . . goddamn all directors anyway.* But I want to see their interpretation of power, not music. If they don't have it in them to dance silent in front of strangers, if they can't compete, if they can't pull all my attention and keep it, then they can't give me what I need. Salome wouldn't hesitate.

The dark-haired woman shrugs, stretches her arms out and down toward her toes. The third woman slowly begins to rock her hips; her arms rise swaying in the cliché of eastern emerald-in-the-navel belly dance. She moves as if embarrassed, and I don't blame her. The dark-haired woman stalls for another moment and then launches into a jerky jazz step with a strangely syncopated beat. I can almost hear her humming her favourite song under her breath; her head tilts up and to the right and she moves in her own world, to her own sound. That's not right, either. I realize that I'm hoping one of them will be what I need, so that I do not have to see Jo dance.

And where is Jo? There, at stage right, watching the other two women, comfortable in her stillness. Then she slides gradually into motion, steps slowly across the stage and stops three feet from the belly dancer, whose stumbling rhythm slows and then breaks as Jo stands, still, watching. Jo looks her straight in the eye, and just as the other woman begins to drop her gaze, Jo suddenly whirls, throwing herself around so quickly that for an instant it's as if her head is facing the opposite direction from her body. It is a nauseating moment, and it's followed by a total body shrug, a shaking off, that is both contemptuous and intently erotic. Now she is facing the house facing the other actors, facing Lucky, facing me: now she shows us what she can do. Her dance says *this is what I am, that you can never be; see my body move as it will never move with yours.* She stoops for an imaginary platter, and from the triumph in her step I begin to see the bloody prize. The curve of her arm shows me the filmed eye and the lolling tongue; the movement of her breast and belly describe for me the wreckage of the neck its trailing cords; her feet draw pictures in the splashed gore as she swirls and turns and snaps her arm out like a discus thrower tossing the invisible trophy straight at me. When I realize that I have raised a hand to catch it, I know that I have to have her no matter what she is. Have to have her for the play. Have to have her.

When the actors are gone, Lucky and I go over the list. We do not discuss Salome. Lucky has already set the other two women's resumés aside.

Before we leave: "God, she was amazing. She'll be great, Mars I'm really glad it turned out this way, you know, that she decided to drop that cross-dressing stuff."

"Mmm."

"It really gave me a start, seeing her that day. She was so convincing as a man. I thought . . . well, nothing. It was stupid."

"It wasn't stupid."

"You didn't seem surprised—did you know that first time when he . . . when she came in that she wasn't . . . ? Why didn't you say?"

"If I'm looking at someone who can play John, I don't really care how they pee or whether they shave under their chins. Gender's not important."

"It is if you think you might want to go to bed with it."

"Mmm," I say again. What I cannot tell Lucky is that all along I have been in some kind of shock; like walking through swamp mud, where the world is warm silky wet but you are afraid to look down for fear of what might be swimming with you in the murk. I know that this is not a game: Joe was a man when he came in and a woman when she came back. I look at our cast list and I know that something impossible and dangerous is trying to happen; but all I really see is that suddenly my play—the one inside me—is possible. She'll blow a hole through every seat in the house. She'll burst their brains.

*　*　*

Three weeks into rehearsal, Lucky has unremembered enough to start sharing coffee and head-together conferences with Jo during breaks. The other actors accept Jo as someone they can't believe they never heard of before, a comrade in the art wars. We are such a happy group; we give great ensemble.

Lance, who plays Herod, regards Jo as some kind of wood sprite, brilliant and fey. He is myopic about her to the point that if she turned into an anaconda, he would stroke her head while she wrapped herself around him. Lance takes a lot of kidding about his name, especially from his boyfriends. During our early rehearsals, he discovered a very effective combination of obsession and revulsion in Herod: as if he would like to eat Salome alive and then throw her up again, a sort of sexual bulimia.

Susan plays Herodias; Salome's mother, Herod's second wife, his brother's widow. She makes complicated seem simple. She works well with Lance, giving him a strong partner who nevertheless dims in comparison to her flaming daughter, a constant reminder to Herod of the destruction that lurks just on the other side of a single *yes* to this stepdaughter/niece/demon-child who dances in his fantasies. Susan watches Jo so disinterestedly that it has taken me most of this time to see how she has imitated and matured the arrogance that Jo brings to the stage. She is a tall black woman, soft muscle where Jo is hard: nothing like Jo, but she has become Salome's mother.

And John the Baptist, whose real name is Frank and who is nothing like Joe: I'm not sure I could have cast him if he had come to the audition with red hair, but his is black this season, Irish black for the O'Neill repertory production that he just finished. Lucky says he has "Jesus feet." Frankie's a method actor, disappointed that he doesn't have any sense memory references for decapitation. "I know it happens offstage," he says earnestly, at least once a week. "But it needs to be there right from the start, I want them to think about it every scene with her." *Them* is always the audience. *Her* is always Jo. Offstage, he looks at her the way a child looks at a harvest moon.

Three weeks is long enough for us all to become comfortable with the process but not with the results: the discoveries the actors made in the first two weeks refuse to gel, refuse to reinvent themselves. It's a frustrating phase. We're all tense but trying not to show it, trying not to undermine anyone else's efforts. It's hard for the actors, who genuinely want to support each other, but don't really want to see someone else break through first. Too scary: no one wants to be left behind.

There's a pseudosexual energy between actors and directors: there's so much deliberate vulnerability, control, desire to please; so much of the stuff that sex is made of. Working with my actors is like handling bolts of cloth: they each have a texture, a tension. Lance is brocade and plush; Susan is smooth velvet, subtle to the touch; Frankie is spun wool, warm and indefinably tough. And Jo: Jo is raw silk and razorblades, so fine that you don't feel the cut.

So we're all tense; except for Jo. Oh, she talks, but she's not worried; she's waiting for something, and I am beginning to turn those audition days over in my memory, sucking the taste from the bones of those encounters and wondering what it was that danced with me in those early rounds, what I have invited in.

And a peculiar thing begins: as I grow more disturbed, Jo's work becomes better and better. In those moments when I suddenly see myself as the trainer with my head in the mouth of the beast, when I slip and show that my hand is sweaty on the leash—in those moments her work is so pungent, so ripe that Jo the world-shaker disappears, and the living Salome looks up from the cut-off T-shirt, flexes her thigh muscles under the carelessly torn jeans. We have more and more of Salome every rehearsal. On Friday nights I bring a cooler of Corona and a bag of limes for whoever wants to share them. This Friday everyone stays. We sit silent for the first cold green-gold swallows. Lance settles back into Herod's large throne. I straddle a folding chair and rest my arms along the back, bottle loose in one hand. Lucky and the other actors settle on the platforms that break the stage into playing areas.

It starts with the actors talking, as they always do, about work. Lance has played another Herod, years ago, in *Jesus Christ Superstar*, and he wants to tell us how different that was.

"I'd like to do *Superstar*," Jo says. It sounds like an idle remark. She is leaning back with her elbows propped against the rise of a platform, her breasts pushing gently against the fabric of her shirt as she raises her bottle to her mouth. I look away because I do not want to watch her drink, don't want to see her throat work as the liquid goes down.

Lance considers a moment. "I think you'd be great, sweetheart," he says, "but Salome to Mary Magdalene is a pretty big stretch. Acid to apple juice. Wouldn't you at least like to play a semi-normal character in between, work up to it a little?"

Jo snorts. "I'm not interested in Magdalene. I'll play Judas."

Lance whoops, Frankie grins, and even the imperturbable Susan smiles. "Well, why not?" Lance says. "Why shouldn't she play Judas if she wants to?"

"Little question of gender," Frankie says, and shrugs.

Susan sits up. "Why shouldn't she have the part if she can do the work?"

Frankie gulps his beer and wipes his mouth. "Why should any director hire a woman to play a man when they can get a real man to do it?"

"What do you think, Mars?" The voice is Jo's. It startles me. I have been enjoying the conversation so much that I have forgotten the danger in relaxing around Jo or anything that interests her. I look at her now, still sprawled back against the platform with an inch of golden beer in the bottle beside her. She has been enjoying herself, too. I'm not sure where this is going, what the safe answer is. I remember saying to Lucky, *Gender's not important.*

"Gender's not important, isn't that right, Mars?"

Lucky told her about it. But I know Lucky didn't. She didn't have to.

"That's right," I say, and I know from Jo's smile that my voice is not as controlled as it should be. Even so, I'm not prepared for what happens next: a jumble of pictures in my head. Images of dancing in a place so dark that I cannot tell if I am moving with men or women. Images of streets filled with androgynous people and people whose gender-blurring surpasses androgyny and leaps into the realm of performance. Women dressed as men making love to men. Men dressed as women hesitating in front of public bathroom doors. Women in high heels and pearls with biceps so large that they split the expensive silk shirts. And the central image, the real point: Jo, naked, obviously female, slick with sweat, moving under me and over me, Jo making love to me until I gasp and then she begins to change, to change, until it is Joe with me, Joe on me—and I open my mouth to shout my absolute, instinctive refusal—and I remember Lucky saying *It is if you think you might want to sleep with it*—and the movie breaks in my head and I am back with the others. No one has noticed that I've been assaulted, turned inside out. They're still talking about it: "Just imagine the difference in all the relationships if Judas were a woman," Susan says earnestly to Frankie. "It would change everything!" Jo smiles and swallows the last of her beer.

The next rehearsal I feel fragile, as if I must walk carefully to keep from breaking myself. I have to rest often.

I am running a scene with Frankie and Lance when I notice Lucky offstage, talking earnestly to Jo. Jo puts one hand up, interrupts her, smiles, speaks, and they both turn to look at me. Lucky suddenly blushes. She walks quickly away from Jo, swerves to avoid me. Jo's smile is bigger. Her work in the next scene is particularly fine and full.

"What did she say to you, Luck?" I ask her as we are closing the house for the evening.

"Nothing," Lucky mumbles.

"Come on."

"Okay, fine. She wanted to know if you ever slept with your actors, okay?"

I know somehow that it's not entirely true: I can hear Jo's voice very clearly, saying to Lucky *So does Mars ever fuck the leading lady?* while she smiles that catlick smile. Jo has the gift of putting pictures into people's heads, and I believe Lucky got a mindful. That's what really sickens me, the idea that Lucky now has an image behind her eyes of what I'm like . . . no, of what Jo wants her to think I'm like. God knows. I don't want to look at her.

* * *

"Did you get my message?" Jo says to me the next evening, when she finally catches me alone in the wings during a break from rehearsal. She has been watching me all night. Lucky won't talk to her.

"I'm not in the script."

"Everybody's in the script."

"Look, I don't get involved with actors. It's too complicated, it's messy. I don't do it."

"Make an exception."

Lucky comes up behind Jo. Whatever the look is on my face, it gets a scowl from her. "Break's over," she says succinctly, turning away from us even before the words are completely out, halfway across the stage before I think to try to keep her with me.

"Let's get back to work, Jo."

"Make a fucking exception."

I don't like being pushed by actors, and there's something else, too, but I don't want to think about it now, I just want Jo off my back, so I give her the director voice, the vocal whip. "Save it for the stage, princess. You want to impress me, get out there and do your fucking job."

She doesn't answer; her silence makes a cold, high-altitude circle around us. When she moves, it's like a snake uncoiling, and then her hand is around my wrist. She's *strong*. When I look down, I see that her hand is changing: the bones thicken under the flesh, the muscles rearrange themselves subtly, and it's Joe's hand on Jo's arm, Joe's hand on mine. "Don't make me angry, Mars," and the voice is genderless and buzzes like a snake. There is no one here to help me, I can't see Lucky, I'm all alone with this hindbrain thing that wants to come out and play with me. Jo's smile is by now almost too big for her face. *Just another actor*, I think crazily, *they're all monsters anyway*.

"What are you?" I am shaking.

"Whatever you need, Mars. Whatever you need. Every director's dream. At the moment, I'm Salome, right down to the bone. I'm what you asked for."

"I didn't ask for this. I don't want this."

"You wanted Salome, and now you've got her. The power, the sex, the hunger, the need, the wanting, it's all here."

"It's a play. It's just . . . it's a play, for chrissake."

"It's real for you." That hand is still locked around my wrist; the other hand, the soft small hand, reaches up to the centre of my chest where my heart tries to skitter away from her touch. "I saw it, that first audition. I came to play John the Baptist, I saw the way Lucky looked at me, and I was going to give her something to remember . . . but your wanting was so strong, so complex. It's delicious, Mars. It tastes like spice and wine and sweat. The play in your head is more real to you than anything, isn't it, more real than your days of bright sun, your friends, your office transactions. I'm going to bring it right to you, into your world, into your life. I'll give you Salome. Onstage, offstage, there doesn't have to be any difference. Isn't that what making love is, giving someone what they really want?"

She's still smiling that awful smile and I can't tell whether she is talking about love because she really means it or because she knows it makes my stomach turn over. Or maybe both.

"Get out of here. Out of here, right now." I am shaking.

"You don't mean that, sweet. If you did, I'd already be gone."

"I'll cancel the show."

She doesn't answer: she looks at me and then, *phht*, I am seeing the stage from the audience perspective, watching Herod and Herodias quarrel and cry and struggle to protect their love, watching John's patient fear as Herod's resolve slips away: watching Salome dance. When she dances, she brings us all with her, the whole audience living inside her skin for those moments. We all whirl and reach and bend, we all promise, we all twist away. We all tempt. We all rage. We stuff ourselves down Herod's throat until he chokes on us. And then we are all suddenly back in our own bodies and we roar until our throats hurt and our voices rasp. All the things that I have felt about this play, she will make them feel. What I am will be in them. What I have inside me will bring them to their feet and leave them full and aching. Oh god, it makes me weep, and then I am back with her, she still holds me with that monster hand and all I can do is cry with wanting so badly what she can give me.

Her eyes are too wide, too round, too pleased. "Oh," she says, still gently, "It's okay. You'll enjoy most of it, I promise." And she's gone, sauntering onstage, calling out something to Lance, and her upstage hand is still too big, still *wrong*. She lets it caress her thigh once before she turns it back into the Jo hand. I've never seen anything more obscene. I have to take a minute to dry my eyes, cool my face. I feel a small, hollow place somewhere deep, as if Jo reached inside and found something she liked enough to take for herself. She's there now, just onstage, ready to dance, that small piece of me humming in her veins. How much more richness do I have within me? How long will it take to eat me, bit by bit? She raises her arms now and smiles, already tasting. Already well fed.

ANGÉLICA GORODISCHER

The Perfect Married Woman

TRANSLATED BY LORRAINE ELENA ROSES

Angélica Gorodischer is an Argentine writer known for short stories and novels with a speculative element as well as a feminist outlook. Although much of her work is not yet available in English, Ursula K. Le Guin translated Gorodischer's short story collection *Kalpa Imperial: The Greatest Empire That Never Was*, published in 2003 by Small Beer Press. She has won many awards for her fiction, including the Dignity award granted by the Permanent Assembly for Human Rights for works and activity in women's rights. In "The Perfect Married Woman," a typical housewife goes along her daily routine while also living a secret alternate life of great freedom. It was first published in the (highly recommended) *Secret Weavers* anthology in 1991.

If you meet her on the street, cross quickly to the other side and quicken your pace. She's a dangerous lady. She's about forty or forty-five, has one married daughter and a son working in San Nicolas; her husband's a sheet-metal worker. She rises very early, sweeps the sidewalk, sees her husband off, cleans, does the wash, shops, cooks. After lunch she watches television, sews or knits, irons twice a week, and at night goes to bed late. On Saturdays she does a general cleaning and washes windows and waxes the floors. On Sunday mornings she washes the clothes her son brings home—his name is Nestor Eduardo—she kneads dough for noodles or ravioli, and in the afternoon either her sister-in-law comes to visit or she goes to her daughter's house. It's been a long time since she's been to the movies, but she reads *TV Guide* and the police report in the newspaper. Her eyes are dark and her hands are rough and her hair is starting to go gray. She catches cold frequently and keeps a photo album in a dresser drawer along with a black crepe dress with lace collar and cuffs.

Her mother never hit her. But when she was six, she got a spanking for coloring on a door, and she had to wash it off with a wet rag. While she was doing it, she thought about doors, all doors, and decided that they were very dumb because they always led to the same places. And the one she was cleaning was definitely the dumbest of all, the one that led to her parents' bedroom. She opened the door and then it didn't go to her parents' bedroom but to the Gobi desert. She wasn't surprised that she knew it was the Gobi desert even though they hadn't even taught her in school where Mongolia was and neither she nor her mother nor her grandmother had ever heard of Nan Shan or Khangai Nuru.

She stepped through the door, bent over to scratch the yellowish grit and saw that there was no one, nothing, and the hot wind tousled her hair, so she went back through the open door, closed it and kept on cleaning. And when she finished, her mother grumbled a little more and told her to wash the rag and take the broom to sweep up that sand and clean her shoes. That day she modified her hasty judgment about doors, though not completely, at least not until she understood what was going on.

What had been going on all her life and up until today was that from time to time doors behaved satisfactorily, though in general they were still acting dumb and leading to dining rooms, kitchens, laundry rooms, bedrooms and offices even in the best of circumstances. But two months after the desert, for example, the door that every day led to the bath opened onto the workshop of a bearded man dressed in a long uniform, pointed shoes, and a cap that tilted on one side of his head. The old man's back was turned as he took something out of a highboy with many small drawers behind a very strange, large wooden machine with a giant steering wheel and screw, in the midst of cold air and an acrid smell. When he turned around and saw her he began to shout at her in a language she didn't understand.

She stuck out her tongue, dashed out the door, closed it, opened it again, went into the bathroom and washed her hands for lunch.

Again, after lunch, many years later, she opened the door of her room and walked into a battlefield. She dipped her hands in the blood of the wounded and dead and pulled from the neck of a cadaver a crucifix that she wore for a long time under high-necked blouses or dresses without plunging necklines.

She now keeps it in a tin box underneath the nightgowns with a brooch, a pair of earrings and a broken wristwatch that used to belong to her mother-in-law. In the same way, involuntarily and by chance, she visited three monasteries, seven libraries, and the highest mountains in the world, and who knows how many theaters, cathedrals, jungles, refrigeration plants, dens of vice, universities, brothels, forests, stores, submarines, hotels, trenches, islands, factories, palaces, hovels, towers and hell.

She's lost count and doesn't care; any door could lead anywhere and that has the same value as the thickness of the ravioli dough, her mother's death, and the life crises that she sees on TV and reads about in *TV Guide*.

Not long ago she took her daughter to the doctor, and seeing the closed door of a bathroom in the clinic, she smiled. She wasn't sure because she can never be sure, but she got up and went to the bathroom. However, it was a bathroom; at least there was a nude man in a bathtub full of water. It was all very large, with a high ceiling, marble floor and decorations hanging from the closed windows. The man seemed to be asleep in his white bathtub, short but deep, and she saw a razor on a wrought iron table with feet decorated with iron flowers and leaves and ending in lion's paws, a razor, a mirror, a curling iron, towels, a box of talcum powder and an earthen bowl with water. She approached on tiptoe, retrieved the razor, tiptoed over to the sleeping man in the tub and beheaded him. She threw the razor on the floor and rinsed her hands in the lukewarm bathtub water. She turned around when she reached the clinic corridor and spied a girl going into the bathroom through the other door. Her daughter looked at her.

"That was quick."

"The toilet was broken," she answered.

A few days afterward, she beheaded another man in a blue tent at night. That man and a woman were sleeping mostly uncovered by the blankets of a low, king-size bed, and the wind beat around the tent and slanted the flames of the oil lamps. Beyond it there would be another camp, soldiers, animals, sweat, manure, orders and weapons. But inside there was a sword by the leather and metal uniforms, and with it she cut off the head of the bearded man. The woman stirred and opened her eyes as she went out the door on her way back to the patio that she had been mopping.

On Monday and Thursday afternoons, when she irons shirt collars, she thinks of the slit necks and the blood, and she waits. If it's summer she goes out to sweep a little after putting away the clothing and until her husband arrives. If it's windy she sits in the kitchen and knits. But she doesn't always find sleeping men or staring cadavers. One rainy morning, when she was twenty, she was at a prison, and she made fun of the chained prisoners;

one night when the kids were kids and were all living at home, she saw in a square a disheveled woman looking at a gun but not daring to take it out of her open purse. She walked up to her, put the gun in the woman's hand and stayed there until a car parked at the corner, until the woman saw a man in gray get out and look for his keys in his pocket, until the woman aimed and fired. And another night while she was doing her sixth grade geography homework, she went to look for crayons in her room and stood next to a man who was crying on a balcony. The balcony was so high, so far above the street, that she had an urge to push him to hear the thud down below, but she remembered the orographic map of South America and was about to leave. Anyhow, since the man hadn't seen her, she did push him and saw him disappear and ran to color in the map so she didn't hear the thud, only the scream. And in an empty theater, she made a fire underneath the velvet curtain; in a riot she opened the cover to a basement hatchway; in a house, sitting on top of a desk, she shredded a two-thousand-page manuscript; in a clearing of a forest she buried the weapons of the sleeping men; in a river she opened the floodgates of a dike.

Her daughter's name is Laura Inés, her son has a fiancée in San Nicolás and he's promised to bring her over on Sunday so she and her husband can meet her. She has to remind herself to ask her sister-in-law for the recipe for orange cake, and Friday on TV is the first episode of a new soap opera. Again, she runs the iron over the front of the shirt and remembers the other side of the doors that are always carefully closed in her house, that other side where the things that happen are much less abominable than the ones we experience on this side, as you can easily understand.

NALO HOPKINSON

The Glass Bottle Trick

Nalo Hopkinson is a Jamaican science fiction writer formerly from Canada now living in the United States. Her first novel, *Brown Girl in the Ring*, received substantial critical acclaim and was shortlisted for the Philip K. Dick Award. In addition to her novels and short fiction, she has also edited various anthologies, including *Skin Folk* and *So Long Been Dreaming*. "The Glass Bottle Trick" details the ingenious qualities of coping and escape by a woman in a difficult situation. This story was first published in 2000 in the anthology *Whispers from the Cotton Tree Root: Caribbean Fabulist Fiction*.

The air was full of storms, but they refused to break.

In the wicker rocking chair on the front verandah, Beatrice flexed her bare feet against the wooden slat floor, rocking slowly back and forth. Another sweltering rainy season afternoon. The arid heat felt as though all the oxygen had boiled out of the parched air to hang as looming rainclouds, waiting.

Oh, but she loved it like this. The hotter the day, the slower she would move, basking. She stretched her arms and legs out to better feel the luxuriant warmth, then guiltily sat up straight again. Samuel would scold if he ever saw her slouching like that. Stuffy Sammy. She smiled fondly, admiring the lacy patterns the sunlight threw on the floor as it filtered through the white gingerbread fretwork that trimmed the roof of their house.

"Anything more today, Mistress Powell? I finish doing the dishes." Gloria had come out of the house and was standing in front of her, wiping her chapped hands on her apron.

Beatrice felt the shyness come over her as it always did when she thought of giving the older woman orders. Gloria was older than Beatrice's mother. "Ah . . . no, I think that's everything, Gloria . . ."

Gloria quirked an eyebrow, crinkling her face like running a fork through molasses. "Then I go take the rest of the afternoon off. You and Mister Samuel should be alone tonight. Is time you tell him."

Beatrice gave an abortive, shamefaced "huh" of a laugh. Gloria had known from the start, she'd had so many babies of her own. She'd been mad to run to Samuel with the news from since. But yesterday, Beatrice had already decided to tell Samuel. Well, almost decided. She felt irritated, like a child whose tricks have been found out. She swallowed the feeling. "I think you right, Gloria," she said, fighting for some dignity before the older woman. "Maybe . . . maybe I cook him a special meal, feed him up nice, then tell him."

"Well, I say is time and past time you make him know. A pickney is a blessing to a family."

"For true," Beatrice agreed, making her voice sound as certain as she could.

"Later, then, Mistress Powell." Giving herself the afternoon off, not even a by-your-leave, Gloria headed off to the maid's room at the back of the house to change into her street clothes. A few minutes later, she let herself out the garden gate.

"That seems like a tough book for a young lady of such tender years."

"Excuse me?" Beatrice threw a defensive cutting glare at the older man. He'd caught her off guard, though she'd seen his eyes following her ever since she entered the bookstore.

"You have something to say to me?" She curled the Gray's Anatomy *possessively into the crook of her arm, price sticker hidden against her body. Two more months of saving before she could afford it.*

He looked shyly at her. "Sorry if I offended, Miss," he said. "My name is Samuel."

Would be handsome, if he'd chill out a bit. Beatrice's wariness thawed a little. Middle of the sun-hot day, and he wearing black wool jacket and pants. His crisp white cotton shirt was buttoned right up, held in place by a tasteful, unimaginative tie. So proper, Jesus. He wasn't that much older than she.

"Is just . . . you're so pretty, and it's the only thing I could think of to say to get you to speak to me."

Beatrice softened more at that, smiled for him and played with the collar of her blouse. He didn't seem too bad, if you could look beyond the stocious, starchy behaviour.

* * *

Beatrice doubtfully patted the slight swelling of her belly. Four months. She was shy to give Samuel her news, but she was starting to show. Silly to put it off, yes? Today she was going to make her husband very happy; break that thin shell of mourning that still insulated him from her. He never said so, but Beatrice knew that he still thought of the wife he'd lost, and tragically, the one before that. She wished she could make him warm up to life again.

Sunlight was flickering through the leaves of the guava tree in the front yard. Beatrice inhaled the sweet smell of the sun-warmed fruit. The tree's branches hung heavy with the pale yellow globes, smooth and round as eggs. The sun reflected off the two blue bottles suspended in the tree, sending cobalt light dancing through the leaves.

When Beatrice first came to Sammy's house, she'd been puzzled by the two bottles that were jammed onto branches of the guava tree.

"Is just my superstitiousness, darling," he'd told her. "You never heard the old people say that if someone dies, you must put a bottle in a tree to hold their spirit, otherwise it will come back as a duppy and haunt you? A blue bottle. To keep the duppy cool, so it won't come at you in hot anger for being dead."

Beatrice had heard something of the sort, but it was strange to think of her Sammy as a superstitious man. He was too controlled and logical for that. Well, grief makes somebody act in strange ways. Maybe the bottles gave him some comfort, made him feel that he'd kept some essence of his poor wives near him.

* * *

"That Samuel is nice. Respectable, hard-working. Not like all them other ragamuffins you always going out with." Mummy picked up the butcher knife and began expertly slicing the goat meat into cubes for the curry.

Beatrice watched the red lumps of flesh part under the knife. Crimson liquid leaked onto the cutting board. She sighed, "But, Mummy, Samuel so boring! Michael and Clifton know how to have fun. All Samuel want to do is go for country drives. Always taking me away from other people."

"You should be studying your books, not having fun," her mother replied crossly.

Beatrice pleaded, "You well know I could do both, Mummy." Her mother just grunted.

Is only truth Beatrice was talking. Plenty men were always courting her, they flocked to her like birds, eager to take her dancing or out for a drink. But somehow she kept her marks up, even though it often meant studying right

*through the night, her head pounding and belly queasy from hangover while
some man snored in the bed beside her. Mummy would kill her if she didn't get
straight A's for medical school.* "You going *have to look after yourself, Beatrice.
Man not going do it for you. Them get their little piece of sweetness and then
them bruk away.*"

"*Two patty and a King Cola, please.*" *The guy who'd given the order had
a broad chest that tapered to a slim waist. Good face to look at, too. Beatrice
smiled sweetly at him, made shift to gently brush his palm with her fingertips
as she handed him the change.*

* * *

A bird screeched from the guava tree, a tiny kiskedee, crying angrily, "*Dit, dit,
qu'est-ce qu'il dit!*" A small snake was coiled around one of the upper branches,
just withdrawing its head from the bird's nest. Its jaws were distended with the
egg it had stolen. It swallowed the egg whole, throat bulging hugely with its
meal. The bird hovered around the snake's head, giving its pitiful wail of, "Say,
say, what's he saying!"

"Get away!" Beatrice shouted at the snake. It looked in the direction of the
sound, but didn't back off. The gulping motion of its body as it forced the egg
farther down its own throat made Beatrice shudder. Then, oblivious to the
fluttering of the parent bird, it arched its head over the nest again. Beatrice
pushed herself to her feet and ran into the yard. "Hsst! Shoo! Come away
from there!" But the snake took a second egg.

Sammy kept a long pole with a hook at one end leaned against the guava
tree for pulling down the fruit. Beatrice grabbed up the pole, started jooking
it at the branches as close to the bird and nest as she dared. "Leave them, you
brute! Leave!" The pole connected with some of the boughs. The two bottles
in the tree fell to the ground and shattered with a crash. A hot breeze sprang
up. The snake slithered away quickly, two eggs bulging in its throat. The bird
flew off, sobbing to itself.

Nothing she could do now. When Samuel came home, he would hunt the
nasty snake down for her and kill it. She leaned the pole back against the tree.

The light breeze should have brought some coolness, but really it only
made the day warmer. Two little dust devils danced briefly around Beatrice.
They swirled across the yard, swung up into the air, and dashed themselves to
powder against the shuttered window of the third bedroom.

Beatrice got her sandals from the verandah. Sammy wouldn't like it if she
stepped on broken glass. She picked up the broom that was leaned against
the house and began to sweep up the shards of bottle. She hoped Samuel

wouldn't be too angry with her. He wasn't a man to cross, could be as stern as a father if he had a mind to.

That was mostly what she remembered about Daddy, his temper—quick to show and just as quick to go. So was he; had left his family before Beatrice turned five. The one cherished memory she had of him was of being swung back and forth through the air, her two small hands clasped in one big hand of his, her feet held tight in another. Safe. And as he swung her through the air, her daddy had been chanting words from an old-time story:

> Yung-Kyung-Pyung, what a pretty basket!
> Margaret Powell Alone, what a pretty basket!
> Eggie-law, what a pretty basket!

Then he had held her tight to his chest, forcing the air from her lungs in a breathless giggle. The dressing-down Mummy had given him for that game! "You want to drop the child and crack her head open on the hard ground? Ee? Why you can't be more responsible?"

"Responsible?" he'd snapped. "Is who working like dog sunup to sundown to put food in oonuh belly?" He'd set Beatrice down, her feet hitting the ground with a jar. She'd started to cry, but he'd just pushed her towards her mother and stormed out of the room. One more volley in the constant battle between them. After he'd left them Mummy had opened the little food shop in town to make ends meet. In the evenings, Beatrice would rub lotion into her mother's chapped, work-wrinkled hands. "See how that man make us come down in the world?" Mummy would grumble. "Look at what I come to."

Privately, Beatrice thought that maybe all Daddy had needed was a little patience. Mummy was too harsh, much as Beatrice loved her. To please her, Beatrice had studied hard all through high school: physics, chemistry, biology, describing the results of her lab experiments in her copy book in her cramped, resigned handwriting. Her mother greeted every A with a noncommittal grunt and anything less with a lecture. Beatrice would smile airily, seal the hurt away, pretend the approval meant nothing to her. She still worked hard, but she kept some time for play of her own. Rounders, netball, and later, boys. All those boys, wanting a chance for a little sweetness with a light-skin browning like her. Beatrice had discovered her appeal quickly.

* * *

"Leggo beast . . ." Loose woman. The hissed words came from a knot of girls that slouched past Beatrice as she sat on the library steps, waiting for Clifton to come

and pick her up. She willed her ears shut, smothered the sting of the words. But she knew some of those girls. Marguerita, Deborah. They used to be friends of hers. Though she sat up proudly, she found her fingers tugging self-consciously at the hem of her short white skirt. She put the big physics textbook in her lap, where it gave her thighs a little more coverage.

The farting vroom of Clifton's motorcycle interrupted her thoughts. Grinning, he slewed the bike to a dramatic halt in front of her. "Study time done now, darling. Time to play."

He looked good this evening, as he always did. Tight white shirt, jeans that showed off the bulges of his thighs. The crinkle of the thin gold chain at his neck set off his dark brown skin. Beatrice stood, tucked the physics text under her arm, smoothed the skirt over her hips. Clifton's eyes followed the movement of her hands. See, it didn't take much to make people treat you nice. She smiled at him.

* * *

Samuel would still show up hopefully every so often to ask her to accompany him on a drive through the country. He was so much older than all her other suitors. And dry? Country drives, Lord! She went out with him a few times; he was so persistent and she couldn't figure out how to tell him no. He didn't seem to get her hints that really she should be studying. Truth to tell, though, she started to find his quiet, undemanding presence soothing. His eggshell-white BMW took the graveled country roads so quietly that she could hear the kiskedee birds in the mango trees, chanting their query: "*Dit, dit, qu'est-ce qu'il dit?*"

One day, Samuel brought her a gift.

"These are for you and your family," he said shyly, handing her a wrinkled paper bag. "I know your mother likes them." Inside were three plump eggplants from his kitchen garden, raised by his own hands. Beatrice took the humble gift out of the bag. The skins of the eggplants had a taut, blue sheen to them. Later she would realise that that was when she'd begun to love Samuel. He was stable, solid, responsible. He would make Mummy and her happy.

Beatrice gave in more to Samuel's diffident wooing. He was cultured and well spoken. He had been abroad, talked of exotic sports: ice hockey, downhill skiing. He took her to fancy restaurants she'd only heard of, that her other, young, unestablished boyfriends would never have been able to afford, and would probably only have embarrassed her if they had taken her. Samuel had polish. But he was humble, too, like the way he grew his own vegetables, or the self-deprecating tone in which he spoke of himself. He was always punctual, always courteous to her and her mother. Beatrice could count on him for little things, like picking her up after class, or driving her mother to the hairdresser's. With the other men, she always had to be on guard: pouting until they took her somewhere else for dinner, not another free meal in her mother's restaurant, wheedling them into using the condoms. She always had to hold something of herself shut away. With Samuel, Beatrice relaxed into trust.

* * *

"Beatrice, come! Come quick, nuh!"

Beatrice ran in from the backyard at the sound of her mother's voice. Had something happened to Mummy?

Her mother was sitting at the kitchen table, knife still poised to crack an egg into the bowl for the pound cake she was making to take to the shop. She was staring in open-mouthed delight at Samuel, who was fretfully twisting the long stems on a bouquet of blood-red roses. "Lord, Beatrice; Samuel say he want to marry you!"

Beatrice looked to Sammy for verification. "Samuel," she asked unbelievingly, "what you saying? Is true?"

He nodded yes. "True, Beatrice."

Something gave way in Beatrice's chest, gently as a long-held breath. Her heart had been trapped in glass, and he'd freed it.

* * *

They'd been married two months later. Mummy was retired now; Samuel had bought her a little house in the suburbs, and he paid for the maid to come in three times a week. In the excitement of planning for the wedding, Beatrice had let her studying slip. To her dismay she finished her final year of university with barely a C average.

"Never mind, sweetness," Samuel told her. "I didn't like the idea of you studying, anyway. Is for children. You're a big woman now." Mummy had agreed with him too, said she didn't need all that now. She tried to argue with them, but Samuel was very clear about his wishes, and she'd stopped, not wanting anything to cause friction between them just yet. Despite his genteel manner, Samuel had just a bit of a temper. No point in crossing him, it took so little to make him happy, and he was her love, the one man she'd found in whom she could have faith.

Too besides, she was learning how to be the lady of the house, trying to use the right mix of authority and jocularity with Gloria, the maid, and Cleitis, the yardboy who came twice a month to do the mowing and the weeding. Odd to be giving orders to people when she was used to being the one taking orders, in Mummy's shop. It made her feel uncomfortable to tell people to do her work for her. Mummy said she should get used to it, it was her right now.

The sky rumbled with thunder. Still no rain. The warmth of the day was nice, but you could have too much of a good thing. Beatrice opened her mouth, gasping a little, trying to pull more air into her lungs. She was a little short of breath nowadays as the baby pressed on her diaphragm. She knew she could go inside for relief from the heat, but Samuel kept the air-conditioning on high, so cold that they could keep the butter in its dish on the kitchen counter. It never went rancid. Even insects refused to come inside. Sometimes Beatrice felt as though the house were really somewhere else, not the tropics. She had been used to waging constant war against ants and cockroaches, but not in Samuel's house. The cold in it made Beatrice shiver, dried her eyes out until they felt like boiled eggs sitting in their sockets. She went outside as often as possible, even though Samuel didn't like her to spend too much time in the sun. He said he feared that cancer would mar her soft skin, that he didn't want to lose another wife. But Beatrice knew he just didn't want her to get too brown. When the sun touched her, it brought out the sepia and cinnamon in her blood, overpowered the milk and honey, and he could no longer pretend she was white. He loved her skin pale. "Look how you gleam in the moonlight," he'd say to her when he made gentle, almost supplicating love to her at night in the four-poster bed. His hand would slide over her flesh, cup her breasts with an air of reverence. The look in his eyes was so close to worship that it sometimes frightened her. To be loved so much! He would whisper to her, "Beauty. Pale Beauty, to my Beast," then blow a cool breath over the delicate membranes of her ear, making her shiver in delight. For her part, she loved to look at him, his molasses-dark skin, his broad chest, the way the planes of flat muscle slid across it. She imagined tectonic plates shifting in the earth. She loved the bluish-black cast the moonlight lent him. Once, gazing up at him as he loomed above her, body working against and in hers, she had seen the moonlight playing glints of deepest blue in his trim beard.

"Black Beauty," she had joked softly, reaching to pull his face closer for a kiss. At the words, he had lurched up off her to sit on the edge of the bed, pulling a sheet over him to hide his nakedness. Beatrice watched him, confused, feeling their blended sweat cooling along her body.

"Never call me that, please, Beatrice," he said softly. "You don't have to draw attention to my colour. I'm not a handsome man, and I know it. Black and ugly as my mother made me."

"But, Samuel . . . !"

"No."

Shadows lay between them on the bed. He wouldn't touch her again that night.

Beatrice sometimes wondered why Samuel hadn't married a white woman. She thought she knew the reason, though. She had seen the way that Samuel behaved around white people. He smiled too broadly, he simpered, he made silly jokes. It pained her to see it, and she could tell from the desperate look in his eyes that it hurt him too. For all his love of creamy white skin, Samuel probably couldn't have brought himself to approach a white woman the way he'd courted her.

The broken glass was in a neat pile under the guava tree. Time to make Samuel's dinner now. She went up the verandah stairs to the front door, stopping to wipe her sandals on the coir mat just outside the door. Samuel hated dust. As she opened the door, she felt another gust of warm wind at her back, blowing past her into the cool house. Quickly, she stepped inside and closed the door, so that the interior would stay as cool as Sammy liked it. The insulated door shut behind her with a hollow sound. It was air-tight. None of the windows in the house could be opened. She had asked Samuel, "Why you want to live in a box like this, sweetheart? The fresh air good for you."

"I don't like the heat, Beatrice. I don't like baking like meat in the sun. The sealed windows keep the conditioned air in." She hadn't argued.

She walked through the elegant, formal living room to the kitchen. She found the heavy imported furnishings cold and stuffy, but Samuel liked them.

In the kitchen she set water to boil and hunted a bit—where did Gloria keep it?—until she found the Dutch pot. She put it on the burner to toast the fragrant coriander seeds that would flavour the curry. She put on water to boil, stood staring at the steam rising from the pots. Dinner was going to be special tonight. Curried eggs, Samuel's favourite. The eggs in their cardboard case put Beatrice in mind of a trick she'd learned in physics class, for getting an egg unbroken into a narrow-mouthed bottle. You had to boil the egg hard and peel it, then stand a lit candle in the bottle. If you put the narrow end of the egg into the mouth of the bottle, it made a seal, and when the candle had burnt up all the air in the bottle, the vacuum it created would suck the egg in, whole. Beatrice had been the only one in her class patient enough to make the trick work. Patience was all her husband needed. Poor, mysterious Samuel had lost two wives in this isolated country home. He'd been rattling about in the airless house like the egg in the bottle. He kept to himself. The closest neighbours were miles away, and he didn't even know their names.

She was going to change all that, though. Invite her mother to stay for a while, maybe have a dinner party for the distant neighbours. Before her pregnancy made her too lethargic to do much.

A baby would complete their family. Samuel *would* be pleased, he would. She remembered him joking that no woman should have to give birth to his ugly black babies, but she would show him how beautiful their children would be, little brown bodies new as the earth after the rain. She would show him how to love himself in them.

It was hot in the kitchen. Perhaps the heat from the stove? Beatrice went out into the living room, wandered through the guest bedroom, the master bedroom, both bathrooms. The whole house was warmer than she'd ever felt it. Then she realised she could hear sounds coming from the outside, the cicadas singing loudly for rain. There was no whisper of cool air through the vents in the house. The air conditioner wasn't running.

Beatrice began to feel worried. Samuel liked it cold. She had planned tonight to be a special night for the two of them, but he wouldn't react well if everything wasn't to his liking. He'd raised his voice at her a few times. Once or twice he had stopped in the middle of an argument, one hand pulled back as if to strike, to take deep breaths, battling for self-control. His dark face would flush almost blue-black as he fought his rage down. Those times she'd stayed out of his way until he was calm again.

What could be wrong with the air conditioner? Maybe it had just come unplugged? Beatrice wasn't even sure where the controls were. Gloria and Samuel took care of everything around the house. She made another circuit through her home, looking for the main controls. Nothing. Puzzled, she went back into the living room. It was becoming thick and close as a womb inside their closed-up home.

There was only one room left to search. The locked third bedroom. Samuel had told her that both his wives had died in there, first one, then the other. He had given her the keys to every room in the house, but requested that she never open that particular door.

"I feel like it's bad luck, love. I know I'm just being superstitious, but I hope I can trust you to honour my wishes in this." She had, not wanting to cause him any anguish. But where else could the control panel be? It was getting so hot!

As she reached into her pocket for the keys she always carried with her, she realised she was still holding a raw egg in her hand. She'd forgotten to put it into the pot when the heat in the house had made her curious. She managed a little smile. The hormones flushing her body were making her so absent-minded! Samuel would tease her, until she told him why. Everything would be all right.

Beatrice put the egg into her other hand, got the keys out of her pocket, opened the door.

A wall of icy, dead air hit her body. It was freezing cold in the room. Her exhaled breath floated away from her in a long, misty curl. Frowning, she took a step inside and her eyes saw before her brain could understand, and when it did, the egg fell from her hands to smash open on the floor at her feet. Two women's bodies lay side by side on the double bed. Frozen mouths gaped open; frozen, gutted bellies, too. A fine sheen of ice crystals glazed their skin, which like hers was barely brown, but laved in gelid, rime-covered blood that had solidified ruby red. Beatrice whimpered.

* * *

"But Miss," Beatrice asked her teacher, "how the egg going to come back out the bottle again?"

"How do you think, Beatrice? There's only one way; you have to break the bottle."

* * *

This was how Samuel punished the ones who had tried to bring his babies into the world, his beautiful black babies. For each woman had had the muscled sac of her womb removed and placed on her belly, hacked open to reveal the purplish mass of her placenta. Beatrice knew that if she were to dissect the thawing tissue, she'd find a tiny foetus in each one. The dead women had been pregnant too.

A movement at her feet caught her eyes. She tore her gaze away from the bodies long enough to glance down. Writhing in the fast congealing yolk was a pin-feathered embryo. A rooster must have been at Mister Herbert's hens. She put her hands on her belly to still the sympathetic twitching of her womb. Her eyes were drawn back to the horror on the beds. Another whimper escaped her lips.

A sound like a sigh whispered in through the door she'd left open. A current of hot air seared past her cheek, making a plume of fog as it entered the room. The fog split into two, settled over the heads of each woman, began to take on definition. Each misty column had a face, contorted in rage. The faces were those of the bodies on the bed. One of the duppy women leaned over her own corpse. She lapped like a cat at the blood thawing on its breast. She became a little more solid for having drunk of her own life blood. The other duppy stooped to do the same. The two duppy women each had a belly slightly swollen with the pregnancies for which Samuel had killed them. Beatrice had broken the bottles that had confined the duppy wives, their bodies held in stasis because their spirits were trapped. She'd freed them. She'd let them into the house. Now there was nothing to cool their fury. The heat of it was warming the room up quickly.

The duppy wives held their bellies and glared at her, anger flaring hot behind their eyes. Beatrice backed away from the beds. "I didn't know," she said to the wives. "Don't vex with me. I didn't know what it is Samuel do to you."

Was that understanding on their faces, or were they beyond compassion?

"I making baby for him too. Have mercy on the baby, at least?"

Beatrice heard the *snik* of the front door opening. Samuel was home. He would have seen the broken bottles, would feel the warmth of the house. Beatrice felt that initial calm of the prey that realises it has no choice but to turn and face the beast that is pursuing it. She wondered if Samuel would be able to read the truth hidden in her body, like the egg in the bottle.

"Is not me you should be vex with," she pleaded with the duppy wives. She took a deep breath and spoke the words that broke her heart. "Is . . . is Samuel who do this."

She could hear Samuel moving around in the house, the angry rumbling of his voice like the thunder before the storm. The words were muffled, but she could hear the anger in his tone. She called out, "What you saying, Samuel?"

She stepped out of the meat locker and quietly pulled the door in, but left it open slightly so the duppy wives could come out when they were ready. Then with a welcoming smile, she went to greet her husband. She would stall him as long as she could from entering the third bedroom. Most of the blood in the wives' bodies would be clotted, but maybe it was only important that it be *warm*. She hoped that enough of it would thaw soon for the duppies to drink until they were fully real.

When they had fed, would they come and save her, or would they take revenge on her, their usurper, as well as on Samuel?

Eggie-Law, what a pretty basket.

LEENA KROHN

Their Mother's Tears: The Fourth Letter

(EXCERPT FROM *TAINARON*)

Leena Krohn is one of the most respected Finnish writers of her generation. Her short
novel *Tainaron: Mail from Another City* was nominated for a World Fantasy Award
and International Horror Guild Award in 2005. In her large body of work for adults and
children, Krohn deals with issues related to the boundary between reality and illusion,
artificial intelligence, and issues of morality and conscience—and also interesting views
on motherhood. "Their Mother's Tears: The Fourth Letter" was first published in 2004.

There are strange houses in one of the suburbs. They are like goblets, very
narrow and high, and to a certain extent they recall piles of ashes; but their
reddish walls are as strong as concrete. In them live a countless mass of
inhabitants, small but very industrious folk, who are in constant motion. They
all resemble each other so closely that I should never learn to recognise any of
them. One, however, is an exception.

It is already a long time since I asked Longhorn whether, one day, he
would take me to one of those houses. "Why do they interest you?" he asked.
"Their architecture is so extraordinary," I said. "Perhaps you know someone
there? Perhaps I could go there with you sometime?"

"If you wish," said Longhorn; but he did not look particularly keen.

Yesterday, at last, Longhorn took me to one of those dwellings. At the
entrance was a doorman with whom he exchanged a few words and who set
off to accompany me. "We shall meet this evening," shouted Longhorn, and
disappeared into the gaudy bustle of Tainaron.

I was led along dim and intricate corridors that opened on halls, ware-houses and living spaces of different sizes. Past me rushed large numbers of people; all of them seemed to be in a hurry and in the midst of important tasks. But I was taken to the innermost room of the house, at whose door stood more guards. There was no window in the room, but it was neverthe-less almost unbearably bright, although I could not see the source of the light.

I certainly realised that there were other people in the room, but I could see only one. She was immeasurably larger than all the others, monumental, all the more so because she stayed in one place, unmoving. Her dimensions were enormous: her egg-shaped head grazed the roof of the vault and, in its half recumbent position, her breadth extended from the doorway to the back of the room. As I stepped inside and stood by the wall (there was hardly room anywhere else), there came from her mouth a creaking sound which I interpreted as a welcome.

"Show respect for the queen," hissed my guide, and knelt down. Unaccustomed to such gestures, I felt embarrassed, but I followed his example.

Some time passed before any attention was paid to me. By the walls of the room, around the queen, rushed creatures whose task was evidently to satisfy all her needs. I soon realised that they were necessary, for the queen was so formless that she herself could hardly take a step. And I concluded that she could not possibly have gone out through the door; she must live and die within these walls, without ever seeing even a flicker of sun. Her plight horrified me, and I wanted to leave the glowing cave quickly.

At that moment the creaking voice startled me. I realised that the queen had turned her head a little so that she was now staring at me languidly, at the same time sipping a milky fluid from a goblet held under her infinitesimal jaw.

The straw fell from her lip, and new croaks followed. With difficulty, I made out the following words: "I know what you're thinking, you little smidgeon."

"I'm sorry," I stammered, and vexation made me flushed.

"You think, don't you, that I am some kind of individual, a person, admit it!"

As she went on speaking, her voice grew deeper, and it was as if it began to buzz. It was a most extraordinary voice, for it seemed to be made up of the murmur of hundreds of voices.

"Yes, indeed, I mean . . ." I grew completely confused for a moment and sat down on my heels, as kneeling on the hard floor was too tiring.

"Quite so, of course," I said rapidly, completely puzzled. "Didn't I guess?" she said, and burst into laughter, which sometimes boomed, sometimes tinkled in the corridors so infectiously that in the end all the inhabitants of the building seemed to be joining in, and the entire house was laughing at my simplicity.

Suddenly complete silence followed, and she said, pointing at me with her long proboscis, "So tell me, who am I?"

Before I could even think of an answer to this question, I realised at last what was happening in the back part of the room, which was filled with the queen's great rear body. I had, in fact, been aware all the while that something was being done incessantly, but the nature of that activity hit me like a thunderbolt. Bundles had been carried past me, but it was only at the third or fourth that I looked more closely and saw: they were newborn babies.

The queen was giving birth! She was giving birth incessantly. And just as I realised that, I seemed to hear from all around me the din of a hammer, commands, the chirrup of a saw, and everywhere there hovered the stench of building mortar. I realised that more and more storeys were being added to the house, and that it was reaching ever higher into the serenity of the sea of air. The sounds of construction reached me even from deep under the ground, and in my mind's eye I could see corridors branching beneath the paving stones like roots, greedily growing from day to day. The tribe was increasing; the house was being extended. The city was growing.

"You are the mother of them all, your majesty," I replied, humbly.

"But what is a mother?" she squealed, and suddenly her voice rose to a piercing height, as one of her antennae lashed through the air above my head like a whip.

I retreated and pressed myself to the wall, although I understood that she would not be able to come any nearer.

"She from whom everything flows is not a someone," the queen hissed through her wide jaws, like a snake. I gazed at her, bewitched. "You came to see me, admit it!" she growled, more deeply than I dared think. "But you will be disappointed! You are already disappointed! Admit it!"

"No, not in the least," I protested, anxiously.

"But there is no me here; look around you and understand that! And here, here in particular, there is less of me than anywhere. You think I fill this room. Wrong! Quite wrong! For I am the great hole out of which the city grows. I am the road everyone must travel! I am the salty sea from which everyone emerges, helpless, wet, wrinkled . . ."

Her voice chided me warmly, like a great ocean swell. As she spoke, she glanced languidly behind her, at her formless, mountainous rear, from whose depths her latest offspring were being helped into the brightness of the lamps. They were all born silently, as if they were dead.

But suddenly I saw something gush from her eyes; it splashed on to the floor and the walls and wetted all my clothes.

She was no longer looking at me, and I rose and left the room, wet with the queen's tears.

JAMES TIPTREE, JR.

The Screwfly Solution

James Tiptree, Jr. was an award-winning American speculative fiction writer whose visionary stories and novels often seemed to have no antecedent. The author's real name, not known publicly until 1977, was Alice Bradley Sheldon, but she considered a male name "good camouflage." Sheldon gained a sterling reputation within the science fiction field, winning the Hugo Award, the Nebula, the World Fantasy Award, and others. In 1991, the James Tiptree, Jr Award was created by Pat Murphy and Karen Joy Fowler to honor her memory and each year recognizes works of fiction that continue to explore issues of gender. "The Screwfly Solution" deals with issues of gender, safety, and danger and was first published in *Analog Science Fiction/Science Fact* in 1977.

The young man sitting at 2°N, 75°W, sent a casually venomous glance up at the nonfunctional shoofly *ventilador* and went on reading his letter. He was sweating heavily, stripped to his shorts in the hotbox of what passed for a hotel room in Cuyapán .

> How do other wives *do* it? I stay busy-busy with the Ann Arbor grant review-programs and the seminar, saying brightly "Oh yes, Alan is in Colombia setting up a biological pest-control program, isn't it wonderful?" But inside I imagine you surrounded by nineteen-year-old raven-haired cooing beauties, every one panting with social dedication and filthy rich. And forty inches of bosom busting out of her delicate lingerie. I even figured it in centimeters, that's 101.6 centimeters of busting. Oh, darling, darling, do what you want only *come home safe*.

Alan grinned fondly, briefly imagining the only body he longed for. His girl, his magic Anne. Then he got up to open the window another cautious notch. A long pale mournful face looked in—a goat. The room opened on the goat pen, the stench was vile. Air, anyway. He picked up the letter.

Everything is just about as you left it, except that the Peedsville horror seems to be getting worse. They're calling it the Sons of Adam cult now. Why can't they *do* something, even if it is a religion? The Red Cross has set up a refugee camp in Ashton, Georgia. Imagine, refugees in the U.S.A. I heard two little girls were carried out all slashed up. Oh, Alan.

Which reminds me, Barney came over with a wad of clippings he wants me to send you. I'm putting them in a separate envelope; I know what happens to very fat letters in foreign POs. He says, in case you don't get them, what do the following have in common? Peedsville, São Paulo, Phoenix, San Diego, Shanghai, New Delhi, Tripoli, Brisbane, Johannesburg, and Lubbock, Texas. He says the hint is, remember where the Intertropical Convergence Zone is now. That makes no sense to me, maybe it will to your superior ecological brain. All I could see about the clippings was that they were fairly horrible accounts of murders or massacres of women. The worst was the New Delhi one, about "rafts of female corpses" in the river. The funniest (!) was the Texas Army officer who shot his wife, three daughters, and his aunt, because God told him to clean the place up.

Barney's such an old dear, he's coming over Sunday to help me take off the downspout and see what's blocking it. He's dancing on air right now; since you left, his spruce budworm-moth antipheromone program finally paid off. You know he tested over 2,000 compounds? Well, it seems that good old 2,097 *really* works. When I asked him what it does he just giggles, you know how shy he is with women. Anyway, it seems that a one-shot spray program will save the forests, without harming a single other thing. Birds and people can eat it all day, he says.

Well, sweetheart, that's all the news except Amy goes back to Chicago to school Sunday. The place will be a tomb, I'll miss her frightfully in spite of her being at the stage where I'm her worst enemy. The sullen sexy subteens, Angie says. Amy sends love to her daddy. I send you my whole heart, all that words can't say.

Your Anne

Alan put the letter safely in his note file and glanced over the rest of the thin packet of mail, refusing to let himself dream of home and Anne. Barney's "fat envelope" wasn't there. He threw himself on the rumpled bed, yanking off the light cord a minute before the town generator went off for the night. In the darkness the list of places Barney had mentioned spread themselves around a misty globe that turned, troublingly, in his mind. Something . . .

But then the memory of the hideously parasitized children he had worked with at the clinic that day took possession of his thoughts. He set himself to considering the data he must collect.

Look for the vulnerable link in the behavioral chain—how often Barney— Dr. Barnhard Braithwaite—had pounded it into his skull. Where was it, where? In the morning he would start work on bigger canefly cages . . .

* * *

At that moment, five thousand miles north, Anne was writing.

Oh, darling, darling, your first three letters are here, they all came together. I *knew* you were writing. Forget what I said about swarthy heiresses, that was all a joke. My darling, I know, I know . . . us. Those dreadful canefly larvae, those poor little kids. If you weren't my husband I'd think you were a saint or something. (I do anyway.)

I have your letters pinned up all over the house, makes it a lot less lonely. No real news here except things feel kind of quiet and spooky. Barney and I got the downspout out, it was full of a big rotted hoard of squirrel nuts. They must have been dropping them down the top, I'll put a wire over it. (Don't worry, I'll use a ladder this time.)

Barney's in an odd, grim mood. He's taking this Sons of Adam thing very seriously, it seems he's going to be on the investigation committee if that ever gets off the ground. The weird part is that nobody seems to be doing anything, as if it's just too big. Selina Peters has been printing some acid comments, like: When one man kills his wife you call it murder, but when enough do it we call it a life-style. I think it's spreading, but nobody knows because the media have been asked to downplay it. Barney says it's being viewed as a form of contagious hysteria. He insisted I send you this ghastly interview, printed on thin paper. It's *not* going to be published, of course. The quietness is worse, though, it's like something terrible was going on just out of sight. After reading Barney's thing I called up Pauline in San Diego to make sure she was all right. She sounded funny, as if she wasn't saying everything . . . my own sister. Just after she said things were great she suddenly asked if she could come and stay here a while next month. I said come right away, but she wants to sell her house first. I wish she'd hurry.

The diesel car is okay now, it just needed its filter changed. I had to go out to Springfield to get one, but Eddie installed it for only $2.50. He's going to bankrupt his garage.

In case you didn't guess, those places of Barney's are all about latitude 30° N or S—the horse latitudes. When I said not exactly, he said remember the Equatorial Convergence Zone shifts in winter, and to add in Libya, Osaka, and a place I forget—wait, Alice Springs, Australia. What has this to do with anything, I asked. He said, "Nothing—I hope." I leave it to you, great brains like Barney can be weird.

Oh my dearest, here's all of me to all of you. Your letters make life possible. But don't feel you *have* to, I can tell how tired you must be. Just know we're together, always everywhere.

                                                                    Your Anne

Oh PS I had to open this to put Barney's thing in, it wasn't the secret police. Here it is. All love again. A.

In the goat-infested room where Alan read this, rain was drumming on the roof. He put the letter to his nose to catch the faint perfume once more, and folded it away. Then he pulled out the yellow flimsy Barney had sent and began to read, frowning.

PEEDSVILLE CULT/SONS OF ADAM SPECIAL. Statement by driver Sgt. Willard Mews, Globe Fork, Ark. We hit the roadblock about 80 miles west of Jacksonville. Major John Heinz of Ashton was expecting us, he gave us an escort of two riot vehicles headed by Capt. T. Parr. Major Heinz appeared shocked to see that the N.I.H. medical team included two women doctors. He warned us in the strongest terms of the danger. So Dr. Patsy Putnam (Urbana, Ill.), the psychologist, decided to stay behind at the Army cordon. But Dr. Elaine Fay (Clinton, N.J.) insisted on going with us, saying she was the epi-something (?epidemiologist).

We drove behind one of the riot cars at 30 m.p.h. for about an hour without seeing anything unusual. There were two big signs Saying SONS OF ADAM—LIBERATED ZONE. We passed some small pecan-packing plants and a citrus-processing plant. The men there looked at us but did not do anything unusual. I didn't see any children or women, of course. Just outside Peedsville we stopped at a big barrier made of oil drums in front of a large citrus warehouse. This area is old, sort of a shantytown and trailer park. The new part of town with the shopping center and

developments is about a mile farther on. A warehouse worker with a shot-
gun came out and told us to wait for the mayor. I don't think he saw Dr.
Elaine Fay then, she was sitting sort of bent down in back.

Mayor Blount drove up in a police cruiser, and our chief, Dr. Premack,
explained our mission from the Surgeon General. Dr. Premack was very
careful not to make any remarks insulting to the mayor's religion. Mayor
Blount agreed to let the party go on into Peedsville to take samples of the
soil and water and so on and talk to the doctor who lives there. The mayor
was about 6'2", weight maybe 230 or 240, tanned, with grayish hair. He
was smiling and chuckling in a friendly manner.

Then he looked inside the car and saw Dr. Elaine Fay and he blew up.
He started yelling we had to all get the hell back. But Dr. Premack talked
to him and cooled him down, and finally the mayor said Dr. Fay should
go into the warehouse office and stay there with the door closed. I had to
stay there too and see she didn't come out, and one of the mayor's men
would drive the party.

So the medical people and the mayor and one of the riot vehicles went
on into Peedsville, and I took Dr. Fay back into the warehouse office and
sat down. It was real hot and stuffy. Dr. Fay opened a window, but then I
heard her trying to talk to an old man outside and I told her she couldn't
do that and closed the window. The old man went away. Then she wanted
to talk to me, but I told her I did not feel like conversing. I felt it was real
wrong, her being there.

So then she started looking through the office files and reading papers
there. I told her that was a bad idea, she shouldn't do that. She said the
government expected her to investigate. She showed me a booklet or
magazine they had there, it was called *Man Listens to God* by Reverend
McIllhenny. They had a carton full in the office. I started reading it, and
Dr. Fay said she wanted to wash her hands. So I took her back along a kind
of enclosed hallway beside the conveyor to where the toilet was. There
were no doors or windows, so I went back. After a while she called out that
there was a cot back there, she was going to lie down. I figured that was all
right because of the no windows; also, I was glad to be rid of her company.

When I got to reading the book it was very intriguing. It was very
deep thinking about how man is now on trial with God and if we fulfill
our duty God will bless us with a real new life on Earth. The signs and
portents show it. It wasn't like, you know, Sunday-school stuff. It was deep.

After a while I heard some music and saw the soldiers from the other
riot car were across the street by the gas tanks, sitting in the shade of
some trees and kidding with the workers from the plant. One of them was

playing a guitar, not electric, just plain. It looked so peaceful.

Then Mayor Blount drove up alone in the cruiser and came in. When he saw I was reading the book he smiled at me sort of fatherly, but he looked tense. He asked me where Dr. Fay was, and I told him she was lying down in back. He said that was okay. Then he kind of sighed and went back down the hall, closing the door behind him. I sat and listened to the guitar man, trying to hear what he was singing. I felt really hungry, my lunch was in Dr. Premack's car.

After a while the door opened and Mayor Blount came back in. He looked terrible, his clothes were messed up, and he had bloody scrape marks on his face. He didn't say anything, he just looked at me hard and fierce, like he might have been disoriented. I saw his zipper was open and there was blood on his clothing and also on his (private parts).

I didn't feel frightened, I felt something important had happened. I tried to get him to sit down. But he motioned me to follow him back down the hall, to where Dr. Fay was. "You must see," he said. He went into the toilet and I went into a kind of little room there, where the cot was. The light was fairly good, reflected off the tin roof from where the walls stopped. I saw Dr. Fay lying on the cot in a peaceful appearance. She was lying straight, her clothing was to some extent different but her legs were together, I was glad to see that. Her blouse was pulled up, and I saw there was a cut or incision on her abdomen. The blood was coming out there, or it had been coming out there, like a mouth. It wasn't moving at this time. Also her throat was cut open.

I returned to the office. Mayor Blount was sitting down, looking very tired. He had cleaned himself off. He said, "I did it for you. Do you understand?"

He seemed like my father. I can't say it better than that. I realized he was under a terrible strain, he had taken a lot on himself for me. He went on to explain how Dr. Fay was very dangerous, she was what they call a cripto-female (crypto?), the most dangerous kind. He had exposed her and purified the situation. He was very straightforward, I didn't feel confused at all, I knew he, had done what was right.

We discussed the book, how man must purify himself and show God a clean world. He said some people raise the question of how can man reproduce without women, but such people miss the point. The point is that as long as man depends on the old filthy animal way, God won't help him. When man gets rid of his animal part which is woman, this is the signal God is awaiting. Then God will reveal the new true clean way, maybe angels will come bringing new souls, or maybe we will live forever, but it is not our place to speculate, only to obey. He said some men here had seen an Angel of the Lord. This was very deep, it seemed like it echoed inside me, I felt it was an inspiration.

Then the medical party drove up and I told Dr. Premack that Dr. Fay had been taken care of and sent away, and I got in the car to drive them out of the Liberated Zone. However, four of the six soldiers from the road-block refused to leave. Capt. Parr tried to argue them out of it but finally agreed they could stay to guard the oil-drum barrier.

I would have liked to stay too, the place was so peaceful, but they needed me to drive the car. If I had known there would be all this hassle I never would have done them the favor. I am not crazy and I have not done anything wrong and my lawyer will get me out. That is all I have to say.

In Cuyapán the hot afternoon rain had temporarily ceased. As Alan's fingers let go of Sgt. Willard Mews's wretched document, he caught sight of pencil-scrawled words in the margin in Barney's spider hand. He squinted.

"Man's religion and metaphysics are the voices of his glands. Schönweiser, 1878."

Who the devil Schönweiser was Alan didn't know, but he knew what Barney was conveying. This murderous crackpot religion of McWhosis was a symptom, not a cause. Barney believed something was physically affecting the Peedsville men, generating psychosis, and a local religious demagogue had sprung up to "explain" it.

Well, maybe. But cause or effect, Alan thought only of one thing: eight hundred miles from Peedsville to Ann Arbor. Anne should be safe. She *had* to be.

He threw himself on the lumpy cot, his mind going back exultantly to his work. At the cost of a million bites and cane cuts he was pretty sure he'd found the weak link in the canefly cycle. The male mass-mating behavior, the comparative scarcity of ovulant females. It would be the screwfly solution all over again with the sexes reversed. Concentrate the pheromone, release sterilized females. Luckily the breeding populations were comparatively isolated. In a couple of seasons they ought to have it. Have to let them go on spraying poison meanwhile, of course; damn pity, it was slaughtering everything and getting in the water, and the caneflies had evolved to immunity anyway. But in a couple of seasons, maybe three, they could drop the canefly populations below reproductive viability. No more tormented human bodies with those stinking larvae in the nasal passages and brain . . . He drifted off for a nap, grinning.

Up north, Anne was biting her lip in shame and pain.

Sweetheart, I shouldn't admit it but your wife is scared a bit jittery. Just female nerves or something, nothing to worry about. Everything is normal up here. It's so eerily normal, nothing in the papers, nothing anywhere except what I hear through Barney and Lillian. But Pauline's phone won't answer out in San Diego; the fifth day some strange man yelled at me and banged the phone down. Maybe she's sold her house—but why wouldn't she call?

Lillian's on some kind of Save-the-Women committee, like we were an endangered species, ha-ha—you know Lillian. It seems the Red Cross has started setting up camps. But she says, after the first rush, only a trickle are coming out of what they call "the affected areas." Not many children, either, even little boys. And they have some air photos around Lubbock showing what look like mass graves. Oh, Alan . . . so far it seems to be mostly spreading west, but something's happening in St. Louis, they're cut off. So many places seem to have just vanished from the news, I had a nightmare that there isn't a woman left alive down there. And nobody's doing anything. They talked about spraying with tranquilizers for a while and then that died out. What could it do? Somebody at the UN has proposed a convention on—you won't believe this—*femicide*. It sounds like a deodorant spray.

Excuse me, honey, I seem to be a little hysterical. George Searles came back from Georgia talking about God's Will—Searles the lifelong atheist. Alan, something crazy is happening.

But there aren't any facts. Nothing. The Surgeon General issued a report on the bodies of the Rahway Rip-Breast Team—I guess I didn't tell you about that. Anyway, they could find no pathology. Milton Baines wrote a letter saying in the present state of the art we can't distinguish the brain of a saint from a psychopathic killer, so how could they expect to find what they don't know how to look for?

Well, enough of these jitters. It'll be all over by the time you get back, just history. Everything's fine here, I fixed the car's muffler again. And Amy's coming home for the vacations, *that'll* get my mind off faraway problems.

Oh, something amusing to end with—Angie told me what Barney's enzyme does to the spruce budworm. It seems it blocks the male from turning around after he connects with the female, so he mates with her *head* instead. Like clockwork with a cog missing. There're going to be some pretty puzzled female spruceworms. Now why couldn't Barney tell me that? He really is such a sweet shy old dear. He's given me some stuff to put in, as usual. I didn't read it.

Now don't worry, my darling, everything's fine.

I love you, I love you so.

Always, all ways your Anne

Two weeks later in Cuyapán when Barney's enclosures slid out of the envelope, Alan didn't read them, either. He stuffed them into the pocket of his bush jacket with a shaking hand and started bundling his notes together on the rickety table, with a scrawled note to Sister Dominique on top. The hell with the canefly, the hell with everything except that tremor in his fearless Anne's firm handwriting. The hell with being five thousand miles away from his woman, his child, while some deadly madness raged. He crammed his meager belongings into his duffel. If he hurried he could catch the bus through to Bogota and maybe make the Miami flight.

He made it to Miami, but the planes north were jammed. He failed a quick standby; six hours to wait. Time to call Anne. When the call got through some difficulty, he was unprepared for the rush of joy and relief that burst along the wires.

"Thank god—I can't believe it—Oh, Alan, my darling, are you really—I can't believe—"

He found he was repeating too, and all mixed up with the canefly data. They were both laughing hysterically when he finally hung up.

Six hours. He settled in a frayed plastic chair opposite Aerolineas Argentinas, his mind half back at the clinic, half on the throngs moving by him. Something was oddly different here, he perceived presently. Where was the decorative fauna he usually enjoyed in Miami, the parade of young girls in crotch-tight pastel jeans? The flounces, boots, wild hats and hairdos, and startling expanses of newly tanned skin, the brilliant fabrics barely confining the bob of breasts and buttocks? Not here—but wait; looking closely, he glimpsed two young faces hidden under unbecoming parkas, their bodies draped in bulky nondescript skirts. In fact, all down the long vista he could see the same thing: hooded ponchos, heaped-on clothes and baggy pants, dull colors. A new style? No, he thought not. It seemed to him their movements suggested furtiveness, timidity. And they moved in groups. He watched a lone girl struggle to catch up with the others ahead of her, apparently strangers. They accepted her wordlessly.

They're frightened, he thought. Afraid of attracting notice. Even that gray-haired matron in a pantsuit resolutely leading a flock of kids was glancing around nervously.

And at the Argentine desk opposite he saw another odd thing; two lines had a big sign over them: *Mujeres*. Women. They were crowded with the shapeless forms and very quiet.

The men seemed to be behaving normally; hurrying, lounging, griping, and joking in the lines as they kicked their luggage along. But Alan felt an undercurrent of tension, like an irritant in the air. Outside the line of store-fronts behind him a few isolated men seemed to be handing out tracts. An airport attendant spoke to the nearest man; he merely shrugged and moved a few doors down.

To distract himself Alan picked up a *Miami Herald* from the next seat. It was surprisingly thin. The international news occupied him for a while; he had seen none for weeks. It too had a strange empty quality, even the bad news seemed to have dried up. The African war which had been going on seemed to be over, or went unreported. A trade summit meeting was hag-gling over grain and steel prices. He found himself at the obituary pages, columns of close-set type dominated by the photo of an unknown defunct ex-senator. Then his eye fell on two announcements at the bottom of the, page. One was too flowery for quick comprehension, but the other stated in bold plain type:

THE FORSETTE FUNERAL HOME REGRETFULLY ANNOUNCES
IT WILL NO LONGER ACCEPT FEMALE CADAVERS

Slowly he folded the paper, staring at it numbly. On the back was an item headed *Navigational Hazard Warning*, in the shipping news. Without really taking it in, he read:

> *AP/Nassau:* The excursion liner *Carib Swallow* reached port under tow today after striking an obstruction in the Gulf Stream off Cape Hatteras. The obstruction was identified as part of a commercial trawler's seine floated by female corpses. This confirms reports from Florida and the Gulf of the use of such seines, some of them over a mile in length. Similar reports coming from the Pacific coast and as far away as Japan indicate a growing hazard to coastwise shipping.

Alan flung the thing into the trash receptacle and sat rubbing his fore-head and eyes. Thank god he had followed his impulse to come home. He felt totally disoriented, as though he had landed by error on another planet. Five hours more to wait . . . At length he recalled the stuff from Barney he had thrust in his pocket, and pulled it out and smoothed it.

The top item seemed to be from the *Ann Arbor News*. Dr. Lillian Dash, together with several hundred other members of her organization, had been arrested for demonstrating without a permit in front of the White House. They had started a fire in a garbage can, which was considered particularly heinous. A number of women's groups had participated; the total struck

Alan as more like thousands than hundreds. Extraordinary security precautions were being taken, despite the fact that the President was out of town at the time.

The next item had to be Barney's acerbic humor.

UP/Vatican City 19 June. Pope John IV today intimated that he does not plan to comment officially on the so-called Pauline Purification cults advocating the elimination of women as a means of justifying man to God. A spokesman emphasized that the Church takes no position on these cults but repudiates any doctrine involving a "challenge" to or from God to reveal His further plans for man.

Cardinal Fazzoli, spokesman for the European Pauline movement, reaffirmed his view that the Scriptures define woman as merely a temporary companion and instrument of man. Women, he states, are nowhere defined as human, but merely as a transitional expedient or state. "The time of transition to full humanity is at hand," he concluded.

The next item appeared to be a thin-paper Xerox from a recent issue of *Science*:

SUMMARY REPORT OF THE AD HOC
EMERGENCY COMMITTEE ON FEMICIDE

The recent worldwide though localized outbreaks of femicide appear to represent a recurrence of similar outbreaks by groups or sects which are not uncommon in world history in times of psychic stress. In this case the root cause is undoubtedly the speed of social and technological change, augmented by population pressure, and the spread and scope are aggravated by instantaneous world communications, thus exposing more susceptible persons. It is not viewed as a medical or epidemiological problem; no physical pathology has been found. Rather it is more akin to the various manias which swept Europe in the seventeenth century, e.g., the Dancing Manias, and like them, should run its course and disappear. The chiliastic cults which have sprung up around the affected areas appear to be unrelated, having in common only the idea that a new means of human reproduction will be revealed as a result of the "purifying" elimination of women.

We recommend that (1) inflammatory and sensational reporting be suspended; (2) refugee centers be set up and maintained for women escapees from the focal areas; (3) containment of affected areas by military cordon be continued and enforced; and (4) after a cooling-down period and the subsidence of the mania, qualified mental-health teams and appropriate professional personnel go in to undertake rehabilitation.

SUMMARY OF THE MINORITY
REPORT OF THE AD HOC COMMITTEE

The nine members signing this report agree that there is no evidence for epidemiological contagion of femicide in the strict sense. *However*, the geographical relation of the focal areas of outbreak strongly suggests that they cannot be dismissed as purely psychosocial phenomena. The initial outbreaks have occurred around the globe near the 30th parallel, the area of principal atmospheric downflow of upper winds coming from the Intertropical Convergence Zone. An agent or condition in the upper equatorial atmosphere would thus be expected to reach ground level along the 30th parallel, with certain seasonal variations. One principal variation is that the downflow moves north over the East Asian continent during the late winter months, and those areas south of it (Arabia, Western India, parts of North Africa) have in fact been free of outbreaks until recently, when the downflow zone moved south. A similar downflow occurs in the Southern Hemisphere, and outbreaks have been reported along the 30th parallel running through Pretoria and Alice Springs, Australia. (Information from Argentina is currently unavailable.)

This geographical correlation cannot be dismissed, and it is therefore urged that an intensified search for a physical cause be instituted. It is also urgently recommended that the rate of spread from known focal points be correlated with wind conditions. A watch for similar outbreaks along the secondary down-welling zones at 60° north and south should be kept.

(signed for the minority)

Barnhard Braithwaite

Alan grinned reminiscently at his old friend's name, which seemed to restore normalcy and stability to the world. It looked as if Barney was on to something, too, despite the prevalence of horses' asses. He frowned, puzzling it out.

Then his face slowly changed as he thought how it would be, going home to Anne. In a few short hours his arms would be around her, the tall, secretly beautiful body that had come to obsess him. Theirs had been a late-blooming love. They'd married, he supposed now, out of friendship, even out of friends' pressure. Everyone said they were made for each other, he big and chunky and blond, she willowy brunette; both shy, highly controlled, cerebral types.

For the first few years the friendship had held, but sex hadn't been all that much. Conventional necessity. Politely reassuring each other, privately—he could say it now—disappointing.

But then, when Amy was a toddler, something had happened. A miraculous inner portal of sensuality had slowly opened to them, a liberation into their own secret unsuspected heaven of fully physical bliss . . . Jesus, but it had been a wrench when the Colombia thing had come up. Only their absolute sureness of each other had made him take it. And now, to be about to have her again, trebly desirable from the spice of separation—feeling-seeing-hearing-smelling-grasping. He shifted in his seat to conceal his body's excitement, half mesmerized by fantasy.

And Amy would be there, too; he grinned at the memory of that pre-pubescent little body plastered against him. She was going to be a handful, all right. His manhood understood Amy a lot better than her mother did; no cerebral phase for Amy . . . But Anne, his exquisite shy one, with whom he'd found the way into the almost unendurable transports of the flesh . . . First the conventional greeting, he thought; the news, the unspoken, savored, mounting excitement behind their eyes; the light touches; then the seeking of their own room, the falling clothes, the caresses, gentle at first—the flesh, the *nakedness*—the delicate teasing, the grasp, the first thrust—

A terrible alarm bell went off in his head. Exploded from his dream, he stared around, then finally down at his hands. *What was he doing with his open clasp knife in his fist?*

Stunned, he felt for the last shreds of his fantasy, and realized that the tactile images had not been of caresses, but of a frail neck strangling in his fist, the thrust had been the plunge of a blade seeking vitals. In his arms, legs, phantasms of striking and trampling bones cracking. And Amy—

Oh, god. Oh, god—

Not sex, blood lust.

That was what he had been dreaming. The sex was there, but it was driving some engine of death.

Numbly he put the knife away, thinking only over and over, it's got me. It's got me. Whatever it is, it's got me. *I can't go home.*

After an unknown time he got up and made his way to the United counter to turn in his ticket. The line was long. As he waited, his mind cleared a little. What could he do, here in Miami? Wouldn't it be better to get back to Ann Arbor and turn himself in to Barney? Barney could help him, if anyone could. Yes, that was best. But first he had to warn Anne.

The connection took even longer this time. When Anne finally answered he found himself blurting unintelligibly, it took a while to make her understand he wasn't talking about a plane delay.

"I tell you, I've caught it. Listen, Anne, for god's sake. If I should come to the house don't let me come near you. I mean it. I mean it. I'm going to the lab, but I might lose control and try to get to you. Is Barney there?"

"Yes, but darling—"

"Listen. Maybe he can fix me, maybe this'll wear off. But I'm not safe. Anne, Anne, I'd kill you, can you understand? Get a—get a weapon. I'll try not to come to the house. But if I do, don't let me get near you. Or Amy. It's a sickness, it's real. Treat me—treat me like a fucking wild animal. Anne, say you understand, say you'll do it."

They were both crying when he hung up.

He went shaking back to sit and wait. After a time his head seemed to clear a little more. *Doctor, try to think.* The first thing he thought of was to take the loathsome knife and throw it down a trash slot. As he did so he realized there was one more piece of Barney's material in his pocket. He uncrumpled it; it seemed to be a clipping from *Nature*.

At the top was Barney's scrawl: "Only guy making sense. U.K. infected now, Oslo, Copenhagen out of communication. Damfools still won't listen. Stay put."

COMMUNICATION FROM PROFESSOR IAN MACLNTYRE, GLASGOW UNIV.

A potential difficulty for our species has always been implicit in the close linkage between the behavioral expression of aggression/predation and sexual reproduction in the male. This close linkage is shown by (a) many of the same neuromuscular pathways which are utilized both in predatory and sexual pursuit, grasping, mounting, etc., and (b) similar states of adrenergic arousal which are activated in both. The same linkage is seen in the males of many other species; in some, the expression of aggression and copulation alternate or even coexist, an all-too-familiar example being the common house cat. Males of many species bite, claw, bruise, tread, or otherwise assault receptive females during the act of intercourse; indeed, in some species the male attack is necessary for female ovulation to occur.

In many if not all species it is the aggressive behavior which appears first, and then changes to copulatory behavior when the appropriate signal is presented (e.g., the three-tined stickleback and the European robin). Lacking the inhibiting signal, the male's fighting response continues and the female is attacked or driven off.

It seems therefore appropriate to speculate that the present crisis might be caused by some substance, perhaps at the viral or enzymatic level, which effects a failure of the switching or triggering function in the higher primates. (Note: Zoo gorillas and chimpanzees have recently been observed to attack or destroy their mates; rhesus not.) Such a dysfunction could be expressed by the failure of mating behavior to modify or supervene over the aggressive/predatory response; i.e., sexual stimulation would produce attack only, the stimulation discharging itself through the destruction of the stimulating object.

In this connection it might be noted that exactly this condition is a commonplace of male functional pathology, in those cases where murder occurs as a response to, and apparent completion of, sexual desire.

It should be emphasized that the aggression/copulation linkage discussed here is specific to the male; the female response (e.g., lordotic reflex) being of a different nature.

Alan sat holding the crumpled sheet a long time; the dry, stilted Scottish phrases seemed to help clear his head, despite the sense of brooding tension all around him. Well, if pollution or whatever had produced some substance, it could presumably be countered, filtered, neutralized. Very very carefully, he let himself consider his life with Anne, his sexuality. Yes; much of their loveplay could be viewed as genitalized, sexually gentled savagery. Play-predation . . . He turned his mind quickly away. Some writer's phrase occurred to him: "The panic element in all sex." Who? Fritz Leiber? The violation of social distance, maybe; another threatening element.

Whatever, it's our weak link, he thought. Our vulnerability . . . The dreadful feeling of *rightness* he had experienced when he found himself knife in hand, fantasizing violence, came back to him. As though it was the right, the only, way. Was that what Barney's budworms felt when they mated with their females wrong-end-to?

At long length, he became aware of body need and sought a toilet. The place was empty, except for what he took to be a heap of clothes blocking the door of the far stall. Then he saw the red-brown pool in which it lay, and the bluish mounds of bare, thin buttocks. He backed out, not breathing, and fled into the nearest crowd, knowing he was not the first to have done so.

Of course. Any sexual drive. Boys, men, too.

At the next washroom he watched to see men enter and leave normally before he ventured in.

Afterward he returned to sit, waiting, repeating over and over to himself: *Go to the lab. Don't go home. Go straight to the lab.* Three more hours; he sat numbly at 26°N, 81°W, breathing, breathing . . .

Dear diary. Big scene tonite, Daddy came home!!! Only he acted so funny, he had the taxi wait and just held on to the doorway, he wouldn't touch me or let us come near him. (I mean funny weird, not funny ha-ha.) He said, I have something to tell you, this is getting worse not better. I'm going to sleep in the lab but I want you to get out, Anne, Anne, I can't trust myself anymore. First thing in the morning you both get on the plane for Martha's and stay there. So I thought he had to be joking, I mean with the dance next week and Aunt Martha lives in Whitehorse where there's nothing nothing nothing. So I was yelling and Mother was yelling and Daddy was groaning, Go now! And then he started crying. Crying!!! So I realized, wow, this is serious, and I started to go over to him but Mother yanked me back and then I saw she had this big *knife*!!! And she shoved me in back of her and started crying too: Oh Alan, Oh Alan, like she was insane. So I said, Daddy, I'll never leave you, it felt like the perfect thing to say. And it was thrilling, he looked at me real sad and deep like I was a grown-up while Mother was treating me like I was a mere infant as usual. But Mother ruined it raving, Alan the child is mad, darling go. So he ran out of the door yelling, Be gone. Take the car. Get out before I come back.

Oh I forgot to say I was wearing what but my gooby *green* with my curl-tites still on, wouldn't you know of all the shitty luck, how could I have known such a beautiful scene was ahead we never know life's cruel whimsy. And Mother is dragging out suitcases yelling, Pack your things hurry! So she's going I guess but I am not repeat not going to spend the fall sitting in Aunt Martha's grain silo and lose the dance and all my summer credits. And Daddy was trying to *communicate* with us, right? I think their relationship is obsolete. So when she goes upstairs I am splitting. I am going to go over to the lab and see Daddy.

Oh PS Diane tore my yellow jeans she promised me I could use her pink ones ha-ha that'll be the day.

I ripped that page out of Amy's diary when I heard the squad car coming. I never opened her diary before, but when I found she'd gone I looked . . . Oh, my darling little girl. She went to him, my little girl, my poor little fool child. Maybe if I'd taken time to explain, maybe—

Excuse me, Barney. The stuff is wearing off, the shots they gave me. I didn't feel anything. I mean, I knew somebody's daughter went to see her father and he killed her. And cut his throat. But it didn't mean anything.

Alan's note, they gave me that but then they took it away. Why did they have to do that? His last handwriting, the last words he wrote before his hand picked up the, before he—

I remember it. *"Sudden and light as that, the bonds gave. And we learned of finalities besides the grave. The bonds of our humanity have broken, we are finished. I love—"*

I'm all right, Barney, really. Who wrote that, Robert Frost? *The bonds gave* . . . Oh, he said, tell Barney: *The terrible rightness.* What does that mean?

You can't answer that, Barney dear. I'm just writing this to stay sane, I'll put it in your hidey-hole. Thank you, thank you, Barney dear. Even as blurry as I was, I knew it was you. All the time you were cutting off my hair and rubbing dirt on my face, I knew it was right because it was you. Barney, I never thought of you as those horrible words you said. You were always Dear Barney.

By the time the stuff wore off I had done everything you said, the gas, the groceries. Now I'm here in your cabin. With those clothes you made me put on—I guess I do look like a boy, the gas man called me "Mister."

I still can't really realize, I have to stop myself from rushing back. But you saved my life, I know that. The first trip in I got a paper, I saw where they bombed the Apostle Islands refuge. And it had about those three women stealing the Air Force plane and bombing Dallas, too. Of course they shot them down, over the Gulf. Isn't it strange how we do nothing? Just get killed by ones and twos. Or more, now they've started on the refuges . . . Like hypnotized rabbits. We're a toothless race.

Do you know I never said "we" meaning women before? "We" was always me and Alan, and Amy of course. Being killed selectively encourages group identification . . . You see how sane-headed I am.

But I still can't really realize.

My first trip in was for salt and kerosene. I went to that little Red Deer store and got my stuff from the old man in the back, as you told me—you see, I remembered! He called me "Boy," but I think maybe he suspects. He knows I'm staying at your cabin.

Anyway, some men and boys came in the front. They were all so *normal*, laughing and kidding. I just couldn't believe, Barney. In fact I started to go out past them when I heard one of them say, "Heinz saw an angel." An *angel*. So I stopped and listened. They said it was big and sparkly. Coming to see if man is carrying out God's Will, one of them said. And he said, Moosenee is now a liberated zone, and all up by Hudson Bay. I turned and got out the back, fast. The old man had heard them, too. He said to me quietly, "I'll miss the kids."

Hudson Bay, Barney, that means it's coming from the north too, doesn't it? That must be about 60°.

But I have to go back once again, to get some fishhooks. I can't live on bread. Last week I found a deer some poacher had killed, just the head and legs. I made a stew. It was a doe. Her eyes; I wonder if mine look like that now.

* * *

I went to get the fishhooks today. It was bad, I can't ever go back. There were some men in front again, but they were different. Mean and tense. No boys. And there was a new sign out in front, I couldn't see it; maybe it says Liberated Zone, too.

The old man gave me the hooks quick and whispered to me, "Boy, them woods'll be full of hunters next week." I almost ran out.

About a mile down the road a blue pickup started to chase me. I guess he wasn't from around there, I ran the VW into a logging draw and he roared on by. After a long while I drove out and came on back, but I left the car about a mile from here and hiked in. It's surprising how hard it is to pile enough brush to hide a yellow VW.

Barney, I can't stay here. I'm eating perch raw so nobody will see my smoke, but those hunters will be coming through. I'm going to move my sleeping bag out to the swamp by that big rock, I don't think many people go there.

Since my last lines I moved out. It feels safer. Oh, Barney, how did this *happen*?

Fast, that's how. Six months ago I was Dr. Anne Alstein. Now I'm a widow and bereaved mother, dirty and hungry, squatting in a swamp in mortal fear. Funny if I'm the last woman left alive on Earth. I guess the last one around here, anyway. Maybe some are holed up in the Himalayas, or sneaking through the wreck of New York City. How can we last?

We can't.

And I can't survive the winter here, Barney. It gets to 40° below. I'd have to have a fire, they'd see the smoke. Even if I worked my way south, the woods end in a couple hundred miles. I'd be potted like a duck. No. No use. Maybe somebody is trying something somewhere, but it won't reach here in time . . . and what do I have to live for?

No. I'll just make a good end, say up on that rock where I can see the stars. After I go back and leave this for you. I'll wait a few days to see the beautiful color in the trees one last time.

Good-bye, dearest dearest Barney.

I know what I'll scratch for an epitaph.

HERE LIES THE SECOND MEANEST PRIMATE ON EARTH

I guess nobody will ever read this, unless I get the nerve and energy to take it back to Barney's. Probably I won't. Leave it in a Baggie, I have one here; maybe Barney will come and look. I'm up on the big rock now. The moon is going to rise soon, I'll do it then. Mosquitoes, be patient. You'll have all you want.

The thing I have to write down is that I saw an angel, too. This morning. It was big and sparkly, like the man said; like a Christmas tree without the tree. But I knew it was real because the frogs stopped croaking and two blue jays gave alarm calls. That's important; it was *really there*.

I watched it, sitting under my rock. It didn't move much. It sort of bent over and picked up something, leaves or twigs, I couldn't see. Then it did something with them around its middle, like putting them into an invisible sample pocket.

Let me repeat—it was *there*. Barney, if you're reading this, *there are things here*. And I think they've done whatever it is to us. Made us kill ourselves off.

Why?

Well, it's a nice place, if it wasn't for the people. How do you get rid of people? Bombs, death rays—all very primitive. Leave a big mess. Destroy everything, craters, radioactivity, ruin the place.

This way there's no muss, no fuss. just like what we did to the screwfly. Pinpoint the weak link, wait a bit while we do it for them. Then only a few bones around; make good fertilizer.

Barney dear, good-bye. I saw it. It was there.

But it wasn't an angel.

I think I saw a real estate agent.

ROSE LEMBERG

Seven Losses of *na Re*

Rose Lemberg is a writer, poet, and editor originally from Ukraine but currently living in the U.S. She is passionate about diversity in SFF and elsewhere, and advocates for diversity through her essays and editorial work. Her work has been published in *Strange Horizons, Beneath Ceaseless Skies, Fantasy Magazine, Apex, Goblin Fruit*, and other places. She is the founder and coeditor of *Stone Telling*, a magazine of boundary-crossing speculative poetry. "Seven Losses of Na Re" tells the story of a young woman and the importance and power of her name. It was first published in *Daily Science Fiction* in 2012.

1.

My life is described by the music of mute violins. When my parents married, my great-grandfather, may the earth be as a feather, ascended the special-guests podium, cradling the old fiddle to his chest. "And now the *zeide* will play the wedding melody," they said. "A special blessing," they said, a *sgule*, a royal blessing. But the bow fell from his fingers.

2.

When I was born, my parents couldn't name me. They wanted a name *na Re*, which means "beginning with the letter R," after my great-grandmother. She was born Rukhl, the brilliant daughter of a penniless *shlimazl* cobbler. As the revolution fumbled all archetypes, they called her Rakhil'ka; a kind of ironed, bronze-buttoned, bright-Soviet-future Rukhl. Later even Rakhil'ka became too bourgeois, and my great-grandmother changed her name to Roza, Roza like the beautiful Jewish communist in the propaganda film *Seekers of*

Happiness. They banned that film long before I was born. And by the time I was born, Rakhil'—or worse yet, Rukhl—was a name never to be uttered in polite company. Roza was reserved for aging fat Odessan fish peddlers with a mole on their upper lip.

In addition to Roza, my parents rejected Regina (pretentious), Renata (pretentious), Rimma (low-brow), Rita (uncultured), Raisa (worse than Rita), Rina (too Jewish), Roxana (too Ukrainian), Rostislava (too Russian), and Raya ("I just don't like it").

Na Re bypasses names—bypasses the rest of the sounds that would make me too pretentious, too low-brow, too bourgeois, too communist, too Jewish, too *goyish*. The letter R doesn't have a history. The letter R does not remember Stalin.

3.

All letters of the alphabet remember Stalin. The repressions started before 1937, and lasted long after. They took my grandfather because he was an historian.

History and memory are not the same. History must be written, made, organized. Memory is herded on trans-Siberian trains, memory disappears in labor camps, memory pines and withers from hunger, memory freezes under fallen lumber, memory thaws and erases all traces. My grandfather remembers. He was composing a dictionary of Russian synonyms in his head, and this is what kept him alive. He couldn't compose history there. Or since.

Snow: blizzard, frost, permafrost, firn, cold shower naked on the snow (see also under *punishment*), snowstorm, graupel, rime, ice, névé, gale, absence, *my little girl is safe elsewhere*, whiteout.

Whiteout.

4.

They let my grandfather go in 1965. Stalin was dead, and so was Beria. My grandmother, Roza's daughter, had prostituted herself, so grandfather believed, because he no longer remembered their little girl. And after the shouting was done, my grandmother became opaque to him, thawing like absence over timber, buried under Siberia, gone. History is events and processes, history is rustling archives, it's oral interviews conducted inside the safety of the future, protected by course assignments and gleaming recording hardware. Memory compacts the permafrost under skin. When skin thaws, we are left with nothing.

My grandfather is leaving—forever leaving, taken away by people who come at night. They say only four words. Always the same. *S vesh'ami na vykhod*. Roughly, it means, "get your things and get out." One small bag. They always come for you at night. In 1937, they came for me, and missed by some seventy years. I keep a small bag with basics under my bed at all times, just in case. Cigarettes—although I've never smoked—the labor camp currency to trade for food or paper.

My grandfather is leaving—forever leaving. In 1965 he is taken away by people in ghost overcoats, so familiar they have become his family. He has no family. He is an orphan of snow in which to bury himself, to find a way back to the packed bag under the bed and the sleepless fear and my grandmother's breathing warmth by his side.

History is not like this.

5.

My mother left when I was five. She is an architect of permafrost. They dig deep—to bury the foundations, she says, so strong under the snow they will persist even when the earth sheds all water, that great thaw that will make past pain run in rivulets and be absorbed into the newly pliant earth.

She is digging for her father.

She doesn't want us to mention his name. I have a letter at least. He has nothing, only the concrete foundations hammered into permafrost, the night people who forever come for you.

6.

When the Germans came, my grandmother sewed all her jewelry into the underside of a white comforter cover. She had a dozen of those, embroidered white on white with snowflakes, flowers, little stars. She packed her bag—before the evacuation. She left with the bag, clutching her treasures—her mother's, aunt's, grandmother's—baubles bought by sweethearts, husbands, mothers who starved to save for a sliver of a diamond, a scrap of a golden watch. Back then *I love you* meant a little piece of herring to last all week, it meant enduring cold and staying up all night to sew an extra pair of pants for sale. My grandmother stitched the family *I love you's* into the comforter cover.

She didn't want to talk about how it got lost.

Sometimes I imagine her running after the ghost guards in her night-gown at night, crying *take it! take it!* for that's how the story takes shape, that you must exchange your treasures for life—and if they bypass your treasures they will take your life, perhaps to return it later, mangled, memory-less; and it will leave again then, leave for good, that life-shaped emptiness that gnaws and cusses at its tormentors: the wife, the child. The should-have-never-beens.

Or perhaps my grandmother exchanged the comforter for bread on the long flight away from the war, from where the sirens wailed; or perhaps she simply took the wrong comforter, her *I love you's* trampled into the earth under the growing heap of bodies.

When my grandmother died, she left me her wedding ring, the only thing that didn't go into the comforter. She left a little paper scrap attached to it. "For my *na Re*," it said.

I do not want to talk about it.

7.

My grandmother wanted to protect me. She spoke Russian to me—purer than permafrost, rigid like her husband's dictionary of salvation. But her father the fiddler taught Yiddish to me in secret. *Gedenk!* he would say. *Remember!* He had his heart packed in the violin case and ready to go, but they never did come for him.

Grandmother found us one day, huddled in the corner of the sofa, whispering forbidden warmth, stitching each other to life with thin threads of memory.

The next day my grandmother took me to the speech pathologist. A woman named Rimma, another never-be-Rukhl like me. "Open your mouth," she said kindly. With anonymous instruments gleaming silver and frost, she scraped my language out.

Afterloss

Everything goes. Rings and languages. Grandparents and bedding. Parents and selves. Names. Even the memory of loss is lost at last. Even snow. Even skin.

We are careless and fumbling. We slide through life—bypassing history, curling memory into smoke from the cigarettes packed for emergency visits from ghosts in the night. *S vesh'ami na vyhod.* Get your things and get out. When the guards came, they could not find me on the list. *Na Re* is not a name. So they took my little bag, carried my *I love you's* away to starve, to freeze, to lose their minds, their speech, to work away the years. And only the ancient fiddler stays behind, a patriarch of loss, fingers numb and weeping in the cold.

Everything thaws. Even my mother's earth-deep construction.

Only that which isn't remembered can never be lost.

OCTAVIA E. BUTLER

The Evening and the Morning and the Night

Octavia E. Butler was an American writer. As a multiple recipient of both the Hugo and Nebula awards, Butler was one of the best-known women in the field and has often been credited with inspiring many other writers both in and out of genre fiction. In 1995, she became the first science fiction writer to receive the MacArthur Fellowship. At the time, Butler was also one of the only African-American women in the science fiction field. In 2010, she was inducted into the Science Fiction Hall of Fame. Butler's novels include *Kindred* (1979) and *Parable of the Sower* (1993). In "The Evening and the Morning and the Night" Butler creates a fictional disease and uses this story to explore how society deals with issues of illness and stigma. It was first published in *OMNI* magazine in 1987.

When I was fifteen and trying to show my independence by getting careless with my diet, my parents took me to a Duryea-Gode disease ward. They wanted me to see, they said, where I was headed if I wasn't careful. In fact, it was where I was headed no matter what. It was only a matter of when: now or later. My parents were putting in their vote for later.

I won't describe the ward. It's enough to say that when they brought me home, I cut my wrists. I did a thorough job of it, old Roman style in a bathtub of warm water. Almost made it. My father dislocated his shoulder breaking down the bathroom door. He and I never forgave each other for that day.

The disease got him almost three years later—just before I went off to college. It was sudden. It doesn't happen that way often. Most people notice themselves beginning to drift—or their relatives notice—and they make arrangements with their chosen institution. People who are noticed and who resist going in can be locked up for a week's observation. I don't doubt that that observation period breaks up a few families. Sending someone away for what turns out to be a false alarm . . . Well, it isn't the sort of thing the victim is likely to forgive or forget. On the other hand, not sending someone away in time—missing the signs or having a person go off suddenly without signs— is inevitably dangerous for the victim. I've never heard of it going as badly, though, as it did in my family. People normally injure only themselves when their time comes—unless someone is stupid enough to try to handle them without the necessary drugs or restraints.

My father had killed my mother, then killed himself. I wasn't home when it happened. I had stayed at school later than usual, rehearsing graduation exercises. By the time I got home, there were cops everywhere. There was an ambulance, and two attendants were wheeling someone out on a stretcher— someone covered. More than covered. Almost . . . bagged.

The cops wouldn't let me in. I didn't find out until later exactly what had happened. I wish I'd never found out. Dad had killed Mom, then skinned her completely. At least that's how I hope it happened. I mean I hope he killed her first. He broke some of her ribs, damaged her heart. Digging.

Then he began tearing at himself, through skin and bone, digging. He had managed to reach his own heart before he died. It was an especially bad example of the kind of thing that makes people afraid of us. It gets some of us into trouble for picking at a pimple or even for daydreaming. It has inspired restrictive laws, created problems with jobs, housing, schools . . . The Duryea-Gode Disease Foundation has spent millions telling the world that people like my father don't exist.

A long time later, when I had gotten myself together as best I could, I went to college—to the University of Southern California—on a Dilg scholarship. Dilg is the retreat you try to send your out-of-control DGD relatives to. It's run by controlled DGDs like me, like my parents while they lived. God knows how any controlled DGD stands it. Anyway, the place has a waiting list miles long. My parents put me on it after my suicide attempt, but chances were, I'd be dead by the time my name came up.

I can't say why I went to college—except that I had been going to school all my life and didn't know what else to do. I didn't go with any particular hope. Hell, I knew what I was in for eventually. I was just marking time. Whatever I did was just marking time. If people were willing to pay me to go to school and mark time, why not do it?

The weird part was, I worked hard, got top grades. If you work hard enough at something that doesn't matter, you can forget for a while about the things that do.

Sometimes I thought about trying suicide again. How was it I'd had the courage when I was fifteen but didn't have it now? Two DGD parents both religious, both as opposed to abortion as they were to suicide. So they had trusted God and the promises of modern medicine and had a child. But how could I look at what had happened to them and trust anything?

I majored in biology. Non-DGDs say something about our disease makes us good at the sciences—genetics, molecular biology, biochemistry . . . That something was terror. Terror and a kind of driving hopelessness. Some of us went bad and became destructive before we had to—yes, we did produce more than our share of criminals. And some of us went good—spectacularly—and made scientific and medical history. These last kept the doors at least partly open for the rest of us. They made discoveries in genetics, found cures for a couple of rare diseases, made advances against other diseases that weren't so rare—including, ironically, some forms of cancer. But they'd found nothing to help themselves. There had been nothing since the latest improvements in the diet, and those came just before I was born. They, like the original diet, gave more DGDs the courage to have children. They were supposed to do for DGDs what insulin had done for diabetics—give us a normal or nearly normal life span. Maybe they had worked for someone somewhere. They hadn't worked for anyone I knew.

Biology school was a pain in the usual ways. I didn't eat in public anymore, didn't like the way people stared at my biscuits—cleverly dubbed "dog biscuits" in every school I'd ever attended. You'd think university students would be more creative. I didn't like the way people edged away from me when they caught sight of my emblem. I'd begun wearing it on a chain around my neck and putting it down inside my blouse, but people managed to notice it anyway. People who don't eat in public, who drink nothing more interesting than water, who smoke nothing at all—people like that are suspicious. Or rather, they make others suspicious. Sooner or later, one of those others, finding my fingers and wrists bare, would fake an interest in my chain. That would be that. I couldn't hide the emblem in my purse. If anything happened to me, medical people had to see it in time to avoid giving me the medications they might use on a normal person. It isn't just ordinary food we have to avoid, but about a quarter of a *Physicians' Desk Reference* of widely used drugs. Every now and then there are news stories about people who stopped carrying their emblems—probably trying to pass as normal. Then they have an accident. By the time anyone realizes there is anything wrong, it's too late. So I wore my emblem. And one way or another, people got a look at it or got the word from someone who had. "She *is!*" Yeah.

At the beginning of my third year, four other DGDs and I decided to rent a house together. We'd all had enough of being lepers twenty-four hours a day. There was an English major. He wanted to be a writer and tell our story from the inside—which had only been done thirty or forty times before. There was a special-education major who hoped the handicapped would accept her more readily than the able-bodied, a premed who planned to go into research, and a chemistry major who didn't really know what she wanted to do.

Two men and three women. All we had in common was our disease, plus a weird combination of stubborn intensity about whatever we happened to be doing and hopeless cynicism about everything else. Healthy people say no one can concentrate like a DGD. Healthy people have all the time in the world for stupid generalizations and short attention spans.

We did our work, came up for air now and then, ate our biscuits, and attended classes. Our only problem was housecleaning. We worked out a schedule of who would clean what when, who would deal with the yard, whatever. We all agreed on it; then, except for me, everyone seemed to forget about it. I found myself going around reminding people to vacuum, clean the bathroom, mow the lawn . . . I figured they'd all hate me in no time, but I wasn't going to be their maid, and I wasn't going to live in filth. Nobody complained. Nobody even seemed annoyed. They just came up out of their academic daze, cleaned, mopped, mowed, and went back to it. I got into the habit of running around in the evening reminding people. It didn't bother me if it didn't bother them.

"How'd you get to be housemother?" a visiting DGD asked.

I shrugged. "Who cares? The house works." It did. It worked so well that this new guy wanted to move in. He was a friend of one of the others, and another premed. Not bad looking.

"So do I get in or don't I?" he asked.

"As far as I'm concerned, you do," I said. I did what his friend should have done—introduced him around, then, after he left, talked to the others to make sure nobody had any real objections. He seemed to fit right in. He forgot to clean the toilet or mow the lawn, just like the others. His name was Alan Chi. I thought Chi was a Chinese name, and I wondered. But he told me his father was Nigerian and that in Ibo the word meant a kind of guardian angel or personal God. He said his own personal God hadn't been looking out for him very well to let him be born to two DGD parents. Him too.

I don't think it was much more than that similarity that drew us together at first. Sure, I liked the way he looked, but I was used to liking someone's looks and having him run like hell when he found out what I was. It took me a while to get used to the fact that Alan wasn't going anywhere.

I told him about my visit to the DGD ward when I was fifteen—and my suicide attempt afterward. I had never told anyone else. I was surprised at how relieved it made me feel to tell him. And somehow his reaction didn't surprise me.

"Why didn't you try again?" he asked. We were alone in the living room.

"At first, because of my parents," I said. "My father in particular. I couldn't do that to him again."

"And after him?"

"Fear. Inertia."

He nodded. "When I do it, there'll be no half measures. No being rescued, no waking up in a hospital later."

"You mean to do it?"

"The day I realize I've started to drift. Thank God we get some warning."

"Not necessarily."

"Yes, we do. I've done a lot of reading. Even talked to a couple of doctors. Don't believe the rumors non-DGDs invent."

I looked away, stared into the scarred, empty fireplace. I told him exactly how my father had died—something else I'd never voluntarily told anyone.

He sighed. "Jesus!"

We looked at each other.

"What are you going to do?" he asked.

"I don't know."

He extended a dark, square hand, and I took it and moved closer to him. He was a dark, square man my height, half again my weight, and none of it fat. He was so bitter sometimes, he scared me.

"My mother started to drift when I was three," he said. "My father only lasted a few months longer. I heard he died a couple of years after he went into the hospital. If the two of them had had any sense, they would have had me aborted the minute my mother realized she was pregnant. But she wanted a kid no matter what. And she was Catholic." He shook his head. "Hell, they should pass a law to sterilize the lot of us."

"They?" I said.

"You want kids?"

"No, but—"

"More like us to wind up chewing their fingers off in some DGD ward."

"I don't want kids, but I don't want someone else telling me I can't have any."

He stared at me until I began to feel stupid and defensive. I moved away from him.

"Do you want someone else telling you what to do with your body?" I asked.

"No need," he said. "I had that taken care of as soon as I was old enough."

This left me staring. I'd thought about sterilization. What DGD hasn't? But I didn't know anyone else our age who had actually gone through with it. That would be like killing part of yourself—even though it wasn't a part you intended to use. Killing part of yourself when so much of you was already dead.

"The damned disease could be wiped out in one generation," he said, "but people are still animals when it comes to breeding. Still following mindless urges, like dogs and cats."

My impulse was to get up and go away, leave him to wallow in his bitterness and depression alone. But I stayed. He seemed to want to live even less than I did. I wondered how he'd made it this far.

"Are you looking forward to doing research?" I probed. "Do you believe you'll be able to—"

"No."

I blinked. The word was as cold and dead a sound as I'd ever heard.

"I don't believe in anything," he said.

I took him to bed. He was the only other double DGD I had ever met, and if nobody did anything for him, he wouldn't last much longer. I couldn't just let him slip away. For a while, maybe we could be each other's reasons for staying alive.

He was a good student—for the same reason I was. And he seemed to shed some of his bitterness as time passed. Being around him helped me understand why, against all sanity, two DGDs would lock in on each other and start talking about marriage. Who else would have us?

We probably wouldn't last very long, anyway. These days, most DGDs make it to forty, at least. But then, most of them don't have two DGD parents. As bright as Alan was, he might not get into medical school because of his double inheritance. No one would tell him his bad genes were keeping him out, of course, but we both knew what his chances were. Better to train doctors who were likely to live long enough to put their training to use.

Alan's mother had been sent to Dilg. He hadn't seen her or been able to get any information about her from his grandparents while he was at home. By the time he left for college, he'd stopped asking questions. Maybe it was hearing about my parents that made him start again. I was with him when he called Dilg. Until that moment, he hadn't even known whether his mother was still alive. Surprisingly, she was.

"Dilg must be good," I said when he hung up. "People don't usually . . . I mean . . ."

"Yeah, I know," he said. "People don't usually live long once they're out of control. Dilg is different." We had gone to my room, where he turned a chair backward and sat down. "Dilg is what the others ought to be, if you can believe the literature."

"Dilg is a giant DGD ward," I said. "It's richer—probably better at sucking in the donations—and it's run by people who can expect to become patients eventually. Apart from that, what's different?"

"I've read about it," he said. "So should you. They've got some new treatment. They don't just shut people away to die the way the others do."

"What else is there to do with them? With us."

"I don't know. It sounded like they have some kind of . . . sheltered workshop. They've got patients doing things."

"A new drug to control the self-destructiveness?"

"I don't think so. We would have heard about that."

"What else could it be?"

"I'm going up to find out. Will you come with me?"

"You're going up to see your mother."

He took a ragged breath. "Yeah. Will you come with me?"

I went to one of my windows and stared out at the weeds. We let them thrive in the backyard. In the front we mowed them, along with the few patches of grass.

"I told you my DGD-ward experience."

"You're not fifteen now. And Dilg isn't some zoo of a ward."

"It's got to be, no matter what they tell the public. And I'm not sure I can stand it."

He got up, came to stand next to me. "Will you try?"

I didn't say anything. I focused on our reflections in the window glass—the two of us together. It looked right, felt right. He put his arm around me, and I leaned back against him. Our being together had been as good for me as it seemed to have been for him. It had given me something to go on besides inertia and fear. I knew I would go with him. It felt like the right thing to do.

"I can't say how I'll act when we get there," I said.

"I can't say how I'll act, either," he admitted. "Especially . . . when I see her."

He made the appointment for the next Saturday afternoon. You make appointments to go to Dilg unless you're a government inspector of some kind. That is the custom, and Dilg gets away with it.

We left L.A. in the rain early Saturday morning. Rain followed us off and on up the coast as far as Santa Barbara. Dilg was hidden away in the hills not far from San Jose. We could have reached it faster by driving up I-5, but neither of us were in the mood for all that bleakness. As it was, we arrived at one P.M. to be met by two armed gate guards. One of these phoned the main building and verified our appointment. Then the other took the wheel from Alan.

"Sorry," he said. "But no one is permitted inside without an escort. We'll meet your guide at the garage."

None of this surprised me. Dilg is a place where not only the patients but much of the staff has DGD. A maximum security prison wouldn't have been as potentially dangerous. On the other hand, I'd never heard of anyone getting chewed up here. Hospitals and rest homes had accidents. Dilg didn't. It was beautiful—an old estate. One that didn't make sense in these days of high taxes. It had been owned by the Dilg family. Oil, chemicals, pharmaceuticals. Ironically, they had even owned part of the late, unlamented Hedeon Laboratories. They'd had a briefly profitable interest in Hedeonco: the magic bullet, the cure for a large percentage of the world's cancer and a number of serious viral diseases—and the cause of Duryea-Gode disease. If one of your parents was treated with Hedeonco and you were conceived after the treatments, you had DGD. If you had kids, you passed it on to them. Not everyone was equally affected. They didn't all commit suicide or murder, but they all mutilated themselves to some degree if they could. And they all drifted—went off into a world of their own and stopped responding to their surroundings.

Anyway, the only Dilg son of his generation had had his life saved by Hedeonco. Then he had watched four of his children die before Doctors Kenneth Duryea and Jan Gode came up with a decent understanding of the problem and a partial solution: the diet. They gave Richard Dilg a way of keeping his next two children alive. He gave the big, cumbersome estate over to the care of DGD patients.

So the main building was an elaborate old mansion. There were other, newer buildings, more like guest houses than institutional buildings. And there were wooded hills all around. Nice country. Green. The ocean wasn't far away. There was an old garage and a small parking lot. Waiting in the lot was a tall, old woman. Our guard pulled up near her, let us out, then parked the car in the half-empty garage.

"Hello," the woman said, extending her hand. "I'm Beatrice Alcantara." The hand was cool and dry and startlingly strong. I thought the woman was DGD, but her age threw me. She appeared to be about sixty, and I had never seen a DGD that old. I wasn't sure why I thought she was DGD. If she was, she must have been an experimental model—one of the first to survive.

"Is it Doctor or Ms.?" Alan asked.

"It's Beatrice," she said. "I am a doctor, but we don't use titles much here."

I glanced at Alan, was surprised to see him smiling at her. He tended to go a long time between smiles. I looked at Beatrice and couldn't see anything to smile about. As we introduced ourselves, I realized I didn't like her. I couldn't see any reason for that either, but my feelings were my feelings. I didn't like her.

"I assume neither of you have been here before," she said, smiling down at us. She was at least six feet tall, and straight.

We shook our heads. "Let's go in the front way, then. I want to prepare you for what we do here. I don't want you to believe you've come to a hospital."

I frowned at her, wondering what else there was to believe. Dilg was called a retreat, but what difference did names make?

The house close up looked like one of the old-style public buildings— massive, baroque front with a single domed tower reaching three stories above the three-story house. Wings of the house stretched for some distance to the right and left of the tower, then cornered and stretched back twice as far. The front doors were huge—one set of wrought iron and one of heavy wood. Neither appeared to be locked. Beatrice pulled open the iron door, pushed the wooden one, and gestured us in.

Inside, the house was an art museum—huge, high-ceilinged, tile floored. There were marble columns and niches in which sculptures stood or paintings hung. There were other sculptures displayed around the rooms. At one end of the rooms there was a broad staircase leading up to a gallery that went around the rooms. There more art was displayed. "All this was made here," Beatrice said. "Some of it is even sold from here. Most goes to galleries in the Bay Area or down around L.A. Our only problem is turning out too much of it."

"You mean the patients do this?" I asked.

The old woman nodded. "This and much more. Our people work instead of tearing at themselves or staring into space. One of them invented the p.v. locks that protect this place. Though I almost wish he hadn't. It's gotten us more government attention than we like."

"What kind of locks?" I asked.

"Sorry. Palmprint-voiceprint. The first and the best. We have the patent." She looked at Alan. "Would you like to see what your mother does?"

"Wait a minute," he said. "You're telling us out-of-control DGDs create art and invent things?"

"And that lock," I said. "I've never heard of anything like that. I didn't even see a lock."

"The lock is new," she said. "There have been a few news stories about it. It's not the kind of thing most people would buy for their homes. Too expensive. So it's of limited interest. People tend to look at what's done at Dilg in the way they look at the efforts of idiot savants. Interesting, incomprehensible, but not really important. Those likely to be interested in the lock and able to afford it know about it." She took a deep breath, faced Alan again. "Oh, yes, DGDs create things. At least they do here."

"Out-of-control DGDs."

"Yes."

"I expected to find them weaving baskets or something—at best. I know what DGD wards are like."

"So do I," she said. "I know what they're like in hospitals, and I know what it's like here." She waved a hand toward an abstract painting that looked like a photo I had once seen of the Orion Nebula. Darkness broken by a great cloud of light and color. "Here we can help them channel their energies. They can create something beautiful, useful, even something worthless. But they create. They don't destroy."

"Why?" Alan demanded. "It can't be some drug. We would have heard."

"It's not a drug."

"Then what is it? Why haven't other hospitals—?"

"Alan," she said. "Wait."

He stood frowning at her.

"Do you want to see your mother?"

"Of course I want to see her!"

"Good. Come with me. Things will sort themselves out."

She led us to a corridor past offices where people talked to one another, waved to Beatrice, worked with computers . . . They could have been anywhere. I wondered how many of them were controlled DGDs. I also wondered what kind of game the old woman was playing with her secrets. We passed through rooms so beautiful and perfectly kept it was obvious they were rarely used. Then at a broad, heavy door, she stopped us.

"Look at anything you like as we go on," she said. "But don't touch anything or anyone. And remember that some of the people you'll see injured themselves before they came to us. They still bear the scars of those injuries. Some of those scars may be difficult to look at, but you'll be in no danger. Keep that in mind. No one here will harm you." She pushed the door open and gestured us in.

Scars didn't bother me much. Disability didn't bother me. It was the act of self-mutilation that scared me. It was someone attacking her own arm as though it were a wild animal. It was someone who had torn at himself and been restrained or drugged off and on for so long that he barely had a recognizable human feature left, but he was still trying with what he did have to dig into his own flesh. Those are a couple of the things I saw at the DGD ward when I was fifteen. Even then I could have stood it better if I hadn't felt I was looking into a kind of temporal mirror.

I wasn't aware of walking through that doorway. I wouldn't have thought I could do it. The old woman said something, though, and I found myself on the other side of the door with the door closing behind me. I turned to stare at her.

She put her hand on my arm. "It's all right," she said quietly. "That door looks like a wall to a great many people."

I backed away from her, out of her reach, repelled by her touch. Shaking hands had been enough, for God's sake.

Something in her seemed to come to attention as she watched me. It made her even straighter. Deliberately, but for no apparent reason, she stepped toward Alan, touched him the way people do sometimes when they brush past—a kind of tactile "Excuse me." In that wide, empty corridor, it was totally unnecessary. For some reason, she wanted to touch him and wanted me to see. What did she think she was doing? Flirting at her age? I glared at her, found myself suppressing an irrational urge to shove her away from him. The violence of the urge amazed me.

Beatrice smiled and turned away. "This way," she said. Alan put his arm around me and tried to lead me after her.

"Wait a minute," I said, not moving.

Beatrice glanced around.

"What just happened?" I asked. I was ready for her to lie—to say nothing happened, pretend not to know what I was talking about.

"Are you planning to study medicine?" she asked.

"What? What does that have to do—?"

"Study medicine. You may be able to do a great deal of good." She strode away, taking long steps so that we had to hurry to keep up. She led us through a room in which some people worked at computer terminals and others with pencils and paper. It would have been an ordinary scene except that some people had half their faces ruined or had only one hand or leg or had other obvious scars. But they were all in control now. They were working. They were intent but not intent on self-destruction. Not one was digging into or tearing away flesh. When we had passed through this room and into a small, ornate sitting room, Alan grasped Beatrice's arm.

"What is it?" he demanded. "What do you do for them?"

She patted his hand, setting my teeth on edge. "I will tell you," she said. "I want you to know. But I want you to see your mother first." To my surprise, he nodded, let it go at that.

"Sit a moment," she said to us.

We sat in comfortable, matching upholstered chairs—Alan looking reasonably relaxed. What was it about the old lady that relaxed him but put me on edge? Maybe she reminded him of his grandmother or something. She didn't remind me of anyone. And what was that nonsense about studying medicine?

"I wanted you to pass through at least one workroom before we talked about your mother—and about the two of you." She turned to face me. "You've had a bad experience at a hospital or a rest home?"

I looked away from her, not wanting to think about it. Hadn't the people in that mock office been enough of a reminder? Horror film office. Nightmare office.

"It's all right," she said. "You don't have to go into detail. Just outline it for me."

I obeyed slowly, against my will, all the while wondering why I was doing it.

She nodded, unsurprised. "Harsh, loving people, your parents. Are they alive?"

"No."

"Were they both DGD?"

"Yes, but . . . yes."

"Of course, aside from the obvious ugliness of your hospital experience and its implications for the future, what impressed you about the people in the ward?"

I didn't know what to answer. What did she want? Why did she want anything from me? She should have been concerned with Alan and his mother.

"Did you see people unrestrained?"

"Yes," I whispered. "One woman. I don't know how it happened that she was free. She ran up to us and slammed into my father without moving him. He was a big man. She bounced off, fell, and . . . began tearing at herself. She bit her own arm and . . . swallowed the flesh she'd bitten away. She tore at the wound she'd made with the nails of her other hand. She . . . I screamed at her to stop." I hugged myself, remembering the young woman, bloody, cannibalizing herself as she lay at our feet, digging into her own flesh. Digging. "They try so hard, fight so hard to get out."

"Out of what?" Alan demanded.

I looked at him, hardly seeing him.

"Lynn," he said gently. "Out of what?"

I shook my head. "Their restraints, their disease, the ward, their bodies . . ."

He glanced at Beatrice, then spoke to me again. "Did the girl talk?"

"No. She screamed."

He turned away from me uncomfortably. "Is this important?" he asked Beatrice.

"Very," she said.

"Well . . . can we talk about it after I see my mother?"

"Then and now." She spoke to me. "Did the girl stop what she was doing when you told her to?"

"The nurses had her a moment later. It didn't matter."

"It mattered. Did she stop?"

"Yes."

"According to the literature, they rarely respond to anyone," Alan said.

"True." Beatrice gave him a sad smile. "Your mother will probably respond to you, though."

"Is she? . . ." He glanced back at the nightmare office. "Is she as controlled as those people?"

"Yes, though she hasn't always been. Your mother works with clay now. She loves shapes and textures and—"

"She's blind," Alan said, voicing the suspicion as though it were fact. Beatrice's words had sent my thoughts in the same direction. Beatrice hesitated. "Yes," she said finally. "And for . . . the usual reason. I had intended to prepare you slowly."

"I've done a lot of reading."

I hadn't done much reading, but I knew what the usual reason was. The woman had gouged, ripped, or otherwise destroyed her eyes. She would be badly scarred. I got up, went over to sit on the arm of Alan's chair. I rested my hand on his shoulder, and he reached up and held it there.

"Can we see her now?" he asked.

Beatrice got up. "This way," she said.

We passed through more workrooms. People painted; assembled machinery; sculpted in wood, stone; even composed and played music. Almost no one noticed us. The patients were true to their disease in that respect. They weren't ignoring us. They clearly didn't know we existed. Only the few controlled-DGD guards gave themselves away by waving or speaking to Beatrice. I watched a woman work quickly, knowledgeably, with a power saw. She obviously understood the perimeters of her body, was not so dissociated as to perceive herself as trapped in something she needed to dig her way out of. What had Dilg done for these people that other hospitals did not do? And how could Dilg withhold its treatment from the others?

"Over there we make our own diet foods," Beatrice said, pointing through a window toward one of the guest houses. "We permit more variety and make fewer mistakes than the commercial preparers. No ordinary person can concentrate on work the way our people can."

I turned to face her. "What are you saying? That the bigots are right? That we have some special gift?"

"Yes," she said. "It's hardly a bad characteristic, is it?"

"It's what people say whenever one of us does well at something. It's their way of denying us credit for our work."

"Yes. But people occasionally come to the right conclusions for the wrong reasons." I shrugged, not interested in arguing with her about it.

"Alan?" she said. He looked at her.

"Your mother is in the next room."

He swallowed, nodded. We both followed her into the room.

Naomi Chi was a small woman, hair still dark, fingers long and thin, graceful as they shaped the clay. Her face was a ruin. Not only her eyes but most of her nose and one ear were gone. What was left was badly scarred. "Her parents were poor," Beatrice said. "I don't know how much they told you, Alan, but they went through all the money they had, trying to keep her at a decent place. Her mother felt so guilty, you know. She was the one who had cancer and took the drug . . . Eventually, they had to put Naomi in one of those state-approved, custodial-care places. You know the kind. For a while, it was all the government would pay for. Places like that . . . well, sometimes if patients were really troublesome—especially the ones who kept breaking free—they'd put them in a bare room and let them finish themselves. The only things those places took good care of were the maggots, the cockroaches, and the rats."

I shuddered. "I've heard there are still places like that."

"There are," Beatrice said, "kept open by greed and indifference." She looked at Alan. "Your mother survived for three months in one of those places. I took her from it myself. Later I was instrumental in having that particular place closed."

"You took her?" I asked.

"Dilg didn't exist then, but I was working with a group of controlled DGDs in L.A. Naomi's parents heard about us and asked us to take her. A lot of people didn't trust us then. Only a few of us were medically trained. All of us were young, idealistic, and ignorant. We began in an old frame house with a leaky roof. Naomi's parents were grabbing at straws. So were we. And by pure luck, we grabbed a good one. We were able to prove ourselves to the Dilg family and take over these quarters."

"Prove what?" I asked.

She turned to look at Alan and his mother. Alan was staring at Naomi's ruined face, at the ropy, discolored scar tissue. Naomi was shaping the image of an old woman and two children. The gaunt, lined face of the old woman was remarkably vivid—detailed in a way that seemed impossible for a blind sculptress.

Naomi seemed unaware of us. Her total attention remained on her work. Alan forgot about what Beatrice had told us and reached out to touch the scarred face.

Beatrice let it happen. Naomi did not seem to notice. "If I get her attention for you," Beatrice said, "we'll be breaking her routine. We'll have to stay with her until she gets back into it without hurting herself. About half an hour."

"You can get her attention?" he asked.

"Yes."

"Can she? . . ." Alan swallowed. "I've never heard of anything like this. Can she talk?"

"Yes. She may not choose to, though. And if she does, she'll do it very slowly."

"Do it. Get her attention."

"She'll want to touch you."

"That's all right. Do it."

Beatrice took Naomi's hands and held them still, away from the wet clay. For several seconds Naomi tugged at her captive hands, as though unable to understand why they did not move as she wished.

Beatrice stepped closer and spoke quietly. "Stop, Naomi." And Naomi was still, blind face turned toward Beatrice in an attitude of attentive waiting. Totally focused waiting.

"Company, Naomi."

After a few seconds, Naomi made a wordless sound.

Beatrice gestured Alan to her side, gave Naomi one of his hands. It didn't bother me this time when she touched him. I was too interested in what was happening. Naomi examined Alan's hand minutely, then followed the arm up to the shoulder, the neck, the face. Holding his face between her hands, she made a sound. It may have been a word, but I couldn't understand it. All I could think of was the danger of those hands. I thought of my father's hands.

"His name is Alan Chi, Naomi. He's your son." Several seconds passed.

"Son?" she said. This time the word was quite distinct, though her lips had split in many places and had healed badly. "Son?" she repeated anxiously. "Here?"

"He's all right, Naomi. He's come to visit."

"Mother?" he said.

She reexamined his face. He had been three when she started to drift. It didn't seem possible that she could find anything in his face that she would remember. I wondered whether she remembered she had a son.

"Alan?" she said. She found his tears and paused at them. She touched her own face where there should have been an eye, then she reached back toward his eyes. An instant before I would have grabbed her hand, Beatrice did it.

"No!" Beatrice said firmly.

The hand fell limply to Naomi's side. Her face turned toward Beatrice like an antique weather vane swinging around. Beatrice stroked her hair, and Naomi said something I almost understood. Beatrice looked at Alan, who was frowning and wiping away tears.

"Hug your son," Beatrice said softly.

Naomi turned, groping, and Alan seized her in a tight, long hug. Her arms went around him slowly. She spoke words blurred by her ruined mouth but just understandable.

"Parents?" she said. "Did my parents . . . care for you?" Alan looked at her, clearly not understanding.

"She wants to know whether her parents took care of you," I said.

He glanced at me doubtfully, then looked at Beatrice.

"Yes," Beatrice said. "She just wants to know that they cared for you."

"They did," he said. "They kept their promise to you, Mother."

Several seconds passed. Naomi made sounds that even Alan took to be weeping, and he tried to comfort her.

"Who else is here?" she said finally.

This time Alan looked at me. I repeated what she had said.

"Her name is Lynn Mortimer," he said. "I'm . . ." He paused awkwardly. "She and I are going to be married."

After a time, she moved back from him and said my name. My first impulse was to go to her. I wasn't afraid or repelled by her now, but for no reason I could explain, I looked at Beatrice.

"Go," she said. "But you and I will have to talk later."

I went to Naomi, took her hand.

"Bea?" she said.

"I'm Lynn," I said softly.

She drew a quick breath. "No," she said. "No, you're . . ."

"I'm Lynn. Do you want Bea? She's here."

She said nothing. She put her hand to my face, explored it slowly. I let her do it, confident that I could stop her if she turned violent. But first one hand, then both, went over me very gently.

"You'll marry my son?" she said finally.

"Yes."

"Good. You'll keep him safe."

As much as possible, we'll keep each other safe. "Yes," I said.

"Good. No one will close him away from himself. No one will tie him or cage him." Her hand wandered to her own face again, nails biting in slightly.

"No," I said softly, catching the hand. "I want you to be safe, too."

The mouth moved. I think it smiled. "Son?" she said.

He understood her, took her hand.

"Clay," she said. Lynn and Alan in clay. "Bea?"

Of course," Beatrice said. "Do you have an impression?"

"No!" It was the fastest that Naomi had answered anything. Then, almost childlike, she whispered. "Yes."

Beatrice laughed. "Touch them again if you like, Naomi. They don't mind."

We didn't. Alan closed his eyes, trusting her gentleness in a way I could not. I had no trouble accepting her touch, even so near my eyes, but I did not delude myself about her. Her gentleness could turn in an instant. Naomi's fingers twitched near Alan's eyes, and I spoke up at once, out of fear for him.

"Just touch him, Naomi. Only touch."

She froze, made an interrogative sound.

"She's all right," Alan said.

"I know," I said, not believing it. He would be all right, though, as long as someone watched her very carefully, nipped any dangerous impulses in the bud.

"Son!" she said, happily possessive. When she let him go, she demanded clay, wouldn't touch her old-woman sculpture again. Beatrice got new clay for her, leaving us to soothe her and ease her impatience. Alan began to recognize signs of impending destructive behavior. Twice he caught her hands and said no. She struggled against him until I spoke to her. As Beatrice returned, it happened again, and Beatrice said, "No, Naomi." Obediently Naomi let her hands fall to her sides.

"What is it?" Alan demanded later when we had left Naomi safely, totally focused on her new work—clay sculptures of us. "Does she only listen to women or something?"

Beatrice took us back to the sitting room, sat us both down, but did not sit down herself. She went to a window and stared out. "Naomi only obeys certain women," she said. "And she's sometimes slow to obey. She's worse than most—probably because of the damage she managed to do to herself before I got her." Beatrice faced us, stood biting her lip and frowning. "I haven't had to give this particular speech for a while," she said. "Most DGDs have the sense not to marry each other and produce children. I hope you two aren't planning to have any—in spite of our need." She took a deep breath. "It's a pheromone. A scent. And it's sex-linked. Men who inherit the disease from their fathers have no trace of the scent. They also tend to have an easier time with the disease. But they're useless to use as staff here. Men who inherit from their mothers have as much of the scent as men get. They can be useful here because the DGDs can at least be made to notice them.

The same for women who inherit from their mothers but not their fathers. It's only when two irresponsible DGDs get together and produce girl children like me or Lynn that you get someone who can really do some good in a place like this." She looked at me. "We are very rare commodities, you and I. When you finish school you'll have a very well-paying job waiting for you."

"Here?" I asked.

"For training, perhaps. Beyond that, I don't know. You'll probably help start a retreat in some other part of the country. Others are badly needed." She smiled humorlessly. "People like us don't get along well together. You must realize that I don't like you any more than you like me."

I swallowed, saw her through a kind of haze for a moment. Hated her mindlessly—just for a moment.

"Sit back," she said. "Relax your body. It helps."

I obeyed, not really wanting to obey her but unable to think of anything else to do. Unable to think at all. "We seem," she said, "to be very territorial. Dilg is a haven for me when I'm the only one of my kind here. When I'm not, it's a prison."

"All it looks like to me is an unbelievable amount of work," Alan said.

She nodded. "Almost too much." She smiled to herself. "I was one of the first double DGDs to be born. When I was old enough to understand, I thought I didn't have much time. First I tried to kill myself. Failing that, I tried to cram all the living I could into the small amount of time I assumed I had. When I got into this project, I worked as hard as I could to get it into shape before I started to drift. By now I wouldn't know what to do with myself if I weren't working."

"Why haven't you . . . drifted?" I asked.

"I don't know. There aren't enough of our kind to know what's normal for us."

"Drifting is normal for every DGD sooner or later."

"Later, then."

"Why hasn't the scent been synthesized?" Alan asked. "Why are there still concentration-camp rest homes and hospital wards?"

"There have been people trying to synthesize it since I proved what I could do with it. No one has succeeded so far. All we've been able to do is keep our eyes open for people like Lynn." She looked at me. "Dilg scholarship, right?"

"Yeah. Offered out of the blue."

"My people do a good job keeping track. You would have been contacted just before you graduated or if you dropped out."

"Is it possible," Alan said, staring at me, "that she's already doing it? Already using the scent to . . . influence people?"

"You?" Beatrice asked.

"All of us. A group of DGDs. We all live together. We're all controlled, of course, but . . ." Beatrice smiled. "It's probably the quietest house full of kids that anyone's ever seen."

I looked at Alan, and he looked away. "I'm not doing anything to them," I said. "I remind them of work they've already promised to do. That's all."

"You put them at ease," Beatrice said. "You're there. You . . . well, you leave your scent around the house. You speak to them individually. Without knowing why, they no doubt find that very comforting. Don't you, Alan?"

"I don't know," he said. "I suppose I must have. From my first visit to the house, I knew I wanted to move in. And when I first saw Lynn, I . . ." He shook his head. "Funny, I thought all that was my idea."

"Will you work with us, Alan?"

"Me? You want Lynn."

"I want you both. You have no idea how many people take one look at one workroom here and turn and run. You may be the kind of young people who ought to eventually take charge of a place like Dilg."

"Whether we want to or not, eh?" he said.

Frightened, I tried to take his hand, but he moved it away. "Alan, this works," I said. "It's only a stopgap, I know. Genetic engineering will probably give us the final answers, but for God's sake, this is something we can do now!"

"It's something *you* can do. Play queen bee in a retreat full of workers. I've never had any ambition to be a drone."

"A physician isn't likely to be a drone," Beatrice said.

"Would you marry one of your patients?" he demanded. "That's what Lynn would be doing if she married me—whether I become a doctor or not."

She looked away from him, stared across the room. "My husband is here," she said softly. "He's been a patient here for almost a decade. What better place for him . . . when his time came?"

"Shit!" Alan muttered. He glanced at me. "Let's get out of here!" He got up and strode across the room to the door, pulled at it, then realized it was locked. He turned to face Beatrice, his body language demanding she let him out. She went to him, took him by the shoulder, and turned him to face the door. "Try it once more," she said quietly. "You can't break it. Try."

Surprisingly, some of the hostility seemed to go out of him. "This is one of those p.v. locks?" he asked.

"Yes."

I set my teeth and looked away. Let her work. She knew how to use this thing she and I both had. And for the moment, she was on my side.

I heard him make some effort with the door. The door didn't even rattle. Beatrice took his hand from it, and with her own hand flat against what appeared to be a large brass knob, she pushed the door open.

"The man who created that lock is nobody in particular," she said. "He doesn't have an unusually high I.Q., didn't even finish college. But sometime in his life he read a science-fiction story in which palmprint locks were a given. He went that story one better by creating one that responded to voice or palm. It took him years, but we were able to give him those years. The people of Dilg are problem solvers, Alan. Think of the problems you could solve!"

He looked as though he were beginning to think, beginning to understand. "I don't see how biological research can be done that way," he said. "Not with everyone acting on his own, not even aware of other researchers and their work."

"It *is* being done," she said, "and not in isolation. Our retreat in Colorado specializes in it and has—just barely—enough trained, controlled DGDs to see that no one really works in isolation. Our patients can still read and write—those who haven't damaged themselves too badly. They can take each other's work into account if reports are made available to them. And they can read material that comes in from the outside. They're working, Alan. The disease hasn't stopped them, *won't* stop them." He stared at her, seemed to be caught by her intensity—or her scent. He spoke as though his words were a strain, as though they hurt his throat. "I won't be a puppet. I won't be controlled . . . by a goddamn smell!"

"Alan—"

"I won't be what my mother is. I'd rather be dead!"

"There's no reason for you to become what your mother is."

He drew back in obvious disbelief.

"Your mother is brain damaged—thanks to the three months she spent in that custodial-care toilet. She had no speech at all when I met her. She's improved more than you can imagine. None of that has to happen to you. Work with us, and we'll see that none of it happens to you."

He hesitated, seemed less sure of himself. Even that much flexibility in him was surprising. "I'll be under your control or Lynn's," he said.

She shook her head. "Not even your mother is under my control. She's aware of me. She's able to take direction from me. She trusts me the way any blind person would trust her guide."

"There's more to it than that."

"Not here. Not at any of our retreats."

"I don't believe you."

"Then you don't understand how much individuality our people retain. They know they need help, but they have minds of their own. If you want to see the abuse of power you're worried about, go to a DGD ward."

"You're better than that, I admit. Hell is probably better than that. But . . ."

"But you don't trust us."

He shrugged.

"You do, you know." She smiled. "You don't want to, but you do. That's what worries you, and it leaves you with work to do. Look into what I've said. See for yourself. We offer DGDs a chance to live and do whatever they decide is important to them. What do you have, what can you realistically hope for that's better than that?"

Silence. "I don't know what to think," he said finally.

"Go home," she said. "Decide what to think. It's the most important decision you'll ever make."

He looked at me. I went to him, not sure how he'd react, not sure he'd want me no matter what he decided.

"What are you going to do?" he asked.

The question startled me. "You have a choice," I said. "I don't. If she's right . . . how could I not wind up running a retreat?"

"Do you want to?"

I swallowed. I hadn't really faced that question yet. Did I want to spend my life in something that was basically a refined DGD ward? "No!"

"But you will."

". . . Yes." I thought for a moment, hunted for the right words. "You'd do it."

"What?"

"If the pheromone were something only men had, you would do it."

That silence again. After a time he took my hand, and we followed Beatrice out to the car. Before I could get in with him and our guard-escort, she caught my arm. I jerked away reflexively. By the time I caught myself, I had swung around as though I meant to hit her. Hell, I did mean to hit her, but I stopped myself in time. "Sorry," I said with no attempt at sincerity.

She held out a card until I took it. "My private number," she said. "Before seven or after nine, usually. You and I will communicate best by phone."

I resisted the impulse to throw the card away. God, she brought out the child in me.

Inside the car, Alan said something to the guard. I couldn't hear what it was, but the sound of his voice reminded me of him arguing with her—her logic and her scent. She had all but won him for me, and I couldn't manage even token gratitude. I spoke to her, low voiced.

"He never really had a chance, did he?"

She looked surprised. "That's up to you. You can keep him or drive him away. I assure you, you *can* drive him away."

"How?"

"By imagining that he doesn't have a chance." She smiled faintly. "Phone me from your territory. We have a great deal to say to each other, and I'd rather we didn't say it as enemies."

She had lived with meeting people like me for decades. She had good control. I, on the other hand, was at the end of my control. All I could do was scramble into the car and floor my own phantom accelerator as the guard drove us to the gate. I couldn't look back at her. Until we were well away from the house, until we'd left the guard at the gate and gone off the property, I couldn't make myself look back. For long, irrational minutes, I was convinced that somehow if I turned, I would see myself standing there, gray and old, growing small in the distance, vanishing.

AUTHOR'S AFTERWORD

"The Evening and the Morning and the Night" grew from my ongoing fascinations with biology, medicine, and personal responsibility.

In particular, I began the story wondering how much of what we do is encouraged, discouraged, or otherwise guided by what we are genetically. This is one of my favorite questions, parent to several of my novels. It can be a dangerous question. All too often, when people ask it, they mean who has the biggest or the best or the most of whatever they see as desirable, or who has the smallest and the least of what is undesirable. Genetics as a board game, or worse, as an excuse for the social Darwinism that swings into popularity every few years. Nasty habit.

And yet the question itself is fascinating. And disease, grim as it is, is one way to explore answers. Genetic disorders in particular may teach us much about who and what we are.

I built Duryea-Gode disease from elements of three genetic disorders. The first is Huntington's disease—hereditary, dominant, and thus an inevitability if one has the gene for it. And it is caused by only one abnormal gene. Also Huntington's does not usually show itself until its sufferers are middle-aged.

In addition to Huntington's, I used phenylketonuria (PKU), a recessive genetic disorder that causes severe mental impairment unless the infant who has it is put on a special diet.

Finally, I used Lesch-Nyhan disease, which causes both mental impairment and self-mutilation.

To elements of these disorders, I added my own particular twists: a sensitivity to pheromones and the sufferers' persistent delusion that they are trapped, imprisoned within their own flesh, and that that flesh is somehow not truly part of them. In that last, I took an idea familiar to us all—present in many religions and philosophies—and carried it to a terrible extreme.

We carry as many as fifty thousand different genes in each of the nuclei of our billions of cells. If one gene among the fifty thousand, the Huntington's gene, for instance, can so greatly change our lives—what we can do, what we can become—then what are we?

What, indeed?

For readers who find this question as fascinating as I do, I offer a brief, unconventional reading list: *The Chimpanzees of Gombe: Patterns of Behavior* by Jane Goodall, *The Boy Who Couldn't Stop Washing: The Experience and Treatment of Obsessive-Compulsive Disorder* by Judith L. Rapoport, *Medical Detectives* by Berton Roueché, *An Anthropologist on Mars: Seven Paradoxical Tales* and *The Man Who Mistook His Wife for a Hat and Other Clinical Tales* by Oliver Sacks.

Enjoy!

ANNE RICHTER

The Sleep of Plants

TRANSLATED BY EDWARD GAUVIN

Anne Richter is a Belgian author, editor, and scholar. Her first collection, written at the age of fifteen, was translated as *The Blue Dog* by Alice B. Toklas, who praised her in the preface. In addition to her own fiction, she is known for editing an international anthology of female fantastical writers, *Le fantastique féminin d'Ann Radcliffe à nos jours* and writing essays about women writers and fantastical literature. In "The Sleep of Plants" a woman transforms into a plant in order to escape a humdrum, predictable life and seek the solitude she desires. It was first published in her collection *Les locataires* (*The Tenants*) in 1967.

"Slowing, we feel the pulse of things." —Henri Michaux, "La Ralentie"

She lived like a plant. The rhythms of her life were more vegetable than human. She was prone, periodically, to sliding slowly into sleep; she remained inactive, immobile, hands crossed on knees, head tilted slightly toward one shoulder, staring straight ahead. Sometimes it was a tiny thing. A wearied bee gone astray in a fold of curtain, patiently, haltingly making the climb, stopping to gather its strength. The bee would hunch up briefly before setting out again; the young woman waited for the moment when the insect would fall, at once wishing for and fearing it, so much a part of the creature's misery that her palms were moist. Or she would observe the exact whirl of dust motes in the light, between dresser and rug, finding secret calm in their constant movement. She followed water droplets gliding down gray panes, or would slip into one of her lengthy afflictions which never threatened her life, which she seemed to prolong for pleasure, from which she returned unhurriedly, eyes widened, a blue tinge to her skin, as if dazzled by the light upon leaving a cave.

* * *

She sank into utter solitude, surrounding herself with a rampart of silence. In these moments, her thoughts were vague, yet followed a precise path. With a spider's patience, she forced herself from behind half-closed eyelids to catch, unawares, things as she felt they must be. This required total stillness, arduous efforts of concentration. Meticulously, she repeated everyday words until they lost their usual meaning. *Spoon, spoon*, she would say, softly and stubbornly. She would polish the word, handling it almost absent-mindedly, yet taking care to treat it as respectfully as she could, never to consider it and see only usefulness. Little by little, it lost all consistency. Then began the meticulous work of a watchmaker. She persisted cautiously, decanted it, slowly breathed new life into the word. Sometimes she saw it come round, get back on its feet; then she would discover an entirely new meaning. She called this undressing words.

* * *

One day, she got engaged. Her fiancé was a likable young man. Sundays they often went for walks in the countryside. They trod carefully, hand in hand, along meadows and hedges. They spoke of this and that, without passion or impatience. One morning, George wanted to show her a place he'd found. They packed a lunch and set out. It was unusually warm. All the trees were in bloom, and the grass was tall in the fields. "There it is!" cried George. "Let's run for it!" They both broke into a sprint, and the young woman flew through the grass, laughing and waving her arms, displaying an unusual vitality. She reached the first trunk, and threw her arms around it; her fiancé caught up and kissed her on the mouth. The woods before them were split between sunlight and shadow. But suddenly she felt faint, and her hands gripped the bark. The young man was worried, surprised.

"Oh, it's nothing," she said.

She sat down in the grass and leaned her head against the trunk. Then she went pale, smoothed her dress, and glanced anxiously at her fiancé.

"What a pretty place!" she said.

But *le déjeuner sur l'herbe* was ruined.

They stopped going for walks. Her fiancé tried to drag her along, but she stubbornly refused, pleading fatigue. Around this time, she did in fact suffer from inexplicable spells of weariness. She was sorry, in all her immobility, that she couldn't sink roots. Bore into the ground for good, surround herself with a quiet cloud of light like those around pines or over certain shrubs in summer. But she had to get up from her chair, go here, go there. She did violence to herself speaking, moving, and afterwards fell back trembling, mouth dry, dying of thirst like a plant denied water.

The activity around her seemed less comprehensible than ever: needless commotion, futile chaos. And yet the regular course of daily affairs troubled her. She furled her leaves, lived on nothing. She was like a cactus, skin tender behind protecting needles, needing little water and light to live.

She saw that, by dint of stillness and withdrawal, you felt yourself become the center of the world, the source of its movement. As a child, she'd played at becoming the center of the world, an extraordinary game she never tired of—secretly aware, perhaps, of its gravity and power. She would walk backward, head thrown back and gazing at the sky until she grew dizzy. That was what she wanted, for dizziness to make her see things differently, herself frozen and the earth yawing, the sun and the clouds whirling about. Or else, sitting in a moving train, feeling the coarseness of the seat cushion beneath her palms, aware of the cadenced pace of travel in every part of her body, the train car stinking of cold ash, wet clothes, and smoke, she would scrutinize the white square of window, and suddenly the world would begin to change. The train had stopped, in the corner of her window she'd watch all the people walking, the meadows leaping past, the fleeing sky, slashed in its flight by taut telephone wires.

This state of grace almost always ended soon. The world grew still again, and her train car clattered along God knew where. Bitterness flooded her; disgust. She believed herself the only living person in a dead world shaken by sound and fury, till the day she understood: in motionlessness, movement found its source. She decided to fall silent, and in silence, animate the world.

* * *

This is what she did: she found a giant stoneware pot, a great bag of humus. She stepped into the basin, covered her legs in a blanket of earth. She vanished up to her hips. How good it felt! Never had she known such ecstasy. She was back in her element. From the depths of herself rose a silence. Still, a certain nervousness persisted, a tingle at the end of her fingers, toes, like expectation. *I'll get used to it*, she thought, wiggling her toes.

But there was a knock at the door; what would she tell her mother? The door opened and their eyes met. What grief in her mother's gaze!

"I always expected the worst from you, but not this—not this!"

"Look, I've always given in, but this time, your tears are wasted!"

In fact, things stayed much the same. After the initial shock, the usual routine set in. She'd never taken up much space in family life. From now on, she took up none at all. An empty chair at dinner was pushed to a corner. A vacant bed was moved to the attic. Clothes were given to the poor. Not once did her mother lift her gaze to the heavy basin upstairs. She vacuumed around it, cleaned the rug without comment, dusted quickly, her face expressionless. Maybe she hoped, by denying her daughter light, to see her wither and die. But plants are hardy. They have all the time in the world, and a gift for frugality.

When her fiancé came to see her, he didn't know what to say. He raised the blinds. She looked pale, her eyes ringed. Her arms hung slack at her sides like dead branches; her neck bowed beneath the moss of her hair. She gazed at him, not without a certain annoyance in her eyes: had his movements always been so brusque? She couldn't recall suffering from them before.

"You always said you wanted me to be happy," she murmured. "Probably you never noticed I was unhappy? This had to happen sooner or later. Isn't it better that it happened before we got married? You're still free now. Don't worry about hurting me."

George tried to take her hand, but it was so cold! As if blood were, ever so slowly, receding from it.

"How can you talk like that? Don't you know I love you? I would've died for you. But I can see that doesn't mean a thing to you; you're deliberately destroying yourself. What can I give you now?"

Despite everything, she was touched. But she was tired. The darkness had been a terrible ordeal for her. She turned her faded eyes to the sun, made an effort to speak.

"You're generous, George. There's something you can do for me, if you want. My mother won't admit it, but I know she wants bring things to an end as soon as she can. But I need food! Bring me things to eat and drink."

She was still a bit of a carnivore. Her fiancé brought her flies, mosquitoes, sometimes spiders. She swallowed them whole, hurriedly, craning her neck forward, snapping at them with sudden movements of her jaw. It was a peculiar sight, which her fiancé had a hard time watching. He turned discreetly away. But she soon lost her taste for meat. All that remained was a yearning for pure water, a dream of springs. Her ideas took the shape of leaves. Vague desires for silence. She spoke less and less. A bit embarrassed by her muteness, the fiancé spoke for them both.

One day he said, "If you'd wanted. Ania . . ."

But he didn't finish his sentence. He saw quite well that she no longer wanted a thing. In fact, she no longer even needed his presence. She possessed it forever, behind closed eyes. But he was still talking. They were all talking. How badly she wanted to drive off this insufferable swarm of words, as if waving away harmful insects!

Downstairs, they were saying, "Where's Ania?"

"Oh, in her room." "At a boarding house." "Traveling." "She's so shy, painfully shy!"

She was waiting for her roots. She shouldered the suffering of plants. The thirst of cut flowers torqueing their stalks toward the light. The moist dream of seaweed abandoned on the sand. The cold of rosebushes in November frost. The passing madness of indoor plants devouring walls and windows. The furious proliferation of exotic blossoms, brought over like slaves, strewing the four corners of the yard with the sinister fruit of their revolt. The sighs of men, stuck in the mud of futile acts.

Her fiancé conscientiously brought her water every day before going to work. He grew discouraged about talking, but she didn't notice. Sometimes he looked worried, but she was too preoccupied to notice. She was waiting. How long it was, the sitting still and waiting! We fill our days with distractions, but perhaps it would be better to be faithful to waiting—to wait without moving, speaking, lifting a finger, in a room bare as this one.

Her roots grew overnight. She felt them everywhere piercing the earth. What joy, alas, and what pain! She felt like she was traveling backward up the river of time. Odors assailed her, shifting essences. Her adolescence had an anxious scent, like bitter linden. Some had grown in the school playground where she'd always felt so bored. Her childhood smelled like sorb trees. She saw herself going down a curving path. A blackbird cackled from deep in a bush. Sorb apples lay bleeding in the grass. She squashed them underfoot. What world would spring forth when she rounded the bend? She advanced cautiously. With one final push, her roots punctured soil. Now she descended, heart pounding, toward an odor, the odor of the day she was born. Her birth had a dull smell, like the smell hanging over iron quarries. Her birth smelled like ferns. She saw a glittering fern, its crozier erect, scratch at the sky with its palm of light.

* * *

The next morning, her leaf hands were open. Her fiancé came to see her, looking vexed. He sat down beside her, head lowered.

"Look . . . I've given this a lot of thought. I think I owe it to you to tell you this. I've met someone . . . a young woman, the sister of someone at work. She's sweet, serious-minded . . . she looks like you a bit. You're the one who told me life goes on. But I can't just abandon you. Our lives are intertwined, Ania: do you want to come to our wedding, come live with us?"

A light breeze came in through the window. It caressed the trunk, played in the branches. The leaves up top bent forward a bit, in silent approbation. George bent over, lifted up the heavy stoneware basin. For a moment, the leaves grew flustered, shuddered. But they soon recovered their dreamy stillness. As Ania crossed the doorsill in the young man's arms, the mother, deep in her kitchen, closed her fist around a saucepan and turned her back to the couple.

* * *

George planted her in his yard, in the middle of the lawn. The roots breathed freely; she thanked him with a happy nod of foliage. One sunny morning not long after, he got married. The little pale-cheeked bride floated among the guests, light as a waterlily. There was dancing beneath leaves bathed in moonlight.

That summer, the tree put forth splendid blossoms.

KELLY BARNHILL

The Men Who Live in Trees

Kelly Barnhill is an American writer. She currently has published three fantasy novels for children: *The Witch's Boy*, *Iron Hearted Violet*, and *The Mostly True Story of Jack*. She has also written several well-received short stories for adults, which can be found in *Postscripts*, Tor.com, *Weird Tales*, *Lightspeed*, *Clarksworld*, and other publications and anthologies. In "The Men Who Live in Trees," Carmina searches for an answer to her father's death. This story was first published in *Postscripts 15* in 2008.

Of all the cultures, subcultures, clans, gangs and sects that are bounded and protected by our Glorious Empire, none is more puzzling than the Molaru, known to the residents of Acanthacae as the men who live in trees. They have no recognized language, save for a complicated pageant of gestures and movements, accompanied by a codified set of facial expressions. Similarly, they have no recognizable tradition of the arts or music. That which, I suppose, is to pass as music is played on instruments not tuned to create melodies, but created instead for the express purpose of making a sound nearly identical to that of the wind pushing ceaselessly through the heavily canopied trees. Sometimes, one can even hear the rain dripping from the jungle's broad leaves, stretching darkly into the world, into the end of the world.

—From the Notes and Journals of Tamino Ailare

* * *

When Carmina Ailare was born, her father laid her in a green cradle. Patterns of vine, leaf, and heavy blossom twined along the curved edge, and twisted their runners into the cavity where the babe slept. When the cradle rocked, the leaves seemed to blow in an effortless wind. And when one looked closely, it sometimes appeared as though a pair of green eyes gazed back—unblinking, flickering, and gone.

The cradle had been fashioned from a thousand interlocking pieces of wood, cut from a single tree, which had crashed into the south side of the house when everyone was asleep, injuring two servants, though only slightly. Her father, in his typical fashion, said that he never liked the south side of the house anyway, and that the servants in question were in need of a much deserved day off, and since recuperation is as good an excuse as any, they were ordered to recuperate. In truth, he cared only for the tree, and believed that its arrival into the servants' quarters was a sign.

"What sort of sign," his wife asked as she leaned into the overstuffed chair, her tawny eyes bloodshot with heat and hope and something else that she could not name.

Tamino shrugged vaguely and stared out into the misty green just past the garden wall.

"What sort of sign," she asked again, but he said nothing and she gave up.

During the length of his wife's pregnancy, as she sweated and moaned for her home and family in the familiar and licentious chaos of the Emperor's City, Tamino Ailare cut wood. He sawed and split and sanded and planed. He baked each piece, allowing the sap to pool out of its veins, sink deep into the wood's firm flesh, giving it a peculiar sheen. Indeed, the wood from the trees of the Oponax river was unlike any that Tamino Ailare had ever seen. Once cured, it was fragrant, luminous and dark. In a quiet room, Tamino swore that one could hear it breathing.

The day the cradle was finished, Carmina was born. Shaking with excitement, he extracted the bound babe from the protesting arms of her mother and laid her in the cradle. Immediately, a breeze blew up from trees just over the garden wall. The babe in the cradle made a sound—a sound like the wind in the overburdened branches. A sound like the creaking of wood.

Carmina's father had been a professor of discrete mathematics and applied philosophy of language. He had served at most of the major universities that spanned the boundless Empire, which is to say, he taught at every university that mattered. Which means, as well, that he was subsequently fired from every university that mattered.

With nowhere else to send him, the sages of the Empire sent him to the farthest corner possible, where he would no longer be a nuisance, and his tendency towards heresy and sedition could be chalked up to jungle fever, and therefore ignored. Acanthacae. Guardian of the penal colony. Gatherer of rubies. Overseer of the wide and fragrant Oponax River. He was sent to study the men who live in trees. He was sent to discover their secrets. He was to report regularly to the Emperor by way of His governors, ministers and mages as to why the Molaru had not been, nor, it would seem, could not be, subdued. He had not been instructed to love them, and yet he did. And then he died. Carmina supposed that she could take a lesson in that, but what that lesson was, and how it applied, well, this was mystery.

* * *

The men who live in trees have no women. Ask anyone. The Governor, the Warden, the Bishop, the Provost of the University, even the proprietress of the estimable House of Ladies: They agree, and have agreed, on nothing, of course, save this. That a tribe or a nation or even a supper club could be comprised only of men, is clearly a mad belief, and yet all assert the same. The men who live in trees are men. No women or children have ever been sighted, mentioned, let alone examined for study and publication.
—From the Notes and Journals of Tamino Ailare

* * *

On the day of her betrothal, Carmina went to the window to look for the men who live in trees. She would see nothing, of course, which is to say that she would see the slicked leaves of the jungle pressing up and over her garden wall, its great green and blossomed bulk sighing, panting, sweating. She shuddered.

Somewhere, beyond—no, *inside*, the skin of the jungle lived the men who live in trees. In her sixteen years she had only seen them four times: Twice for the protocol and pomp that surrounds the signing of a treaty, once for the show of friendship with the slaughter and roast of a wild pig—or perhaps it was a bear—and a demonstration of song and dance, met with much wincing and gritting of teeth for most everyone involved. Most everyone but Carmina, who loved the stylized bow and sashay, the overly gestured hunt and evasion, slicked as always with sheen upon sheen of sweet sweat.

The last time that she saw the men who live in trees was two years ago, when they climbed the walls of the city, sliced the bellies of the guards and laid the grin of their blades against her father's throat. She stood in the door-way, her white nightdress fluttering about her body like translucent wings. She opened her mouth, felt her lips stretch against her teeth, but no sound came. The men who live in trees clustered around her kneeling father. One held his sparse hair, one his shoulders, and one the blade. Her father choked, then gasped, then grunted something that sounded like, *forgive me, please, forgive me.* The men who live in trees had faces that did not move. Their mouths were stone, their faces, sky. With a quick flick of the wrist, the blade slid neatly into her father's neck, and sliced a clean arc from one side to the other.

Her father did not weep, nor did he scream. Instead he spread his fin-gers, curved the pinkie and ring finger inward with a fluttering motion, and brought both hands to his chest. Carmina knew the sign. Her father had taught it to her. The men who lived in trees knew it too. They spoke not in words. They spoke with their hands. Carmina's father, in their language, told them one thing. *Thank you.*

* * *

It is said that each man lives for three hundred years. That they emerge, fully formed and rational, from a slit in the side of the tree. That they do not die as we do, but rot from the center outwards as they inch towards death, dropping limbs as they do so. This, of course, is ludicrous, and yet. And yet. Once I saw a man while I traveled deep into the jungle's green heart. He had no left arm and no nose. He inched down the overgrown path. He creaked in the wind.
    —From the journals of Tamino Ailare

* * *

Given that this was the day that she would be presented to her future husband and her future husband's family (which is to say, this was the day that she was to be presented to her future mother-in-law, who would, in a series of codified gestures, display her approval, indifference, grudging acceptance, open distain, downright hostility, or abject refusal), Carmina was particularly alone. Normally, she would be escorted from the garden doors of the compound with her mother at her left hand and her father at her right. She would have a cacophony of relatives giggling behind her, covering their white teeth and spreading lips with the backs of their salty hands. Behind that would be the household servants, leading the household animals, and likely, after that would be a musician and singer, or even a choir, hired specially for the occasion.

Instead, it would only be Carmina and her aunt, which meant that Carmina would be completely alone.

Deborah, the servant waited quietly at the dressing table. This was not surprising. Deborah never spoke. None of the servants did. She simply waited for Carmina arranging and rearranging the various tools for the intricate performance that was Carmina's toilette: A boar's bristle brush, a jar of grease made from the fat of a lamb, scented with bergamot, jasmine and lime. She had fourteen silver combs and ten ropes of tiny pearls that would shortly twine through her black hair, binding it fast. There were eight jars of fine powder in varying degrees of pallor. With each successive application, Carmina would become paler and paler until she was the color of stone. There were also jars holding an assortment of fine, smooth pastes, as silky as custard with a pleasing grit. There was a berry colored paste that would be applied to her lips (on her wedding night, this would be applied to her nipples as well), a seashell pink paste for her high cheekbones, and a sunset of blues and purples and iridescent greens for around her eyes.

There was, of course, much to do, but she stood at the window instead, watching the mounded green exhale in clouds of heat and mist towards the high, white sky.

It was in this moment that the door to the room opened as though by a force of nature and hit the opposite wall so hard that it cracked the plaster in a dusty puff.

"Clean that up," Carmina's aunt said to the silent servant without glancing over. Deborah stood, bowed and went for a broom. "This," her aunt said, hooking her head downwards like a vulture, "is what I am to present to your future mother-in-law? I came here looking for a bride-to-be. If it weren't for that ill-behaved tongue in your wretched mouth, I might have mistaken you for one of the servants."

Carmina leaned against the window sill, tilted her head and smiled mildly at her aunt.

"It shouldn't matter either way," she said. "I could meet his family wearing nothing but fig leaves and they'll still pant for the match." Her aunt snorted and reached for the powder, but Carmina continued, emboldened mostly because she knew she was right.

"I think I'll do just that," she said as sweat pooled and dripped between her bound breasts and down the fine ribs of sliced whale bones that caged her middle. "I'll make a dress of leaves and burlap. And I'll anoint my hair with last year's tallow. Oh and *ashes* too." Her aunt laid a long-nailed hand at the small of Carmina's back and led her—with more than a bit of firm insistence at the tips—to the chair. "Behold the bride," Carmina said bitterly as her aunt began with the first jar of powder.

"Selfish," her aunt said with a hiss at her teeth. "Selfish and stupid. Just like your father. Think of your mother, for a change. Think of your mother, and do your duty."

Carmina's mother lay in bed, weak with fever. She had suffered from fevers for the last two years. When she saw her husband lying on the ground, his blood pooling on the cool flagstones, she fell into a swoon. Her body fell hard upon the stones, her father's blood flowing towards and around her head like a halo. Later, when the doctors and apothecaries, and even twelve women from the penal colony who were jailed as witches, examined the barely conscious woman, the diagnosis was unanimous, which is to say that each had his or her own particular theory, and they agreed in their utter lack of agreement. The doctors blamed a parasitic infection, and prescribed a draft of quinine, drunk morning, noon and night, followed by a second draft of strong spirits, and followed again by a tincture of morphine. The apothecaries blamed an over abundance of humor, and insisted that she be bled for fifteen minutes every day until her condition improved. At half past two every afternoon, she was to have a draft made from the petals of lilies, hibiscus and bitterroot, combined, of course, with the dried petals of roses imported from the beating heart of the Empire, to feed the poor woman's dying heart. The witches declared that it was from the shock of heartbreak and the unintentional ingestion of blood. They required a measure of seawater to be flushed to the eyes every day to wash away sorrow, the oil of poppy to be placed under the tongue to replace joy, and the presence of a singer in her bedchamber every day for at least two hours, to clear the head and soothe the heart.

As a result, Carmina's mother went blind, her skin ghosted and faded until she was nearly transparent, and she was rarely conscious. Her aunt, to her credit, followed the instructions to the letter. All, except for the singer, which she felt was an ostentatious addition to a household populated by women.

As it happens, the singing was the one thing that could have saved her, if brought in immediately. Without song, Carmina's mother, though she breathed, was already dead.

* * *

Death does not exist in the minds of the men who live in trees. Nor birth. There is no sign for either. In my first dealings with the Molaru, after my initial tours of the penal colony, as well as our small, but growing, University of the Upper Opponax, I was introduced to a man who was a healer of the Molaru. He had been called to the Central Mansion to see to the child of the Governor's most beloved and most beautiful mistress. The child had suffered from fevers, which had grown progressively worse, until he lay, white faced, on the crisp, linen sheet, as near to death as one could be without actually being dead. The healer entered the inner room where the child lay. My lady commanded that I ask if the child would die. My knowledge of their hand speech was far from adept, but I did my best regardless. "End. This. Small Man." I asked with my hands. The old healer stared at me. He brought his middle finger of his right hand to his mouth and let it fly gently away, like a butterfly. He looked at me meaningfully. I said to my lady, "It appears that he is saying, 'the small man is free,' though I cannot possibly know what that means." That night, the child died. That night, a Molaru prisoner at the penal colony escaped—the first person to do so. He was a very small man.

—From the journals of Tamino Ailare

* * *

Carmina ground her teeth as her aunt lashed on the heavy red dress. She imagined that in the Northern and only slightly barbaric cities of the Empire, such a dress would make sense. Or, at least it would make sense in winter. Carmina's mother, originally from the cities in the North, was the original owner of the dress, and doubtless looked beautiful in it. Carmina held her breath as her aunt stretched the thick, luminous velvet around her merciless corset. The fabric cut cruelly into the tender flesh of her breasts, and the flounce of skirt, as heavy as church drapes, from her hips to the floor made it difficult to walk. Her aunt attached the stiff collar and attached it with pins that bit at Carmina's shoulders and upper back. She winced and said nothing, though she knew she bled. Her feet were strapped into tiny, beaded shoes that whispered against the stone floors as she walked.

Her aunt eyed her critically. "Not fit for a bride of God, but you'll do for a man," she said. "Especially that man," she added with a half smile and glittering eyes. Carmina decided to ignore this, and went to see her mother instead.

Carmina's aunt did not marry, but made vows to the Sisters of the Western Sky and came to live in the province at the mouth of the Opponax river, separated from the world by Abbey walls, four feet thick and twenty feet high. In spite of the wall, the Abbey was destroyed only two years later during the unpleasantness between Empire forces and the rag-tag armies of anarchists, expelled students, displaced aboriginals, and defrocked clergy.

The Empire forces, led to believe that the Abbess was harboring terrorists within its sacred walls, blasted a hole in the western edge and poured inside. All its residents were slaughtered, save one—Carmina's aunt. No one knew who told the general that dissidents hid in the Abbey. In truth, no dissidents were found. As a result, the Church released Carmina's aunt from her vows. *For your grief*, they said.

✳ ✳ ✳

The men who live in trees do not grieve as we do. Since death does not exist, grief is altered as well. Recently, the Molaru sanctioned me to live with one of their own for a period of three weeks. I was not allowed to visit the communal dwelling of their people—even if there is such a thing. Some say that the men who live in trees build nests like birds and sing out their territory. I don't believe this to be true, but since I've never seen their homeplace, I suppose that anything is possible. Instead, we slept on the ground each night, facing the sky. The man taught me the intricacies of Molaru storytelling, and how to draw their handpictures on the ground. On the eleventh day, he brought me to the walls of the penal colony. The soldiers walking the wall did not observe us, though we stood in the open. He instructed me to lay one hand upon the wall and another hand on his palm. I did, and instantly felt a stab of grief that pierced my poor heart. Through my one hand I felt the groans of the prisoners, their dry mouths and empty bellies, their rotting limbs and broken backs, and their crushing despair. Through the other hand, I felt my new friend's shocked horror, numb acceptance and breaking heart. We left without a sound. We were not seen.
   —From the journals of Tamino Ailare

✳ ✳ ✳

After kissing her mother on her shrunken, shriveled lips, and arranging the bedclothes around her tiny body, Carmina went to the front door, placed her hand in the hand of her grim lipped aunt and walked out into the thick sunshine, Deborah the servant trailing behind, holding up a very small parasol, which did little to block the crushing heat.

Although she was not accompanied, people on the busy street knew from the red velvet gripping her damp body, they knew from the beaded swirl of her heavy hair and the layer upon layer of powder on her face, neck and bosom that she was a bride-to-be. And, in truth, many had begun to wonder when a suitable match would be found—one that would satisfy the girl's aunt, and would satisfy the future mother-in-law. Since, as relatives of a Banished

Individual, that being Carmina's beloved father, by law they were not permitted to access the vast resources of his family's coffers. Ever since Tamino Ailare was sent to the upper Opponax, he and his dependants were allowed a monthly stipend, which saw to their general well-being and provided the necessary luxury for maintaining a certain level in the larger society, but it was not enough for a dowry.

However, anyone who married Carmina, would have access, as a relative once removed, to the largely untouched fortune, and would thus be very rich.

The man standing on the opposite end of the square wanted to be very rich, which is to say that his mother wanted him to be very rich.

The extra weight braided into her hair pulled on Carmina's scalp, giving her a headache. She looked the young man up and down as she approached. She had seen him before, of course, but it had been a while, as his mother sent him to the university in the Emperor's City, though how she afforded it, no one really knew. The young man came from a family as old family, nearly, though not quite, as old and glorious as the Beloved Emperor himself. But his grandfather, one of the progenitors of the concept of the penal colony and its lucrative business pulling rubies from the ground, had sold all of his family's lands and sunk the proceeds into two ruby mines that produced for five years and fifteen years, respectively. Now there were no more rubies, and the family's fortunes dwindled.

He wore a silk shirt that was bound with lace at the throat and riding pants made from the skin of something soft and young. A rabbit, perhaps. Or a young doe. His high boots wore thick layers of polish and gleamed impressively in the noonday sun. But this, Carmina could see, was only for show. The boots, though polished, were old, perhaps his father's, and they buckled deeply at the toes as though walked too long with feet that never grew to their limit. The doeskin, freshly dyed cornflower blue (hope's color), was creased and cracked, its seams pockmarked from excessive mending. And the dye bled upon the rim of the shirt, a blue that would never wash away. He didn't look at Carmina. Not at all. He looked instead at his overlarge boots and sighed deeply, moping his brow with a monogrammed handkerchief.

Carmina looked into the face of the woman on his left. Despite the heat, she looked dry, bloodless as dusty bones. Her thin lips cracked into a frown.

"Your dress is creased," she said in a dry voice.

Carmina's aunt nodded ruefully. "Indeed it is," she said. "She dressed in haste. She is an anxious thing."

The mother's eyes wrinkled to slits. "And she sweats like a servant. Didn't she know to bathe before an occasion such as this?" Carmina flushed, caught her anger in her teeth and bit down hard. It was true, she sweat openly. It gathered at her hairline, ringed her neck, flowed downward past her breasts and navel. What was worse, she knew by the ache, heat and flow at her thighs that she bled as well.

"Then send me away in shame," Carmina said in a low voice, "or bind our hands and be done with it."

Both mother and aunt gasped, but Carmina sighed in relief.

"She is young," her aunt gasped. "Young enough to be molded. Bound."

* * *

It is the tradition when the Molaru make the transformation from men of power to men of age, to bind their hands and feet as they pray to the river. If the river floods, he is taken away, and they say that is voice can be heard in the first gurgles of spring. If it does not, he is unbound after three days. His hair is white where it once was not and his face is lined where it once was smooth. He is no longer a sapling, but bears a strange resemblance to the twisted grooves in the oldest trees—that which only the strongest wind can ever master.

—From the journals of Tamino Ailare

* * *

Upstairs, Carmina's aunt recounted to her unconscious mother the sins committed that day. Her aunt did this every day, of course, but given the magnitude of today's sins, Carmina knew she would remain in the sick room until late afternoon.

Not that her sins had made any difference, either way. She was summarily betrothed. Bound. Her well being, and that of her mother and aunt were now in the hands of the man she would marry, which is to say, they were now at the mercy of her mother-in-law. Carmina slipped out the back door and followed the path that snaked past the apothecary's tent, past the House of Eight Scribes, past the house of ladies, and past the sad hut of the Governor's first rejected mistress and her many children, until she reached the banks of the Opponax. She followed the thin trail that led upstream until she reached the mouth of a narrow, though deep, tributary, nearly hidden in a canopy of heavy leaved branches. The red velvet and the beads were already gone—the first hung to air in the courtyard, the second counted wrapped and locked in her aunt's bedroom. She removed her white muslin, her corset, her many layered undergarments. She removed each stocking, each shoe. She removed the ring that was her father's, the bracelet that was her mother's. She stood, mother naked by the water, her thighs glistening with sweat and bright blood, and slowly lowered herself into the water, hanging onto a large root to keep from floating away.

As she watched the tender curve of the trees' limbs swaying gently overhead, she heard the sharp groan of bending wood and a blinding crack. Above the water's skin, she smelled the sharp tang of flowing sap—a smell that instantly made her think of green eyes peering through a green wood, though she did not know why. She held more tightly to the submerged root and pulled close to the overgrown bank, her legs still floating freely in the swift water.

On the other bank, next to a large tree, was a man. A Molaru man who turned to the tree, and patted it gently. He was tall, taller than Carmina, though by how much she could not say. Like the rest she had seen, he wore a head-dress made from the oiled inner skin of the Looma tree, its seams bound up with the gut of a panther. From the forehead, fresh leaves wove with the hair of the dead—both human and animal, creating something of a crown. The breastplate was made of wood, dark, with a strange sheen, carved throughout in patterns of blossom and branch and leaf, and the boots were made of rushes.

Carmina, naked in the water, watched him as he touched the tree. His hands were small, smaller than her father's, with narrow fingers and soft, brown palms. He moved as a tree moves, gently, irrevocably, whispering to the wind. He removed his headdress, and the stretched dome of his scalp gleamed in the dappled light. He slipped each leg from the boots of rushes, and Carmina marveled at the delicate arch of the feet, the neatly cinched heels. After untying the eight straps that held it in place, he pulled the breastplate over his head and leaned it against the tree, draping the leafy cloth from around his waist over the top. Carmina's mouth opened, then closed. His nipples, dark as dates, hovered above the swell of two breasts. His thighs, like hers, were damp with sweat and the flow of blood from the dark scoop between.

Carmina let out a cry, scrambled to the bank and stood opposite from the Molaru man who was not a man at all. The man who was not simply gazed back at Carmina, unblinking and unsurprised.

"You," Carmina said, but the man who was not simply raised her eyebrows. "Oh," she said. "Of course." She thought a minute, and tried the signs she knew. "You," she signed. "Man. Not a man." Carmina pressed her lips together. Surely she could do better than this. Had not her father taught her the poetry of handsigning? Had she learned nothing?

"I am a man," the naked girl across the water signed back. "We are all men."

Carmina thought for a moment. Then she signed, "Then what am I?"

"You?" The girl who was a man shrugged her shoulders. "A child. Son of a wise child."

"My father, you mean."

"Both of your fathers were wise children. Your father whose blood lives in the stones. And your father who is living and dead at once. Wise children."

"Who is your father?" Carmina signed.

"The trees," the girl replied.

* * *

The men who live in trees have many stories. Some I remember. Others washed away like water. One story is claimed to be their oldest, though who can tell? As a member of the empire and a distant relative to the Emperor himself, I am afraid they may be more guarded with me than with another. And thus, this, my last great research, may also fail. Regardless, here is the tale they told me: Once there was a man with fourteen fathers. Like all other men, this man was noble and honest and fair. He was a skilled hunter, a moral and merciless judge, a terrible warrior. He was so great that the rest of the people were awed in their respect for him. They backed away when he came, shielded their eyes from his gaze, and would not communicate with him without invitation. As a result, the man was friendless, peerless and utterly lonely. He went to the oldest man and knelt before him. "My spear is unsurpassed in all this endless wood," he said. "My judgment is sound and unyielding, and I have kept my people fed and safe since I first became a man, which is to say, always. But I am alone, and therefore I have failed. I ask your permission to yield my life to the river, that my spirit may join in the lifeblood of the world and I may protect my people forever." The oldest man thought on this, and as he thought, drew a circle on the ground. Within that circle, he wove another circle. And within that another. He continued until fourteen circles entwined in a tight knot. The man did not notice. Finally, the oldest man spoke. "Any permission would not be mine to give. Such a decision lies in the hands of your fourteen fathers. Ask them." But the man did not know where his fathers could be found, so he prepared himself to journey into the heart of the wood. He took a single spear, which he strapped to his back. He brought no food, nor clothing, nor water skins. "I shall go forth into the world as I first entered—naked, hungry, but powerful." The people listened and lowered their heads. They feared his gaze.

The man traveled upstream towards the river's beating heart—the beating heart of the known world. He traveled for fourteen days and fourteen nights. He neither slept nor ate. When he was hungry, he bent his knees to the ground and opened his mouth to the sky, biting down a small piece to chew. Back home, his people noticed bite marks in the high, white sky. Small ones at first, but as

*the days wore on, they were larger and full of teeth. By the fourteenth day, the
rains came, and water poured in heavy gushes from the holes bitten in the sky.*
 —*From the journals of Tamino Ailare*

* * *

"Come across," the man who was a girl who apparently lived in the trees
or under the trees, or perhaps was actually a tree, had said with a gentle
movement of her right hand, her left arm outstretched over the water.

"I can't," Carmina said with her palms facing her chest, and flicking plain-
tively to the ground. This was one of the first signs she ever learned. She sat
down on a rock and attempted to shove her feet into her wet undergarments,
now washed nearly clean.

"Come across," the girl said again, using both hands for emphasis.

"I cannot," Carmina signed back. "My father." There was no sign for
mother.

"His blood is in the stones. Ask the stones."

"No," Carmina said out loud. She buttoned her white shift over her damp
breasts. The girl across the water remained as she was—damp with sweat
and blood and muck. From where she fussed with sashes and laces, Carmina
could smell her—a lush, woody, damp earth smell. Carmina shivered. "His
blood is in his body. He breathes."

"One breathes, though dead. The other calls to you every time you walk by.
The trees hear it. We hear it. You do not."

Carmina nodded. "Did my father know that some of you are men and
some are not?" She did not like the girl who pretended to be a man, she
decided. But, then, she didn't like a lot of people.

"Your father knew that we all were men. He knew it with his last breath."
Carmina picked up a stone the size of a mango and threw it into the water.
It dropped with a satisfying splash and disappeared. She wasn't aiming at
anyone, of course, nor did she intend to hurt the girl—or the man—or what
ever it was. She simply wanted to throw something. The girl who called
herself a man raised one eyebrow but remained silent. Carmina turned and
hurried back down the path, rubbing her palm against her hip as though it
burned. When she leaned down she heard a whisper—so faint, she wondered
if she had heard it before without noticing. *Listen*, it said as she leaned. *In the
stones*, it said as she reared back. And it arced upwards, its pale heft curving
through the damp and dappled light of the afternoon, it said, *The one true
stone*, before disappearing with a plop.

* * *

On his tenth day on the river, the man began to talk to the water. On the fourteenth day, the river answered back.

"I was hungry, so I ate a portion of the sky," he said.

"And when you did so, the land wept."

The man pushed against his pole, and the hollowed out boat—the one he had scraped himself—drifted to the shore. He stepped into the muck and waded into the flowering weeds along the river's edge. He released the boat into the river and watched the river take it away.

"A wicked man," he said, "knelt before me. He begged for mercy. He begged for justice. I told him he could not have both. He asked me to choose. So I laid my blade upon the stretch of his neck and sliced it neatly away."

The river said nothing.

"His body was laid among the trees. By morning it was gone."

"And the sky wept," the river said.

"Yes. Yes, it did. Why did it weep?"

"It wept because it weeps. Why did the wicked man do wicked? Why did the merciless man lack mercy? Every true thing acts according to its nature."

"Then," said the man, "why, today, does the river speak, when such an action defies its nature?"

"Every true thing acts according to its nature," repeated the river. "Except when it does not. Then, it does not." And with that, the river fell silent.

The man tried again to speak to the river, but it communicated only in whorls and ripples and the occasional gurgle. A language he did not know. Weak with hunger, he ate another piece of the sky. He waited for the land to weep. It never did.

—From the journals of Tamino Ailare

* * *

When Carmina returned home, she found four surveyors, six carpenters, two architects, nine apprentices and sixteen servants crawling around the house and garden and walls like ants. The woman who was to be her mother-in-law leaned over the desk in the arched alcove that once served as her father's study and now was a dusty reminder of a dead man's quiet learning. Carmina stopped, her white shift fluttering around her now-sweating legs in a faint breeze. The woman who would be her mother-in-law leaned shoulder to shoulder with Carmina's aunt. On the other side of the desk stood a very small, very nervous architect, hands and face smudged with graphite and ink. He bobbed his head and curled his shoulders as he unfurled page after page of plans and drawings. He simpered; he whined; he showed his teeth. The two women clicked their heels against the broad stone floor impatiently, pointing *here*, and *here*, and *here*. Carmina cleared her throat.

Both women stood with a hiss. They regarded Carmina while simultaneously raising their chins and arching their brows. They brought their hands together in front of their chests and stroked their fingers gently, like insects preparing for a meal. "You," her future mother-in-law said. "You're here."

"Of course I am," Carmina said. "I live here."

The older women gave one another a knowing glance. The architect stared at the ground apparently looking for something to squish.

"For now," the aunt said. The future mother-in-law smiled.

"Please explain," Carmina said sweetly as she ground her teeth.

"Well, can't expect to stay here once you are married. This house was bestowed upon your wretched father as part of his banishment. The law prohibits you to profit from its sale, but your husband—"

"Future husband," Carmina corrected.

"*So rude*," the aunt hissed.

Her future mother-in-law thinned her lips into a brittle smile. "Your *husband* will be permitted to sell the house, the grounds, and all its possessions as he sees fit."

"As *you* see fit."

"Same thing."

Carmina placed her fists at the small of her back and dug in hard. Her hips hurt, her womb hurt, her breasts hurt. She wanted to lie down.

"But not the books. And my father's papers. They will stay with me."

"The books will be appraised by the bookseller next week. Anything of value will be sold. The rest you may keep."

Carmina spoke quietly, and closed her eyes to keep from shouting. "The books belong to my mother, who still lives. The books will not be appraised without her permission."

"Nonsense! How can an unconscious woman give permission," her aunt exclaimed, raising her hands heavenward.

"Indeed," said Carmina.

"In any case, they can't all belong to your mother. Unless they are marked, ownership is assumed by the male and passed to his heir which in this case—"

"They are marked. Each one. My father did so himself."

Carmina had watched him do it. Eighteen pots of sticky glue, nine brushes, and over a thousand identical, hand pressed plates, embossed with gold, declaring, *"From the library of Petra Ailare,"* all lovingly affixed inside the front covers. This he had done in the week before his death. As though he knew something was coming.

"I was never told of this," the future mother-in-law hissed to the aunt.

The aunt stammered and whined. "I—I'm certainly—Well, I never—Honestly they couldn't all—" Quickly she began removing books from the shelves and checking inside the covers. They were all marked with Petra's name. Every single one.

* * *

After twenty-eight days of journey, the man fell to his knees at the center of the world. He raised his hands to the broken sky. "I cannot travel any further," he cried. "My feet are torn, my hands are torn, my heart is torn." He sunk his fingers into the mud and scooped it to his mouth. "If my fathers meant for my life to end, then I shall lie here, and here will be my grave, a shallow maw in the worthless muck at the center of the world!"

"A shallow grave for a shallow man," said a voice behind him.

"A merciless end to one who had no time for mercy. Is this our plan for our son, my brothers?"

"All true things act according to their natures."

"True, but only if the thing, itself, is true."

"Who are you," said the man, still cradling mud in his hands.

"Your father," said fourteen voices. The man stood in a circle of fourteen trees. Each tree had a gash at the base, two friendly knots on either side and two large, red stones set, peering out. The stones blinked.

"My fathers," the man said, straightening up. "My spear is unsurpassed in all this endless wood. My judgment is sound and unyielding, and I have kept my people fed and safe since I first became a man, which is to say, always."

"And what have you to show for this?"

"Nothing," the man said.

"Nothing," repeated the trees, and they blinked their glittering eyes.

—From the journals of Tamino Ailare

* * *

When Carmina Ailare was a little child, her father took her into the forest to gather rocks. It was a welcome change from the merciless glare of the constant sun in town. She could remember the long, sweaty walk from the front door, along the bleached glare of the cobblestone street to the high wall that circled the city. The nearest exit point from their house was the smallest of the four ports, and was set low like a pleading, open mouth. It only had one guard, who was often too drunk to bother arriving at his post, and the door would remain locked for days at a time. Carmina remembered holding her father's cool palm, and wondering at how dry it was while her own was hot and sticky with sweat and dust.

They ducked under the low stone arch, sidled past the guard who stank of vinegar and grime and old meat. The guard grunted what Carmina assumed must have been a hello. Her father responded with a sound like the creaking of wood. Between the forest and the wall was a thin circle of bare earth that the Governor, in his terror of the green world beyond, insisted on clearing to keep the trees at bay. Each day, laborers, conscripted from the Penal Colony, grunted and heaved with tillers, scythes and plows, under the watchful eyes of their guards. They cleared the green to the root, and yet it resprouted under their feet. By evening the trees unfurled thin leaves towards the darkening sky, and were knee high by morning when the next group of laborers arrived.

Carmina and her father tripped across the stubbled ground and slipped into the shadow of the wood. It was cool and damp and dark. Carmina let go of her father's cool palm and struggled over root and branch and fallen trunk. Her father seemed to sway with ease of windy limbs. With each foot fall, he seemed to take a green hue, then brown, then green again. Finally, they reached a small, clear stream, one of the many arms that reach for the broad middle of the forest—the flowing Opponax River. The stream was swift and clear, though narrow. When she waded in, it only reached her waist, though she had to hold onto her father's hands to keep from slipping away. The stream's bottom was spangled entirely with small, oval stones—just large enough to fit inside of her small fists. She submerged herself again and again, filling her sodden skirts with as many stones as the fabric would bear.

Afterwards, she sat with her father on the stream's rocky edge, their feet still dangling in the water, as they examined the pile of stones between them. Checking each one for a purity of color, they made piles of blue stones, green stones and black stones. White stones and muddled stones were thrown back. As they did this, Tamino Ailare told his daughter a story:

"Once upon a time, my darling, there lived a man who fell in love with a tree."

"What sort of tree," Carmina asked.

"What sort of tree? Any sort! What does it matter what sort it was?"

Carmina thought on this. "Well, was it a good tree? A kind tree? Or was it a selfish and wicked tree?"

"A good tree," Carmina's father said quietly. "The very best of trees."

"Good," Carmina said. "Because I want to like this story."

"Anyway, a man loved a tree very much. The tree grew at the center of the forest at the center of the world. It was not easy for the man to see his love. He had obligations. He was an honored citizen with a wife and a child. He had duties that he must do."

"How could he love something that was not his wife and family."

"Because he did."

"So he was a wicked man."

"Yes. But also a good man. Sometimes, a man can be both. Sometimes, they are the same."

Carmina said nothing. She watched the way her father watched the wood. His hair shone black, then gold, then green in the dappled sun.

"One day, the man prepared himself to leave his beloved and found that he could not. He laid his hands in the tender grooves along the bark, buried his face at the mossy roots. The tree quaked and sighed. It waved its limbs mournfully in the crushing wind, and as the man's heart broke within his breast, the tree shuddered and split down its very middle, crashing down on either side of the man. At the center of the trunk lay a stone, dark red and glittering—like this." He reached into the pile of stones and extracted one that was teardrop shaped—smooth and red and twice the size of Carmina's thumb. He deposited it into her hand. "The one true stone."

"Did he go home, then?" Carmina asked.

"I don't know," her father said.

"Did he die?"

"I don't know," he said again.

Carmina looked at the stone in her hand. It glittered. It blinked. "What should I do with this stone?"

"Keep it," her father said standing up and hunting for his boots. "Don't lose it."

But she did lose it. That very day. As they left the wood, the stone slid through a hole in her pocket and landed on the overgrown trail. She never told her father.

✳ ✳ ✳

To Our Noble and Gracious Emperor, Beloved of Generations, Protector of the Faith, Healer of Nations, Headmaster of Errant Tribes and Bearer of Knowledge, Reason and Truth: Greetings, Cousin.

It has been fourteen years since last we met, and fourteen years since last

I wounded your Honor and dared to impede on the Blessed Sanctity of your most Holy Office. It is only by your Grace and Blessings that I still live to pen this letter, and that my wife and child still remain as a delight and comfort for this, your most Humble Servant. You sent me to, with all Diligence and Purpose, endeavor to study and document the pernicious Molaru—known locally as the men who live in trees—and thus provide needed Insight for your Grace in your Considerations for the future of the Molaru, the colony, and the State of Trade along the glorious Opponax.

Because of the Love that once we shared, oh Cousin, oh Sovereign, oh Patron to us all; because it is with only the fondest memories do I recall our days as young lads together, suffering the same punishments after the wrongs we did to that poor Governess—may she rest in peace—that I must confess my failures in this matter. The task you set, cousin, is impossible. The Molaru will not—nay, they cannot—be dominated. Strangely, they cannot be a threat to you either. For fourteen years, I have followed, transcribed, documented and interviewed. I have used every known method of espionage, coercion, argument and trickery. I believe I know more about the language, history, culture and movements of the Molaru than any other man in the Empire. And I know nothing. Nothing! For fifteen years I have labored as a lover labors, quivering over the arch of my Beloved's eyebrow, moaning for one backward glance. They have given me little. And I, now, am a weakened, broken, and broken-hearted man.

The reason for my poor epistle to you, Dear Cousin, is this: any information I have learned, any detail that may—though this is doubtful—assist you in your quest to crush the Molaru, I will not give. For fourteen years I have sweated in this swamp, suffered under the weight of dull minds in this empty hull that calls itself a university, and for fourteen years I have loved the Molaru. If they knew your full intention for sending me, they have never let on. They will now, for I shall tell them. Whether or not they will let me live is an open question. Regardless, I would rather offer my throat to the blades of friends than to the hooded minions of a tyrant. I loved you once, Cousin, but your wickedness has forced me to despise you. I love the Molaru, and my treachery will likely cause them to despise me. So it goes.

My notes have been burned, my journal hidden in the depths of the forest, and my books have been removed from every library in the Empire by the stealthy hands of my remaining allies. All is destroyed or lost or hidden. All I have left now to lay claim to, is my life. So it is for any man. Even you, dear Cousin.

With all due Courtesy, Honor and Respect, I remain,

Your loyal servant,
Tamino Ailare

* * *

Carmina went into the garden. Two servants stood under the orange trees, gathering fruit into four large baskets.

"These are not ready to be picked," Carmina scolded. "They aren't ripe. Did *she* tell you to do this?" The servants simply looked at the ground, their large, mournful eyes heavy lidded and sullen. She looked to the edge of the garden. Her future husband stood facing the wall, throwing rocks over the top. Above the wall's rim the trees hovered and pressed, their leaves clouded with mist.

"You won't be allowed to speak to the servants once we are married," he said without looking at her. He reached down and picked up another stone, throwing it neatly over. The trees shuddered.

"Why not," Carmina asked.

"Mother says that as the daughter of a known heretic and fear-monger, you would likely upset the staff and spread your father's doctrine of laziness and crass immorality."

"She says that, does she?" She watched him reach down and pick up another stone, about the size and shape of a mango. He hefted it once, then twice, and glanced sidelong in her direction before hurling it over the lip of the wall. He threw it with such force, such focused intention, that she assumed he must have been thinking of throwing the stone at her head. It was a sentiment she shared. His head was, after all, rather large, and would be easy to hit.

On the other side of the wall, the trees gathered into a mass of green. Mist hung from the skin of the leaves and tumbled like drapes to the ground. Carmina coughed. She watched his hunched shoulders, his slack middle, the pasty skin just barely clinging to his fleshy neck. He bit his lower lip—pink as raw meat—as he reached down and hefted two more stones. His front teeth sank deep into the lip, creasing it neatly at the top. Carmina wondered if he would draw blood. She looked back over the wall. The heavily greened branches seemed even closer now, as though they were creeping over. The limbs swayed insistently though no discernable wind blew. Her husband to be still didn't look at her, but stared over the wall, preparing to throw his stone.

"I shouldn't worry about it though. It's not like you won't be cared for. Mother's got it all planned. We'll sell this hovel—honestly, I don't know how you can live here."

"I like it here," Carmina said. He didn't notice.

"We will be able to purchase a sizable stake in the ruby mine, and will have funds left over to renovate my grandfather's estate—"

"Excuse me," Carmina interrupted. "That's my rock." In his left hand was a stone, teardrop-shaped and red. It flickered in the light. "My father told me not to lose it."

"Your father is dead." Her husband to be examined the stone. "And anyway, anything that's yours is mine. That's how it works. Besides, there's nothing special about this. It's just a stupid rock." He threw it high into the air. Carmina watched it arc cleanly over the wall and disappear into the mass of leaves. The trees were over the wall now—leaves and sticks tumbled into the courtyard, piling along the edge. The green gathered and swelled like clouds—or a wave, and Carmina wondered briefly if they would be submerged.

"There," he said. "You see? Problem solved. There's nothing—" But he did not finish his sentence. There was a sound on the other side of the wall. A sound like the creaking of wood. A sound of wood bending, swelling, and snapping open, followed by the sharp note of sap in the air.

"The trees," her husband to be said, and though he pulled at her arm, his voice seemed to be coming from very far away. "The *trees*," he said again. But she couldn't hear him. She was too busy listening to the music of limb and branch and wood.

Six trees crashed into the wall, crushing it to the ground. From a thousand places inside the breathing forest, trees sighed, cracked, and yawned open. Men wearing polished breastplates and leafy tunics crawled through the gaps, scurried over the sides and leapt from the leaning branches.

"Run," her husband to be yelled as he ran. He turned, his broad face slack and slick from fear before a blade sliced him first in the thigh, then at the chest, then at the neck. He crumpled in a dappling of red and green and red, red, red. Carmina knelt beside him. Men with knives and spears and clubs ran by. Somewhere, a bell rang. And another answered it. And a third. These bells only rang in case of catastrophe, and Carmina had only heard them twice in her life—once when a man escaped from the penal colony, and once when the men who live in trees swarmed into her house and killed her father.

The man who would be her husband lay, face up, on the ground. His mouth ran with blood, and his breath was harsh and shallow. Carmina took his hand. She picked up a leaf and laid it on his chest wound. She laid another on his thigh. She laid another at his throat. He blinked. His breathing slowed and became easy.

"Once," she said, "there was a man who journeyed to the center of the wide world to find his fourteen fathers."

He looked at her face. Slowly, he brought his other hand to hers and squeezed weakly.

"Once, there was a man who was good and wicked at the same time. He loved a tree. He loved her so much, he thought he'd die."

Eight more trees fell over the wall. Carmina looked around and instead of a courtyard, they sat in a forest. Nineteen trees grew up through the house, their canopies piercing and arching over the roof. One of the Molaru men went by wearing her aunt's boots and carrying her favorite fan. Carmina did not move.

"Once there was a man who was not a man. Once there was a man who was me." The man who would be her husband shuddered and sighed and his hands dropped away from hers and onto the ground. Carmina stood and walked to a gap in the wall and climbed through. Forty trees stood with their middles slit open. Carmina approached the nearest tree and laid her hands on the exposed wood. It was yellow, veined with green and brown and smelled sweet and sharp with sap and dust. She found two handholds and lifted herself up and inside, finding that she just fit. Finding that she was quite comfortable. And when the bark closed behind her, she did not cry out. She was not afraid. And she did not look back.

HIROMI GOTO

Tales from the Breast

Hiromi Goto is a Japanese-Canadian writer and editor of novels, poetry, and short fiction. She has written for both children, young adults and adults. Her work has been recognized with numerous awards, including the James Tiptree, Jr. Award, the Sunburst Award, and the Carl Brandon Society Parallax Award. *Darkest Light* is her latest novel. "Tales from the Breast" is a fresh, perhaps darkly twisted, look at the roles and responsibilities of new parents. It was first published in *absinthe*, winter 1995, then reprinted in *Ms. Magazine*.

The questions that were never asked may be the most important. You don't think of this. You never do. When you were little, your mother used to tell you that asking too many questions could get you into trouble. You realize now that not asking enough has landed you in the same boat, in the same river of shit without the same paddle. You phone your mother long distance to tell her this and she says, "Well, two wrongs don't make a right, dear," and gives you a dessert recipe that is reported as being Prince Charles's favourite in the September issue of *Royalty* magazine.

Your Child's First Journey, page 173:
Your success in breastfeeding depends greatly on your desire to nurse as well as the encouragement you receive from those around you.

"Is there anything coming out?" He peers curiously at the baby's head, my covered breast.
"I don't know, I can't tell," I wince.

"What do you mean, you can't tell? It's your body, isn't it? I mean, you must be able to feel something," scratching his head. "Nope, only pain." "Oh." Blinks twice. "I'm sorry. I'm very proud of you, you know."

The placenta slips out from between your legs like the hugest blood clot of your life. The still-wet baby is strong enough to nurse but cannot stagger to her feet like a fawn or a colt. You will have to carry her in your arms for a long time. You console yourself with the fact that at least you are not an elephant who would be pregnant for close to another year. This is the first and last time she will nurse for the next twelve hours.

"Nurse, could you please come help me wake her up? She hasn't breastfed for five hours now."

The nurse has a mole with a hair on it. You can't help but look at it a little too long each time you glance up at her face. She undresses the baby but leaves the toque on. The infant is red and squirmy and you hope no one who visits says she looks just like you.

"Baby's just too comfortable," the nurse chirps. "And sometimes they're extra tired after the delivery. It's hard work for them too, you know!"

"Yeah, I suppose you're right."

"Of course. Oh, and when you go to the washroom, I wouldn't leave Baby by herself. Especially if the door is open." The nurse briskly rubs the red baby until she starts squirming, eyes still closed in determined sleep.

"What do you mean?"

"Well, we have security, but really, anyone could just waltz in and leave with Baby." The nurse smiles, like she's joking.

"Are you serious?"

"Oh, yes. And you shouldn't leave valuables around, either. We've been having problems with theft, and I know you people have nice cameras."

You have endured twelve hours of labour and gone without sleep for twenty-eight. You do not have the energy to tell the nurse of the inappropriateness of her comment. The baby does not wake up.

Your mother-in-law, from Japan, has come to visit. She is staying for a month to help with the older child. She gazes at the sleeping infant you hold to your chest. You tell her that the baby won't feed properly and that you are getting a little worried.

"Your nipples are too flat and she's not very good at breastfeeding," she says, and angry tears fill your eyes.

"Are you people from Tibet?" the nurse asks.

Page 174:
Breastmilk is raw and fresh.

You are at home. You had asked if you could stay longer in the hospital if you paid, but they just laughed and said no. Your mother-in-law makes lunch for herself and the firstborn but does not make any for you because she does not know if you will like it. You eat shredded wheat with NutraSweet and try breastfeeding again.

The pain is raw and fresh.

She breastfeeds for three hours straight, and when you burp her, there is a pinkish froth in the corners of her lips that looks like strawberry milk-shake. You realize your breast milk is blood-flavoured and wonder if it is okay for her to drink. Secretly, you hope that it is bad for her so that you will have to quit breastfeeding. When you call a friend and tell her about the pain and blood and your concerns for the baby's health, you learn, to your dismay, that the blood will not hurt her. That your friend had problems too, that she even had blood blisters on her nipples, but she kept right on breastfeeding through it, the doctor okayed it and ohhhh the blood, the pain, when those blood blisters popped, but she went right on breastfeeding until the child was four years old.

When you hang up, you are even more depressed. Because the blood is not a problem and your friend suffered even more than you do now. You don't come in first on the tragic nipple story. You don't even come close.

"This isn't going very well." I try smiling, but give up the effort.

"Just give it some time. Things'll get better." He snaps off the reading light at the head of the bed. I snap it back on.

"I don't think so. I don't think *things* are going to get better at all."

"Don't be so pessimistic," he smiles, trying not to offend me.

"Have you read the pamphlet for fathers of breastfed babies?"

"Uhhhhm, no. Not yet." Shrugs his shoulders and tries reaching for the lamp again. I swing out my hand to catch his wrist in midair.

"Well, read the damn thing and you might have some idea of what I'm going through."

"Women have been breastfeeding since there have been women."

"What!"

"You know what I mean. It's natural. Women have been breastfeeding ever since their existence, ever since ever having a baby," he lectures, glancing down once at my tortured breasts.

"That doesn't mean they've all been enjoying it, ever since existing and having done it since their existence! Natural isn't the same as liking it or being good at it," I hiss.

"Why do you have to be so complicated?"

"Why don't you just marry someone who isn't, then?"

"Are you hungry?" My mother-in-law whispers from the other side of the closed bedroom door. "I could fix you something if you're hungry."

Page 183:
Engorgement

The baby breastfeeds for hours on end. This is not the way the manual reads. You phone the emergency breastfeeding number they gave to you at the hospital. The breastfeeding professionals tell you that Baby is only doing what is natural. That the more she sucks, the more breast milk you will produce, how it works on a supply and demand system and how everything will be better when the milk comes in. On what kind of truck, you wonder.

They tell you that if you are experiencing pain of the nipples, it's because Baby isn't latched on properly. How the latch has to be just right for proper nursing. You don't like the sounds of that. You don't like how *latch* sounds like something that's suctioned on and might never come off again. You think of lamprey eels and leeches. Notice how everything starts with an "l."

When the milk comes in, it comes in on a semi-trailer. There are even marbles of milk under the surface of the skin in your armpits, hard as glass and painful to the touch. Your breasts are as solid as concrete balls and the pressure is so great that the veins around the nipple are swollen, bulging. Like the stuff of horror movies, they are ridged, expanded to the point of blood splatter explosion.

"Feel this, feel how hard my breasts are," I say, gritting my teeth.

"Oh my god!"

"It hurts," I whisper.

"Oh my god." He is horrified. Not with me, but at me.

"Can you suck them a little, so they're not so full? I can't go to sleep."

"What!" He looks at me like I've asked him to suck from a vial of cobra venom.

"Could you please suck some out? It doesn't taste bad. It's kinda like sugar water."

"Uhhh, I don't think so. It's so . . . incestuous."

"We're married, for god's sake, not blood relations. How can it be incestuous? Don't be so weird about it. Please! It's very painful."

"I'm sorry. I just can't." Clicks off the lamp and turns over to sleep.

Page 176:
Advantages also exist for you, the nursing mother . . . it is easy for you to lose weight without dieting and regain your shape sooner.

"You look like you're still pregnant," he jokes. "Are you sure there isn't another one still in there?"

"Just fuck off, okay?"

Your belly has a loose fold of skin and fat that impedes the sight of your pubic hair. You have a beauty mark on your lower abdomen you haven't seen for five years. You wonder if you would have had a better chance at being slimmer if you had breastfed the first child. There is a dark stain that runs vertically over the skin of your belly, from the pubic mound to the belly button and almost in line with the bottom of your breasts. Perversely, you imagined it to be the marker for the doctor to slice if the delivery had gone bad. The stain isn't going away and you don't really care because, what with the flab and all, it doesn't much make a difference. You are hungry all the time from producing breast milk and eat three times as much as you normally would, therefore you don't lose weight at all.

"You should eat as much as you want," your mother-in-law says. She spoons another slice of eggplant onto your plate and your partner passes his over as well. The baby starts to wail from the bedroom and your mother-in-law rushes to pick her up.

"Don't cry," you hear her say. "Breast milk is coming right away."

You want to yell down the hall that you have a name and it isn't Breast-Milk.

You eat the eggplant.

Page 176:

The hormone prolactin, which causes the secretion of milk, helps you to feel "motherly."

Just how long can the pain last, you ask yourself. It is the eleventh day of nipple torture and maternal hell. You phone a friend and complain about the pain, the endless pain. Your friend says that some people experience so much pleasure from breastfeeding that they have orgasms. If that were the case, you say, you would do it until the kid was big enough to run away from you.

The middle-of-the-night feed is the longest and most painful part of the breastfeeding day. It lasts from two to six hours. You alternate from breast to breast, from an hour at each nipple dwindling down to a half hour, fifteen minutes, eight minutes, two, one, as your nipples get so sore that even the soft brush of the baby's bundling cloth is enough to make your toes squeeze up into fists of pain, tears streaming down your cheeks. You try thinking about orgasms as the slow tick tick of the clock prolongs your misery. You try thinking of S&M. The pain is so intense, so slicing real, that you are unable to think of it as pleasurable. You realize that you are not a masochist.

Page 176:

Because you must sit down or lie down to nurse, you are assured of getting the rest you need postpartum.

You can no longer sit to breastfeed. You try lying down to nurse her like a puppy, but the shape of your breasts are not suitable for this method. You prop her up on the back of the easy chair and feed her while standing. Her legs dangle but she is able to suck on your sore nipples. You consider hanging a sign on your back: The Milk Stand.

Your ass is killing you. You take a warm sitz bath because it helps for a little while, and you touch yourself in the water as carefully as you can. You feel several new nubs of flesh between your vagina and your rectum and hopefully imagine that you are growing a second, third, fourth clitoris. When you visit your doctor, you find out that they're only hemorrhoids.

"I'm quitting. I hate this."

"You've only been at it for two weeks. This is the worst part and it'll only get better from here on," he encourages. Smiles gently and tries to kiss me on my nose.

"I quit, I tell you. If I keep on doing this, I'll start hating the baby."

"You're only thinking about yourself," he accuses, pointing a finger at my chest. "Breastfeeding is the best for her and you're giving up, just like that. I thought you were tougher."

"Don't you guilt me! It's my goddamn body and I make my own decisions on what I will and will not do with it!"

"You always have to do what's best for yourself! What about my input? Don't I have a say on how we raise our baby?" he shouts, Mr Sensible and let's-talk-about-it-like-two-adults.

"Is everything alright?" his mother whispers from outside the closed bedroom door. "Is anybody hun—"

"We're fine! Just go to bed!" he yells.

The baby snorts, hiccups into an incredible wail. Nasal and distressed.

"Listen, it's me who has to breastfeed her, me who's getting up every two hours to have my nipples lacerated and sucked on till they bleed while you just snore away. You haven't even got up once in the middle of the night to change her goddamn diaper even as a token fucking gesture of support, so don't you tell me what I should do with my breasts. There's nothing wrong with formula. I was raised on formula. You were raised on formula. Our whole generation was raised on formula and we're fine. So just shut up about it. Just shut up. Because this isn't about you. This is about me!"

"If I could breastfeed, I would do it gladly!" he hisses. Flings the blankets back and stomps to the crib.

And I laugh. I laugh because the sucker said the words out loud.

* * *

3:27 A.M. The baby has woken up. Your breasts are heavy with milk but you supplement her with formula. 5:15. You supplement her again and your breasts are so full, so tight, that they lie like marble on your chest. They are ready.

You change the baby's diapers and put her into the crib. In the low glow of the baby light, you can see her lips pursed around an imaginary nipple. She even sucks in her sleep. You sit on the bed, beside your partner, and unsnap the catches of the nursing bra. The pads are soaked and once the nipples are exposed, they spurt with sweet milk. The skin around your breasts stretches tighter than a drum, so tight that all you need is one little slice for the skin to part. Like a pressured zipper, it tears, spreading across the surface of your chest, directed by your fingers, tears in a complete circle around the entire breast.

There is no blood.

You lean slightly forward and the breast falls gently into your cupped hands. The flesh is a deep red and you wonder at its beauty, how flesh becomes food without you asking or even wanting it. You set the breast on your lap and slice your other breast. Two pulsing orbs still spurting breast milk. You gently tug the blankets down from the softly clenched fingers of your partner's sleep, unbutton his pyjamas, and fold them back so his chest is exposed. You stroke the hairless skin, then lift one breast, then the other, to lie on top of his flat penny nipples. The flesh of your breasts seeps into his skin, soft whisper of cells joining cells, your skin into his, tissue to tissue, the intimate melding before your eyes, your mouth an "o" of wonder and delight.

The unfamiliar weight of engorged breasts makes him stir, restless, a soft moan between parted lips. They are no longer spurting with milk, but they drip evenly, runnels down his sides. The cooling wet becomes uncomfortable and his eyelids flutter. Open. He focuses on my face peering down and blinks rapidly.

"What's wrong?" he asks, voice dry with sleep.

"Nothing. Not a thing. How do you feel?"

"Funny," he answers, perplexed. "My chest feels funny. I feel all achy. Maybe I'm coming down with something. My chest is wet! I'm bleeding!"

"Shhhhh. You'll wake the baby," I caution. Gently press my forefinger over his lips.

He was groggy with sleep, but he now he's wide awake. Sitting up. Looks down at his chest, his two engorged breasts. He looks at my face. Then back at his breasts.

"Oh my god," he moans.

"It's okay," I nurture him. "Don't worry. Everything is fine. Just do what comes naturally."

A sudden look of shock slams into his face and he reaches, panicked, with his hands to touch himself between his legs. When he feels himself intact, his eyes flit with relief only to be permanently replaced with bewilderment.

I smile. Beam in the dim glow of light. Turn on to my side and sleep sweetly, soundly.

ANGELA CARTER

The Fall River Axe Murders

Angela Carter was an English writer of fantastical fiction ranked tenth by *The Times* in 2008 on their list of "The 50 greatest British writers since 1945." Always a maverick, Carter filtered a love for weird fiction, folktales, and surrealists like Leonora Carrington through a feminist lens to create abidingly unique stories and novels that rank among the best of the twentieth century. Carter's classics include *The Infernal Desire Machines of Doctor Hoffman* (1972) and *Nights at the Circus* (1984), along with several iconic story collections, especially *Fireworks* (1974) and *The Bloody Chamber* (1979). Lizzie Borden has been remembered in history as a cold-blooded murderer and perhaps a woman who had reached her limit. "The Fall River Axe Murders" provides a different viewpoint of this unknowable, and most likely wronged, woman. It was first published in the *London Review of Books* in 1981.

Lizzie Borden with an axe
Gave her father forty whacks
When she saw what she had done
She gave her mother forty-one.
—Children's rhyme

Early in the morning of the fourth of August, 1892, in Fall River, Massachusetts.
    Hot, hot, hot . . . very early in the morning, before the factory whistle, but, even at this hour, everything shimmers and quivers under the attack of white,

furious sun already high in the still air.

Its inhabitants have never come to terms with these hot, humid sum-mers—for it is the humidity more than the heat that makes them intolerable; the weather clings like a low fever you cannot shake off. The Indians who lived here first had the sense to take off their buckskins when hot weather came and sit up to their necks in ponds; not so the descendants of the indus-trious, self-mortifying saints who imported the Protestant ethic wholesale into a country intended for the siesta and are proud, proud! of flying in the face of nature. In most latitudes with summers like these, everything slows down, then. You stay all day in penumbra behind drawn blinds and closed shutters; you wear clothes loose enough to make your own breeze to cool yourself when you infrequently move. But the ultimate decade of the last century finds us at the high point of hard work, here; all will soon be bustle, men will go out into the furnace of the morning well wrapped up in flannel underclothes, linen shirts, vests and coats and trousers of sturdy woollen cloth, and they garrotte themselves with neckties, too, they think it is so vir-tuous to be uncomfortable.

And today it is the middle of a heat wave; so early in the morning and the mercury has touched the middle eighties, already, and shows no sign of slowing down its headlong ascent.

As far as clothes were concerned, women only appeared to get off more lightly. On this morning, when, after breakfast and the performance of a few household duties, Lizzie Borden will murder her parents, she will, on rising, don a simple cotton frock—but, under that, went a long, starched cotton petticoat; another short, starched cotton petticoat; long drawers; woollen stockings; a chemise; and a whalebone corset that took her viscera in a stern hand and squeezed them very tightly. She also strapped a heavy linen napkin between her legs because she was menstruating.

In all these clothes, out of sorts and nauseous as she was, in this dement-ing heat, her belly in a vice, she will heat up a flat-iron on a stove and press handkerchiefs with the heated iron until it is time for her to go down to the cellar woodpile to collect the hatchet with which our imagination—"Lizzie Borden with an axe"—always equips her, just as we always visualise St Catherine rolling along her wheel, the emblem of her passion.

Soon, in just as many clothes as Miss Lizzie wears, if less fine, Bridget, the servant girl, will slop kerosene on a sheet of last night's newspaper crumpled with a stick or two of kindling. When the fire settles down, she will cook break-fast; the fire will keep her suffocating company as she washes up afterwards.

In a serge suit, one look at which would be enough to bring you out in prickly heat, Old Borden will perambulate the perspiring town, truffling for money like a pig until he will return home mid-morning to keep a pressing appointment with destiny.

But nobody here is up and about, yet; it is still early morning, before the factory whistle, the perfect stillness of hot weather, a sky already white, the shadowless light of New England like blows from the eye of God, and the sea, white, and the river, white.

If we have largely forgotten the physical discomforts of the itching, oppressive garments of the past and the corrosive effects of perpetual physical discomfort on the nerves, then we have mercifully forgotten, too, the smells of the past, the domestic odours—ill-washed flesh; infrequently changed underwear; chamber-pots; slop-pails; inadequately plumbed privies; rotting food; unattended teeth; and the streets are no fresher than indoors, the omnipresent acridity of horse piss and dung, drains, sudden stench of old death from butchers' shops, the amniotic horror of the fishmonger.

You would drench your handkerchief with cologne and press it to your nose. You would splash yourself with parma violet so that the reek of fleshly decay you always carried with you was overlaid by that of the embalming parlour. You would abhor the air you breathed.

Five living creatures are asleep in a house on Second Street, Fall River. They comprise two old men and three women. The first old man owns all the women by either marriage, birth or contract. His house is narrow as a coffin and that was how he made his fortune—he used to be an undertaker but he has recently branched out in several directions and all his branches bear fruit of the most fiscally gratifying kind.

But you would never think, to look at his house, that he is a successful and a prosperous man. His house is cramped, comfortless, small and mean—"unpretentious," you might say, if you were his sycophant—while Second Street itself saw better days some time ago. The Borden house—see "Andrew J. Borden" in flowing script on the brass plate next to the door— stands by itself with a few scant feet of yard on either side. On the left is a stable, out of use since he sold the horse. In the back lot grow a few pear trees, laden at this season.

On this particular morning, as luck would have it, only one of the two Borden girls sleeps in their father's house. Emma Lenora, his oldest daughter, has taken herself off to nearby New Bedford for a few days, to catch the ocean breeze, and so she will escape the slaughter.

Few of their social class stay in Fall River in the sweating months of June, July and August but, then, few of their social class live on Second Street, in the low part of town where heat gathers like fog. Lizzie was invited away, too, to a summer house by the sea to join a merry band of girls but, as if on purpose to mortify her flesh, as if important business kept her in the exhausted town, as if a wicked fairy spelled her in Second Street, she did not go.

The other old man is some kind of kin of Borden's. He doesn't belong here; he is visiting, passing through, he is a chance bystander, he is irrelevant.

Write him out of the script.

Even though his presence in the doomed house is historically unimpeachable, the colouring of this domestic apocalypse must be crude and the design profoundly simplified for the maximum emblematic effect.

Write John Vinnicum Morse out of the script.

One old man and two of his women sleep in the house on Second Street.

The City Hall clock whirrs and sputters the prolegomena to the first stroke of six and Bridget's alarm clock gives a sympathetic skip and click as the minute-hand stutters on the hour; back the little hammer jerks, about to hit the bell on top of her clock, but Bridget's damp eyelids do not shudder with premonition as she lies in her sticking flannel nightgown under one thin sheet on an iron bedstead, lies on her back, as the good nuns taught her in her Irish girlhood, in case she dies during the night, to make less trouble for the undertaker.

She is a good girl, on the whole, although her temper is sometimes uncertain and then she will talk back to the missus, sometimes, and will be forced to confess the sin of impatience to the priest. Overcome by heat and nausea—for everyone in the house is going to wake up sick today—she will return to this little bed later in the morning. While she snatches a few moments rest, upstairs, all hell will be let loose, downstairs.

A rosary of brown glass beads, a cardboard-backed colour print of the Virgin bought from a Portuguese shop, a flyblown photograph of her solemn mother in Donegal—these lie or are propped on the mantelpiece that, however sharp the Massachusetts winter, has never seen a lit stick. A banged tin trunk at the foot of the bed holds all Bridget's worldly goods.

There is a stiff chair beside the bed with, upon it, a candlestick, matches, the alarm clock that resounds the room with a dyadic, metallic clang, for it is a joke between Bridget and her mistress that the girl could sleep through anything, *anything*, and so she needs the alarm as well as all the factory whistles that are just about to blast off, just this very second about to blast off...

A splintered deal washstand holds the jug and bowl she never uses; she isn't going to lug water up to the third floor just to wipe herself down, is she? Not when there's water enough in the kitchen sink.

Old Borden sees no necessity for baths. He does not believe in total immersion. To lose his natural oils would be to rob his body.

A frameless square of mirror reflects in corrugated waves a cracked, dusty soap dish containing a quantity of black metal hairpins.

On bright rectangles of paper blinds move the beautiful shadows of the pear trees.

Although Bridget left the door open a crack in forlorn hopes of coaxing a draught into the room, all the spent heat of the previous day has packed itself tightly into her attic. A dandruff of spent whitewash flakes from the ceiling where a fly drearily whines.

The house is thickly redolent of sleep, that sweetish, clinging smell. Still, all still; in all the house nothing moving except the droning fly. Stillness on the staircase. Stillness pressing against the blinds. Stillness, mortal stillness in the room below, where Master and Mistress share the matrimonial bed.

Were the drapes open or the lamp lit, one could better observe the differences between this room and the austerity of the maid's room. Here is a carpet splashed with vigorous flowers, even if the carpet is of the cheap and cheerful variety; there are mauve, ochre and harsh cerise flowers on the wallpaper, even though the wallpaper was old when the Bordens arrived in the house. A dresser with another distorting mirror; no mirror in this house does not take your face and twist it. On the dresser, a runner embroidered with forget-me-nots; on the runner, a bone comb missing three teeth and lightly threaded with grey hairs, a hairbrush backed with ebonised wood, and a number of lace mats underneath small china boxes holding safety-pins, hairnets etc. The little hairpiece that Mrs Borden attaches to her balding scalp for daytime wear is curled up like a dead squirrel. But of Borden's male occupation of this room there is no trace because he has a dressing room of his own, through *that* door, on the left . . .

What about the other door, the one next to it?

It leads to the back stairs.

And that yet other door, partially concealed behind the head of the heavy, mahogany bed?

If it were not kept securely locked, it would take you into Miss Lizzie's room.

One peculiarity of this house is the number of doors the rooms contain and, a further peculiarity, how all these doors are always locked. A house full of locked doors that open only into other rooms with other locked doors, for, upstairs and downstairs, all the rooms lead in and out of one another like a maze in a bad dream. It is a house without passages. There is no part of the house that has not been marked as some inmate's personal territory; it is a house with no shared, no common spaces between one room and the next. It is a house of privacies sealed as close as if they had been sealed with wax on a legal document.

The only way to Emma's room is through Lizzie's. There is no way out of Emma's room. It is a dead end.

The Bordens' custom of locking all the doors, inside and outside, dates from a time, a few years ago, shortly before Bridget came to work for them, when the house was burgled. A person unknown came through the side door while Borden and his wife had taken one of their rare trips out together; he had loaded her into a trap and set out for the farm they owned at Swansea to ensure his tenant was not bilking him. The girls stayed at home in their rooms, napping on their beds or repairing ripped hems or sewing loose buttons more securely or writing letters or contemplating acts of charity among the deserving poor or staring vacantly into space.

I can't imagine what else they might do.

What the girls do when they are on their own is unimaginable to me.

Emma is more mysterious by far than Lizzie, for we know much less about her. She is a blank space. She has no life. The door from her room leads only into the room of her sister.

"Girls" is, of course, a courtesy term. Emma is well into her forties, Lizzie in her thirties, but they did not marry and so live in their father's house, where they remain in a fictive, protracted childhood.

While the master and the mistress were away and the girls asleep or otherwise occupied, some person or persons unknown tiptoed up the back stairs to the matrimonial bedroom and pocketed Mrs Borden's gold watch and chain, the coral necklace and silver bangle of her remote childhood, and a roll of dollar bills Old Borden kept under clean union suits in the third drawer of the bureau on the left. The intruder attempted to force the lock of the safe, that featureless block of black iron like a slaughtering block or an altar sitting squarely next to the bed on Old Borden's side, but it would have taken a crowbar to penetrate adequately the safe and the intruder tackled it with a pair of nail scissors that were lying handy on the dresser so *that* didn't come off.

Then the intruder pissed and shat on the cover of the Bordens' bed, knocked the clutter of this and that on the dresser to the floor, smashing everything, swept into Old Borden's dressing room there to maliciously assault the funeral coat as it hung in the moth-balled dark of his closet with the self-same nail scissors that had been used on the safe (the nail scissors now split in two and were abandoned on the closet floor), retired to the kitchen, smashed the flour crock and the treacle crock, and then scrawled an obscenity or two on the parlour window with the cake of soap that lived beside the scullery sink.

What a mess! Lizzie stared with vague surprise at the parlour window; she heard the soft bang of the open screen door, swinging idly, although there was no breeze. What was she doing, standing clad only in her corset in the middle of the sitting room? How had she got there? Had she crept down when she heard the screen door rattle? She did not know. She could not remember.

All that happened was: all at once here she is, in the parlour, with a cake of soap in her hand.

She experienced a clearing of the senses and only then began to scream and shout.

"Help! We have been burgled! Help!"

Emma came down and comforted her, as the big sister had comforted the little one since babyhood. Emma it was who cleared from the sitting-room carpet the flour and treacle Lizzie had heedlessly tracked in from the kitchen on her bare feet in her somnambulist trance. But of the missing jewellery and dollar bills no trace could be found.

I cannot tell you what effect the burglary had on Borden. It utterly disconcerted him; he was a man stunned. It violated him, even. He was a man raped. It took away his hitherto unshakeable confidence in the integrity inherent in things.

The burglary so moved them that the family broke its habitual silence with one another in order to discuss it. They blamed it on the Portuguese, obviously, but sometimes on the Canucks. If their outrage remained constant and did not diminish with time, the focus of it varied according to their moods, although they always pointed the finger of suspicion at the strangers and newcomers who lived in the gruesome ramparts of the company housing a few squalid blocks away. They did not always suspect the dark strangers exclusively; sometimes they thought the culprit might very well have been one of the mill-hands fresh from saucy Lancashire across the ocean who committed the crime, for a slum landlord has few friends among the criminal classes.

However, the possibility of a poltergeist occurs to Mrs Borden, although she does not know the word; she knows, however, that her younger stepdaughter is a strange one and could make the plates jump out of sheer spite, if she wanted to. But the old man adores his daughter. Perhaps it is then, after the shock of the burglary, that he decides she needs a change of scene, a dose of sea air, a long voyage, for it was after the burglary he sent her on the grand tour.

After the burglary, the front door and the side door were always locked three times if one of the inhabitants of the house left it for just so much as to go into the yard and pick up a basket of fallen pears when pears were in season or if the maid went out to hang a bit of washing or Old Borden, after supper, took a piss under a tree.

From this time dated the custom of locking all the bedroom doors on the inside when one was on the inside oneself or on the outside when one was on the outside. Old Borden locked his bedroom door in the morning, when he left it, and put the key in sight of all on the kitchen shelf.

The burglary awakened Old Borden to the evanescent nature of private property. He thereafter undertook an orgy of investment. He would forthwith invest his surplus in good brick and mortar, for who can make away with an office block?

A number of leases fell in simultaneously at just this time on a certain street in the downtown area of the city and Borden snapped them up. He owned the block. He pulled it down. He planned the Borden building, an edifice of shops and offices, dark red brick, deep tan stone, with cast-iron detail, from whence, in perpetuity, he might reap a fine harvest of unsaleable rents, and this monument, like that of Ozymandias, would long survive him—and, indeed, stands still, foursquare and handsome, the Andrew Borden Building, on South Main Street.

Not bad for a fish peddler's son, eh?

For, although Borden is an ancient name in New England and the Borden clan between them owned the better part of Fall River, our Borden, Old Borden, these Bordens, did not spring from a wealthy branch of the family. There were Bordens and Bordens and he was the son of a man who sold fresh fish in a wicker basket from house to house to house. Old Borden's parsimony was bred of poverty but learned to thrive best on property, for thrift has a different meaning for the poor; they get no joy of it, it is stark necessity to them. Whoever heard of a penniless miser?

Morose and gaunt, this self-made man is one of few pleasures. His vocation is capital accumulation.

What is his hobby?

Why, grinding the faces of the poor.

First, Andrew Borden was an undertaker, and death, recognising an accomplice, did well by him. In the city of spindles, few made old bones; the little children who laboured in the mills died with especial frequency. When he was an undertaker, no!—it was not true he cut the feet off corpses to fit into a job lot of coffins bought cheap as Civil War surplus! That was a rumour put about by his enemies!

With the profits from his coffins, he bought up a tenement or two and made fresh profit off the living. He bought shares in the mills. Then he invested in a bank or two, so that now he makes a profit on money itself, which is the purest form of profit of all.

Foreclosures and evictions are meat and drink to him. He loves nothing better than a little usury. He is halfway on the road to his first million.

At night, to save the kerosene, he sits in lampless dark. He waters the pear trees with his urine; waste not, want not. As soon as the daily newspapers are done with, he rips them up in geometric squares and stores them in the cellar privy so that they all can wipe their arses with them. He mourns the loss of the good organic waste that flushes down the WC. He would like to charge the very cockroaches in the kitchen rent. And yet he has not grown fat on all this; the pure flame of his passion has melted off his flesh, his skin sticks to his bones out of sheer parsimony. Perhaps it is from his first profession that he has acquired his bearing, for he walks with the stately dignity of a hearse.

To watch Old Borden bearing down the street towards you was to be filled with an instinctual respect for mortality, whose gaunt ambassador he seemed to be. And it made you think, too, what a triumph over nature it was when we rose up to walk on two legs instead of four, in the first place! For he held himself upright with such ponderous assertion it was a perpetual reminder to all who witnessed his progress how it is not natural to be upright, that it is a triumph of will over gravity, in itself a transcendence of the spirit over matter.

His spine is like an iron rod, forged, not born, impossible to imagine that spine of Old Borden's curled up in the womb in the big C of the foetus; he walks as if his legs had joints at neither knee nor ankle so that his feet hit the trembling earth like a bailiff pounding a door.

He has a white, chin-strap beard, old-fashioned already in those days He looks as if he'd gnawed his lips off. He is at peace with his god for he has used his talents as the Good Book says he should.

Yet do not think he has no soft spot. Like Old Lear, his heart—and more than that, his cheque-book—is putty in his youngest daughter's hands. On his pinky—you cannot see it, it lies under the covers—he wears a gold ring, not a wedding ring but a high-school ring, a singular trinket for a fabulously misanthropic miser. His youngest daughter gave it to him when she left school and asked him to wear it, always, and so he always does, and will wear it to the grave to which she is going to send him later in the morning of this combustible day.

He sleeps fully dressed in a flannel nightshirt over his long-sleeved underwear, and a flannel nightcap, and his back is turned towards his wife of thirty years, as is hers to his.

They are Mr and Mrs Jack Spratt in person, he tall and gaunt as a hanging judge and she, such a spreading, round little doughball. He is a miser, while she is a glutton, a solitary eater, most innocent of vices and yet the shadow or parodic vice of his, for he would like to eat up all the world, or, failing that, since fate has not spread him a sufficiently large table for his ambitions, he is a mute, inglorious Napoleon, he does not know what he might have done because he never had the opportunity—since he has not access to the entire world, he would like to gobble up the city of Fall River. But she, well, she just gently, continuously stuffs herself, doesn't she; she's always nibbling away at something, at the cud, perhaps.

Not that she gets much pleasure from it, either; no gourmet she forever meditating the exquisite difference between a mayonnaise sharpened with a few drops of Orleans vinegar or one pointed up with a squeeze of fresh lemon juice. No. Abby never aspired so high, nor would she ever think to do so even if she had the option; she is satisfied to stick to simple gluttony and she eschews all overtones of the sensuality of indulgence. Since she relishes not one single mouthful of the food she eats, she knows her ceaseless gluttony is no transgression.

Here they lie in bed together, living embodiments of two of the Seven Deadly Sins, but he knows his avarice is no offence because he never spends any money and she knows she is not greedy because the grub she shovels down gives her dyspepsia.

She employs an Irish cook and Bridget's rough-and-ready hand in the kitchen fulfils Abby's every criterion. Bread, meat, cabbage, potatoes—Abby was made for the heavy food that made her. Bridget merrily slaps on the table boiled dinners, boiled fish, cornmeal mush, Indian pudding johnny-cakes, cookies.

But those cookies . . . ah! there you touch on Abby's little weakness. Molasses cookies, oatmeal cookies, raisin cookies. But when she tackles a sticky brownie, oozing chocolate, then she feels a queasy sense of having gone almost too far, that sin might be just around the corner if her stomach did not immediately palpitate like a guilty conscience.

Her flannel nightdress is cut on the same lines as his nightshirt except for the limp flannel frill round the neck. She weighs two hundred pounds. She is five feet nothing tall. The bed sags on her side. It is the bed in which his first wife died.

Last night, they dosed themselves with castor oil, due to the indisposition that kept them both awake and vomiting the whole night before that; the copious results of their purges brim the chamber-pots beneath the bed. It is fit to make a sewer faint.

Back to back they lie. You could rest a sword in the space between the old man and his wife, between the old man's backbone, the only rigid thing he ever offered her, and her soft, warm, enormous bum. Their purges flailed them. Their faces show up decomposing green in the gloom of the curtained room, in which the air is too thick for flies to move.

The youngest daughter dreams behind the locked door.

Look at the sleeping beauty!

She threw back the top sheet and her window is wide open but there is no breeze, outside, this morning, to shiver deliciously the screen. Bright sun floods the blinds so that the linen-coloured light shows us how Lizzie has gone to bed as for a levee in a pretty, ruffled nightdress of snatched white muslin with ribbons of pastel pink satin threaded through the eyelets of the lace, for is it not the "naughty Nineties" everywhere but dour Fall River? Don't the gilded steamships of the Fall River Line signify all the squandered luxury of the Gilded Age within their mahogany and chandeliered interiors? But don't they sail *away* from Fall River, to where, elsewhere, it is the Belle Epoque? In New York, Paris, London, champagne corks pop, in Monte Carlo the bank is broken, women fall backwards in a crisp meringue of petticoats for fun and profit, but not in Fall River. Oh, no. So, in the immutable privacy of her bedroom, for her own delight, Lizzie puts on a rich girl's pretty night-dress, although she lives in a mean house, because she is a rich girl, too.

But she is plain.

The hem of her nightdress is rucked up above her knees because she is a restless sleeper. Her light, dry, reddish hair, crackling with static, slipping loose from the night-time plait, crisps and stutters over the square pillow at which she clutches as she sprawls on her stomach, having rested her cheek on the starched pillowcase for coolness' sake at some earlier hour.

Lizzie was not an affectionate diminutive but the name with which she had been christened. Since she would always be known as "Lizzie," so her father reasoned, why burden her with the effete and fancy prolongation of "Elizabeth"? A miser in everything, he even cropped off half her name before he gave it to her. So Lizzie it was, stark and unadorned, and she is a mother-less child, orphaned at two years old, poor thing.

Now she is two-and-thirty and yet the memory of that mother she cannot remember remains an abiding source of grief: "If mother had lived, every-thing would have been different."

How? Why? Different in what way? She wouldn't have been able to answer that, lost in a nostalgia for unknown love. Yet how could she have been loved better than by her sister, Emma, who lavished the pent-up treasures of a New England spinster's heart upon the little thing? Different, perhaps, because her natural mother, the first Mrs Borden, subject as she was to fits of sudden, wild, inexplicable rage, might have taken the hatchet to Old Borden on her own account? But Lizzie *loves* her father. All are agreed on that. Lizzie adores the adoring father who, after her mother died, took to himself another wife.

Her bare feet twitch a little, like those of a dog dreaming of rabbits. Her sleep is thin and unsatisfying, full of vague terrors and indeterminate menaces to which she cannot put a name or form once she is awake. Sleep opens within her a disorderly house. But all she knows is, she sleeps badly, and this last, stifling night has been troubled, too, by vague nausea and the gripes of her female pain; her room is harsh with the metallic smell of menstrual blood.

Yesterday evening she slipped out of the house to visit a woman friend. Lizzie was agitated; she kept picking nervously at the shirring on the front of her dress.

"I am afraid . . . that somebody . . . will *do* something," said Lizzie.

"Mrs Borden . . ." and here Lizzie lowered her voice and her eyes looked everywhere in the room except at Miss Russell . . . "Mrs Borden—oh! will you ever believe? Mrs Borden thinks somebody is trying to *poison* us!"

She used to call her stepmother "mother," as duty bade, but, after a quarrel about money after her father deeded half a slum property to her stepmother five years before, Lizzie always, with cool scrupulosity, spoke of "Mrs Borden" when she was forced to speak of her, and called her "Mrs Borden" to her face, too.

"Last night, Mrs Borden and poor father were so sick! I heard them, through the wall. And, as for me, I haven't felt myself all day, I have felt so strange. So very . . . strange."

For there were those somnambulist fits. Since a child, she endured occasional "peculiar spells," as the idiom of the place and time called odd lapses of behaviour, unexpected, involuntary trances, moments of disconnection. Those times when the mind misses a beat. Miss Russell hastened to discover an explanation within reason; she was embarrassed to mention the "peculiar spells." Everyone knew there was nothing odd about the Borden girls.

"Something you ate? It must have been something you have eaten. What was yesterday's supper?" solicitously queried kind Miss Russell.

"Warmed-over swordfish. We had it hot for dinner though I could not take much. Then Bridget heated up the leftovers for supper but, again, for myself, I could only get down a forkful. Mrs Borden ate up the remains and scoured her plate with her bread. She smacked her lips but then was sick all night." (Note of smugness, here.)

"Oh, Lizzie! In all this heat, this dreadful heat! Twice-cooked fish! You know how quickly fish goes off in this heat! Bridget should have known better than to give you twice-cooked fish!"

It was Lizzie's difficult time of the month, too; her friend could tell by a certain haggard, glazed look on Lizzie's face. Yet her gentility forbade her to mention that. But how could Lizzie have got it into her head that the entire household was under siege from malign forces without?

"There have been threats," Lizzie pursued remorselessly, keeping her eyes on her nervous fingertips. "So many people, you understand, dislike father."

This cannot be denied. Miss Russell politely remained mute.

"Mrs Borden was so very sick she called the doctor in and Father was abusive towards the doctor and shouted at him and told him he would not pay a doctor's bills whilst we had our own good castor oil in the house. He shouted at the doctor and all the neighbours heard and I was so ashamed. There is a man, you see . . ." and here she ducked her head, while her short, pale eyelashes beat on her cheek bones . . . "such a man, *dark* man, with the aspect, yes of death upon his face, Miss Russell, a dark man I've seen outside the house at odd, at unexpected hours, early in the morning, late at night, whenever I cannot sleep in this dreadful shade if I raise the blind and peep out, there I see him in the shadows of the pear trees, in the yard, a dark man . . . perhaps he puts poison in the milk, in the mornings, after the milkman fills his can. Perhaps he poisons the ice, when the iceman comes."

"How long has he been haunting you?" asked Miss Russell, properly dismayed.

"Since . . . the burglary," said Lizzie and suddenly looked Miss Russell full in the face with a kind of triumph. How large her eyes were; prominent, yet veiled. And her well-manicured fingers went on pecking away at the front of her dress as if she were trying to unpick the shirring.

Miss Russell knew, she just *knew*, this dark man was a figment of Lizzie's imagination. All in a rush, she lost patience with the girl; dark men standing outside her bedroom window, indeed! Yet she was kind and cast about for ways to reassure.

"But Bridget is up and about when the milkman, the iceman call and the whole street is busy and bustling, too; who would dare to put poison in either milk or ice-bucket while half of Second Street looks on? Oh, Lizzie, it is the dreadful summer, the heat, the intolerable heat that's put us all out of sorts, makes us fractious and nervous, makes us sick. So easy to imagine things in this terrible weather, that taints the food and sows worms in the mind . . . I thought you'd planned to go away, Lizzie, to the ocean. Didn't you plan to take a little holiday, by the sea? Oh, do go! Sea air would blow away these silly fancies!"

Lizzie neither nods nor shakes her head but continues to worry at her shirring. For does she not have important business in Fall River? Only that morning, had she not been down to the drug-store to try to buy some prussic acid herself? But how can she tell kind Miss Russell she is gripped by an imperious need to stay in Fall River and murder her parents?

She went to the drug-store on the corner of Main Street in order to buy prussic acid but nobody would sell it to her, so she came home empty-handed.

Had all that talk of poison in the vomiting house put her in mind of poison? The autopsy will reveal no trace of poison in the stomachs of either parent. She did not try to poison them; she only had it in mind to poison them. But she had been unable to buy poison. The use of poison had been denied her; so what can she be planning, now?

"And this dark man," she pursued to the unwilling Miss Russell, "oh! I have seen the moon glint upon an *axe*!"

When she wakes up, she can never remember her dreams; she only remembers she slept badly.

Hers is a pleasant room of not ungenerous dimensions, seeing the house is so very small. Besides the bed and the dresser, there is a sofa and a desk; it is her bedroom and also her sitting room and her office, too, for the desk is stacked with account books of the various charitable organisations with which she occupies her ample spare time. The Fruit and Flower Mission, under whose auspices she visits the indigent old in hospital with gifts; the Women's Christian Temperance Union, for whom she extracts signatures for petitions against the Demon Drink; Christian Endeavour, whatever that is— this is the golden age of good works and she flings herself into committees with a vengeance. What would the daughters of the rich do with themselves if the poor ceased to exist?

There is the Newsboys Thanksgiving Dinner Fund; and the Horse-trough Association; and the Chinese Conversion Association—no class nor kind is safe from her merciless charity.

Bureau; dressing-table; closet; bed; sofa. She spends her days in this room, moving between each of these dull items of furniture in a circumscribed, undeviating, planetary round. She loves her privacy, she loves her room, she locks herself up in it all day. A shelf contains a book or two: *Heroes of the Mission Field*, *The Romance of Trade*, *What Katy Did*. On the walls, framed photographs of high-school friends, sentimentally inscribed, with, tucked inside one frame, a picture postcard showing a black kitten peeking through a horseshoe. A watercolour of a Cape Cod seascape executed with poignant amateur incompetence. A monochrome photograph or two of works of art, a Delia Robbia madonna and the Mona Lisa; these she bought in the Uffizi and the Louvre respectively when she went to Europe.

Europe!

For don't you remember what Katy did next? The storybook heroine took the steamship to smoky old London, to elegant, fascinating Paris, to sunny, antique Rome and Florence, the story-book heroine sees Europe reveal itself before her like an interesting series of magic-lantern slides on a gigantic screen. All is present and all unreal. The Tower of London; click.

Notre Dame; click. The Sistine Chapel; click. Then the lights go out and she is in the dark again.

Of this journey she retained only the most circumspect of souvenirs, that madonna, that Mona Lisa, reproductions of objects of art consecrated by a universal approval of taste. If she came back with a bag full of memories stamped "Never to be Forgotten," she put the bag away under the bed on which she had dreamed of the world before she set out to see it and on which, at home again, she continued to dream, the dream having been transformed not into lived experience but into memory, which is only another kind of dreaming.

Wistfully: "When I was in Florence . . ."

But then, with pleasure, she corrects herself: "When *we* were in Florence . . ."

Because a good deal, in fact most, of the gratification the trip gave her came from having set out from Fall River with a select group of the daughters of respectable and affluent mill-owners. Once away from Second Street, she was able to move comfortably in the segment of Fall River society to which she belonged by right of old name and new money but from which, when she was at home, her father's plentiful personal eccentricities excluded her. Sharing bedrooms, sharing state-rooms, sharing berths, the girls travelled together in a genteel gaggle that bore its doom already upon it, for they were the girls who would not marry, now, and any pleasure they might have obtained from the variety and excitement of the trip was spoiled in advance by the knowledge they were eating up what might have been their own wedding-cake, using up what should have been, if they'd had any luck, their marriage settlements.

All girls pushing thirty, privileged to go out and look at the world before they resigned themselves to the thin condition of New England spinsterhood; but it was a case of look, don't touch. They knew they must not get their hands dirtied or their dresses crushed by the world, while their affectionate companionship en route had a certain steadfast, determined quality about it as they bravely made the best of the second-best.

It was a sour trip, in some ways, sour; and it was a round trip, it ended at the sour place from where it had set out. Home, again; the narrow house, the rooms all locked like those in Bluebeard's castle, and the fat, white stepmother whom nobody loves sitting in the middle of the spider web, she has not budged a single inch while Lizzie was away but she has grown fatter.

This stepmother oppressed her like a spell.

The days open their cramped spaces into other cramped spaces and old furniture and never anything to look forward to, nothing.

When Old Borden dug in his pocket to shell out for Lizzie's trip to Europe, the eye of God on the pyramid blinked to see daylight, but no extravagance is too excessive for the miser's younger daughter who is the wild card in his house and, it seems, can have anything she wants, play ducks and drakes with her father's silver dollars if it so pleases her. He pays all her dressmakers' bills on the dot and how she loves to dress up fine! She is addicted to dandyism. He gives her each week in pin-money the same as the cook gets for wages and Lizzie gives that which she does not spend on personal adornment to the deserving poor.

He would give his Lizzie anything, anything in the world that lives under the green sign of the dollar.

She would like a pet, a kitten or a puppy, she loves small animals and birds, too, poor, helpless things. She piles high the bird-table all winter. She used to keep some white pouter pigeons in the disused stable, the kind that look like shuttlecocks and go "vroo croo," soft as a cloud.

Surviving photographs of Lizzie Borden show a face it is difficult to look at as if you knew nothing about her; coming events cast their shadow across her face, or else you see the shadows these events have cast—something terrible, something ominous in this face with its jutting, rectangular jaw and those mad eyes of the New England saints, eyes that belong to a person who does not listen to you . . . fanatic's eyes, you might say, if you knew nothing about her. If you were sorting through a box of old photographs in a junk shop and came across this particular, sepia, faded face above the choked collars of the 1890s, you might murmur when you saw her: "Oh, what big eyes you have!" as Red Riding Hood said to the wolf, but then you might not even pause to pick her out and look at her more closely, for hers is not, in itself, a striking face.

But as soon as the face has a name, once you recognise her, when you know who she is and what it was she did, the face becomes as if of one possessed, and now it haunts you, you look at it again and again, it secretes mystery.

This woman, with her jaw of a concentration-camp attendant, and such eyes . . .

In her old age, she wore pince-nez, and truly with the years the mad light has departed from those eyes or else is deflected by her glasses—if, indeed, it *was* a mad light, in the first place, for don't we all conceal somewhere photographs of ourselves that make us look like crazed assassins? And, in those early photographs of her young womanhood, she herself does not look so much like a crazed assassin as somebody in extreme solitude, oblivious of that camera in whose direction she obscurely smiles, so that it would not surprise you to learn that she is blind.

There is a mirror on the dresser in which she sometimes looks at those times when time snaps in two and then she sees herself with blind, clairvoyant eyes, as though she were another person.

"Lizzie is not herself, today."

At those times, those irremediable times, she could have raised her muzzle to some aching moon and howled.

At other times, she watches herself doing her hair and trying her clothes on. The distorting mirror reflects her with the queasy fidelity of water. She puts on dresses and then she takes them off. She looks at herself in her corset. She pats her hair. She measures herself with the tape-measure. She pulls the measure tight. She pats her hair. She tries on a hat, a little hat, a chic little straw toque. She punctures it with a hatpin. She pulls the veil down. She pulls it up. She takes the hat off. She drives the hatpin into it with a strength she did not know she possessed.

Time goes by and nothing happens.

She traces the outlines of her face with an uncertain hand as if she were thinking of unfastening the bandages on her soul but it isn't time to do that, yet: she isn't ready to be seen, yet.

She is a girl of Sargasso calm.

She used to keep her pigeons in the loft above the disused stable and feed them grain out of the palms of her cupped hands. She liked to feel the soft scratch of their beaks. They murmured "vroo croo" with infinite tenderness. She changed their water every day and cleaned up their leprous messes but Old Borden took a dislike to their cooing, it got on his nerves, who'd have thought he *had* any nerves but he invented some, they got on them, one afternoon he took out the hatchet from the woodpile in the cellar and chopped those pigeons' heads right off, he did.

Abby fancied the slaughtered pigeons for a pie but Bridget the servant girl put her foot down, at that: what?!? make a pie out of Miss Lizzie's beloved turtledoves? JesusMaryandJoseph!!! she exclaimed with characteristic impetuousness, what can they be thinking of! Miss Lizzie so nervy with her funny turns and all! (The maid is the only one in the house with any sense and that's the truth of it.) Lizzie came home from the Fruit and Flower Mission for whom she had been reading a tract to an old woman in a poorhouse: "God bless you, Miss Lizzie." At home all was blood and feathers.

She doesn't weep, this one, it isn't her nature, she is still waters, but, when moved, she changes colour, her face flushes, it goes dark, angry, mottled red. The old man loves his daughter this side of idolatry and pays for everything she wants, but all the same he killed her pigeons when his wife wanted to gobble them up.

That is how she sees it. That is how she understands it. She cannot bear to watch her stepmother eat, now. Each bite the woman takes seems to go: "Vroo croo."

Old Borden cleaned off the hatchet and put it back in the cellar, next to the woodpile. The red receding from her face, Lizzie went down to inspect the instrument of destruction. She picked it up and weighed it in her hand.

That was a few weeks before, at the beginning of the spring.

Her hands and feet twitch in her sleep; the nerves and muscles of this complicated mechanism won't relax, just won't relax, she is all twang, all tension, she is taut as the strings of a wind-harp from which random currents of the air pluck out tunes that are not our tunes.

At the first stroke of the City Hall clock, the first factory hooter blares, and then, on another note, another, and another, the Metacomet Mill, the American Mill, the Mechanics Mill . . . until every mill in the entire town sings out aloud in a common anthem of summoning and hot alleys where the factory folk live blacken with the hurrying throng: hurry! scurry! to loom, to bobbin, to spindle, to dye-shop as to places of worship, men, and women, too, and children, the streets blacken, the sky darkens as the chimneys now belch forth, the clang, bang, clatter of the mills commences.

Bridget's clock leaps and shudders on its chair, about to sound its own alarm. Their day, the Bordens' fatal day, trembles on the brink of beginning.

Outside, above, in the already burning air, see! the angel of death roosts on the roof-tree.

PAT MURPHY

Love and Sex
Among the Invertebrates

Pat Murphy is an American writer and scientist. In addition to novels and short fiction, she has also written a children's book, *The Wild Ones*. Her work has won numerous awards including the Nebula Award, the World Fantasy Award, and the Philip K. Dick Award. She also cofounded the James Tiptree, Jr. Memorial Award with Karen Joy Fowler. Her latest project is *Bad Grrlz' Guide to Reality*, an omnibus of two connected novels, *Wild Angel* and *Adventures in Time and Space with Max Merriwell*. "Love and Sex Among the Invertebrates" explores sexuality and gender roles in the animal kingdom and their application to human beings. It was first published in the anthology *Alien Sex* in 1990.

This is not science. This has nothing to do with science. Yesterday, when the bombs fell and the world ended, I gave up scientific thinking. At this distance from the blast site of the bomb that took out San Jose, I figure I received a medium-sized dose of radiation. Not enough for instant death, but too much for survival. I have only a few days left, and I've decided to spend this time constructing the future. Someone must do it.

It's what I was trained for, really. My undergraduate studies were in biology—structural anatomy, the construction of body and bone. My graduate studies were in engineering. For the past five years, I have been designing and constructing robots for use in industrial processing. The need for such industrial creations is over now. But it seems a pity to waste the equipment and materials that remain in the lab that my colleagues have abandoned.

I will put robots together and make them work. But I will not try to understand them. I will not take them apart and consider their inner workings and poke and pry and analyze. The time for science is over.

* * *

The pseudoscorpion, *Lasiochernes pilosus*, is a secretive scorpion-like insect that makes its home in the nests of moles. Before pseudoscorpions mate, they dance—a private underground minuet, observed only by moles and voyeuristic entomologists. When a male finds a receptive female, he grasps her claws in his and pulls her toward him. If she resists, he circles, clinging to her claws and pulling her after him, refusing to take no for an answer. He tries again, stepping forward and pulling the female toward him with trembling claws. If she continues to resist, he steps back and continues the dance: circling, pausing to tug on his reluctant partner, then circling again.

After an hour or more of dancing, the female inevitably succumbs, convinced by the dance steps that her companion's species matches her own. The male deposits a packet of sperm on the ground that has been cleared of debris by their dancing feet. His claws quiver as he draws her forward, positioning her over the package of sperm. Willing at last, she presses her genital pore to the ground and takes the sperm into her body.

Biology texts note that the male scorpion's claws tremble as he dances, but they do not say why. They do not speculate on his emotions, his motives, his desires. That would not be scientific.

I theorize that the male pseudoscorpion is eager. Among the everyday aromas of mole shit and rotting vegetation, he smells the female, and the perfume of her fills him with lust. But he is fearful and confused: a solitary insect, unaccustomed to socializing, he is disturbed by the presence of another of his kind. He is caught by conflicting emotions: his all-encompassing need, his fear, and the strangeness of the social situation.

I have given up the pretense of science. I speculate about the motives of the pseudoscorpion, the conflict and desire embodied in his dance.

* * *

I put the penis on my first robot as a kind of joke, a private joke, a joke about evolution. I suppose I don't really need to say it was a private joke—all my jokes are private now. I am the last one left, near as I can tell. My colleagues fled—to find their families, to seek refuge in the hills, to spend their last days running around, here and there. I don't expect to see anyone else around anytime soon. And if I do, they probably won't be interested in my jokes. I'm sure that most people think the time for joking is past. They don't see that the bomb and the war are the biggest jokes of all. Death is the biggest joke. Evolution is the biggest joke.

I remember learning about Darwin's theory of evolution in high school biology. Even back then, I thought it was kind of strange, the way people talked about it. The teacher presented evolution as a *fait accompli*, over and done with. She muddled her way through the complex speculations regarding human evolution, talking about *Ramapithecus, Australopithecus, Homo erectus, Homo sapiens*, and *Homo sapiens neanderthalensis*. At *Homo sapiens* she stopped, and that was it. The way the teacher looked at the situation, we were the last word, the top of the heap, the end of the line.

I'm sure the dinosaurs thought the same, if they thought at all. How could anything get better than armor plating and a spiked tail? Who could ask for more?

Thinking about the dinosaurs, I build my first creation on a reptilian model, a lizard-like creature constructed from bits and pieces that I scavenge from the industrial prototypes that fill the lab and the storeroom. I give my creature a stocky body, as long as I am tall; four legs, extending to the side of the body then bending at the knee to reach the ground; a tail as long as the body, spiked with decorative metal studs; a crocodilian mouth with great curving teeth.

The mouth is only for decoration and protection; this creature will not eat. I equip him with an array of solar panels, fixed to a sail-like crest on his back. The warmth of sunlight will cause the creature to extend his sail and gather electrical energy to recharge his batteries. In the cool of the night, he will fold his sail close to his back, becoming sleek and streamlined.

I decorate my creature with stuff from around the lab. From the trash beside the soda machine, I salvage aluminum cans. I cut them into a colorful fringe that I attach beneath the creature's chin, like the dewlap of an iguana. When I am done, the words on the soda cans have been sliced to nonsense: Coke, Fanta, Sprite, and Dr Pepper mingle in a collision of bright colors. At the very end, when the rest of the creature is complete and functional, I make a cock of copper tubing and pipe fittings. It dangles beneath his belly, copper bright and obscene-looking. Around the bright copper, I weave a rat's nest of my own hair, which is falling out by the handful. I like the look of that: bright copper peeking from a clump of wiry black curls.

Sometimes, the sickness overwhelms me. I spend part of one day in the ladies room off the lab, lying on the cool tile floor and rousing myself only to vomit into the toilet. The sickness is nothing that I didn't expect. I'm dying, after all. I lie on the floor and think about the peculiarities of biology.

* * *

For the male spider, mating is a dangerous process. This is especially true in the spider species that weave intricate orb-shaped webs, the kind that catch the morning dew and sparkle so nicely for nature photographers. In these species, the female is larger than the male. She is, I must confess, rather a bitch; she'll attack anything that touches her web.

At mating time, the male proceeds cautiously. He lingers at the edge of the web, gently tugging on a thread of spider silk to get her attention. He plucks in a very specific rhythm, signaling to his would-be lover, whispering softly with his tugs: "I love you. I love you."

After a time, he believes that she has received his message. He feels confident that he has been understood. Still proceeding with caution, he attaches a mating line to the female's web. He plucks the mating line to encourage the female to move onto it. "Only you, baby," he signals. "You are the only one."

She climbs onto the mating line—fierce and passionate, but temporarily soothed by his promises. In that moment, he rushes to her, delivers his sperm, then quickly, before she can change her mind, takes a hike. A dangerous business, making love.

* * *

Before the world went away, I was a cautious person. I took great care in my choice of friends. I fled at the first sign of a misunderstanding. At the time, it seemed the right course.

I was a smart woman, a dangerous mate. (Odd—I find myself writing and thinking of myself in the past tense. So close to death that I consider myself already dead.) Men would approach with caution, delicately signalling from a distance: "I'm interested. Are you?" I didn't respond. I didn't really know how.

An only child, I was always wary of others. My mother and I lived together. When I was just a child, my father had left to pick up a pack of cigarettes and had never returned. My mother, protective and cautious by nature, warned me that men could not be trusted. People could not be trusted. She could trust me and I could trust her, and that was all.

When I was in college, my mother died of cancer. She had known of the tumor for more than a year; she had endured surgery and chemotherapy, while writing me cheery letters about her gardening. Her minister told me that my mother was a saint—she hadn't told me because she hadn't wanted to disturb my studies. I realized then that she had been wrong. I couldn't really trust her after all.

I think perhaps I missed some narrow window of opportunity. If, at some point along the way, I had had a friend or a lover who had made the effort to coax me from hiding, I could have been a different person. But it never happened. In high school, I sought the safety of my books. In college, I studied alone on Friday nights. By the time I reached graduate school, I was, like the pseudoscorpion, accustomed to a solitary life.

I work alone in the laboratory, building the female. She is larger than the male. Her teeth are longer and more numerous. I am welding the hip joints into place when my mother comes to visit me in the laboratory.

"Katie," she says. "Why didn't you ever fall in love? Why didn't you ever have children?"

I keep on welding, despite the trembling of my hands. I know she isn't there. Delirium is one symptom of radiation poisoning. But she keeps watching me as I work.

"You're not really here," I tell her, and realize immediately that talking to her is a mistake. I have acknowledged her presence and given her more power.

"Answer my questions, Katie," she says. "Why didn't you?"

I do not answer. I am busy and it will take too long to tell her about betrayal, to explain the confusion of a solitary insect confronted with a social situation, to describe the balance between fear and love. I ignore her just as I ignore the trembling of my hands and the pain in my belly, and I keep on working. Eventually, she goes away.

I use the rest of the soda cans to give the female brightly colored scales: Coca-Cola red, Sprite green, Fanta orange. From soda cans, I make an oviduct, lined with metal. It is just large enough to accommodate the male's cock.

✳ ✳ ✳

The male bowerbird attracts a mate by constructing a sort of art piece. From sticks and grasses, he builds two close-set parallel walls that join together to make an arch. He decorates this structure and the area around it with gaudy trinkets: bits of bone, green leaves, flowers, bright stones, and feathers cast off by gaudier birds. In areas where people have left their trash, he uses bottle caps and coins and fragments of broken glass.

He sits in his bower and sings, proclaiming his love for any and all females in the vicinity. At last, a female admires his bower, accepts his invitation, and they mate.

The bowerbird uses discrimination in decorating his bower. He chooses his trinkets with care—selecting a bit of glass for its glitter, a shiny leaf for its natural elegance, a cobalt-blue feather for a touch of color. What does he think about as he builds and decorates? What passes through his mind as he sits and sings, advertising his availability to the world?

* * *

I have released the male and I am working on the female when I hear rattling and crashing outside the building. Something is happening in the alley between the laboratory and the nearby office building. I go down to investigate. From the mouth of the alley, I peer inside, and the male creature runs at me, startling me so that I step back. He shakes his head and rattles his teeth threateningly.

I retreat to the far side of the street and watch him from there. He ventures from the alley, scuttling along the street, then pauses by a BMW that is parked at the curb. I hear his claws rattling against metal. A hubcap clangs as it hits the pavement. The creature carries the shiny piece of metal to the mouth of the alley and then returns for the other three, removing them one by one. When I move, he rushes toward the alley, blocking any attempt to invade his territory. When I stand still, he returns to his work, collecting the hubcaps, carrying them to the alley, and arranging them so that they catch the light of the sun.

As I watch, he scavenges in the gutter and collects things he finds appealing: a beer bottle, some colorful plastic wrappers from candy bars, a length of bright yellow plastic rope. He takes each find and disappears into the alley with it.

I wait, watching. When he has exhausted the gutter near the mouth of the alley, he ventures around the corner and I make my move, running to the alley entrance and looking inside. The alley floor is covered with colored bits of paper and plastic; I can see wrappers from candy bars and paper bags from Burger King and McDonald's. The yellow plastic rope is tied to a pipe running up one wall and a protruding hook on the other. Dangling from it, like clean clothes on the clothesline, are colorful pieces of fabric: a burgundy-colored bathtowel, a paisley-print bedspread, a blue satin bedsheet.

I see all this in a glance. Before I can examine the bower further, I hear the rattle of claws on pavement. The creature is running at me, furious at my intrusion. I turn and flee into the laboratory, slamming the door behind me. But once I am away from the alley, the creature does not pursue me.

From the second-story window, I watch him return to the alley and I suspect that he is checking to see if I have tampered with anything. After a time, he reappears in the alley mouth and crouches there, the sunlight glittering on his metal carapace.

In the laboratory, I build the future. Oh, maybe not—but there's no one here to contradict me, so I will say that it is so. I complete the female and release her.

The sickness takes over then. While I still have the strength, I drag a cot from a backroom and position it by the window, where I can look out and watch my creations.

What is it that I want from them? I don't know exactly.

I want to know that I have left something behind. I want to be sure that the world does not end with me. I want the feeling, the understanding, the certainty that the world will go on.

I wonder if the dying dinosaurs were glad to see the mammals, tiny rat-like creatures that rustled secretively in the underbrush.

* * *

When I was in seventh grade, all the girls had to watch a special presentation during gym class one spring afternoon. We dressed in our gym clothes, then sat in the auditorium and watched a film called *Becoming a Woman*. The film talked about puberty and menstruation. The accompanying pictures showed the outline of a young girl. As the film progressed, she changed into a woman, developing breasts. The animation showed her uterus as it grew a lining, then shed it, then grew another. I remember watching with awe as the pictures showed the ovaries releasing an egg that united with a sperm, and then lodged in the uterus and grew into a baby.

The film must have delicately skirted any discussion of the source of the sperm, because I remember asking my mother where the sperm came from and how it got inside the woman. The question made her very uncomfortable. She muttered something about a man and woman being in love—as if love were somehow all that was needed for the sperm to find its way into the woman's body.

After that discussion, it seems to me that I was always a little confused about love and sex—even after I learned about the mechanics of sex and what goes where. The penis slips neatly into the vagina—but where does the love come in? Where does biology leave off and the higher emotions begin?

Does the female pseudoscorpion love the male when their dance is done? Does the male spider love his mate as he scurries away, running for his life? Is there love among the bowerbirds as they copulate in their bower? The textbooks fail to say. I speculate, but I have no way to get the answers.

* * *

My creatures engage in a long, slow courtship. I am getting sicker. Sometimes, my mother comes to ask me questions that I will not answer. Sometimes, men sit by my bed—but they are less real than my mother. These are men I cared about—men I thought I might love, though I never got beyond the thought. Through their translucent bodies, I can see the laboratory walls. They never were real, I think now.

Sometimes, in my delirium, I remember things. A dance back at college; I was slow-dancing, with someone's body pressed close to mine. The room was hot and stuffy and we went outside for some air. I remember he kissed me, while one hand stroked my breast and the other fumbled with the buttons of my blouse. I kept wondering if this was love—this fumbling in the shadows.

In my delirium, things change. I remember dancing in a circle with someone's hands clasping mine. My feet ache, and I try to stop, but my partner pulls me along, refusing to release me. My feet move instinctively in time with my partner's, though there is no music to help us keep the beat. The air smells of dampness and mold; I have lived my life underground and I am accustomed to these smells.

Is this love?

I spend my days lying by the window, watching through the dirty glass. From the mouth of the alley, he calls to her. I did not give him a voice, but he calls in his own way, rubbing his two front legs together so that metal rasps against metal, creaking like a cricket the size of a Buick.

She strolls past the alley mouth, ignoring him as he charges toward her, rattling his teeth. He backs away, as if inviting her to follow. She walks by. But then, a moment later, she strolls past again and the scene repeats itself. I understand that she is not really oblivious to his attention. She is simply taking her time, considering her situation. The male intensifies his efforts, tossing his head as he backs away, doing his best to call attention to the fine home he has created.

I listen to them at night. I cannot see them—the electricity failed two days ago and the streetlights are out. So I listen in the darkness, imagining. Metal legs rub together to make a high creaking noise. The sail on the male's back rattles as he unfolds it, then folds it, then unfolds it again, in what must be a sexual display. I hear a spiked tail rasping over a spiny back in a kind of caress. Teeth chatter against metal—love bites, perhaps. (The lion bites the lioness on the neck when they mate, an act of aggression that she accepts as affection.) Claws scrape against metal hide, clatter over metal scales. This, I think, is love. My creatures understand love.

I imagine a cock made of copper tubing and pipe fittings sliding into a canal lined with sheet metal from a soda can. I hear metal sliding over metal. And then my imagination fails. My construction made no provision for the stuff of reproduction: the sperm, the egg. Science failed me there. That part is up to the creatures themselves.

* * *

My body is giving out on me. I do not sleep at night; pain keeps me awake. I hurt everywhere, in my belly, in my breasts, in my bones. I have given up food. When I eat, the pains increase for a while, and then I vomit. I cannot keep anything down, and so I have stopped trying.

When the morning light comes, it is gray, filtering through the haze that covers the sky. I stare out the window, but I can't see the male. He has abandoned his post at the mouth of the alley. I watch for an hour or so, but the female does not stroll by. Have they finished with each other?

I watch from my bed for a few hours, the blanket wrapped around my shoulders. Sometimes, fever comes and I soak the blanket with my sweat. Sometimes, chills come, and I shiver under the blankets. Still, there is no movement in the alley.

It takes me more than an hour to make my way down the stairs. I can't trust my legs to support me, so I crawl on my knees, making my way across the room like a baby too young to stand upright. I carry the blanket with me, wrapped around my shoulders like a cape. At the top of the stairs, I rest, then I go down slowly, one step at a time.

The alley is deserted. The array of hubcaps glitters in the dim sunlight. The litter of bright papers looks forlorn and abandoned. I step cautiously into the entrance. If the male were to rush me now, I would not be able to run away. I have used all my reserves to travel this far.

The alley is quiet. I manage to get to my feet and shuffle forward through the papers. My eyes are clouded, and I can just make out the dangling bedspread halfway down the alley. I make my way to it. I don't know why I've come here. I suppose I want to see. I want to know what has happened. That's all.

I duck beneath the dangling bedspread. In the dim light, I can see a doorway in the brick wall. Something is hanging from the lintel of the door.

I approach cautiously. The object is gray, like the door behind it. It has a peculiar, spiralling shape. When I touch it, I can feel a faint vibration inside, like the humming of distant equipment. I lay my cheek against it and I can hear a low-pitched song, steady and even.

When I was a child, my family visited the beach and I spent hours exploring the tidepools. Among the clumps of blue-black mussels and the black turban snails, I found the egg casing of a horn shark in a tidepool. It was spiral-shaped, like this egg, and when I held it to the light, I could see a tiny embryo inside. As I watched, the embryo twitched, moving even though it was not yet truly alive.

* * *

I crouch at the back of the alley with my blanket wrapped around me. I see no reason to move—I can die here as well as I can die anywhere. I am watching over the egg, keeping it safe.

Sometimes, I dream of my past life. Perhaps I should have handled it differently. Perhaps I should have been less cautious, hurried out on the mating line, answered the song when a male called from his bower. But it doesn't matter now. All that is gone, behind us now.

My time is over. The dinosaurs and the humans—our time is over. New times are coming. New types of love. I dream of the future, and my dreams are filled with the rattle of metal claws.

JOANNA RUSS

When It Changed

Joanna Russ was an important American writer, academic, and critic whose dystopian novel *The Female Man* (1975) and influential nonfiction tract *How to Suppress Women's Writing* (1983) have overshadowed a body of short fiction as various and rich as that of Angela Carter or Shirley Jackson. Russ wrote both science fiction and fantasy, with a number of stories coming from a horror or weird fiction slant. Collections include *The Zanzibar Cat* (1983), *(Extra)Ordinary People* (1985) and *The Hidden Side of the Moon* (1987). "When It Changed" was considered a groundbreaking story when first published over forty years ago. Its message of gender politics and the differences in how the sexes view and wield power still resonates strongly today. The story was first published in *Again, Dangerous Visions* in 1972.

Katy drives like a maniac; we must have been doing over 120 kilometers per hour on those turns. She's good, though, extremely good, and I've seen her take the whole car apart and put it together again in a day. My birthplace on Whileaway was largely given to farm machinery and I refuse to wrestle with a five-gear shift at unholy speeds, not having been brought up to it, but even on those turns in the middle of the night, on a country road as bad as only our district can make them, Katy's driving didn't scare me.

The funny thing about my wife, though: she will not handle guns. She has even gone hiking in the forests above the forty-eighth parallel without firearms, for days at a time. And that *does* scare me.

Katy and I have three children between us, one of hers and two of mine. Yuriko, my eldest, was asleep in the back seat, dreaming twelve-year-old dreams of love and war: running away to sea, hunting in the North, dreams of strangely beautiful people in strangely beautiful places, all the wonderful guff you think up when you're turning twelve and the glands start going. Some day soon, like all of them, she will disappear for weeks on end to come back grimy and proud, having knifed her first cougar or shot her first bear, dragging some abominably dangerous dead beastie behind her, which I will never forgive for what it might have done to my daughter. Yuriko says Katy's driving puts her to sleep.

For someone who has fought three duels, I am afraid of far, far too much. I'm getting old. I told this to my wife.

"You're thirty-four," she said. Laconic to the point of silence, that one. She flipped the lights on, on the dash—three kilometers to go and the road getting worse all the time. Far out in the country. Electric-green trees rushed into our headlights and around the car. I reached down next to me where we bolt the carrier panel to the door and eased my rifle into my lap. Yuriko stirred in the back. My height but Katy's eyes, Katy's face. The car engine is so quiet, Katy says, that you can hear breathing in the back seat. Yuki had been alone in the car when the message came, enthusiastically decoding her dot-dashes (silly to mount a wide frequency transceiver near an I.C. engine, but most of Whileaway is on steam). She had thrown herself out of the car, my gangly and gaudy offspring, shouting at the top of her lungs, so of course she had had to come along. We've been intellectually prepared for this ever since the Colony was founded, ever since it was abandoned, but this is different. This is awful.

"Men!" Yuki had screamed, leaping over the car door. "They've come back! Real Earth men!"

* * *

We met them in the kitchen of the farmhouse near the place where they had landed; the windows were open, the night air very mild. We had passed all sorts of transportation when we parked outside—steam tractors, trucks, an I.C. flatbed, even a bicycle. Lydia, the district biologist, had come out of her Northern taciturnity long enough to take blood and urine samples and was sitting in a corner of the kitchen shaking her head in astonishment over the results; she even forced herself (very big, very fair, very shy, always painfully blushing) to dig up the old language manuals—though I can talk the old tongues in my sleep. And do. Lydia is uneasy with us; we're Southerners and too flamboyant. I counted twenty people in that kitchen, all the brains of North Continent. Phyllis Spet, I think, had come in by glider. Yuki was the only child there.

Then I saw the four of them.

They are bigger than we are. They are bigger and broader. Two were taller than I, and I am extremely tall, one meter eighty centimeters in my bare feet. They are obviously of our species but *off*, indescribably off, and as my eyes could not and still cannot quite comprehend the lines of those alien bodies, I could not, then, bring myself to touch them, though the one who spoke Russian—what voices they have—wanted to "shake hands," a custom from the past, I imagine. I can only say they were apes with human faces. He seemed to mean well, but I found myself shuddering back almost the length of the kitchen—and then I laughed apologetically—and then to set a good example (*interstellar amity*, I thought) did "shake hands" finally. A hard, hard hand. They are heavy as draft horses. Blurred, deep voices. Yuriko had sneaked in between the adults and was gazing at *the men* with her mouth open.

He turned *his* head—those words have not been in our language for six hundred years—and said, in bad Russian:

"Who's that?"

"My daughter," I said, and added (with that irrational attention to good manners we sometimes employ in moments of insanity), "My daughter, Yuriko Janetson. We use the patronymic. You would say matronymic."

He laughed, involuntarily. Yuki exclaimed, "I thought they would be good looking!" greatly disappointed at this reception of herself. Phyllis Helgason Spet, whom someday I shall kill, gave me across the room a cold, level, venomous look, as if to say: *Watch what you say. You know what I can do.* It's true that I have little formal status, but Madam President will get herself in serious trouble with both me and her own staff if she continues to consider industrial espionage good clean fun. Wars and rumors of wars, as it says in one of our ancestors' books. I translated Yuki's words into *the man's* dog-Russian, once our *lingua franca*, and *the man* laughed again.

"Where are all your people?" he said conversationally.

I translated again and watched the faces around the room; Lydia embarrassed (as usual), Spet narrowing her eyes with some damned scheme, Katy very pale.

"This is Whileaway," I said.

He continued to look unenlightened.

"Whileaway," I said. "Do you remember? Do you have records? There was a plague on Whileaway,"

He looked moderately interested. Heads turned in the back of the room, and I caught a glimpse of the local professions-parliament delegate; by morning every town meeting, every district caucus, would be in full session.

"Plague?" he said. "That's most unfortunate."

"Yes," I said. "Most unfortunate. We lost half our population in one generation."

He looked properly impressed.

"Whileaway was lucky," I said. "We had a big initial gene pool, we had been chosen for extreme intelligence, we had a high technology and a large remaining population in which every adult was two-or-three experts in one. The soil is good. The climate is blessedly easy. There are thirty millions of us now. Things are beginning to snowball in industry—do you understand?— give us seventy years and we'll have more than one real city, more than a few industrial centers, full-time professions, full-time radio operators, full-time machinists, give us seventy years and not everyone will have to spend three-quarters of a lifetime on the farm." And I tried to explain how hard it is when artists can practice full-time only in old age, when there are so few, so very few who can be free, like Katy and myself. I tried also to outline our government, the two houses, the one by professions and the geographic one; I told him the district caucuses handled problems too big for the individual towns. And that population control was not a political issue, not yet, though give us time and it would be. This was a delicate point in our history; give us time. There was no need to sacrifice the quality of life for an insane rush into industrialization. Let us go our own pace. Give us time.

"Where are all the people?" said that monomaniac.

I realized then that he did not mean people, he meant *men*, and he was giving the word the meaning it had not had on Whileaway for six centuries.

"They died," I said. "Thirty generations ago."

I thought we had poleaxed him. He caught his breath. He made as if to get out of the chair he was sitting in; he put his hand to his chest; he looked around at us with the strangest blend of awe and sentimental tenderness. Then he said, solemnly and earnestly:

"A great tragedy."

I waited, not quite understanding.

"Yes," he said, catching his breath again with the queer smile, that adult-to-child smile that tells you something is being hidden and will be presently produced with cries of encouragement and joy, "a great tragedy. But it's over." And again he looked around at all of us with the strangest deference. As if we were invalids.

"You've adapted amazingly," he said.

"To what?" I said. He looked embarrassed. He looked inane. Finally he said, "Where I come from, the women don't dress so plainly."

"Like you?" I said. "Like a bride?" for the men were wearing silver from head to foot. I had never seen anything so gaudy. He made as if to answer and then apparently thought better of it; he laughed at me again. With an odd exhilaration—as if we were something childish and something wonderful, as if he were doing us an enormous favor—he took one shaky breath and said, "Well, we're here."

I looked at Spet, Spet looked at Lydia, Lydia looked at Amalia, who is the head of the local town meeting, Amalia looked at I don't know whom. My throat was raw. I cannot stand local beer, which the farmers swill as if their stomachs had iridium linings, but I took it anyway, from Amalia (it was her bicycle we had seen outside as we parked), and swallowed it all. This was going to take a long time. I said, "Yes, here you are," and smiled (feeling like a fool), and wondered seriously if male-Earth-people's minds worked so very differently from female-Earth-people's minds, but that couldn't be so or the race would have died out long ago. The radio network had got the news around planet by now and we had another Russian speaker, flown in from Varna; I decided to cut out when *the man* passed around pictures of his wife, who looked like the priestess of some arcane cult. He proposed to question Yuki, so I barreled her into a back room in spite of her furious protests, and went out on the front porch. As I left, Lydia was explaining the difference between parthenogenesis (which is so easy that anyone can practice it) and what we do, which is the merging of ova. That is why Katy's baby looks like me. Lydia went on to the Ansky Process and Katy Ansky, our one full-polymath genius and the great-great I don't know how many times great-grandmother of my own Katharina.

A dot-dash transmitter in one of the outbuildings chattered faintly to itself—operators flirting and passing jokes down the line.

There was a man on the porch. The other tall man. I watched him for a few minutes—I can move very quietly when I want to and when I allowed him to see me, he stopped talking into the little machine hung around his neck. Then he said calmly, in excellent Russian, "Did you know that sexual equality has been reestablished on Earth?"

"You're the real one," I said, "aren't you? The other one's for show." It was a great relief to get things cleared up. He nodded affably.

"As a people, we are not very bright," he said. "There's been too much genetic damage in the last few centuries. Radiation. Drugs. We can use Whileaway's genes, Janet." Strangers do not call strangers by the first name.

"You can have cells enough to drown in," I said. "Breed your own."

He smiled. "That's not the way we want to do it." Behind him I saw Katy come into the square of light that was the screened-in door. He went on, low and urbane, not mocking me, I think, but with the self-confidence of someone who has always had money and strength to spare, who doesn't know what it is to be second-class or provincial. Which is very odd, because the day before, I would have said that was an exact description of me.

"I'm talking to you, Janet," he said, "because I suspect you have more popular influence than anyone else here. You know as well as I do that parthenogenetic culture has all sorts of inherent defects, and we do not—if we can help it—mean to use you for anything of the sort. Pardon me; I should not have said 'use.' But surely you can see that this kind of society is unnatural."

"Humanity is unnatural," said Katy. She had my rifle under her left arm. The top of that silky head does not quite come up to my collarbone, but she is as tough as steel; he began to move, again with that queer smiling deference (which his fellow had showed to me but he had not), and the gun slid into Katy's grip as if she had shot with it all her life.

"I agree," said the man. "Humanity is unnatural. I should know. I have metal in my teeth and metal pins here." He touched his shoulder. "Seals are harem animals," he added, "and so are men; apes are promiscuous and so are men; doves are monogamous and so are men; there are even celibate men and homosexual men. There are homosexual cows, I believe. But Whileaway is still missing something." He gave a dry chuckle. I will give him the credit of believing that it had something to do with nerves.

"I miss nothing," said Katy, "except that life isn't endless."

"You are—?" said the man, nodding from me to her.

"Wives," said Katy. "We're married." Again the dry chuckle.

"A good economic arrangement," he said, "for working and taking care of the children. And as good an arrangement as any for randomizing heredity, if your reproduction is made to follow the same pattern. But think, Katharina Michaelason, if there isn't something better that you might secure for your daughters. I believe in instincts, even in Man, and I can't think that the two of you—a machinist, are you? and I gather you are some sort of chief of police—don't feel somehow what even you must miss. You know it intellectually, of course. There is only half a species here. Men must come back to Whileaway."

Katy said nothing.

"I should think, Katharina Michaelason," said the man gently, "that you, of all people, would benefit most from such a change," and he walked past Katy's rifle into the square of light coming from the door. I think it was then that he noticed my scar, which really does not show unless the light is from the side: a fine line that runs from temple to chin. Most people don't even know about it.

"Where did you get that?" he said, and I answered with an involuntary grin. "In my last duel." We stood there bristling at each other for several seconds (this is absurd but true) until he went inside and shut the screen door behind him. Katy said in a brittle voice, "You damned fool, don't you know when we've been insulted?" and swung up the rifle to shoot him through the screen, but I got to her before she could fire and knocked the rifle out of aim; it burned a hole through the porch floor. Katy was shaking. She kept whispering over and over, "That's why I never touched it, because I knew I'd kill someone. I knew I'd kill someone." The first man—the one I'd spoken with first—was still talking inside the house, something about the grand movement to recolonize and rediscover all the Earth had lost. He stressed the advantages to Whileaway: trade, exchange of ideas, education. He, too, said that sexual equality had been reestablished on Earth.

* * *

Katy was right, of course; we should have burned them down where they stood. Men are coming to Whileaway. When one culture has the big guns and the other has none, there is a certain predictability about the outcome. Maybe men would have come eventually in any case. I like to think that a hundred years from now my great-grandchildren could have stood them off or fought them to a standstill, but even that's no odds; I will remember all my life those four people I first met who were muscled like bulls and who made me—if only for a moment—feel small. A neurotic reaction, Katy says. I remember everything that happened that night; I remember Yuki's excitement in the car, I remember Katy's sobbing when we got home as if her heart would break, I remember her lovemaking, a little peremptory as always, but wonderfully soothing and comforting. I remember prowling restlessly around the house after Katy fell asleep with one bare arm hung into a patch of light from the hall. The muscles of her forearms are like metal bars from all that driving and testing of her machines. Sometimes I dream about Katy's arms. I remember wandering into the nursery and picking up my wife's baby, dozing for a while with the poignant, amazing warmth of an infant in my lap, and finally returning to the kitchen to find Yuriko fixing herself a late snack. My daughter eats like a Great Dane.

"Yuki," I said, "do you think you could fall in love with a man?" and she whooped derisively. "With a ten-foot toad!" said my tactful child.

But men are coming to Whileaway. Lately I sit up nights and worry about the men who will come to this planet, about my two daughters and Betta Katharinason, about what will happen to Katy, to me, to my life. Our ancestors' journals are one long cry of pain and I suppose I ought to be glad now, but one can't throw away six centuries, or even (as I have lately discovered) thirty-four years. Sometimes I laugh at the question those four men hedged about all evening and never quite dared to ask, looking at the lot of us, hicks in overalls, farmers in canvas pants and plain shirts: *Which of you plays the role of the man?* As if we had to produce a carbon copy of their mistakes! I doubt very much that sexual equality has been reestablished on Earth. I do not like to think of myself mocked, of Katy deferred to as if she were weak, of Yuki made to feel unimportant or silly, of my other children cheated of their full humanity or turned into strangers. And I'm afraid that my own achievements will dwindle from what they were—or what I thought they were—to the not-very-interesting curiosa of the *human* race, the oddities you read about in the back of the book, things to laugh at sometimes because they are so exotic, quaint but not impressive, charming but not useful. I find this more painful than I can say. You will agree that for a woman who has fought three duels, all of them kills, indulging in such fears is ludicrous. But what's around the corner now is a duel so big that I don't think I have the guts for it; in Faust's words: *Verweile doch, du bist so schön!* Keep it as it is. Don't change.

Sometimes at night I remember the original name of this planet, changed by the first generation of our ancestors, those curious women for whom, I suppose, the real name was too painful a reminder after the men died. I find it amusing, in a grim way, to see it all so completely turned around. This, too, shall pass. All good things must come to an end.

Take my life but don't take away the meaning of my life.

For-A-While.

VANDANA SINGH

The Woman Who Thought She Was a Planet

Vandana Singh is an Indian writer of speculative fiction and a scientist living and working in the United States. Her work has been published in numerous magazines and anthologies and has frequently been reprinted in year's-best publications. She is a winner of the Carl Brandon Parallax Award. Her most recent publications include stories for *Lightspeed* magazine and for Tor.com. "The Woman Who Thought She Was a Planet" concerns a relationship shaped by changes that lead a wife to question her marriage. It was first published in *Trampoline* in 2003.

Ramnath Mishra's life changed forever one morning, when, during his perusal of the newspaper on the verandah, a ritual that he had observed for the last forty years, his wife set down her cup of tea with a crash and announced:

"I know at last what I am. I am a planet."

Ramnath's retirement was a source of displeasure to them both. He had been content to know his wife from a distance, to acknowledge her as the benign despot of the household and mother of his now-grown children, but he had desired no intimacy beyond that. As for Kamala herself, she seemed grumpy and uncomfortable with his proximity—her façade of the dutiful Indian wife had dropped after the first week. Now he lowered his newspaper, scowling, prepared to lecture her sternly for interrupting his peace, but instead his mouth fell open in silent astonishment.

His wife had gotten to her feet and was unwinding her sari.

Ramnath nearly knocked over his chair.

"What are you doing—have you lost your mind?" He leaped at her, grabbing a scrap of blue cotton sari with one hand and her arm with the other, looking around wildly to see if the servants were around, or the gardener, or whether the neighbors were peeping through the sprays of bougainvillea that sheltered the verandah from the summer heat. His wife, arrested in his arms, glared at him balefully.

"A planet does not need clothes," she said with great dignity.

"You are not a planet, you are crazy," Ramnath said. He propelled her into the bedroom. Thankfully the washerwoman had left and the cook was in the kitchen, singing untunefully to the radio. "Arrange your sari for heaven's sake."

She complied. Ramnath saw that tears were glistening in her eyes. He felt a stab of concern mingled with irritation.

"Have you been feeling ill, Kamala? Should I phone Dr. Kumar?"

"I am not ill," she said. "I have had a revelation. I am a planet. I used to be a human, a woman, a wife and mother. All the time I wondered if there was more to me than that. Now I know. Being a planet is good for me. I have stopped taking my liver pills."

"Well, if you were a planet," Ramnath said in exasperation, "you would be an inanimate object circling a star. You would probably have an atmosphere and living things crawling about you. You would be very large, like Earth or Jupiter. You are not a planet but a living soul, a woman. A lady from a respectable household who holds the family honor in her hands."

He was gratified that he had explained it so well because she smiled at him and smoothed her hair, nodding. "I must go see to lunch," she said in her normal voice. Ramnath went back to reading his newspaper on the verandah, shaking his head at the things a man had to do. But he could not concentrate on the prime minister's latest antics. It came to him suddenly that it could be a rather frightening thing not to know the person with whom he had lived for forty years. Where had she been getting such strange ideas? He remembered the scandal when, many years ago, a great-aunt of his had gone mad, locked herself in the outdoor toilet of the ancestral home and begun shrieking like a sarus crane in the mating season. They had finally got her out while curious neighbors thronged the courtyard, muttering with false sympathy and shouting encouragement. He remembered how quiet she had seemed after they helped her over the broken door, how there had been no warning before she bent her head, apparently in meek surrender, and bit her husband on his arm. She had ended up in the insane asylum in Ranchi. What terrible dishonor the family had suffered, what indignity—a mad person in a respectable upper middle class family—he shuddered suddenly, set down his newspaper and went to call Dr. Kumar. Dr. Kumar would be discreet, he was a family friend . . .

But when he went into the drawing room, it was dark—somebody had closed the curtains, shutting out the morning light. Disturbed by the unnatural silence—the cook had stopped singing—he groped blindly towards the light-switch, which was closer to him than any of the windows. "Kamala!" he called, irritated to find his voice trembling.

Abruptly a curtain at the other end of the room was drawn violently back, letting in a burst of sunshine that hurt his eyes. There stood his wife, naked, facing the sun with her arms spread wide. She began to turn slowly. There was a beatific expression on her face. The sunlight washed her ample body, the generous terraces and folds of flesh that cascaded down to her sagging belly and buttocks. Ramnath was transfixed with horror. He ran up to the curtain, drew it closed, put his hands on his wife's plump shoulders and shook her hard.

"You have gone mad! What will the neighbors think? What did I do to deserve this!"

He dragged her to the bedroom and looked around for her sari. The blouse, petticoat and sari lay in crumpled folds on the bed. This in itself was disturbing because she was usually obsessive about tidiness. He realized that he had no idea how to put the sari on her. He saw the nightgown hanging neatly folded on the mosquito-netting bar, and grabbed it. His wife was struggling in his arms.

"Are you completely shameless? Put this on!"

After a while he managed to get the nightgown on her, but it was back-to-front. That didn't matter. He sat her down on the bed.

"Stay here and don't move. I am going to call the doctor. Has the cook gone out?"

Her nod reassured him, but she would not look at him. As Ramnath went into the drawing room, he hesitated, then turned on the light instead of drawing open the curtains. He was irritated to find that a part of his body had responded to her nakedness and his struggle with her. Resolutely he put all distracting thoughts aside and went to the phone.

Dr. Kumar was out attending to a hospital emergency. Ramnath thought unkind thoughts about his friend. "Tell him he must phone the moment he returns—it is a matter of great urgency," he told the servant. He slammed down the phone. He went back to the bedroom. His wife was lying down, apparently asleep.

All that day Ramnath kept guard over his wife. By lunch she had changed back into her sari and combed her hair. The cook served them a stew of chickpeas simmered in a sauce of onions, cumin, ginger and chilies. There was basmati rice which they kept only for special occasions, and tiny fried eggplants stuffed with tomatoes and spices. Ramnath, having no idea what his wife's favorite dishes were, had asked the cook to make whatever she liked, hoping that food would distract her from this insanity. But she picked at her food absently, a dreamy look on her face. It was obvious that her thoughts were miles away. Ramnath felt a surge of anger and self-pity. What had he done to deserve this? He had worked hard for forty years or more, risen up to the ranks of a senior bureaucrat in the state government. He had fathered two sons. Now it occurred to him that it would have been nice to have a daughter, somebody whom he could call on at times like this. His mind did a quick survey of elderly female relatives—but they were either all dead, or lived in other towns and villages. Why didn't that damned doctor phone?

Ramnath's day was completely ruined. In the evenings he liked to go to the senior club and play chess with other retirees, but today he dared not leave his wife. She, for her part, spoke only when spoken to. She seemed outwardly calm, instructing the cook and herself dusting the pictures and bric-a-brac in the drawing room, but occasionally he would catch her gazing dreamily into a private world, a smile on her lips. He phoned the doctor again but the damn fool had come home only briefly, dressed for a party and left without receiving the urgent message.

That night was one of the worst that Ramnath had ever experienced. His wife tossed in her sleep, straining against some invisible restraining force like a moored ship trying to break free. Ramnath himself was beset by nightmares of planets and matronly naked women. He woke several times, looking warily at his wife as she slept fitfully, her graying hair all over the pillow, half-covering her open mouth. A wisp of hair blew out of her mouth with her breath, and it seemed to him as though it took on the aspect of some awful living thing. He brushed the hair off her face, trying not to tremble. In the moonlight from the window, her face was like the surface of the moon: pitted and cratered, fissured with age. She looked like a stranger.

The next morning his wife was rather subdued. She did not go out in the middle of the day to visit Mrs. Chakravarti or Mrs. Jain, as she used to do. She let the phone ring until Ramnath, maddened by her indifference, picked up the receiver and shouted into it, only to be embarrassed by the cool voice of Mrs. Jain. "My wife is not well," he said, immediately regretting it. Mrs. Jain, all concern, showed up ten minutes later with Mrs. Chakravarti, bearing fruits and a special herbal concoction that Mrs. Chakravarti's mother-in-law had made. For a minute Ramnath felt like telling them to go away and leave him in peace, but their matronly figures resplendent in crisp, starched cotton saris, their perfumed, hennaed hair tied so neatly into buns, their air of righteous sisterly concern quite defeated him. Kamala came out of the bedroom, where she had been lying down, greeted them with surprised pleasure and led them all back into the room. Ramnath, thus displaced, sat and fretted on the hot verandah, first refusing and then accepting the cook's offer of home-made lemon water. Inside the bedroom the women were all sprawled on the bed like beached whales, sipping lemon water and talking and giggling. He could not tell what they were gossiping about. But slowly he became comforted by the notion that his wife was at least acting normally. Perhaps having her friends over was a good thing. Perhaps he could manage a visit to the club this evening.

As soon as the women left, Kamala reverted to her old air of quiet indifference. Meanwhile Dr. Kumar called. The idiot insisted on asking exactly what the matter was with Mrs. Mishra. Ramnath, feeling his wife's eyes on him, did not know what to say. "It's a lady matter," he said finally, embarrassed. "I can't explain over the phone. Can you come?"

Dr. Kumar came that evening and stayed to dinner. He checked Kamala's blood pressure, listened to her heart. His assistant, a taciturn young man, withdrew blood for further testing. During all this Kamala was serene, hospitable, asking after the doctor's family with sweet concern. It occurred to Ramnath that she had already acquired the infamous cunning of the insane, which enables them to conceal their madness at will.

"You must be mistaken, Mishra-ji," the doctor said on the phone two days later. "Everything is normal—she is, in fact, much healthier than before. If she has been behaving strangely, it is probably mental. Not always the sign of disease. Women are odd—they act strangely when they are hankering after something. She should go out, maybe go visit one of your sons. Grandchildren would do her good."

But Kamala refused to leave town. At last Ramnath, acting on the doctor's advice, persuaded her to walk with him in the evenings, hoping that the open air would do her good. He kept a steely eye on her—if she as much as touched the free end of her sari hanging over her shoulder, he would grunt warningly and slap her hand. The narrow lanes of their neighborhood were lined with amaltash trees heavy with cascades of golden flowers. In the playground the older boys finished the last round of cricket in the failing light, while smaller children squatted in the dust, playing with marbles, ignoring wandering cows and sedate, elderly citizens taking the air. Neighbors sitting on the verandahs of their bungalows called out greetings. Torn between hope and dread, Ramnath frequently and surreptitiously examined his wife's face for signs of incipient madness. She remained calm and sociable, although as they walked on it seemed as though she were falling into a trance, interrupted only by sighs of deep rapture as she gazed at the sunset.

In the week that followed, Kamala attempted twice to take off her clothes. Both times Ramnath managed to restrain her, although the second time she almost managed to escape from him. He caught her just as she was about to run out into the driveway in nothing but a petticoat and blouse, in full view of street vendors, cricket-playing children and respectable elderly gentlemen. He wrestled her into the bedroom and tried to slap some sense into her, but she continued to struggle and weep. At last, frustrated, he pulled half a dozen saris out from the big steel cupboard and flung them on the bed.

"Kamala," he said desperately, "even planets have atmospheres. See here, this gray sari, it looks like a swirl of clouds. How about it?"

She calmed down at once. She began to put on the gray sari although the fabric, georgette, was unsuitable for summer.

"At last you believe me, Ramnath," she said. Her voice seemed to have changed. It was deeper, more powerful. He looked at her, aghast. She had addressed him by his name! That was all very well for the new generation of young adults, but respectable, traditional women never addressed their husbands by their names. He decided not to do anything about it for now. At least she was clothed.

At night Ramnath lay wrestling with doubts and fears. A breeze blew in through the open window, stirring the mosquito-netting. In the starlight his wife, the room, everything looked alien. He propped himself on one elbow and looked at the stranger beside him. A thought came to him that if he could get her confined to the asylum in Ranchi without a scandal, he would do it. But she had that idiot Kumar charmed. The way she had asked so nicely about his ailing mother, congratulated him on his recent membership of a prestigious medical organization. Kumar had known the family for years— and, it occurred to Ramnath, had always had a soft spot for his wife. Who would have thought she'd had so much cunning in her? Now, as he watched her sleep, her hair in disarray and her mouth open like some hideous cavern, it occurred to him how easy his life would be if she would simply die. He was ashamed of the thought as soon as it formed but he could not take it back. It called to him and seduced him and resounded in his head until he was convinced that if he could not have her committed, he would have to kill her himself. He could not live like this.

Every night it became a ritual for him to look at her and imagine the different ways he could commit murder. He had been shocked at himself at first—him, a fine, upstanding ex-bureaucrat contemplating something as hideous as the murder of the mother of his sons—but there was no denying that the thought—the fantasy, he told himself—gave him pleasure. A secret, shameful sort of pleasure, like sex before marriage, but pleasure nonetheless.

He began to count the ways. Suffocation with a pillow while she slept would be the easiest, but he had no idea if the forensics people could infer from that what had happened. Strangulation had the same problem. Poison— but where to procure it? And now that she had stopped taking her liver pills he could no longer perform some artful substitution. Damn the woman!

One night, as he watched her sleeping, he put his hand very gently on her neck. She stirred a little, frightening him, but he made himself keep his hand there, feeling the pulse in her throat. He began to stroke her neck with his thumb. Abruptly she coughed and he jerked his hand away in terror. But she did not wake. She was coughing up something dark from her mouth. For a moment he thought it was blood, that he should call the doctor; his next thought was that perhaps she was dying of her own accord. Maybe it had been enough to wish it so strongly. She coughed again and again but she did not wake. Now the dark stuff had gathered about her mouth, on her chin, like a jelly. To his horror he saw that the darkness was not blood but composed of small, moving things. One stood up on its hind legs for a moment, surveying him, and he drew back in horror. It was insectoid, alien, about as tall as his index finger. There was an army of those things coming out of her mouth.

The mosquito netting was tucked under the bed on all sides—he pushed at it, trying to tear it with his hands, but they were upon him before he could get out of the bed. He tried to cry out but all he could manage was a whim- per. They covered his body, crawling inside his clothes, beating and biting at him with short, sharp appendages. He tried to brush them off but there were too many of them. They made a sound like crickets singing, but softer. He howled in despair, calling to Kamala to save him, but she lay peacefully beside him as the things came out of her. After a while he fainted.

Much later he opened his eyes, with some difficulty—they were sticky with dried tears. A pale morning light came in through the window. There was no sign of the creatures. There was a large tear in the mosquito netting and a mosquito was humming in his ear. His wife lay sleeping beside him. Perhaps what he had experienced had been a nightmare, he told himself, that it was his conscience punishing him for his impious thoughts. But he knew that the soreness all over his body, the marks of bites and the bruises, were real. He turned fearfully towards his wife. Abruptly her eyes snapped open.

"Hai bhagwaan!" She was looking at the tear on his white sleepshirt, the pinpricks of blood. He flinched as she reached out a hand to touch the tiny wounds. They had spared his face. More cunning, he thought. "Why didn't you wake me? I would have told them—they would have understood, not hurt you."

"What are those things?" he whispered.

"Inhabitants," she said. "I'm a planet, remember?"

She smiled at the look on his face.

"Don't be afraid, Ramnath." Again, the free use of his name! Was she possessed? Should he consult an astrologer? An exorcist? He, a rational man, reduced to this!

"Don't be afraid," she said again. "The younger ones probably want to find a place to colonize. If you ever want to be a satellite, Ramnath, let me know. The little animals are good for a planet. They have restored my health."

"Do you want to go visit your mother?" he whispered. "You haven't been home for a while. I will make all the arrangements . . ."

He had not let her go home to her ancestral village for the past five years—there was always something going on that needed her attention. The marriage of their sons, his retirement and the fact that somebody had to run the house and supervise the servants.

"Oh Ramnath," she said, her eyes softening. "You were never this generous before. I think you have quite changed. No, I don't want to leave you, not yet."

She bathed his wounds with Dettol and warm water. She watched over him solicitously as he ate his breakfast. Later, her distracted look returned as she moved about the house, dusting and rearranging things mechanically. Ramnath felt the need to escape.

"Do you mind if I go to the club this evening?"

"No, of course not," she said amiably. "Go enjoy yourself."

When he went to his club he made a private and very expensive phone call to his older son.

"But Papa, I just heard from Ma. She sounded quite normal. Are you sure you are feeling well? . . . No I can't come now, there is a very important case at court. My senior partner has put me in charge . . ."

The younger son was in Germany on an engineering assignment. Defeated, Ramnath immersed himself in a game of chess with an acquaintance who beat him easily.

"Losing your touch, sir?" said the younger man annoyingly.

When Ramnath got home, he felt he was returning to prison. The house was quite silent except for the cook singing in the kitchen. It occurred to him to tell the fellow to shut up. But where was his wife?

"She went to the park, Sahib," the cook said.

He wondered whether to go after her. But five minutes later she was coming up the driveway clutching a balloon. She waved and smiled at him quite shamelessly. He saw with relief that she was clothed. She was eating an ice cream bar.

"I had such fun, Ramnath," she told him. "I played with the little ones. I bought them all balloons. I haven't had a balloon in such a long time."

Later, after the cook had retired, he spoke to her.

"Kamala, those . . . things, those creatures inside you . . . I think we should get you checked up. It is not right to keep all this from Dr. Kumar. You have a terrible disease . . ."

"But, Ramnath, I have no sickness. I am well, very well. After years."

"But . . ."

"And the things, as you call them are not things but my own creation. They came from me, Ramnath."

She slapped his face playfully.

"You look pulled down and grumpy," she said, pinching his thin cheek. "My little animals would do you so much good, Ramnath, if only you would rid yourself of your prejudice."

He backed away from her, outraged and horrified.

"Never! Kamala, I am going to sleep on the sofa. I cannot . . ."

"As you wish," she said indifferently.

That night he lay awake for a long time. He could hear the crickets singing outside the window, but was too nervous to get up and shut out the sound. All the small night-time sounds—the whisper of the curtain in the breeze, the asthmatic squeak of the ceiling fan, the rustle of the leaves of the bougainvillea outside—all this made him think of the insect-like creatures. Once he woke up and fancied that some of them were standing on the top of the narrow sofa, looking down at him and gesturing in a very human way, as he lay there, helpless. He began to edge off the sofa, his heart hammering wildly, but a sudden gust of wind filled the curtains so they billowed out like ghostly sails, letting in the moonlight—and he saw that there was nothing on the top of the sofa after all. At last he fell asleep, exhausted.

Over the next few days Ramnath kept hold of his sanity with great difficulty. He wondered whether he should renounce the world and retire to the Himalayas. Perhaps the gods he had so casually dismissed the past few years were getting their revenge now. He still toyed with the idea of murder, although it seemed impossible now, at least at close range. Looking at his wife over dinner, he began to wonder for the first time about her. What was she really like? What did she want that he had not given her? How had he come to this?

"Kamala," he said one day. He was in a strange mood. He had lit an incense stick in front of the household gods that morning. The scent of sandalwood still pervaded the house. It made him feel humble, virtuous, as though he was at last letting go of his ego and surrendering to the divine. "Tell me, what is it like . . . to have those . . . animals inside you . . ."

She smiled. Her teeth were very white.

"I hardly feel them most of the time, Ramnath," she said. "I wish you would agree to be colonized. It would do you good and it would help them—the younger ones have been clamoring for a new world. I hear them singing sometimes, chirping sounds like crickets. It is a language I am beginning to understand."

He thought he heard it faintly then, too.

"What are they saying?"

She frowned, listening. She sighed.

"A planet needs a sun, Ramnath," she said evasively. "My journey is just beginning."

After this interchange he noticed an increased restlessness in his wife. She kept going out to the garden to sun herself in the 40 degree centigrade heat, among the wilting guava trees. In the house she moved from room to room, making little chirping sounds and humming tunelessly to herself. Ramnath felt his pious resolve shatter. Irritated, he spent that evening at his club.

The next evening, remembering his duty, Ramnath dragged his wife out for a walk. She protested a little feebly but let him pull her into the street. By the time they reached the park a soft twilight had fallen. A few stars and a pale moon hung in the sky. Kamala lingered at the edge of the park.

"Come on," Ramnath said, impatient to continue walking.

But instead his wife gave a cry of pleasure and turned into the park, where in the semidarkness a man was selling balloons. She began to run towards the balloon man, gesturing like an excited child. Embarrassed and annoyed, he followed her at a more dignified pace.

"More balloons," he heard her say. Coins tinkled. A small crowd of street urchins appeared from nowhere. He could hear the rhythmic squeak of a swing in the semidarkness ahead.

Now she was handing balloons out to the gaggle of brats, who jumped and chattered excitedly around her.

"Me too, Auntie-ji!"

The balloons bobbed over their heads like dim little orbs in the moonlight. Ramnath pushed aside the children and grabbed his wife by the shoulder.

"Enough," he said impatiently. "You are spoiling these good-for-nothings!"

She shrugged off his hand. She let go of one of her balloons and watched it float lazily up into the starlit sky. A sudden gust of wind came up and dislodged the free end of her sari from her shoulder, baring her blouse. The balloon man stared at her ample cleavage.

"Adjust your sari for heaven's sake," Ramnath said in a desperate whisper. He looked around to see if anyone else was watching this spectacle and was horrified to see the ramrod figure of Judge Pandey walking towards them on the path through the park, his cane tap-tapping. Fearful that the judge would see him and associate him with this madwoman, Ramnath retreated into the inadequate shadow of an Ashok tree. Fortunately Judge Pandey didn't see him. He saw what seemed to be a wanton looking woman and walked quickly past her in case anyone noticed him staring. Ramnath, sweaty with relief, emerged from the shadows and grabbed the end of his wife's sari that lay on the dusty ground. His wife had released three other balloons into the air and was watching them go up with childish pleasure. The children were shouting in their shrill voices.

"Let another one go, Auntie-ji!"

"Come home, Kamala," Ramnath said pleadingly. "This is madness!"

But instead of answering, Kamala let go of all the balloons, some seven or eight of them. They floated up into the sky. She stretched her arms out to them, her face full of a blissful yearning. Slowly and majestically she began to rise over the ground—an inch, two inches.

"What are you doing?" Ramnath said to her in a horrified whisper.

Three feet, four feet. Ramnath's mouth fell open. He pulled on the end of the sari he was holding but she continued to rise, turning slowly, trailing two yards, then five yards of cotton. Too late, Ramnath let go of the sari. His wife rose into the night air, her white petticoat filling with air like the sails of a ship.

"Oooh! Look what the Auntie is doing!"

Some of the urchins had drawn back. The balloon man's face was a round circle of astonishment.

"Come back!" Ramnath shouted.

The children were yelling and pointing and jumping with glee. She was well up now, higher than the trees and houses. The balloons scattered above her like a flotilla of tiny escort ships. People were running out of their houses now, pointing and staring. Something white and ghostly came slipping down from the sky—her petticoat! Her blouse and undergarments were next. Ramnath stood transfixed with horror while the urchins cavorted about, trying to catch the garments in the darkness. Somebody—Mrs. Jain, perhaps—began wailing. "Hai Bhagwaan, that is Kamala, Kamala Mishra!"

The cry was taken up all around. With each shout Ramnath felt his family name and honor sinking into the ground. He tried to slink away, keeping to the shadows of trees like a thief, hoping nobody would recognize him. But then, on the road, Judge Pandey tapped him on the shoulder. The veteran judge's solemn, impassive face was the last thing he wanted to see.

"Most reprehensible, Mishra! Most reprehensible!"

Ramnath moaned and fled to his house, throwing dignity to the winds. All around people were saying his wife's name—the neighbors, the street urchins, the servants, the man selling roasted corn at the end of the street. The house was dark and empty. No doubt the cook had gone to see the show as well. Ramnath felt he could face nobody after this. He stood in the middle of the dark drawing room, thinking wildly of escape, or suicide.

He went to the window and looked out apprehensively. There she was, a tiny, bright blob still rising into the sky. How dare she leave him like this!

It occurred to him that there was only one option—to take enough things from the house, leave by the late train and disappear. He could even change his name, he thought. Begin anew. The house was willed to his sons. He would not let his dishonor touch them. Let them all think he was dead!

She was out of sight now. For a moment he almost envied her, out there among the stars. He imagined, despite himself, the little alien creatures running over the wild terrain of her body, exploring the mountains, gullies and varied habitats of that mysterious and unknowable geography. What sun would she find? What vistas would she see? A sob caught in his throat. How would he manage now, with nobody to look after him?

A small sound caught his attention. Perhaps it was the cook returning, or the neighbors coming to feast on the remains of his dignity. There was no time. He rushed to the bedroom, turned on the light. Breathing hard, he started to pull things out of the steel cupboard, things he would need, like money, her jewelry, and clothes. It was then that he felt something on his shoulder.

He would have screamed if he had remembered how; the insectoids were already marching up his back, over his shoulder and into his terrified, open mouth.

SUSAN PALWICK

Gestella

Susan Palwick is an American writer and editor. She is also a professor of English teaching creative writing and literature. Her most recent novel is *Mending the Moon*. Her first published story was "The Woman Who Saved the World" for *Isaac Asimov's Science Fiction Magazine* in 1985. Her fiction has been recognized with numerous awards, including the William L. Crawford Award from the International Association for the Fantastic in the Arts, an Alex Award from the American Library Association, and a Silver Pen Award from the Nevada Writers Hall of Fame. A female werewolf is tamed by her human lover in "Gestella." The story explores love, exploitation, and betrayal and what must be sacrificed in order to be considered human. It was first published in the anthology *Starlight 3* in 2001.

Time's the problem. Time and arithmetic. You've known from the beginning that the numbers would cause trouble, but you were much younger then— much, much younger—and far less wise. And there's culture shock, too. Where you come from, it's okay for women to have wrinkles. Where you come from, youth's not the only commodity.

You met Jonathan back home. Call it a forest somewhere, near an Alp. Call it a village on the edge of the woods. Call it old. You weren't old, then: you were fourteen on two feet and a mere two years old on four, although already fully grown. Your kind are fully grown at two years, on four feet. And experienced: oh, yes. You knew how to howl at the moon. You knew what to do when somebody howled back. If your four-footed form hadn't been sterile, you'd have had litters by then—but it was, and on two feet, you'd been just smart enough, or lucky enough, to avoid continuing your line.

But it wasn't as if you hadn't had plenty of opportunities, enthusiastically taken. Jonathan liked that. A lot. Jonathan was older than you were: thirty-five, then. Jonathan loved fucking a girl who looked fourteen and acted older, who acted feral, who *was* feral for three to five days a month, centered on the full moon. Jonathan didn't mind the mess that went with it, either: all that fur, say, sprouting at one end of the process and shedding on the other, or the aches and pains from various joints pivoting, changing shape, redistributing weight, or your poor gums bleeding all the time from the monthly growth and recession of your fangs. "At least that's the only blood," he told you, sometime during that first year.

You remember this very clearly: you were roughly halfway through the four-to-two transition, and Jonathan was sitting next to you in bed, massaging your sore shoulder blades as you sipped mint tea with hands still nearly as clumsy as paws, hands like mittens. Jonathan had just filled two hot water bottles, one for your aching tailbone and one for your aching knees. Now you know he wanted to get you in shape for a major sportfuck—he loved sex even more than usual, after you'd just changed back—but at the time, you thought he was a real prince, the kind of prince girls like you weren't supposed to be allowed to get, and a stab of pain shot through you at his words. "I didn't kill anything," you told him, your lower lip trembling. "I didn't even hunt."

"Gestella, darling, I know. That wasn't what I meant." He stroked your hair. He'd been feeding you raw meat during the four-foot phase, but not anything you'd killed yourself. He'd taught you to eat little pieces out of his hand, gently, without biting him. He'd taught you to wag your tail, and he was teaching you to chase a ball, because that's what good four-foots did where he came from. "I was talking about—"

"Normal women," you told him. "The ones who bleed so they can have babies. You shouldn't make fun of them. They're lucky." You like children and puppies; you're good with them, gentle. You know it's unwise for you to have any of your own, but you can't help but watch them, wistfully.

"*I* don't want kids," he says. "I had that operation. I told you."

"Are you sure it took?" you ask. You're still very young. You've never known anyone who's had an operation like that, and you're worried about whether Jonathan really understands your condition. Most people don't. Most people think all kinds of crazy things. Your condition isn't communicable, for instance, by biting or any other way, but it is hereditary, which is why it's good that you've been so smart and lucky, even if you're just fourteen.

Well, no, not fourteen anymore. It's about halfway through Jonathan's year of folklore research—he's already promised not to write you up for any of the journals, and keeps assuring you he won't tell anybody, although later you'll realize that's for his protection, not yours—so that would make you, oh, seventeen or eighteen. Jonathan's still thirty-five. At the end of the year, when he flies you back to the United States with him so the two of you can get married, he'll be thirty-six. You'll be twenty-one on two feet, three years old on four.

Seven to one. That's the ratio. You've made sure Jonathan understands this. "Oh, sure," he says. "Just like for dogs. One year is seven human years. Everybody knows that. But how can it be a problem, darling, when we love each other so much?" And even though you aren't fourteen anymore, you're still young enough to believe him.

* * *

At first it's fun. The secret's a bond between you, a game. You speak in code. Jonathan splits your name in half, calling you Jessie on four feet and Stella on two. You're Stella to all his friends, and most of them don't even know that he has a dog one week a month. The two of you scrupulously avoid scheduling social commitments for the week of the full moon, but no one seems to notice the pattern, and if anyone does notice, no one cares. Occasionally someone you know sees Jessie, when you and Jonathan are out in the park playing with balls, and Jonathan always says that he's taking care of his sister's dog while she's away on business. His sister travels a lot, he explains. Oh, no, Stella doesn't mind, but she's always been a bit nervous around dogs—even though Jessie's such a *good* dog—so she stays home during the walks.

Sometimes strangers come up, shyly. "What a beautiful dog!" they say. "What a *big* dog!" "What kind of dog is that?"

"A Husky-wolfhound cross," Jonathan says airily. Most people accept this. Most people know as much about dogs as dogs know about the space shuttle.

Some people know better, though. Some people look at you, and frown a little, and say, "Looks like a wolf to me. Is she part wolf?"

"Could be," Jonathan always says with a shrug, his tone as breezy as ever. And he spins a little story about how his sister adopted you from the pound because you were the runt of the litter and no one else wanted you, and now look at you! No one would ever take you for a runt now! And the strangers smile and look encouraged and pat you on the head, because they like stories about dogs being rescued from the pound.

You sit and down and stay during these conversations; you do whatever Jonathan says. You wag your tail and cock your head and act charming. You let people scratch you behind the ears. You're a *good* dog. The other dogs in the park, who know more about their own species than most people do, aren't fooled by any of this; you make them nervous, and they tend to avoid you, or to act supremely submissive if avoidance isn't possible. They grovel on their bellies, on their backs; they crawl away backwards, whining.

Jonathan loves this. Jonathan loves it that you're the alpha with the other dogs—and, of course, he loves it that he's your alpha. Because that's another thing people don't understand about your condition: they think you're vicious, a ravening beast, a fanged monster from hell. In fact, you're no more bloodthirsty than any dog not trained to mayhem. You haven't been trained to mayhem: you've been trained to chase balls. You're a pack animal, an animal who craves hierarchy, and you, Jessie, are a one-man dog. Your man's Jonathan. You adore him. You'd do anything for him, even let strangers who wouldn't know a wolf from a wolfhound scratch you behind the ears.

The only fight you and Jonathan have, that first year in the States, is about the collar. Jonathan insists that Jessie wear a collar. "Otherwise," he says, "I could be fined." There are policemen in the park. Jessie needs a collar and an ID tag and rabies shots.

"Jessie," you say on two feet, "needs so such thing." You, Stella, are bristling as you say this, even though you don't have fur at the moment. "Jonathan," you tell him, "ID tags are for dogs who wander. Jessie will never leave your side, unless you throw a ball for her. And I'm not going to get rabies. All I eat is Alpo, not dead raccoons: How am I going to get rabies?"

"It's the law," he says gently. "It's not worth the risk, Stella."

And then he comes and rubs your head and shoulders *that* way, the way you've never been able to resist, and soon the two of you are in bed having a lovely sportfuck, and somehow by the end of the evening, Jonathan's won. Well, of course he has: he's the alpha.

So the next time you're on four feet, Jonathan puts a strong chain choke collar and an ID tag around your neck, and then you go to the vet and get your shots. You don't like the vet's office much, because it smells of too much fear and pain, but the people there pat you and give you milk bones and tell you how beautiful you are, and the vet's hands are gentle and kind.

The vet likes dogs. She also knows wolves from wolfhounds. She looks at you, hard, and then looks at Jonathan. "A gray wolf?" she asks.

"I don't know," says Jonathan. "She could be a hybrid."

"She doesn't look like a hybrid to me." So Jonathan launches into his breezy story about how you were the runt of the litter at the pound: you wag your tail and lick the vet's hand and act utterly adoring.

The vet's not having any of it. She strokes your head; her hands are kind, but she smells disgusted. "Mr. Argent, gray wolves are endangered."

"At least one of her parents was a dog," Jonathan says. He's starting to sweat. "Now, *she* doesn't look endangered, does she?"

"There are laws about keeping exotics as pets," the vet says. She's still stroking your head; you're still wagging your tail, but now you start to whine, because the vet smells angry and Jonathan smells afraid. "Especially endangered exotics."

"She's a dog," Jonathan says.

"If she's a dog," the vet says, "may I ask why you haven't had her spayed?"

Jonathan splutters. "Excuse me?"

"You got her from the pound. Do you know how animals wind up at the pound, Mr. Argent? They land there because people breed them and then don't want to take care of all those puppies or kittens. They land there—"

"We're here for a rabies shot," Jonathan says. "Can we get our rabies shot, please?"

"Mr. Argent, there are regulations about breeding endangered species—"

"I understand that," Jonathan says. "There are also regulations about rabies shots. If you don't give my *dog* her rabies shot—"

The vet shakes her head, but she gives you the rabies shot, and then Jonathan gets you out of there, fast. "Bitch," he says on the way home. He's shaking. "Animal-rights fascist bitch! Who the hell does she think she is?"

She thinks she's a vet. She thinks she's somebody who's supposed to take care of animals. You can't say any of this, because you're on four legs. You lie in the back seat of the car, on the special sheepskin cover Jonathan bought to protect the upholstery from your fur, and whine. You're scared. You liked the vet, but you're afraid of what she might do. She doesn't understand your condition; how could she?

The following week, after you're fully changed back, there's a knock at the door while Jonathan's at work. You put down your copy of *Elle* and pad, barefooted, over to the door. You open it to find a woman in uniform; a white truck with "Animal Control" written on it is parked in the driveway.

"Good morning," the officer says. "We've received a report that there may be an exotic animal on this property. May I come in, please?"

"Of course," you tell her. You let her in. You offer her coffee, which she doesn't want, and you tell her that there aren't any exotic animals here. You invite her to look around and see for herself.

Of course there's no sign of a dog, but she's not satisfied. "According to our records, Jonathan Argent of this address had a dog vaccinated last Saturday. We've been told that the dog looked very much like a wolf. Can you tell me where that dog is now?"

"We don't have her anymore," you say. "She got loose and jumped the fence on Monday. It's a shame: she was a lovely animal."

The animal-control lady scowls. "Did she have ID?"

"Of course," you say. "A collar with tags. If you find her, you'll call us, won't you?"

She's looking at you, hard, as hard as the vet did. "Of course. We recommend that you check the pound at least every few days, too. And you might want to put up flyers, put an ad in the paper."

"Thank you," you tell her. "We'll do that." She leaves; you go back to reading *Elle*, secure in the knowledge that your collar's tucked into your underwear drawer upstairs and that Jessie will never show up at the pound.

Jonathan's incensed when he hears about this. He reels off a string of curses about the vet. "Do you think you could rip her throat out?" he asks.

"No," you say, annoyed. "I don't want to, Jonathan. I liked her. She's doing her job. Wolves don't just attack people: you know better than that. And it wouldn't be smart even if I wanted to: it would just mean people would have to track me down and kill me. Now look, relax. We'll go to a different vet next time, that's all."

"We'll do better than that," Jonathan says. "We'll move."

So you move to the next county over, to a larger house with a larger yard. There's even some wild land nearby, forest and meadows, and that's where you and Jonathan go for walks now. When it's time for your rabies shot the following year, you go to a male vet, an older man who's been recommended by some friends of friends of Jonathan's, people who do a lot of hunting. This vet raises his eyebrows when he sees you. "She's quite large," he says pleasantly. "Fish and Wildlife might be interested in such a large dog. Her size will add another, oh, hundred dollars to the bill, Johnny."

"I see." Jonathan's voice is icy. You growl, and the vet laughs.

"Loyal, isn't she? You're planning to breed her, of course."

"Of course," Jonathan snaps.

"Lucrative business, that. Her pups will pay for her rabies shot, believe me. Do you have a sire lined up?"

"Not yet." Jonathan sounds like he's strangling.

The vet strokes your shoulders. You don't like his hands. You don't like the way he touches you. You growl again, and again the vet laughs. "Well, give me a call when she goes into heat. I know some people who might be interested."

"Slimy bastard," Jonathan says when you're back home again. "You didn't like him, Jessie, did you? I'm sorry."

You lick his hand. The important thing is that you have your rabies shot, that your license is up to date, that this vet won't be reporting you to Animal Control. You're legal. You're a *good* dog.

You're a good wife, too. As Stella, you cook for Jonathan, clean for him, shop. You practice your English while devouring *Cosmopolitan* and *Martha*

Stewart Living, in addition to *Elle*. You can't work or go to school, because the week of the full moon would keep getting in the way, but you keep yourself busy. You learn to drive and you learn to entertain; you learn to shave your legs and pluck your eyebrows, to mask your natural odor with harsh chemicals, to walk in high heels. You learn the artful uses of cosmetics and clothing, so that you'll be even more beautiful than you are *au naturel*. You're stunning: everyone says so, tall and slim with long silver hair and pale, piercing blue eyes. Your skin's smooth, your complexion flawless, your muscles lean and taut: you're a good cook, a great fuck, the perfect trophy wife. But of course, during that first year, while Jonathan's thirty-six going on thirty-seven, you're only twenty-one going on twenty-eight. You can keep the accelerated aging from showing: you eat right, get plenty of exercise, become even more skillful with the cosmetics. You and Jonathan are blissfully happy, and his colleagues, the old fogies in the Anthropology Department, are jealous. They stare at you when they think no one's looking. "They'd all love to fuck you," Jonathan gloats after every party, and after every party, he does just that.

Most of Jonathan's colleagues are men. Most of their wives don't like you, although a few make resolute efforts to be friendly, to ask you to lunch. Twenty-one going on twenty-eight, you wonder if they somehow sense that you aren't one of them, that there's another side to you, one with four feet. Later you'll realize that even if they knew about Jessie, they couldn't hate and fear you any more than they already do. They fear you because you're young, because you're beautiful and speak English with an exotic accent, because their husbands can't stop staring at you. They know their husbands want to fuck you. The wives may not be young and beautiful anymore, but they're no fools. They lost the luxury of innocence when they lost their smooth skin and flawless complexions.

The only person who asks you to lunch and seems to mean it is Diane Harvey. She's forty-five, with thin gray hair and a wide face that's always smiling. She runs her own computer repair business, and she doesn't hate you. This may be related to the fact that her husband Glen never stares at you, never gets too close to you during conversation; he seems to have no desire to fuck you at all. He looks at Diane the way all the other men look at you: as if she's the most desirable creature on earth, as if just being in the same room with her renders him scarcely able to breathe. He adores his wife, even though they've been married for fifteen years, even though he's five years younger than she is and handsome enough to seduce a younger, more beautiful woman. Jonathan says that Glen must stay with Diane for her salary, which is considerably more than his. You think Jonathan's wrong; you think Glen stays with Diane for herself.

Over lunch, as you gnaw an overcooked steak in a bland fern bar, all glass and wood, Diane asks you kindly when you last saw your family, if you're homesick, whether you and Jonathan have any plans to visit Europe again soon. These questions bring a lump to your throat, because Diane's the only one who's ever asked them. You don't, in fact, miss your family—the parents who taught you to hunt, who taught you the dangers of continuing the line, or the siblings with whom you tussled and fought over scraps of meat—because you've transferred all your loyalty to Jonathan. But two is an awfully small pack, and you're starting to wish Jonathan hadn't had that operation. You're starting to wish you could continue the line, even though you know it would be a foolish thing to do. You wonder if that's why your parents mated, even though they knew the dangers.

"I miss the smells back home," you tell Diane, and immediately you blush, because it seems like such a strange thing to say, and you desperately want this kind woman to like you. As much as you love Jonathan, you yearn for someone else to talk to.

But Diane doesn't think it's strange. "Yes," she says, nodding, and tells you about how homesick she still gets for her grandmother's kitchen, which had a signature smell for each season: basil and tomatoes in the summer, apples in the fall, nutmeg and cinnamon in winter, thyme and lavender in the spring. She tells you that she's growing thyme and lavender in her own garden; she tells you about her tomatoes.

She asks you if you garden. You say no. In truth, you're not a big fan of vegetables, although you enjoy the smell of flowers, because you enjoy the smell of almost anything. Even on two legs, you have a far better sense of smell than most people do; you live in a world rich with aroma, and even the scents most people consider noxious are interesting to you. As you sit in the sterile fern bar, which smells only of burned meat and rancid grease and the harsh chemicals the people around you have put on their skin and hair, you realize that you really do miss the smells of home, where even the gardens smell older and wilder than the woods and meadows here.

You tell Diane, shyly, that you'd like to learn to garden. Could she teach you?

So she does. One Saturday afternoon, much to Jonathan's bemusement, Diane comes over with topsoil and trowels and flower seeds, and the two of you measure out a plot in the backyard, and plant and water and get dirt under your nails, and it's quite wonderful, really, about the best fun you've had on two legs, aside from sportfucks with Jonathan. Over dinner, after Diane's left, you try to tell Jonathan how much fun it was, but he doesn't seem particularly interested. He's glad you had a good time, but really, he doesn't want to hear about seeds. He wants to go upstairs and have sex.

So you do.

Afterwards, you go through all of your old issues of *Martha Stewart Living*, looking for gardening tips.

You're ecstatic. You have a hobby now, something you can talk to the other wives about. Surely some of them garden. Maybe, now, they won't hate you. So at the next party, you chatter brightly about gardening, but somehow all the wives are still across the room, huddled around a table, occasionally glaring in your direction, while the men cluster around you, their eyes bright, nodding eagerly at your descriptions of weeds and aphids.

You know something's wrong here. Men don't like gardening, do they? Jonathan certainly doesn't. Finally one of the wives, a tall blonde with a tennis tan and good bones, stalks over and pulls her husband away by the sleeve. "Time to go home now," she tells him, and curls her lip at you.

You know that look. You know a snarl when you see it, even if the wife's too civilized to produce an actual growl.

You ask Diane about this the following week, while you're in her garden, admiring her tomato plants. "Why do they hate me?" you ask Diane.

"Oh, Stella," she says, and sighs. "You really don't know, do you?" You shake your head, and she goes on. "They hate you because you're young and beautiful, even though that's not your fault. The ones who have to work hate you because you don't, and the ones who don't have to work, whose husbands support them, hate you because they're afraid their husbands will leave them for younger, more beautiful women. Do you understand?"

You don't, not really, even though you're now twenty-eight going on thirty-five. "Their husbands can't leave them for me," you tell Diane. "I'm married to Jonathan. I don't *want* any of their husbands." But even as you say it, you know that's not the point.

A few weeks later, you learn that the tall blonde's husband has indeed left her, for an aerobics instructor twenty years his junior. "He showed me a picture," Jonathan says, laughing. "She's a big-hair bimbo. She's not *half* as beautiful as you are."

"What does that have to do with it?" you ask him. You're angry, and you aren't sure why. You barely know the blonde, and it's not as if she's been nice to you. "His poor wife! That was a terrible thing for him to do!"

"Of course it was," Jonathan says soothingly.

"Would you leave me if I wasn't beautiful anymore?" you ask him.

"Nonsense, Stella. You'll always be beautiful."

But that's when Jonathan's going on thirty-eight and you're going on thirty-five. The following year, the balance begins to shift. He's going on thirty-nine; you're going on forty-two. You take exquisite care of yourself, and really, you're as beautiful as ever, but there are a few wrinkles now, and it takes hours of crunches to keep your stomach as flat as it used to be.

Doing crunches, weeding in the garden, you have plenty of time to think. In a year, two at the most, you'll be old enough to be Jonathan's mother, and you're starting to think he might not like that. And you've already gotten wind of catty faculty-wife gossip about how quickly you're showing your age. The faculty wives see every wrinkle, even through artfully applied cosmetics.

During that thirty-five to forty-two year, Diane and her husband move away, so now you have no one with whom to discuss your wrinkles or the catty faculty wives. You don't want to talk to Jonathan about any of it. He still tells you how beautiful you are, and you still have satisfying sportfucks. You don't want to give him any ideas about declining desirability.

You do a lot of gardening that year: flowers—especially roses—and herbs, and some tomatoes in honor of Diane, and because Jonathan likes them. Your best times are the two-foot times in the garden and the four-foot times in the forest, and you think it's no coincidence that both of these involve digging around in the dirt. You write long letters to Diane, on e-mail or, sometimes, when you're saying something you don't want Jonathan to find on the computer, on old-fashioned paper. Diane doesn't have much time to write back, but does send the occasional e-mail note, the even rarer postcard. You read a lot, too, everything you can find: newspapers and novels and political analysis, literary criticism, true crime, ethnographic studies. You startle some of Jonathan's colleagues by casually dropping odd bits of information about their field, about other fields, about fields they've never heard of: forensic geography, agricultural ethics, poststructuralist mining. You think it's no coincidence that the obscure disciplines you're most interested in involve digging around in the dirt.

Some of Jonathan's colleagues begin to comment not only on your beauty, but on your intelligence. Some of them back away a little bit. Some of the wives, although not many, become a little friendlier, and you start going out to lunch again, although not with anyone you like as much as Diane.

The following year, the trouble starts. Jonathan's going on forty; you're going on forty-nine. You both work out a lot; you both eat right. But Jonathan's hardly wrinkled at all yet, and your wrinkles are getting harder to hide. Your stomach refuses to stay completely flat no matter how many crunches you do; you've developed the merest hint of cottage-cheese thighs. You forego your old look, the slinky, skin-tight look, for long flowing skirts and dresses, accented with plenty of silver. You're going for exotic, elegant, and you're getting there just fine; heads still turn to follow you in the supermarket. But the sportfucks are less frequent, and you don't know how much of this is normal aging and how much is lack of interest on Jonathan's part. He doesn't seem quite as enthusiastic as he once did. He no longer brings you herbal tea and hot water bottles during your transitions; the walks in the woods are a little shorter than they used to be, the ball-throwing sessions in the meadows more perfunctory.

And then one of your new friends, over lunch, asks you tactfully if anything's wrong, if you're ill, because, well, you don't look quite yourself. Even as you assure her that you're fine, you know she means that you look a lot older than you did last year.

At home, you try to discuss this with Jonathan. "We knew it would be a problem eventually," you tell him. "I'm afraid that other people are going to notice, that someone's going to figure it out—"

"Stella, sweetheart, no one's going to figure it out." He's annoyed, impatient. "Even if they think you're aging unusually quickly, they won't make the leap to Jessie. It's not in their worldview. It wouldn't occur to them even if you were aging a hundred years for every one of theirs. They'd just think you had some unfortunate metabolic condition, that's all."

Which, in a manner of speaking, you do. You wince. It's been five weeks since the last sportfuck. "Does it bother you that I look older?" you ask Jonathan.

"Of *course* not, Stella!" But since he rolls his eyes when he says this, you're not reassured. You can tell from his voice that he doesn't want to be having this conversation, that he wants to be somewhere else, maybe watching TV. You recognize that tone. You've heard Jonathan's colleagues use it on their wives, usually while staring at you.

You get through the year. You increase your workout schedule, mine *Cosmo* for bedroom tricks to pique Jonathan's flagging interest, consider and reject liposuction for your thighs. You wish you could have a facelift, but the recovery period's a bit too long, and you're not sure how it would work with your transitions. You read and read and read, and command an increasingly subtle grasp of the implications of, the interconnections between, different areas of knowledge: ecotourism, Third-World famine relief, art history, automobile design. Your lunchtime conversations become richer, your friendships with the faculty wives more genuine.

You know that your growing wisdom is the benefit of aging, the compensation for your wrinkles and for your fading—although fading slowly, as yet—beauty.

You also know that Jonathan didn't marry you for wisdom.

And now it's the following year, the year you're old enough to be Jonathan's mother, although an unwed teenage one: you're going on fifty-six while he's going on forty-one. Your silver hair's losing its luster, becoming merely gray. Sportfucks coincide, more or less, with major national holidays. Your thighs begin to jiggle when you walk, so you go ahead and have the liposuction, but Jonathan doesn't seem to notice anything but the outrageous cost of the procedure.

You redecorate the house. You take up painting, with enough success to sell some pieces in a local gallery. You start writing a book about gardening as a cure for ecotourism and agricultural abuses, and you negotiate a contract with a prestigious university press. Jonathan doesn't pay much attention to any of this. You're starting to think that Jonathan would only pay attention to a full-fledged Lon Chaney imitation, complete with bloody fangs, but if that was ever in your nature, it certainly isn't now. Jonathan and Martha Stewart have civilized you.

On four legs, you're still magnificent, eliciting exclamations of wonder from other pet owners when you meet them in the woods. But Jonathan hardly ever plays ball in the meadow with you anymore; sometimes he doesn't even take you to the forest. Your walks, once measured in hours and miles, now clock in at minutes and suburban blocks. Sometimes Jonathan doesn't even walk you. Sometimes he just shoos you out into the backyard to do your business. He never cleans up after you, either. You have to do that yourself, scooping old poop after you've returned to two legs.

A few times you yell at Jonathan about this, but he just walks away, even more annoyed than usual. You know you have to do something to remind him that he loves you, or loved you once; you know you have to do something to reinsert yourself into his field of vision. But you can't imagine what. You've already tried everything you can think of.

There are nights when you cry yourself to sleep. Once, Jonathan would have held you; now he rolls over, turning his back to you, and scoots to the farthest edge of the mattress.

During that terrible time, the two of you go to a faculty party. There's a new professor there, a female professor, the first one the Anthropology Department has hired in ten years. She's in her twenties, with long black hair and perfect skin, and the men cluster around her the way they used to cluster around you.

Jonathan's one of them.

Standing with the other wives, pretending to talk about new films, you watch Jonathan's face. He's rapt, attentive, totally focused on the lovely young woman, who's talking about her research into ritual scarification in New Guinea. You see Jonathan's eyes stray surreptitiously, when he thinks no one will notice, to her breasts, her thighs, her ass.

You know Jonathan wants to fuck her. And you know it's not her fault, any more than it was ever yours. She can't help being young and pretty. But you hate her anyway. Over the next few days, you discover that what you hate most, hate even more than Jonathan wanting to fuck this young woman, is what your hate is doing to you: to your dreams, to your insides. The hate's your problem, you know; it's not Jonathan's fault, any more than his lust for the young professor is hers. But you can't seem to get rid of it, and you can sense it making your wrinkles deeper, shriveling you as if you're a piece of newspaper thrown into a fire.

You write Diane a long, anguished letter about as much of this as you can safely tell her. Of course, since she hasn't been around for a few years, she doesn't know how much older you look, so you simply say that you think Jonathan's fallen out of love with you since you're over forty now. You write the letter on paper, and send it through the mail.

Diane writes back, and not a postcard this time: she sends five single-spaced pages. She says that Jonathan's probably going through a midlife crisis. She agrees that his treatment of you is, in her words, "barbaric." "Stella, you're a beautiful, brilliant, accomplished woman. I've never known anyone who's grown so much, or in such interesting ways, in such a short time. If Jonathan doesn't appreciate that, then he's an ass, and maybe it's time to ask yourself if you'd be happier elsewhere. I hate to recommend divorce, but I also hate to see you suffering so much. The problem, of course, is economic: Can you support yourself if you leave? Is Jonathan likely to be reliable with alimony? At least—small comfort, I know—there are no children who need to be considered in all this. I'm assuming that you've already tried couples therapy. If you haven't, you should."

This letter plunges you into despair. No, Jonathan isn't likely to be reliable with alimony. Jonathan isn't likely to agree to couples therapy, either. Some of your lunchtime friends have gone that route, and the only way they ever got their husbands into the therapist's office was by threatening divorce on the spot. If you tried this, it would be a hollow threat. Your unfortunate metabolic condition won't allow you to hold any kind of normal job, and your writing and painting income won't support you, and Jonathan knows all that as well as you do. And your continued safety's in his hands. If he exposed you—

You shudder. In the old country, the stories ran to peasants with torches. Here, you know, laboratories and scalpels would be more likely. Neither option's attractive.

You go to the art museum, because the bright, high, echoing rooms have always made it easier for you to think. You wander among abstract sculpture and impressionist paintings, among still lifes and landscapes, among portraits. One of the portraits is of an old woman. She has white hair and many wrinkles; her shoulders stoop as she pours a cup of tea. The flowers on the china are the same pale, luminous blue as her eyes, which are, you realize, the same blue as your own.

The painting takes your breath away. This old woman is beautiful. You know the painter, a nineteenth-century English duke, thought so too.

You know Jonathan wouldn't.

You decide, once again, to try to talk to Jonathan. You make him his favorite meal, serve him his favorite wine, wear your most becoming outfit, gray silk with heavy silver jewelry. Your silver hair and blue eyes gleam in the candlelight, and the candlelight, you know, hides your wrinkles.

This kind of production, at least, Jonathan still notices. When he comes into the dining room for dinner, he looks at you and raises his eyebrows. "What's the occasion?"

"The occasion's that I'm worried," you tell him. You tell him how much it hurts you when he turns away from your tears. You tell him how much you miss the sportfucks. You tell him that since you clean up his messes more than three weeks out of every month, he can damn well clean up yours when you're on four legs. And you tell him that if he doesn't love you anymore, doesn't want you anymore, you'll leave. You'll go back home, to the village on the edge of the forest near an Alp, and try to make a life for yourself.

"Oh, Stella," he says. "Of course I still love you!" You can't tell if he sounds impatient or contrite, and it terrifies you that you might not know the difference. "How could you even *think* of leaving me? After everything I've given you, everything I've done for you—"

"That's been changing," you tell him, your throat raw. "The changes are the *problem*. Jonathan—"

"I can't believe you'd try to hurt me like this! I can't believe—"

"Jonathan, I'm *not* trying to hurt you! I'm reacting to the fact that you're hurting me! Are you going to stop hurting me, or not?"

He glares at you, pouting, and it strikes you that after all, he's very young, much younger than you are. "Do you have any idea how ungrateful you're being? Not many men would put up with a woman like you!"

"*Jonathan!*"

"I mean, do you have any idea how hard it's been for *me*? All the secrecy, all the lying, having to walk the damn dog—"

"You used to enjoy walking the damn dog." You struggle to control your breathing, struggle not to cry. "All right, look, you've made yourself clear. I'll leave. I'll go home."

"You'll do no such thing!"

You close your eyes. "Then what do you want me to do? Stay here, knowing you hate me?"

"I don't hate you! You hate me! If you didn't hate me, you wouldn't be threatening to leave!" He gets up and throws his napkin down on the table; it lands in the gravy boat. Before leaving the room, he turns and says, "I'm sleeping in the guestroom tonight."

"Fine," you tell him dully. He leaves, and you discover that you're trembling, shaking the way a terrier would, or a poodle. Not a wolf.

Well. He's made himself very plain. You get up, clear away the uneaten dinner you spent all afternoon cooking, and go upstairs to your bedroom. Yours, now: not Jonathan's anymore. You change into jeans and a sweatshirt. You think about taking a hot bath, because all your bones ache, but if you allow yourself to relax into warm water, you'll fall apart; you'll dissolve into tears, and there are things you have to do. Your bones aren't aching just because your marriage has ended; they're aching because the transition is coming up, and you need to make plans before it starts.

So you go into your study, turn on the computer, call up an internet travel agency. You book a flight back home for ten days from today, when you'll definitely be back on two feet again. You charge the ticket to your credit card. The bill will arrive here in another month, but by then you'll be long gone. Let Jonathan pay it.

Money. You have to think about how you'll make money, how much money you'll take with you—but you can't think about it now. Booking the flight has hit you like a blow. Tomorrow, when Jonathan's at work, you'll call Diane and ask her advice on all of this. You'll tell her you're going home. She'll probably ask you to come stay with her, but you can't, because of the transitions. Diane, of all the people you know, might understand, but you can't imagine summoning the energy to explain.

It takes all the energy you have to get yourself out of the study, back into your bedroom. You cry yourself to sleep, and this time Jonathan's not even across the mattress from you. You find yourself wondering if you should have handled the dinner conversation differently, if you should have kept yourself from yelling at him about the turds in the yard, if you should have tried to seduce him first, if—

The ifs could go on forever. You know that. You think about going home. You wonder if you'll still know anyone there. You realize how much you'll miss your garden, and you start crying again.

Tomorrow, first thing, you'll call Diane.

But when tomorrow comes, you can barely get out of bed. The transition has arrived early, and it's a horrible one, the worst ever. You're in so much pain you can hardly move. You're in so much pain that you moan aloud, but if Jonathan hears, he doesn't come in. During the brief pain-free intervals when you can think lucidly, you're grateful that you booked your flight as soon as you did. And then you realize that the bedroom door is closed, and that Jessie won't be able to open it herself. You need to get out of bed. You need to open the door.

You can't. The transition's too far advanced. It's never been this fast; that must be why it hurts so much. But the pain, paradoxically, makes the transition seem longer than a normal one, rather than shorter. You moan, and whimper, and lose all track of time, and finally howl, and then, blessedly, the transition's over. You're on four feet.

You can get out of bed now, and you do, but you can't leave the room. You howl, but if Jonathan's here, if he hears you, he doesn't come.

There's no food in the room. You left the master bathroom toilet seat up, by chance, so there's water, full of interesting smells. That's good. And there are shoes to chew on, but they offer neither nourishment nor any real comfort. You're hungry. You're lonely. You're afraid. You can smell Jonathan in the room—in the shoes, in the sheets, in the clothing in the closet—but Jonathan himself won't come, no matter how much you howl.

And then, finally, the door opens. It's Jonathan. "Jessie," he says. "Poor Jessie. You must be so hungry; I'm sorry." He's carrying your leash; he takes your collar out of your underwear drawer and puts it on you and attaches the leash, and you think you're going for a walk now. You're ecstatic. Jonathan's going to walk you again. Jonathan still loves you.

"Let's go outside, Jess," he says, and you dutifully trot down the stairs to the front door. But instead he says, "Jessie, this way. Come on, girl," and leads you on your leash to the family room at the back of the house, to the sliding glass doors that open onto the back yard. You're confused, but you do what Jonathan says. You're desperate to please him. Even if he's no longer quite Stella's husband, he's still Jessie's alpha.

He leads you into the backyard. There's a metal pole in the middle of the backyard. That didn't used to be there. Your canine mind wonders if it's a new toy. You trot up and sniff it, cautiously, and as you do, Jonathan clips one end of your leash onto a ring in the top of the pole.

You yip in alarm. You can't move far; it's not that long a leash. You strain against the pole, the leash, the collar, but none of them give; the harder you pull, the harder the choke collar makes it for you to breathe. Jonathan's still next to you, stroking you, calm, reassuring. "It's okay, Jess. I'll bring you food and water, all right? You'll be fine out here. It's just for tonight. Tomorrow we'll go for a nice long walk, I promise."

Your ears perk up at "walk," but you still whimper. Jonathan brings your food and water bowls outside and puts them within reach.

You're so glad to have the food that you can't think about being lonely or afraid. You gobble your Alpo, and Jonathan strokes your fur and tells you what a good dog you are, what a beautiful dog, and you think maybe everything's going to be all right, because he hasn't stroked you this much in months, hasn't spent so much time talking to you, admiring you.

Then he goes inside again. You strain towards the house, as much as the choke collar will let you. You catch occasional glimpses of Jonathan, who seems to be cleaning. Here he is dusting the picture frames; here he is running the vacuum cleaner. Now he's cooking—beef stroganoff, you can smell it—and now he's lighting candles in the dining room.

You start to whimper. You whimper even more loudly when a car pulls into the driveway on the other side of the house, but you stop when you hear a female voice, because you want to hear what it says.

". . . so terrible that your wife left you. You must be devastated."

"Yes, I am. But I'm sure she's back in Europe now, with her family. Here, let me show you the house." And when he shows her the family room, you see her: in her twenties, with long black hair and perfect skin. And you see how Jonathan looks at her, and you start to howl in earnest.

"*Jesus,*" Jonathan's guest says, peering out at you through the dusk. "What the hell *is* that? A wolf?"

"My sister's dog," Jonathan says. "Husky-wolfhound mix. I'm taking care of her while my sister's away on business. She can't hurt you: don't be afraid." And he touches the woman's shoulder to silence her fear, and she turns towards him, and they walk into the dining room. And then, after a while, the bedroom light flicks on, and you hear laughter and other noises, and you start to howl again.

You howl all night, but Jonathan doesn't come outside. The neighbors yell at Jonathan a few times—*Shut that dog up, goddammit!*—but Jonathan will never come outside again. You're going to die here, tethered to this stake.

But you don't. Towards dawn you finally stop howling; you curl up and sleep, exhausted, and when you wake up the sun's higher and Jonathan's coming through the open glass doors. He's carrying another dish of Alpo, and he smells of soap and shampoo. You can't smell the woman on him.

You growl anyway, because you're hurt and confused. "Jessie," he says. "Jessie, it's all right. Poor, beautiful Jessie. I've been mean to you, haven't I? I'm so sorry."

He does sound sorry, truly sorry. You eat the Alpo, and he strokes you, the same way he did last night, and then he unsnaps your leash from the pole and says, "Okay, Jess, through the gate into the driveway, okay? We're going for a ride."

You don't want to go for a ride. You want to go for a walk. Jonathan promised you a walk. You growl.

"Jessie! Into the car, *now*! We're going to another meadow, Jess. It's farther away than our old one, but someone told me he saw rabbits there, and he said it's really big. You'd like to explore a new place, wouldn't you?"

You don't want to go to a new meadow. You want to go to the old meadow, the one where you know the smell of every tree and rock. You growl again.

"Jessie, you're being a *very bad dog*! Now get in the car. Don't make me call Animal Control."

You whine. You're scared of Animal Control, the people who wanted to take you away so long ago, when you lived in that other county. You know that Animal Control kills a lot of animals, in that county and in this one, and if you die as a wolf, you'll stay a wolf. They'd never know about Stella. As Jessie, you'd have no way to protect yourself except your teeth, and that would only get you killed faster.

So you get into the car, although you're trembling.

In the car, Jonathan seems more cheerful. "Good Jessie. Good girl. We'll go to the new meadow and chase balls now, eh? It's a big meadow. You'll be able to run a long way." And he tosses a new tennis ball into the backseat, and you chew on it, happily, and the car drives along, traffic whizzing past. When you lift your head from chewing on the ball, you can see trees, so you put your head back down, satisfied, and resume chewing. And then the car stops, and Jonathan opens the door for you, and you hop out, holding your ball in your mouth.

This isn't a meadow. You're in the parking lot of a low concrete building that reeks of excrement and disinfectant and fear, *fear*, and from the building you hear barking and howling, screams of misery, and in the parking lot are parked two white Animal Control trucks.

You panic. You drop your tennis ball and try to run, but Jonathan has the leash, and he starts dragging you inside the building, and you can't breathe because of the choke collar. You cough, gasping, trying to howl. "Don't fight, Jessie. Don't fight me. Everything's all right."

Everything's not all right. You can smell Jonathan's desperation, can taste your own, and you should be stronger than he is but you can't breathe, and he's saying, "Jessie, don't bite me, it will be worse if you bite me, Jessie," and the screams of horror still swirl from the building and you're at the door now, someone's opened the door for Jonathan, someone says, "Let me help you with that dog," and you're scrabbling on the concrete, trying to dig your claws into the sidewalk just outside the door, but there's no purchase, and they've dragged you inside, onto the linoleum, and everywhere are the smells and sounds of terror. Above your own whimpering you hear Jonathan saying, "She jumped the fence and threatened my girlfriend, and then she tried to bite me, so I have no choice, it's such a shame, she's always been such a good dog, but in good conscience I can't—"

You start to howl, because he's lying, *lying*, you never did any of that!

Now you're surrounded by people, a man and two women, all wearing colorful cotton smocks that smell, although faintly, of dog shit and cat pee. They're putting a muzzle on you, and even though you can hardly think through your fear—and your pain, because Jonathan's walked back out the door, gotten into the car, and driven away, Jonathan's *left* you here—even with all of that, you know you don't dare bite or snap. You know your only hope is in being a good dog, in acting as submissive as possible. So you whimper, crawl along on your stomach, try to roll over on your back to show your belly, but you can't, because of the leash.

"Hey," one of the women says. The man's left. She bends down to stroke you. "Oh, God, she's so scared. Look at her."

"Poor thing," the other woman says. "She's *beautiful*."

"I know."

"Looks like a wolf mix."

"I know." The first woman sighs and scratches your ears, and you whimper and wag your tail and try to lick her hand through the muzzle. Take me home, you'd tell her if you could talk. Take me home with you. You'll be my alpha, and I'll love you forever. I'm a *good* dog.

The woman who's scratching you says wistfully, "We could adopt her out in a minute, I bet."

"Not with that history. Not if she's a biter. Not even if we had room. You know that."

"I know." The voice is very quiet. "Wish I could take her myself, though."

"Take home a biter? Lily, you have kids!"

Lily sighs. "Yeah, I know. Makes me sick, that's all."

"You don't need to tell me that. Come on, let's get this over with. Did Mark go to get the room ready?"

"Yeah."

"Okay. What'd the owner say her name was?"

"Stella."

"Okay. Here, give me the leash. Stella, come. Come on, Stella."

The voice is sad, gentle, loving, and you want to follow it, but you fight every step, anyway, until Lily and her friend have to drag you past the cages of other dogs, who start barking and howling again, whose cries are pure terror, pure loss. You can hear cats grieving, somewhere else in the building, and you can smell the room at the end of the hall, the room to which you're getting inexorably closer. You smell the man named Mark behind the door, and you smell medicine, and you smell the fear of the animals who've been taken to that room before you. But overpowering everything else is the worst smell, the smell that makes you bare your teeth in the muzzle and pull against the choke collar and scrabble again, helplessly, for a purchase you can't get on the concrete floor: the pervasive, metallic stench of death.

CAROL EMSHWILLER

Boys

Carol Emshwiller is an American writer of short stories and novels of speculative fiction. Her work has been recognized with numerous awards ranging from the Nebula Award to the Philip K. Dick Award. She was honored with the World Fantasy Lifetime Achievement award in 2005. Ursula K. Le Guin has called her "a major fabulist, a marvelous magical realist, one of the strongest, most complex, most consistently feminist voices in fiction." Her short fiction was recently collected in two volumes: *The Collected Stories of Carol Emshwiller*, Vols. 1 and 2. A controversial story, "Boys" takes the idea of gender roles to its extreme with surprising results. It was originally published in *Scifiction* in 2003.

We need a new batch of boys. Boys are so foolhardy, impetuous, reckless, rash. They'll lead the way into smoke and fire and battle. I've seen one of my own sons, aged twelve, standing at the top of the cliff shouting, daring the enemy. You'll never win a medal for being too reasonable.

We steal boys from anywhere. We don't care if they come from our side or theirs. They'll forget soon enough which side they used to be on, if they ever knew. After all, what does a seven-year-old know? Tell them this flag of ours is the best and most beautiful, and that we're the best and smartest, and they believe it. They like uniforms. They like fancy hats with feathers. They like to get medals. They like flags and drums and war cries.

Their first big test is getting to their beds. You have to climb straight up to the barracks. At the top you have to cross a hanging bridge. They've heard rumors about it. They know they'll have to go home to mother if they don't do it. They all do it.

You should see the look on their faces when we steal them. It's what they've always wanted. They've seen our fires along the hills. They've seen us marching back and forth across our flat places. When the wind is right, they've heard the horns that signal our getting up and going to bed and they've gotten up and gone to bed with our sounds or those of our enemies across the valley.

In the beginning they're a little bit homesick (you can hear them smothering their crying the first few nights) but most have anticipated their capture and look forward to it. They love to belong to us instead of to the mothers.

If we'd let them go home they'd strut about in their uniforms and the stripes of their rank. I know because I remember when I first had my uniform. I was wishing my mother and my big sister could see me. When I was taken, I fought, but just to show my courage. I was happy to be stolen—happy to belong, at long last, to the men.

* * *

Once a year in summer we go down to the mothers and copulate in order to make more warriors. We can't ever be completely sure which of the boys is ours and we always say that's a good thing, for then they're all ours and we care about them equally, as we should. We're not supposed to have family groups. It gets in the way of combat. But every now and then, it's clear who the father is. I know two of my sons. I'm sure they know that I, the colonel, am their father. I think that's why they try so hard. I know them as mine because I'm a small, ugly man. I know many must wonder how someone like me got to be a colonel.

(We not only steal boys from either side but we copulate with either side. When I go down to the villages, I always look for Una.)

TO DIE FOR YOUR TRIBE IS TO LIVE FOREVER. That's written over our headquarters entrance. Under it, NEVER FORGET. We know we mustn't forget but we suspect maybe we have. Some of us feel that the real reasons for the battles have been lost. No doubt but that there's hate, so we and they commit more atrocities in the name of the old ones, but how it all began is lost to us.

We've not only forgotten the reasons for the conflict, but we've also forgotten our own mothers. Inside our barracks, the walls are covered with mother jokes and mother pictures. Mother bodies are soft and tempting. "Pillows," we call them. "Nipples" and "pillows." And we insult each other by calling ourselves the same.

* * *

The valley floor is full of women's villages. One every fifteen miles or so. On each side are mountains. The enemy's, at the far side, are called The

Purples. Our mountains are called The Snows. The weather is worse in our mountains than in theirs. We're proud of that. We sometimes call ourselves The Hailstones or The Lightnings. We think the hailstones harden us up. The enemy doesn't have as many caves over on their side. We always tell the boys they were lucky to be stolen by us and not those others.

* * *

When I was first taken, our mothers came up to the caves to get us back. That often happens. Some had weapons. Laughable weapons. My own mother was there, in the front of course. She probably organized the whole thing, her face, red and twisted with resolve. She came straight at me. I was afraid of her. We boys fled to the back of the barracks and our squad leader stood in front of us. Other men covered the doorway. It didn't take long for the mothers to retreat. None were hurt. We try never to do them any harm. We need them for the next crop of boys.

Several days later my mother came again by herself—sneaked up by moonlight. Found me by the light of the night lamp. She leaned over my sleeping mat and breathed on my face. At first I didn't know who it was. Then I felt breasts against my chest and I saw the glint of a hummingbird pin I recognized. She kissed me. I was petrified. (Had I been a little older I'd have known how to choke and kick to the throat. I might have killed her before I realized it was my mother.) What if she took me from my squad? Took away my uniform? (By then I had a red and blue jacket with gold buttons. I had already learned to shoot. Something I'd always wanted to do. I was the first of my group to get a sharpshooters medal. They said I was a natural. I was trying hard to make up for my small size.)

The night my mother came she lifted me in her arms. There, against her breasts, I thought of all the pillow jokes. I yelled. My comrades, though no older than I and only a little larger, came to my aid. They picked up whatever weapon was handy, mostly their boots. (Thank goodness we had not received our daggers yet.) My mother wouldn't hit out at the boys. She let them batter at her. I wanted her to hit back, to run, to save herself. After she finally did run, I found I had bitten my lower lip. In times of stress I'm inclined to do that. I have to watch out. When you're a colonel, it's embarrassing to be found with blood on your chin.

* * *

So now, off to steal boys. We're a troop of older boys and younger men. The oldest maybe twenty-two, half my age. I think of them all as boys, though I would never call them boys to their faces. I'm in charge. My son, Hob, he's seventeen now, is with us.

But we no sooner creep down to the valley than we see things have changed since last year. The mothers have put up a wall. They've built themselves a fort.

I immediately change our plans. I decide this will be copulation day, not boys day. Good military strategy: Always be ready for a quick change of plan.

The minute I think this, I think Una. This is her town. My men look happy, too. This is not only easier, but lots more fun than herding a new crop of boys.

Last time I came down at copulation time I found her—or she found me, she usually does. She's a little old for copulation day, but I didn't want anybody but her. After copulation, I did things for her, repaired a roof leak, fixed a broken table leg . . . Then I took her over again, though it wasn't needed, and caused my squad to have to wait for me. Got me a lot of lewd remarks, but I felt extraordinarily happy anyway.

Sometimes on boys night I wonder, what if I stole Una along with boys? What if I dressed her as a boy and brought her to some secret hiding place on our side of the mountain? There are lots of unused caves. Once our armies occupied them all, but that was long ago. Both us and our enemies seem to be dwindling. Every year there are fewer and fewer suitable boys.

Una always seems glad to see me even though I'm ugly and small. (My size is a disadvantage for a soldier, though less so now that I have rank, but the ugliness . . . that's how I can tell which are my sons . . . small, ugly boys, both of them. Too bad for them. But I've managed well even so, all the way up to colonel.)

Una was my first. I was her first, too. I felt sorry for her, having to have me for her beginning to be a woman. We were little more than children. We hardly knew what we were doing or how to do it. Afterwards she cried. I felt like crying myself but I had learned not to. Not just learned it with the squad, but I had learned it even before they took me from my mother. I wanted to be taken. I roamed far out into the scrub, waiting for them to come and get me.

The pain in my hip started when I was one of those boys. It wasn't from a wound in a skirmish with the enemy, but from a fight among ourselves. Our leaders were happy when we fought each other. We'd have gotten soft and lazy if we didn't. I keep my mouth shut about my injury. I kept my mouth shut even when I got it. I thought if they knew I could be so easily hurt they'd send me back. Later, I thought if they knew about it, I might not be allowed to come on our raids. Later still I thought I might not be able to be a colonel. I don't let myself limp though sometimes that makes me more breathless than I should be. So far it doesn't seem as if anybody's noticed.

* * *

We regroup. I say, "Fellow nipples and fellow pillows . . ." Everybody laughs. "When have they ever stopped men? Look how womanish the walls are. They'll crumble as we climb." I scrape at a part with the tip of my cane. (As a colonel, I'm allowed to have a cane if I wish instead of a swagger stick.)

We're not sure if the women want to stop copulation day or boy gathering day. We hope it's the latter.

Boost up the smallest boy with a rope on hooks. The rest of us follow.

I used to be that smallest boy. I always went first and highest. Times like this I was glad for my size. I got medals for that. I don't wear any of them. I like playing at being one of the boys. Being small and being a colonel is a good example for some. If they knew about my bum leg I'd be an even better example of how far you can get with disabilities.

* * *

We scale the walls and drop into the edges of a vegetable garden. We walk carefully around tomatoes and strawberry plants, squash and beans. After that, raspberry bushes tear at our pants and untie our high-tops as we go by. There's a row of barbed wire just beyond the raspberries. Easy to push down.

I feel sad that the women want to keep us out so badly. I wonder, does Una want me not to come? Except they know we're as determined as mothers. At least I am when it comes to Una.

* * *

Una has always been nice to me. I often wonder why she likes me. I can understand somebody liking me now that I'm a colonel with silver on my epaulets, and a silver handled cane, but she liked me when I was nothing but a runty boy. She's small, too. I always think Una and I fit together except for one thing, she's beautiful.

* * *

We swarm in, turn, each to our favorite place, the younger ones to what's left over, usually other young ones. But then here we are, swarming back again, into their central square, the place with the well, and stone benches, and their one and only tree. Around the tree are the graves of babies. The benches are the mourning benches. We sit on them or on the ground. There's nobody here, not a single woman nor girl nor baby.

Then there's the sound of shooting. We move from the central square—we can't see anything from there. We hide behind the houses at the edges of the gardens. Our enemy stands along the top of the wall. We're ambushed. We flop down. We have no rifles with us and only two pistols, mine and my lieutenant's. This wasn't supposed to be a skirmish. We have our daggers, of course.

Those along the wall don't seem to be very good shots. I raised my pistol. I'm thinking to show them what a good shot really is. But my lieutenant yells, "Stop! Don't shoot. It's mothers!"

Women all along the wall! And with guns. Hiding under wall-colored shields. Whoever heard of such a thing.

They shoot, but a lot are missing, I think on purpose. After all, we may be the enemy, but we're the fathers of many of their girls and many of them. I wonder which one is Una.

The women are angrier than we thought. Perhaps they're tired of losing their boys to us and to the other side. I wouldn't put it past them not to be on any side whatsoever.

Our boys begin to yell their war cry but in a half-hearted way. But then . . . one shot . . . a real shot this time. Good shot, too. One wonders how a woman could have done it. One wonders if it was a man who taught her. The boys are stunned. To think that one of their mothers or one of their sisters would shoot to kill. This is real. We hadn't thought they'd harm us any more than we ever really harm them.

It was my lieutenant they killed. One bloodless shot to the head. For that boy's sake I'm glad at least no pain. He was wearing his ceremonial hat. I wasn't wearing mine. I never liked that fancy heavy hat. I suppose they really wanted to kill me, but had to take second best since they couldn't tell which one I was. Una would know which one was me.

The boys scatter—back to the center square with its mourning tree. The women can't see them back there. I stay to check on the dead lieutenant and to get his dagger and pistol. Then I limp back to where the boys are waiting for me to tell them what to do. Limp. I relax into it. I don't care who sees. I haven't exactly given up, though perhaps I have when it comes to my future. I'll most likely be demoted. To be captured by women . . . All twenty of us. If I can't get out of this in an efficient and capable way, there goes my career.

I hope they have the sense to come rescue us with a large group. They'll have to make a serious effort. I hope they don't try to fight and at the same time try to save the women for future use.

But then we hear shooting again and we look out from behind the huts near the wall and see the women have turned their guns outwards. At first we think it's us, come to rescue us, but it's not. That's not our battle cry, not our drum beats . . . We can't see from behind the walls so some of us go up on the roofs. There's no danger, all the rifles are facing outwards, but our boys would have braved the roof without a word, as they always do.

It's not our red and blue banners. It's their ugly green and white. It's the enemy come to take advantage of our capture. We wish the women would get out of the way and let us go so we could fight for ourselves. Those women are breaking every rule of battle. They're lying flat along their wall. Nobody can get a fair shot at them.

It goes on and on. We get tired of watching and retreat to the square. We reconnoiter food from the kitchens. We eat better than we usually do. The food is so good we wish the women would let up a bit so we can enjoy it without that racket. Where did they get all these weapons? They must have found our ammunition caves and those of our enemy, too.

* * *

The women do a pretty good job. By nightfall our enemy has fled back into their mountains and the women are still on top of their wall. It looks as if they're going to spend the night up there. It's a wide wall. Not as badly built as I told the boys it was.

We find beds for ourselves, all of them better than our usual sleeping pads. I go to Una's hut and lie where I had hoped to have a copulation.

Cats prowl and yowl. All sorts of things live with the women. Goats wander the streets and come in any house they want to. All the animals expect food everywhere. Like the women, our boys are soft-hearted. They feed every creature that comes by. I don't let on that I do too.

This whole thing makes me sad. Worried. If I could just have Una in my arms, I might be able to sleep. I have a "day dream" of her creeping in to me in the middle of the night. I wouldn't even care if we had a copulation or not.

* * *

In the morning boys climb to the roofs again to see what's up. They describe women lying under shields all along the walls and they can see some of the enemy lying dead away from the walls. I need to climb up and see for myself. Besides it's good for the boys to see me taking the same chances they do.

I send the boys off and I take their place. I look down on the women along the wall. I see several rifles pointed at me. I stand like a hero. I dare them to shoot. I take all the time I want. I see wall sections less crowded with women. I take out my notebook (no leader is ever without one) and draw a diagram. I take my time until I have the whole wall mapped out.

I could take out my pistol and threaten them. I could shoot one but it wouldn't be very manly to take advantage of my high point. Were they men I'd do it. But then they do the unmanly thing. They shoot me. My leg. My good leg. I go down, flat on the roof. At first I feel nothing but the shock . . . as if I'd been hit with a hammer. All I know is I can't stand up. Then I see blood.

Though they're on the wall, they're lower. They can't see me as long as I keep down. I crawl to the edge where boys help me. They carry me back to Una's bed. I feel I'm about to pass out or throw up and I become aware that I've soiled myself. I don't want the boys to see. I've always been a source of strength and inspiration in spite of or because of my size.

One of those boys is Hob, come to help me, my arm across his shoulders. I lean in pain but keep my groans to myself.

"Sir? Colonel?"

"I'm fine. Will be. Go."

I wish I could ask him if he really is my son. They say sometimes the women know and tell the boys.

"Don't you want us to . . ."

"No. Go. Now. And shut the door."

They leave just in time. I throw up over the side of the bed. I lie back— Una's pillow all sweated up not to mention what I've done to her quilt.

Una can make potions for pain. I wish I knew which, of the herbs hanging from her ceiling, might help me. But I'd not be able to reach them anyway.

I lie, half conscious, for I don't know how long. Every time I sit up to examine my leg, I feel nausea again and have to lie back. I wonder if I'll ever be able to lead a charge or a raid for boys or a copulation day. And I always thought, when I became a general (and lately I felt sure I'd be one) maybe I'd find out what we're fighting for—beyond, that is, the usual rhetoric we use to make ourselves feel superior. Now I suppose I'll never know the real reasons.

* * *

The boys knock. I rouse myself and say, "Come." Try, that is. At first my voice won't sound out at all and then it sounds more like a groan than a word. The boys tell me the women have called down from the wall. They want to send in a spokesman. The boys want to let him in and then hold him hostage so that we'll all be let out safely.

I tell them the women will probably send in a woman.

That bothers the boys. They must have had torture or killing in mind but now they look worried.

"Tell them yes," I say.

It must smell terrible in here. I even smell terrible to myself, and it's uncomfortable sitting in my own mess. I prop myself up as best I can. I hope I can keep to my senses. I hope I don't throw up in the middle of it. I put my dagger, unsheathed, under the pillow.

At first I think the boys were right, it's a man, of course a man. Where would they have found him, and is he from our side or theirs? That's important. I can't tell by the colors. He's all in tan and gray. He's not wearing any stripes at all so I can't tell his rank. He stands, at ease. More than at ease, utterly relaxed, and in front of a colonel.

But then . . . I can't believe it, it's Una. I should have known. Dressed as a man down to the boots. I have such a sense of relief and after that joy. Everything will be all right now.

I tell the boys to get out and shut the door.

I reach for her, but the look on her face stops me.

"You shot me in the leg on purpose, didn't you! My good leg!"

"I meant to shoot the bad one."

She opens all the windows, and the door again, too, and shoos the boys away.

"Let me see."

She's gentle. As I knew she'd be.

"I'll get the bullet out, but first I'll clean you up." She hands me leaves to chew for pain.

As she leans, so close above me, her hair falls out of her cap and brushes my face, gets in my mouth as it does when we have copulation day. I reach to touch her breast but she pushes me away.

I should kill her for the glory of it . . . the leader of the women. I'd not be thought a failure then. I'd be made a general in no time.

But, as she pulls away the soiled quilts, she finds my dagger first thing. She puts it in the drawer with her kitchen knives.

I think again how . . . (and we all know, only too well) how love is a dangerous thing and can spoil the best of plans. Even as I think it, I want to spoil the very plans I think of. I mean if she's the leader then I could deal with her right now, as she leans over me—even without my dagger. They may be good shots, but can they wrestle a man? Even a wounded one?

"I chose you because I thought, of all of them, you might listen."

"You know I won't ever be let come down to copulation day again."

"Don't go back then. Stay here and copulate."

"I have often thought to bring you up to the mountain dressed as a man. I have a place all picked out."

"Stay here. Let everybody stay here and be as women."

I can't answer such a thing. I can't even think about it.

"But then what else do you know except how to be a colonel?"

She washes me, changes the bed, and throws the bed clothes and my clothes out the door. Then she gets the bullet out. I'm half out of my head from the leaves she had me chew so the pain is dulled. She bandages me, covers me with a clean blanket, puts her lips against my cheek for a moment.

Then stands up, legs apart. She looks like one of our boys getting ready to prove himself. "We'll not stand for this anymore," she says. "It has to end and we'll end it, if not one way, then another."

"But this is how it's always been."

"You could be our spokesman."

How can she even suggest such a thing? "Pillows," I say. "Spokesman for the nipples."

Goodness knows what the mothers are capable of. They never stick to any rules.

"If the answer is no, we'll not have any more boy babies. You can come down and copulate all you want but there'll be no boys. We'll kill them."

"You wouldn't. You couldn't. Not you, Una."

"Have you noticed how there are fewer and fewer boys? Many have already done it."

But I'm in too much pain and dizzy from the leaves she gave me, to think clearly. She sees that. She sits beside me, takes my hand. "Just rest," she says. How can I rest with such ideas in my head? "But the rules."

"Hush. Women don't care about rules. You know that."

"Come back with me." I pull her down against me. This time she lets me. How good it feels to have us chest to chest, my arms around her. "I have a secret place. It's not a hard climb to get there."

She pulls back. "Colonel, sir!"

"Please don't call me that."

Then I say . . . what we're not allowed to say or even think. It's a mother/child thing, not to be said between a man and a woman. I say, "I love you."

She leans back and looks at me. Then wipes at my chin. "Try not to bite your lip like that."

"It doesn't matter anymore."

"It does to me."

"I liked . . . I like . . ." I already used the other word, why not yet again. "I love copulation day only when with you."

I wonder if she feels the same about me. I wish I dared ask her. I wonder if my son . . . Is Hob hers and mine together? I've always hoped he was. She's made no gesture towards him. She hasn't even looked at him any more than any other boy. This would have been his first copulation day had the women not built their wall.

"Rest," she says. "We'll discuss later."

"Is it just us? Or are you saying the same thing to the enemy? They could win the war like that. It would be your fault."

"Stop thinking."

"What if no more boys on either side, ever?"

"What if?"

She gives me more of those leaves to chew. They're bitter. I was in too much pain to notice that the first time. I feel even sleepier right away.

* * *

I dream I'm the last of all the boys. Ever. I have to get somewhere in a hurry, but there's a wall so high I'll never get over it. Beside, my legs are not there at all. I'm nothing but a torso. Women watch me. Women, off across the valley floor as far as I can see and none will help. There's nothing to do but lie there and give the war cry.

I wake shouting and with Una holding me down. Hob is there, helping her. Other boys are in the doorway looking worried.

I've thrown the blanket and the pillow to the floor and now I seem to be trying to throw myself out of bed. Una has a long scratch across her cheek. I must have done that.

"Sorry. Sorry."

I'm still as if in a dream. I pull Una down against me. Hold her hard and then I reach out for Hob, too. My poor ugly boy. I ask the unaskable. "Tell me, is Hob mine and yours together?"

Hob looks shocked that I would ask such a thing, as well he should. Una pulls away and gets up. She answers as if she was one of the boys. "Colonel, sir, how can you, of all people, ask a thing like that." Then she throws my own words back at me. "This is how it's always been."

"Sorry. Sorry."

"Oh, for Heaven's sake stop being so sorry!"

She shoos the boys from the doorway but she lets Hob stay. Together they rearrange the bed. Together she and Hob make broth for me and food for themselves. Hob seems at home here. It's true, I'm sure. This is our son.

But I suppose all this yearning, all this wondering, is due to the leaves Una had me chew. It's not the real me. I'll not pay any attention to myself.

But there's something else. I didn't get a good look at my leg yet, but it feels like a serious wound. If I can't climb up to our stronghold, I'll not ever be able to go home. I shouldn't, even so, and though my career is in a shambles . . . I shouldn't let myself be lured into staying here as a copulator for the rest of my life. I can't think of anything more dishonorable. I should send Hob back to the citadel to report on what's happened and to get help. If he was found trying to escape, would Una let the women kill him?

I try to get Hob alone so I can whisper his orders to him. Only when Una goes out to the privy do I get the chance. "Get back to the citadel. Cross the wall tonight. There's no moon." I show him my map and where I think there are fewer women. I want to tell him to take care, but we don't ever say such things.

* * *

In the morning I tell Una to tell my leaders to come in to me. I'm in pain, in a sweat, my beard is itchy. I ask Una to clean me up. She treats me as a mother would. Back when my mother did it, I pulled away. I wouldn't let her get close to me. I especially wouldn't let her hug or kiss me. I wanted to be a soldier. I wanted nothing to do with mother things.

All the boys are looking scruffy. We take pride in our cleanliness, in shaving everyday, in our brush cuts, and our enemy is as spic and span as we are. I hope they don't launch an offensive today and see us so untidy.

I'm glad to see Hob isn't with them.

I find it hard to rouse myself to my usual humor. I say, "Pillows, nipples," but I'm too uncomfortable to play at being one of the boys.

I'd prefer to recuperate some, but the boys are restless already. I can't be thinking of myself. We'll storm the wall. I show them the map. I point out the less guarded spots. I grab Una. Both her wrists. "Men, we'll need a battering ram."

Wood isn't easy to get out here on the valley floor. This is a desert except along the streams, but every village has one tree in the center square that they've nurtured along. As here, baby's graves are always around it. In other villages, most are cottonwood, but this one is oak. It's so old I wouldn't be surprised if it hadn't been here since before the village. I think the village was built up around it later.

"Chop the tree. Ram the wall," I tell them. "Go back to the citadel. Don't wait around for me. Tell the generals never to come here again, neither for boys nor for copulation. Tell them I'm of no use to us anymore."

The women won't be able to shoot at the boys chopping it down. It's hidden from all parts of the wall.

When they hear the chopping, the women begin to ululate. Our boys stop chopping, but only for a moment. I hear them begin again with even more vigor.

Here beside me Una ululates, too. She struggles against me but I hang on.

"How could you? That's the tree of dead boys."

I let go.

"All the babies buried there are boys. Some are yours."

I can't let this new knowledge color my thinking. I have to think of the safety of my boys. "Let us go, then."

"Tell them to stop."

"Would you let us go for the sake of a tree?"

"We would."

I give the order.

* * *

The women move away from a whole section of the wall, they even provide their ladders. I tell the boys to go. There's no way they could carry me back and no way I could ever climb to the citadel again.

No sooner are the boys gone, even to the last tootle of the fifes, the last triumphant drum beat . . . (We always march home as though victorious whether victorious or not.) Hearing them go, I can't help but groan, though not from pain this time. No sooner have the mothers come down from the wall, but that I hear, ululating again. Una stamps in to me.

"What now?"

"It's Hob. Your enemy . . . Your enemy has dropped him off at the edge of your foothills."

I can see it on her face.

"He's dead."

"Of course he's dead. You are all as good as dead."

She blames me for Hob. "I blame myself."

"I hate you. I hate you all."

I don't believe we'll be seeing many boys anymore. I would warn us if I was able, I would be the spokesman, though I don't suppose I'll ever have the chance.

"What will the women do with me?"

"You were always kind. I'll not be any less to you."

What am I good for? What use am I but to stay here as the father of females? All those small, ugly, black-haired girls . . . I suppose all of them biting their lower lips until they bleed.

EILEEN GUNN

Stable Strategies for Middle Management

Eileen Gunn is an American writer and editor. She is the author of a small but distinguished body of short fiction published over the last three decades. Her other work in science fiction includes editing the pioneering webzine *The Infinite Matrix* and producing the website *The Difference Dictionary,* a concordance to *The Difference Engine* by William Gibson and Bruce Sterling. A graduate of Clarion, Gunn now serves as a director of Clarion West. Her fiction has been recognized with awards such as the Nebula. "Stable Strategies for Middle Management" deals with the lengths an executive will go to fit into the corporate culture and show her loyalty to the company. It was first published in *Asimov's Science Fiction Magazine* in 1988 and was nominated for a Hugo Award.

Our cousin the insect has an external skeleton made of shiny brown chitin, a material that is particularly responsive to the demands of evolution. Just as bioengineering has sculpted our bodies into new forms, so evolution has changed the early insect's chewing mouthparts into her descendants' chisels, siphons, and stilettos, and has molded from the chitin special tools—pockets to carry pollen, combs to clean her compound eyes, notches on which she can fiddle a song.

—From the popular science program *Insect People!*

I awoke this morning to discover that bioengineering had made demands upon me during the night. My tongue had turned into a stiletto, and my left hand now contained a small chitinous comb, as if for cleaning a compound eye. Since I didn't have compound eyes, I thought that perhaps this presaged some change to come.

I dragged myself out of bed, wondering how I was going to drink my coffee through a stiletto. Was I now expected to kill my breakfast, and dispense with coffee entirely? I hoped I was not evolving into a creature whose survival depended on early-morning alertness. My circadian rhythms would no doubt keep pace with any physical changes, but my unevolved soul was repulsed at the thought of my waking cheerfully at dawn, ravenous for some wriggly little creature that had arisen even earlier.

I looked down at Greg, still asleep, the edge of our red and white quilt pulled up under his chin. His mouth had changed during the night too, and seemed to contain some sort of a long probe. Were we growing apart?

I reached down with my unchanged hand and touched his hair. It was still shiny brown, soft and thick, luxurious. But along his cheek, under his beard, I could feel patches of sclerotin, as the flexible chitin in his skin was slowly hardening to an impermeable armor.

He opened his eyes, staring blearily forward without moving his head. I could see him move his mouth cautiously, examining its internal changes. He turned his head and looked up at me, rubbing his hair slightly into my hand.

"Time to get up?" he asked. I nodded. "Oh God," he said. He said this every morning. It was like a prayer.

"I'll make coffee," I said. "Do you want some?"

He shook his head slowly. "Just a glass of apricot nectar," he said. He unrolled his long, rough tongue and looked at it, slightly cross-eyed. "This is real interesting, but it wasn't in the catalog. I'll be sipping lunch from flowers pretty soon. That ought to draw a second glance at Duke's."

"I thought account execs were *expected* to sip their lunches," I said.

"Not from the flower arrangements . . . ," he said, still exploring the odd shape of his mouth. Then he looked up at me and reached up from under the covers. "Come here."

It had been a while, I thought. And I had to get to work. But he did smell terribly attractive. Perhaps he was developing aphrodisiac scent glands. I climbed back under the covers and stretched my body against his. We were both developing chitinous knobs and odd lumps that made this less than comfortable. "How am I supposed to kiss you with a stiletto in my mouth?" I asked.

"There are other things to do. New equipment presents new possibilities." He pushed the covers back and ran his unchanged hands down my body from shoulder to thigh. "Let me know if my tongue is too rough."

It was not.

* * *

Fuzzy-minded, I got out of bed for the second time and drifted into the kitchen.

Measuring the coffee into the grinder, I realized that I was no longer interested in drinking it, although it was diverting for a moment to spear the beans with my stiletto. What was the damn thing for, anyhow? I wasn't sure I wanted to find out.

Putting the grinder aside, I poured a can of apricot nectar into a tulip glass. Shallow glasses were going to be a problem for Greg in the future, I thought. Not to mention solid food.

My particular problem, however, if I could figure out what I was supposed to eat for breakfast, was getting to the office in time for my 10 A.M. meeting. Maybe I'd just skip breakfast. I dressed quickly and dashed out the door before Greg was even out of bed.

* * *

Thirty minutes later, I was more or less awake and sitting in the small conference room with the new marketing manager, listening to him lay out his plan for the Model 2000 launch.

In signing up for his bioengineering program, Harry had chosen specialized primate adaptation, B-E Option No. 4. He had evolved into a text-book example: small and long-limbed, with forward-facing eyes for judging distances and long, grasping fingers to keep him from falling out of his tree.

He was dressed for success in a pinstriped three-piece suit that fit his simian proportions perfectly. I wondered what premium he paid for custom-made. Or did he patronize a ready-to-wear shop that catered especially to primates?

I listened as he leaped agilely from one ridiculous marketing premise to the next. Trying to borrow credibility from mathematics and engineering, he used wildly metaphoric bizspeak, "factoring in the need for pipeline throughput," "fine-tuning the media mix," without even cracking a smile.

Harry had been with the company only a few months, straight out of business school. He saw himself as a much-needed infusion of talent. I didn't like him, but I envied him his ability to root through his subconscious and toss out one half-formed idea after another. I know he felt it reflected badly on me that I didn't join in and spew forth a random selection of promotional suggestions.

I didn't think much of his marketing plan. The advertising section was a textbook application of theory with no practical basis. I had two options: I could force him to accept a solution that would work, or I could yes him to death, making sure everybody understood it was his idea. I knew which path I'd take.

"Yeah, we can do that for you," I told him. "No problem." We'd see which of us would survive and which was hurtling to an evolutionary dead end.

Although Harry had won his point, he continued to belabor it. My attention wandered—I'd heard it all before. His voice was the hum of an air conditioner, a familiar, easily ignored background noise. I drowsed and new emotions stirred in me, yearnings to float through moist air currents, to land on bright surfaces, to engorge myself with warm, wet food.

Adrift in insect dreams, I became sharply aware of the bare skin of Harry's arm, between his gold-plated watchband and his rolled-up sleeve, as he manipulated papers on the conference room table. He smelled delicious, like a pepperoni pizza or a charcoal-broiled hamburger. I realized he probably wouldn't taste as good as he smelled. But I was hungry. My stiletto-like tongue was there for a purpose, and it wasn't to skewer cubes of tofu. I leaned over his arm and braced myself against the back of his hand, probing with my stylets to find a capillary.

Harry noticed what I was doing and swatted me sharply on the side of the head. I pulled away before he could hit me again.

"We were discussing the Model 2000 launch. Or have you forgotten?" he said, rubbing his arm.

"Sorry. I skipped breakfast this morning." I was embarrassed.

"Well, get your hormones adjusted, for chrissake." He was annoyed, and I couldn't really blame him. "Let's get back to the media allocation issue, if you can keep your mind on it. I've got another meeting at eleven in Building Two."

Inappropriate feeding behavior was not unusual in the company, and corporate etiquette sometimes allowed minor lapses to pass without pursuit. Of course, I could no longer hope that he would support me on moving some money out of the direct-mail budget . . .

* * *

During the remainder of the meeting, my glance kept drifting through the open door of the conference room, toward a large decorative plant in the hall, one of those oases of generic greenery that dot the corporate landscape. It didn't look succulent exactly—it obviously wasn't what I would have preferred to eat if I hadn't been so hungry—but I wondered if I swung both ways?

I grabbed a handful of the broad leaves as I left the room and carried them back to my office. With my tongue, I probed a vein in the thickest part of a leaf. It wasn't so bad. Tasted green. I sucked them dry and tossed the husks in the wastebasket.

I was still omnivorous, at least—female mosquitoes don't eat plants. So the process wasn't complete . . .

I got a cup of coffee, for company, from the kitchenette and sat in my office with the door closed and wondered what was happening to me. The incident with Harry disturbed me. Was I turning into a mosquito? If so, what the hell kind of good was that supposed to do me? The company didn't have any use for a whining loner, a bloodsucker.

There was a knock at the door, and my boss stuck his head in. I nodded and gestured him into my office. He sat down in the visitor's chair on the other side of my desk. From the look on his face, I could tell Harry had talked to him already.

Tom Samson was an older guy, pre-bioengineering. He was well versed in stimulus-response techniques, but had somehow never made it to the top job. I liked him, but then that was what he intended. Without sacrificing authority, he had pitched his appearance, his gestures, the tone of his voice, to the warm end of the spectrum. Even though I knew what he was doing, it worked.

He looked at me with what appeared to be sympathy, but was actually a practiced sign stimulus, intended to defuse any fight-or-flight response. "Is there something bothering you, Margaret?"

"Bothering me? I'm hungry, that's all. I get short-tempered when I'm hungry."

Watch it, I thought. He hasn't referred to the incident; leave it for him to bring up. I made my mind go bland and forced myself to see his eyes. A shifty gaze is a guilty gaze.

Tom just looked at me, biding his time, waiting for me to put myself on the spot. My coffee smelt burnt, but I stuck my tongue in it and pretended to drink. "I'm just not human until I've had my coffee in the morning." Sounded phoney. Shut up, I thought.

This was the opening that Tom was waiting for. "That's what I wanted to talk to you about, Margaret." He sat there, hunched over in a relaxed way, like a mountain gorilla, unthreatened by natural enemies. "I just talked to Harry Winthrop, and he said you were trying to suck his blood during a meeting on marketing strategy." He paused for a moment to check my reaction, but the neutral expression was fixed on my face and I said nothing. His face changed to project disappointment. "You know, when we noticed you were developing three distinct body segments, we had great hopes for you. But your actions just don't reflect the social and organizational development we expected."

He paused, and it was my turn to say something in my defense. "Most insects are solitary, you know. Perhaps the company erred in hoping for a termite or an ant. I'm not responsible for that."

"Now, Margaret," he said, his voice simulating genial reprimand. "This isn't the jungle, you know. When you signed those consent forms, you agreed to let the B-E staff mold you into a more useful corporate organism. But this isn't nature, this is man reshaping nature. It doesn't follow the old rules. You can truly be anything you want to be. But you have to cooperate."

"I'm doing the best I can," I said, cooperatively. "I'm putting in eighty hours a week."

"Margaret, the quality of your work is not an issue. It's your interactions with others that you have to work on. You have to learn to work as part of the group. I just cannot permit such backbiting to continue. I'll have Arthur get you an appointment this afternoon with the B-E counselor." Arthur was his secretary. He knew everything that happened in the department and mostly kept his mouth shut.

"I'd be a social insect if I could manage it," I muttered as Tom left my office. "But I've never known what to say to people in bars."

* * *

For lunch I met Greg and our friend David Detlor at a health-food restaurant that advertises fifty different kinds of fruit nectar. We'd never eaten there before, but Greg knew he'd love the place. It was already a favorite of David's, and he still has all his teeth, so I figured it would be okay with me.

David was there when I arrived, but not Greg. David works for the company too, in a different department. He, however, has proved remarkably resistant to corporate blandishment. Not only has he never undertaken B-E, he hasn't even bought a three-piece suit. Today he was wearing chewed-up blue jeans and a flashy Hawaiian shirt, of a type that was cool about ten years ago.

"Your boss lets you dress like that?" I asked.

"We have this agreement. I don't tell her she has to give me a job, and she doesn't tell me what to wear."

David's perspective on life is very different from mine. I don't think it's just that he's in R&D and I'm in Advertising—it's more basic than that. Where he sees the world as a bunch of really neat but optional puzzles put there for his enjoyment, I see it as . . . well, as a series of SATs.

"So what's new with you guys?" he asked, while we stood around waiting for a table.

"Greg's turning into a goddamn butterfly. He went out last week and bought a dozen Italian silk sweaters. It's not a corporate look."

"He's not a corporate *guy*, Margaret."

"Then why is he having all this B-E done if he's not even going to use it?"

"He's dressing up a little. He just wants to look nice. Like Michael Jackson, you know?"

I couldn't tell whether David was kidding me or not. Then he started telling me about his music, this barbershop quartet that he sings in. They were going to dress in black leather for the next competition and sing Shel Silverstein's "Come to Me, My Masochistic Baby."

"It'll knock them on their tails," he said gleefully. "We've already got a great arrangement."

"Do you think it will win, David?" It seemed too weird to please the judges in that sort of a show.

"Who cares?" said David. He didn't look worried.

Just then Greg showed up. He was wearing a cobalt blue silk sweater with a copper green design on it. Italian. He was also wearing a pair of dangly earrings shaped like bright blue airplanes. We were shown to a table near a display of carved vegetables.

"This is great," said David. "Everybody wants to sit near the vegetables. It's where you sit to be *seen* in this place." He nodded to Greg. "I think it's your sweater."

"It's the butterfly in my personality," said Greg. "Waiters never used to do stuff like this for me. I always got the table next to the espresso machine."

If Greg was going to go on about the perks that come with being a butterfly, I was going to change the subject.

"David, how come you still haven't signed up for B-E?" I asked. "The company pays half the cost, and they don't ask questions."

David screwed up his mouth, raised his hands to his face, and made small, twitching, insect gestures, as if grooming his nose and eyes. "I'm doing okay the way I am."

Greg chuckled at this, but I was serious. "You'll get ahead faster with a little adjustment. Plus you're showing a good attitude, you know, if you do it."

"I'm getting ahead faster than I want to right now—it looks like I won't be able to take the three months off that I wanted this summer."

"Three months?" I was astonished. "Aren't you afraid you won't have a job to come back to?"

"I could live with that," said David calmly, opening his menu.

The waiter took our orders. We sat for a moment in a companionable silence, the self-congratulation that follows ordering high-fiber foodstuffs. Then I told them the story of my encounter with Harry Winthrop.

"There's something wrong with me," I said. "Why suck his blood? What good is that supposed to do me?"

"Well," said David, "*you* chose this schedule of treatments. Where did you want it to go?"

"According to the catalog," I said, "the No. 2 Insect Option is supposed to make me into a successful competitor for a middle-management niche, with triggerable responses that can be useful in gaining entry to upper hierarchical levels. Unquote." Of course, that was just ad talk—I didn't really expect it to do all that. "That's what I want. I want to be in charge. I want to be the boss."

"Maybe you should go back to BioEngineering and try again," said Greg. "Sometimes the hormones don't do what you expect. Look at my tongue, for instance." He unfurled it gently and rolled it back into his mouth. "Though I'm sort of getting to like it." He sucked at his drink, making disgusting slurping sounds. He didn't need a straw.

"Don't bother with it, Margaret," said David firmly, taking a cup of rose-hip tea from the waiter. "Bioengineering is a waste of time and money and millions of years of evolution. If human beings were intended to be managers, we'd have evolved pin-striped body covering."

"That's cleverly put," I said, "but it's dead wrong."

The waiter brought our lunches, and we stopped talking as he put them in front of us. It seemed like the anticipatory silence of three very hungry people, but was in fact the polite silence of three people who have been brought up not to argue in front of disinterested bystanders. As soon as he left, we resumed the discussion.

"I mean it," David said. "The dubious survival benefits of management aside, bioengineering is a waste of effort. Harry Winthrop, for instance, doesn't really need B-E at all. Here he is, fresh out of business school, audibly buzzing with lust for a high-level management position. Basically he's just marking time until a presidency opens up somewhere. And what gives him the edge over you is his youth and inexperience, not some specialized primate adaptation."

"Well," I said with some asperity, "he's not constrained by a knowledge of what's failed in the past, that's for sure. But saying that doesn't solve my problem, David. Harry's signed up. I've signed up. The changes are under way and I don't have any choice."

I squeezed a huge glob of honey into my tea from a plastic bottle shaped like a teddy bear. I took a sip of the tea; it was minty and very sweet. "And now I'm turning into the wrong kind of insect. It's ruined my ability to deal with Product Marketing."

"Oh, give it a rest!" said Greg suddenly. "This is *so* boring. I don't want to hear any more talk about corporate hugger-mugger. Let's talk about something that's fun."

I had had enough of Greg's lepidopterate lack of concentration. "Something that's *fun?* I've invested all my time and most of my genetic material in this job. This is all the goddamn fun there is."

The honeyed tea made me feel hot. My stomach itched—I wondered if I was having an allergic reaction. I scratched, and not discreetly. My hand came out from under my shirt full of little waxy scales. What the hell was going on under there? I tasted one of the scales; it was wax all right. Worker bee changes? I couldn't help myself—I stuffed the wax into my mouth.

David was busying himself with his alfalfa sprouts, but Greg looked disgusted. "That's gross, Margaret." He made a face, sticking his tongue part way out. Talk about gross. "Can't you wait until after lunch?"

I was doing what came naturally, and did not dignify his statement with a response. There was a side dish of bee pollen on the table. I took a spoonful and mixed it with the wax, chewing noisily. I'd had a rough morning, and bickering with Greg wasn't making the day more pleasant.

Besides, neither he nor David had any respect for my position in the company. Greg doesn't take my job seriously at all. And David simply does what he wants to do, regardless of whether it makes any money, for himself or anyone else. He was giving me a back-to-nature lecture, and it was far too late for that.

This whole lunch was a waste of time. I was tired of listening to them, and felt an intense urge to get back to work. A couple of quick stings distracted them both: I had the advantage of surprise. I ate some more honey and quickly waxed them over. They were soon hibernating side by side in two large octagonal cells.

I looked around the restaurant. People were rather nervously pretending not to have noticed. I called the waiter over and handed him my credit card. He signaled to several bus boys, who brought a covered cart and took Greg and David away. "They'll eat themselves out of that by Thursday afternoon," I told him. "Store them on their sides in a warm, dry place, away from direct heat." I left a large tip.

* * *

I walked back to the office, feeling a bit ashamed of myself. A couple days of hibernation weren't going to make Greg or David more sympathetic to my problems. And they'd be real mad when they got out.

I didn't used to do things like that. I used to be more patient, didn't I?
More appreciative of the diverse spectrum of human possibility. More interested in sex and television.

This job was not doing much for me as a warm, personable human being.
At the very least, it was turning me into an unpleasant lunch companion.
Whatever had made me think I wanted to get into management anyway?

The money, maybe.

But that wasn't all. It was the challenge, the chance to do something new,
to control the total effort instead of just doing part of a project . . .

The money too, though. There were other ways to get money. Maybe
I should just kick the supports out from under the damned job and start
over again.

I saw myself sauntering into Tom's office, twirling his visitor's chair
around and falling into it. The words "I quit" would force their way out,
almost against my will. His face would show surprise—feigned, of course.
By then I'd have to go through with it. Maybe I'd put my feet up on his desk.
And then—

But was it possible to just quit, to go back to being the person I used to
be? No, I wouldn't be able to do it. I'd never be a management virgin again.

I walked up to the employee entrance at the rear of the building. A suc-
tion device next to the door sniffed at me, recognized my scent, and clicked
the door open. Inside, a group of new employees, trainees, were clustered
near the door, while a personnel officer introduced them to the lock and let it
familiarize itself with their pheromones.

On the way down the hall, I passed Tom's office. The door was open. He
was at his desk, bowed over some papers, and looked up as I went by.

"Ah, Margaret," he said. "Just the person I want to talk to. Come in for
a minute, would you." He moved a large file folder onto the papers in front
of him on his desk, and folded his hands on top of them. "So glad you were
passing by." He nodded toward a large, comfortable chair. "Sit down.

"We're going to be doing a bit of restructuring in the department," he
began, "and I'll need your input, so I want to fill you in now on what will be
happening."

I was immediately suspicious. Whenever Tom said, "I'll need your input,"
he meant everything was decided already.

"We'll be reorganizing the whole division, of course," he continued, drawing little boxes on a blank piece of paper. He'd mentioned this at the department meeting last week.

"Now, your area subdivides functionally into two separate areas, wouldn't
you say?"

"Well—"

"Yes," he said thoughtfully, nodding his head as though in agreement. "That would be the way to do it." He added a few lines and a few more boxes. From what I could see, it meant that Harry would do all the interesting stuff, and I'd sweep up afterwards.

"Looks to me as if you've cut the balls out of my area and put them over into Harry Winthrop's," I said.

"Ah, but your area is still very important, my dear. That's why I don't have you actually reporting to Harry." He gave me a smile like a lie.

He had put me in a tidy little bind. After all, he was my boss. If he was going to take most of my area away from me, as it seemed he was, there wasn't much I could do to stop him. And I would be better off if we both pretended that I hadn't experienced any loss of status. That way I kept my title and my salary.

"Oh, I see," I said. "Right."

It dawned on me that this whole thing had been decided already, and that Harry Winthrop probably knew all about it. He'd probably even wangled a raise out of it. Tom had called me in here to make it look casual, to make it look as though I had something to say about it. I'd been set up.

This made me mad. There was no question of quitting now. I'd stick around and fight. My eyes blurred, unfocused, refocused again. Compound eyes! The promise of the small comb in my hand was fulfilled! I felt a deep chemical understanding of the ecological system I was now a part of. I knew where I fit in. And I knew what I was going to do. It was inevitable now, hard-wired in at the DNA level.

The strength of this conviction triggered another change in the chitin, and for the first time I could actually feel the rearrangement of my mouth and nose, a numb tickling like inhaling seltzer water. The stiletto receded and mandibles jutted forth, rather like Katharine Hepburn. Form and function achieved an orgasmic synchronicity. As my jaw pushed forward, mantis-like, it also opened, and I pounced on Tom and bit his head off.

He leaped from his desk and danced headless about the office.

I felt in complete control of myself as I watched him and continued the conversation. "About the Model 2000 launch," I said. "If we factor in the demand for pipeline throughput and adjust the media mix just a bit, I think we can present a very tasty little package to Product Marketing by the end of the week."

Tom continued to strut spasmodically, making vulgar copulative motions. Was I responsible for evoking these mantid reactions? I was unaware of a sexual component in our relationship.

I got up from the visitor's chair and sat behind his desk, thinking about what had just happened. It goes without saying that I was surprised at my own actions. I mean, irritable is one thing, but biting people's heads off is quite another. But I have to admit that my second thought was, well, this certainly is a useful strategy, and should make a considerable difference in my ability to advance myself. Hell of a lot more productive than sucking people's blood.

Maybe there was something after all to Tom's talk about having the proper attitude.

And, of course, thinking of Tom, my third reaction was regret. He really had been a likeable guy, for the most part. But what's done is done, you know, and there's no use chewing on it after the fact.

I buzzed his assistant on the intercom. "Arthur," I said, "Mr. Samson and I have come to an evolutionary parting of the ways. Please have him re-engineered. And charge it to Personnel."

Now I feel an odd itching on my forearms and thighs. Notches on which I might fiddle a song?

TANITH LEE

Northern Chess

Tanith Lee is a highly respected English writer of science fiction, horror, and fantasy, with over seventy novels and hundreds of short stories to her credit. She has been a regular contributor over many years to *Weird Tales* magazine. She has won the World Fantasy Award, the British Fantasy Award, and the Nebula Award multiple times. "Northern Chess" is great example of how a traditional sword and sorcery tale can surprise and subvert, and features an early strong female character in a subgenre not known for such characters at the time. It was first published in *Women as Demons* in 1979.

Sky and land had the same sallow bluish tinge, soaked in cold light from a vague white sun. It was late summer, but summer might never have come here. The few trees were bare of leaves and birds. The cindery grassless hills rolled up and down monotonously. Their peaks gleamed dully, their dips were full of mist. It was a land for sad songs and dismal rememberings. and, when the night came, for nightmares and hallucinations.

Fifteen miles back, Jaisel's horse had died. Not for any apparent cause. It had been healthy and active when she rode from the south on it, the best the dealer had offered her, though he had tried to cheat her in the beginning. She was aiming to reach a city in the far north, on the sea coast there, but not for any particular reason. She had fallen into the casual habit of the wandering adventurer. Destination was an excuse, never a goal. And when she saw the women at their looms or in their greasy kitchens, or tangled with babies, or broken with field work, or leering out of painted masks from shadowy town doorways, Jaisel's urge to travel, to ride, to fly, to run away, increased. Generally she was running from something in fact as well as in the metaphysical. The last city she had vacated abruptly, having killed two footpads who had jumped her in the street. One had turned out to be a lordling, who had taken up robbery and rape as a hobby. In those parts, to kill a lord, with whatever justice, meant hanging and quartering. So Jaisel departed on her new horse, aiming for a city in the north. And in between had come this bleak northern empty land where her mount collapsed slowly under her and died without warning. Where the streams tasted bitter and the weather looked as if it wished to snow in summer.

She had seen only ruins. Only a flock of grayish wild sheep materialized from mist on one hand and plunged away into mist on the other. Once she heard a raven cawing. She was footsore and growing angry, with the country, with herself, and with God. While her saddle and pack gained weight on her shoulders with every mile.

Then she reached the top of one of the endless slopes, looked over and saw something new.

Down in a pool of the yellowish-bluish mist lay a village. Primitive and melancholy it was, but alive, for smokes spiraled from roof-holes, drifting into the cloudless sky. Mournful and faint, too, there came the lowing of cattle. Beyond the warren of cots, a sinister unleafed spider web of trees. Beyond them, barely seen, transparent in mist, something some distance away, a mile perhaps—a tall piled hill, or maybe a stony building of bizarre and crooked shape . . .

Jaisel started and her eyes refocused on the closer vantage of the village and the slope below.

The fresh sound was unmistakable: jingle-jangle of bells on the bridles of war horses. The sight was exotic, also, unexpected here. Two riders on steelblue mounts, the scarlet caparisons flaming up through the quarter-tone atmosphere like bloody blades. And the shine of mail, the blink of gems.

"Render your name!" one of the two knights shouted.

She half smiled, visualizing what they would see, what they would assume, the surprise in store.

"My name is Jaisel," she shouted back.

And heard them curse.

"What sort of a name is that, boy?"

Boy. Yes, and not the only time.

She started to walk down the slope toward them.

And what they had supposed to be a boy from the top of the incline, gradually resolved itself into the surprise. Her fine flaxen hair was certainly short as a boy's, somewhat shorter. A great deal shorter than the curled manes of knights. Slender in her tarnished chain mail, with slender strong hands dripping with frayed frosty lace at the wrists. The white lace collar lying out over the mail with dangling drawstrings each ornamented by a black pearl. The left ear-lobe pierced and a gold sickle moon flickering sparks from it under the palely electric hair. The sword belt was gray leather, worn and stained. Dagger on right hip with a fancy gilt handle, thin sword on left hip, pommel burnished by much use. A girl knight with intimations of the reaver, the showman, and, (for what it was worth), the prince.

When she was close enough for the surprise to have commenced, she stopped and regarded the two mounted knights. She appeared gravely amused, but really the joke had palled by now. She had had twelve years to get bored with it. And she was tired, and still angry with God.

"Well," one of the knights said at last, "it takes all kinds to fill the world. But I think you've mistaken your road, lady."

He might mean an actual direction. He might mean her mode of living.

Jaisel kept quiet, and waited. Presently the second knight said chillily: "Do you know of this place? Understand where you are?"

"No," she said. "It would be a courteous kindness if you told me."

The first knight frowned. "It would be a courteous kindness to send you home to your father, your husband and your children."

Jaisel fixed her eyes on him. One eye was a little narrower than the other. This gave her face a mocking, witty slant.

"Then, sir," she said, "send me. Come. I invite you."

The first knight gesticulated theatrically.

"I am Renier of Towers," he said. "I don't fight women."

"You do," she said. "You are doing it now. Not successfully."

The second knight grinned; she had not anticipated that.

"She has you, Renier. Let her be. No girl travels alone like this one, and dressed as she is, without skills to back it. Listen, Jaisel. This land is cursed. You've seen, the life's sucked out of it. The village here. Women and beasts birth monsters. The people fall sick without cause. Or with some cause. There was an alchemist who claimed possession of this region. Maudras. A necromancer, a worshipper of old unholy gods. Three castles of his scabbed the countryside between here and Towers in the west. Those three are no more—taken and razed. The final castle is here, a mile off to the northeast. If the mist would lift, you might see it. The Prince of Towers means to expunge all trace of Maudras from the earth. We are the prince's knights, sent here to deal with the fourth castle as with the rest."

"And the castle remains untaken," said Renier. "Months we've sat here in this unwholesome plague-ridden wilderness."

"Who defends the castle?' Jaisel asked. "Maudras himself?"

"Maudras was burned in Towers a year ago," the second knight said. "His familiar, or his curse, holds the castle against God's knights." His face was pale and grim. Both knights indeed were alike in that. But Renier stretched his mouth and said to her sweetly: "Not a spot for a maid. A camp of men. A haunted castle in a blighted country. Better get home."

"I have no horse," said Jaisel levelly. "But coins to buy one."

"We've horses and to spare," said the other knight. "Dead men don't require mounts. I am called Cassant. Vault up behind me and I'll bring you to the camp."

She swung up lightly, despite the saddle and pack on her shoulders.

Renier watched her, sneering, fascinated.

As they turned the horses' heads into the lake of mist, he rode near and murmured: "Beware, lady. The women in the village are sickly and revolting. A knight's honor may be forgotten. But probably you have been raped frequently."

"Once," she said, "ten years back. I was his last pleasure. I dug his grave myself, being respectful of the dead." She met Renier's eyes again and added gently, "and when I am in the district I visit his grave and spit on it."

* * *

The mist was denser below than Jaisel had judged from the slope. In the village a lot was hidden, which was maybe as well. At a turning among the cots she thought she spied a forlorn hunched-over woman, leading by a tether a shadowy animal, which seemed to be a cow with two heads.

They rode between the trees and out the other side, and picccmeal the war camp of Towers evolved through the mist. Blood-blotch red banners hung lankly; the ghosts of tents clawed with bright heraldics that penetrated the obscurity. Horses puffed breath like dragon-smoke at their pickets. A couple of Javelot-cannon emplacements, the bronze tubes sweating on their wheels, the javelins stacked by, the powder casks wrapped in sharkskin but probably damp.

At this juncture, suddenly the mist unravelled. A vista opened away from the camp for two hundred yards northeast, revealing the castle of the necromancer-alchemist, Maudras.

It reared up, stark and peculiar against a tin-colored sky.

The lower portion was carved from the native rock-base of a conical hill. This rose into a plethora of walls and craning, squinnying towers, that seemed somehow like the petrification of a thing once unnaturally growing.

A causeway flung itself up the hill and under an arched doormouth, barri-
caded by iron.

No movements were discernible on battlements or roofs. No pennant flew.
The castle had an aura of the tomb. Yet not necessarily a tomb of the dead.

It was the camp which had more of the feel of a mortuary about it. From
an oblique quarter emanated groanings. Where men were to be found outside the tents, they crouched listlessly over fires. Cook-pots and heaps of
accoutrements plainly went unattended. By a scarlet pavilion two knights
sat at chess. The game was sporadic and violent and seemed likely to end
in blows.

Cassant drew rein a space to the side of the scarlet pavilion, whose cloth
was blazoned with three gold turrets—the insignia of Towers. A boy ran to
take charge of the horse as its two riders dismounted. But Renier remained
astride his horse, staring at Jaisel. Soon he announced generally, in a herald's
carrying tone: "Come, gentlemen, welcome a new recruit. A peerless knight.
A damsel in breeches."

All around, heads lifted. A sullen interest bloomed over the apathy of the
camp: the slurred spiteful humor of men who were ill, or else under sentence
of execution. They began to get up from the pallid fires and shamble closer.
The fierce knights paused and gazed arrogantly across with extravagant oaths.

"Mistress, you're in for trouble," said Cassant ruefully. "But be fair, he
warned you of it."

Jaisel shrugged. She glanced at Renier, nonchalantly posed on the steelblue horse, right leg loose of the stirrup now and hooked across the saddle-
bow. At ease, malevolently, he beamed at her. Jaisel slipped the gaudy dagger
from her belt, let him catch the flash of the gilt, then tossed it at him. The
little blade, with its wasp-sting point, sang through the air, singeing the hairs
on his right cheek. It buried itself, where she had aimed it, in the picket post
behind him. But Renier, reacting to the feint as she had intended, lunged
desperately aside for the sake of his pretty face, took all his own weight on
the yet-stirruped leg and off the free one, unbalanced royally, and plunged
crashing to the ground. At the same instant, fully startled, the horse tried to
rear. Still left-leggedly trapped in the stirrup, Renier of Towers went slither-
ing through the hot ashes of a fire.

A hubbub resulted—delighted unfriendly mirth. The soldiers were as
prepared to make sport of a boastful lord on his ears in the ash as of a helpless girl.

And the helpless girl was not quite finished. Renier was fumbling for
his sword. Jaisel leaped over him like a lion kicking his hands away as
she passed. Landing, she wrenched his foot out of the stirrup and, having

liberated him, jumped to the picket to retrieve her dagger. As Renier gained his knees, he beheld her waiting for him, quiet as a statue, her pack slung on the ground, the thin sword, slick with light, ready as a sixth long murderous finger to her hand.

A second he faltered, while the camp, ferociously animated, buzzed. Then his ringed hand went to the hilt of his own sword. It was two to three thirds its length from the scabbard when a voice bellowed from the doorway of the scarlet and gold pavilion: "Dare to draw upon a woman, Renier, and I'll flay you myself."

Gasping, Renier let the sword grate home again. Jaisel turned and saw a man incarnadine with anger as the tent he had stepped from. Her own dormant anger woke and filled her, white anger not red, bored anger, cold anger.

"Don't fear him slain, sir," she said. "I will give him only a slight cut, and afterward spare him."

The incarnadine captain of the camp of Towers bent a baleful shaggy lour on her.

"Strumpet, or witch?" he thundered.

"Tell me first," said Jaisel coolly, "your title. Is it coward or imbecile?"

Silence was settling like flies on honey.

The captain shook himself.

"I never yet struck a wench—" he said.

"Nor will you now, by God's wounds."

His mouth dropped ajar. He disciplined it and asked firmly: "Why coward and why imbecile?"

"Humoring me, are you?' she inquired. She strolled toward him and let the sword tip weave a delicate pattern about his nose. To his credit, having calmed himself, he retained the calm. "Coward or imbecile," she said, drawing lines of glinting fire an inch from his nostrils, "because you cannot take a castle that offers no defenders."

A response then. A beefy paw thrust up to flick the sword away from him and out of her hand. But the sword was too quick. Now it rested horizontally on the air, tip twitching a moment at his throat And now it was gone back into its scabbard, and merely a smiling strange-eyed girl was before him.

"I already know enough of you," the captain said, "that you are a trial to men and an affront to heaven is evident. Despite that, I will answer your abuse. Maudras's last castle is defended by some sorcery he conjured to guard it. Three assaults were attempted. The result you shall witness. Follow, she-wolf."

And he strode off through the thick of the men who parted to let him by, and to let the she-wolf by in his wake. No one touched her but one fool, who had observed, but learned nothing. The pommel of her dagger in his ribs, bruising through mail and shirt, put pain to his flirtation.

"Here," the captain barked.

He drew aside the flap of a dark tent, and she saw twenty men lying on rusty mattresses and the two surgeons going up and down. The casualties of some savage combat. She beheld things she had beheld often, those things which sickened less but appalled more with repetition. Near to the entrance a boy younger than herself, dreaming horribly in a fever, called out. Jaisel slipped into the tent. She set her icy palm on the boy's forehead and felt his raging heat burn through it. But her touch seemed to alleviate his dream at least. He grew quieter.

"Again," she said softly, "coward, or imbecile. And these are the sacrificial victims on the altar of cowardice or imbecility."

Probably, the captain had never met such merciless eyes. Or, perhaps not so inexplicably, from between the smooth lids of a young girl.

"Enchantment," he said gruffly. "And sorcery. We were powerless against it. Do you drink wine, you virago? Yes, no doubt. Come and drink it with me then in my pavilion and you shall have the full story. Not that you deserve it. But you are the last thrown stone that kills a man. Injustice atop all the rest, and from a *woman*."

Abruptly she laughed at him, her anger spent.

* * *

Red wine and red meat were served in the red pavilion. All the seven knights of the Towers camp were present, Cassant and Renier among the rest. Outside, their men went on sitting around the fires. A dreary song had been struck up, and was repeated, over and over, as iron snow-light radiated from the northern summer sky.

The captain of the knights had told again the story Cassant had recounted to Jaisel on the slope: The three castles razed, the final castle which proved unassailable. Gruff and bellicose, the captain found it hard to speak of supernatural items and growled the matter into his wine.

"Three assaults were offered the walls of the castle. Montaube led the first of these. He died, and fifty men with him. Of what? We saw no swordsmen on the battlements, no javelots were fired, no arrows. Yet men sprinkled the ground, bloody and dying, as if an army twice our numbers had come to grips with them unseen. The second assault, I led. I escaped by a miracle. I saw a man, his mail split as if by a bolt shot from a great distance. He dropped with a cry and blood bursting from a terrible wound. Not a soul was near but I, his captain. No weapon or shot was visible. The third assault—was planned, but never carried through. We reached the escarpment, and my soldiers began falling like scythed grain. No shame in our retreat. Another thing. Last month, three brave fools, men of dead Montaube's, decided secretly to effect entry by night over the walls. A sentry perceived them vanish within. They were not attacked. Nor did they return."

There was a long quiet in the pavilion. Jaisel glanced up and encountered the wrathful glare of the captain.

"Ride home to Towers, then," she said. "What else is there to do?"

"And what other council would you predict from a woman?" broke in Renier. "We are *men*, madam. We'll take that rock, or die. Honor, lady. Did you never hear of it in the whorehouse where you were whelped?'

"You have had too much wine, sir," said Jaisel. "But by all means have some more." She poured her cup, measured and deliberate, over his curling hair. Two or three guffawed, enjoying this novelty. Renier leapt up. The captain bellowed familiarly, and Renier again relapsed.

Wine ran in rosy streams across his handsome brow.

"Truly, you do right to reprove me, and the she-wolf is right to anoint me with her scorn. We sit here like cowards, as she mentioned. There's one way to take the castle. A challenge. Single combat between God and Satan. Can the haunting of Maudras refuse that?" Renier got to his feet with precision now.

"You are drunk, Renier," the captain snapped.

"Not too drunk to fight." Renier was at the entrance. The captain roared. Renier only bowed. "I am a knight. Only so far can you command me."

"You fool—" said Cassant.

"I am, however, my own fool," said Renier.

The knights stood, witnesses to his departure. Respect, sorrow and dread showed in their eyes, their nervous fingers fiddling with jewels, wine cups, chess figures.

Outside, the dreary song had broken off. Renier was shouting for his horse and battle gear.

The knights crowded to the flap to watch him armed. Their captain elect joined them. No further protest was attempted, as if a divine ordinance were being obeyed.

Jaisel walked out of the pavilion. The light was thickening as if to hem them in. Red fires, red banners, no other color able to pierce the gloom. Renier sat his horse like a carved chess figure himself, an immaculate knight moving against a castle on a misty board.

The horse fidgeted, trembled. Jaisel ran her hand peacefully down its nose amid the litter of straps and buckles. She did not look at Renier, swaggering above her. She sensed too well his panic under the pride.

"Don't," she said to him softly, "ride into the arms of death because you think I shamed your manhood. It's too large a purge for so small an ill."

"Go away, girl," he jeered at her. "Go and have babies as God fashioned you to do."

"God did not fashion you to die, Renier of Towers."

"Maybe you're wrong in that," he said wildly, and jerked the horse around and away from her.

He was galloping from the camp across the plain toward the rock. A herald dashed out and followed, but prudently hanging some yards behind, and when he sounded the brass, the notes cracked, and his horse shied at the noise. But Renier's horse threw itself on as if in preparation for a massive jump at the end of its running.

"He's mad; will die," Cassant mumbled.

"And my fault," Jaisel answered.

A low horrified moan went through the ranks of the watchers. The iron barricades of the huge castle's mouth were sluggishly folding aside. Nothing rode forth. It was, on the contrary, patently an invitation.

One man yelled to Renier across a hundred yards of gray ground. Several swelled the cry. Suddenly, three quarters of the camp of Towers was howling. To make sport of a noble was one thing. To see him seek annihilation was another. They screamed themselves hoarse, begging him to choose reason above honor.

Jaisel, not uttering a word, turned from the spectacle. When she heard Cassant swearing, she knew Renier had galloped straight in the iron portal. The commotion of shouting crumbled into breathings, oaths. And then came the shock and clangor of two iron leaves meeting together again across the mouth of hell.

Impossible to imagine what he might be confronting now. Perhaps he would triumph, re-emerge in glory. Perhaps the evil in Maudras' castle had faded, or had never existed. Was an illusion. Or a lie.

They waited. The soldiers, the knights. The woman. A cold wind blew up, raking plumes, pennants, the long curled hair, plucking bridle bells, the gold sickle moon in Jaisel's left ear, the fragile lace at her wrists, and the foaming lace at the wrists of others.

The white sun westered, muddied, disappeared. Clouds like curds forming in milk formed in the sky.

Darkness slunk in on all fours. Mist boiled over, hiding the view of the castle. The fires burned, the horses coughed at their pickets.

There was the smell of a wet rottenness, like marshland—the mist—or rotting hope.

A young knight whose name Jaisel had forgotten was at her elbow. He thrust in her face a chess piece of red amber.

"The white queen possessed the red knight," he hissed at her. "Put him in the box then. Slam the lid. Fine chess game here in the north. Castles unbreachable and bitches for queens. Corpses for God's knights."

Jaisel stared him down till he went away. From the corner of her eye, she noticed Cassant was weeping tears, frugally, one at a time.

* * *

It was too easy to get by the sentries in the mist and dark. Of course, they were alert against the outer environs, not the camp itself. But, still too easy. Discipline was lax. Honor had become everything, and honor was not enough.

Yet it was her own honor that drove her, she was not immune. Nor immune to this sad region. She was full of guilt she had no need to feel, and full of regret for a man with whom she had shared only a mutual dislike, distrust, and some quick verbal cuts and quicker deeds of wrath. Renier had given himself to the castle, to show himself valiant, to shame her. She was duly shamed. Accordingly, she was goaded to breach the castle also, to plumb its vile secret. To save his life if she could, avenge him if not. And die if the castle should outwit her? No. Here was the strangest fancy of all. Somewhere in her bones she did not believe Maudras's castle could do that. After all, her entire life had been a succession of persons, things, fate itself, trying to vanquish her and her aims. From the first drop of menstrual blood, the first husband chosen for her at the age of twelve, the first (and last) rape, the first swordmaster who had mocked her demand to learn and ended setting wagers on her—there had been so many lions in her way. And she had systematically overcome each of them. Because she did not, *would* not, accept that destiny was unchangeable. Or that what was merely named unconquerable could not be conquered.

Maudras's castle then, just another symbol to be thrown down. And the sick-sweet twang of fear in her vitals was no more than before any battle, like an old scar throbbing, simple to ignore.

She padded across the plain noiselessly in the smoky mist. Sword on left hip, dagger on the right. Saddle and pack had been left behind beneath her blanket. Some would-be goat might suffer astonishment if he ventured to her sleeping place. Otherwise they would not detect her absence till sunrise.

The mist ceased thirty feet from the causeway.

She paused a moment, and considered the eccentric edifice pouring aloft into overcast black sky. Now the castle had a choice. It could gape invitingly as it had before Renier the challenger. Or leave her to climb the wall seventy feet high above the door mouth.

The iron barricades stayed shut.

She went along the causeway.

Gazing up, the cranky towers seemed to reel, sway. Certainly it had an aura of wickedness, of impenetrable lingering hate . . .

White queen against bishop of darkness.

Queen takes castle, a rare twist to an ancient game.

The wall.

Masonry jutted, stonework creviced, protruded. Even weeds had rooted there. It was a gift, this wall, to any who would climb it. Which implied a maleficent joke, similar to the opening doors. *Enter. Come, I welcome you. Enter me and be damned within me.*

She jumped, caught hold, began to ascend. Loose-limbed and agile from a hundred trees, some other less lordly walls, one cliff-face five years ago— Jaisel could skim up vertical buildings like a cat. She did not really require all the solicitous help Maudras's wall pressed on her.

She gained the outer battlements in minutes and was looking in. Beyond this barrier, the curtain, a courtyard with its central guard—but all pitch black, difficult to assess. Only that configuration of turrets and crooked bastions breaking clear against the sky. As before, she thought of a growth, petrified.

The sound was of ripped cloth. But it was actually ripped atmosphere. Jaisel threw her body flat on the broad parapet and something kissed the nape of her neck as it rushed by into the night. Reminiscent of a javelot bolt. Or the thicker swan-flighted arrows of the north. Without sentience, yet meant for the heart, and capable of stilling it.

She tilted herself swiftly over the parapet, hung by her fingers, and dropped seven feet to a platform below. As she landed, the tearing sound was reiterated. A violent hand tugged her arm. She glanced and beheld shredded lace barely to be seen in the blackness. The mail above her wrist was heated.

Some power which could make her out when she was nearly blind, but which seemed to attack randomly, inaccurately. She cast herself flat again and crawled on her belly to the head of a stair.

Here, descending, she became the perfect target. No matter. Her second swordmaster had been something of an acrobat—

Jaisel launched herself into air and judging where the rims of the steps should be, executed three bold erratic somersaults, arriving ultimately in a hedgehog-like roll in the court.

As she straightened from this roll, she was aware of a sudden dim glow. She spun to meet it, sword and dagger to hand, then checked, heart and gorge passing each other as they traveled in the wrong directions.

The glow was worse than sorcery. It was caused by a decaying corpse half propped in a ruined cubby under the stairs. Putrescent, the remnants gave off a phosphorescent shine, matched by an intolerable stench that seemed to intensify with recognition. And next, something else. Lit by the witch-light of dead flesh, an inscription apparently chiseled in the stone beside it. Against her wits, Jaisel could not resist studying it. In pure clerical calligraphy it read:

MAUDRAS SLEW ME.

One of Montaube's men.

Only the fighter's seventh sense warned Jaisel. It sent her ducking, darting, her sword arm sweeping up—and a great blow smashed against the blade, singing through her arm into her breast and shoulder. A great invisible blow.

The thought boiled in her—*How can I fight what I cannot see?* And the second inevitable thought: *I have always fought that way, combat with abstracts.* And in that extraordinary instant, wheeling to avoid the slashing lethal blows of a murderous nonentity, Jaisel realized that though she could not *see*, yet she could *sense*.

Perhaps twenty further backings bailed against her sword, chipped the stones around. Her arm was almost numbed, but organized and obedient as a war machine, kept up its parries, feints, deflectings, thrusts. And then, eyes nearly closed, seeing better through her instinct with a hair's-breadth, dancing-with-death accuracy, she paid out her blade the length of her arm, her body hurtling behind it, and *felt* tissue part on either side of the steel. And immediately there followed a brain-slicing shriek, more like breath forced from a bladder than the protest of a dying throat.

The way was open. She sensed this too, and shot forward, doubled over, blade swirling its precaution. A fresh doorway, the gate into the guard, yawning unbarred, and across this gate, to be leaped, a glow, a reeking skeleton, the elegant chiselling in the stone floor on this occasion:

MAUDRAS SLEW ME.

"Maudras," Jaisel shouted as she leaped.

She was in the wide hollow of the castle guard. In the huge black, which tingled and burned and flashed with colors thrown by her own racing blood against the discs of her eyes.

Then the darkness screamed, an awful shattering of notes, which brought on an avalanche, a cacophony, as if the roof fell. It took her an extra heartbeat to understand, to fling herself from the path of a charging destruction no less potent for being natural. As the guard wall met her spine, the scream-ing nightmare, Renier's horse, exploded by her and out into the court beyond the door.

She lay quiet, taking air, and something stirred against her arm. She wrenched away and raised her sword, but Montaube's ultimate glowing sol-dier was there, draped on the base of what looked to be a pillar trunk. A lamp, he shone for her as the circulatory flashes died from the interior of her eyes. So she saw Renier of Towers sprawled not a foot from her.

She kneeled, and tested the quality of the tension about her. And she interpreted from it a savoring, a cat's-paw willingness to play, to let out the leash before dragging it tight once more.

The corpse (MAUDRAS SLEW ME inscribed on the pillar) appeared to glow brighter to enable her to see the mark on Renier's forehead, like the bruise caused by some glancing bolt. A trickle of blood where formerly wine had trickled. The lids shivering, the chest rising and falling shallowly.

She leaned to him and whispered: "You live then. Your luck's kinder than I reckoned. To be stunned rather than slaughtered. And Maudras's magic waiting for you to get up again. Not liking to kill when you would not know it. Preferring to make a meal of killing you, unfair and unsquare."

Then, without preface, terror swamped the hollow pillared guard of Maudras's castle.

A hundred, ten hundred, whirling slivers of steel carved the nothingness. From the blind vault, blades swooped, seared, wailed. Jaisel was netted in a sea of death. Waves of death broke over her, gushed aside, were negated by vaster waves. She sprang from one edge and reached another. The slashing was like the beaks of birds, scoring hands, cheeks; scratches as yet, but peck-ing, diligent. While, in its turn, her sword sank miles deep in substances like mud, like powder. Subhuman voices squalled. Unseen shapes tottered. But the rain of bites of pecks, of scratches, whirled her this way, that way, against pillars, broken stones, downward, upward. And she was in terror. Fought in terror. Terror lent her miraculous skills, feats, and a crazy flailing will to survive, and a high wild cry which again and again she smote the darkness with, along with dagger and sword.

Till abruptly she could no longer fight. Her limbs melted and terror melted with them into a worse state of abject exhaustion, acceptance, resig-nation. Her spirit sank, she sank, the sword sank from one hand, the dagger from the other. Drowning, she thought stubbornly: Die fighting, at least. But she did not have the strength left her.

Not until that moment did she grow aware of the cessation of blows, the silence.

She had stumbled against, was partly leaning on, some upright block of stone that had been in her way when she dropped. Dully, her mind struggled with a paradox that would not quite resolve. She had been battling shadows, which had slain others instantly, but had not slain Jaisel. Surely what she supposed was a game had gone on too long for a game. While in earnest, now she was finished, the mechanism for butchery in this castle might slay her, yet did not. And swimming wonder surfaced scornfully: Am I charmed?

There was a light. Not the phosphorus of Montaube's soldiers. It was a light the color the wretched country had been by day, a sallow snow-blue glaze, dirty silver on the columns, coming up like a Sabbat moon from out of nowhere.

Jaisel stared into the light, and perceived a face floating in it. No doubt. It must be the countenance of burned Maudras, the last malicious dregs of his spirit on holiday from hell to effect menace. More skull than man. Eye sockets faintly gleaming, mouth taut as if in agony.

With loathing and aversion, and with horror, the skull regarded her. It seemed, perversely, to instruct her to shift her gaze downward, to the stone block where she leaned powerlessly.

And something in the face ridiculously amused her, made her shake with laughter, shudder with it, so that she knew before she looked.

The light was snuffed a second later.

Then the castle began, in rumbling stages, to collapse on every side. Matter-of-factly, she went to Renier and lay over his unconscious body to protect him from the cascading granite.

* * *

He was not grateful as she bathed his forehead at the chill pool equidistant between the ruin and the camp of Towers.

Nearby, the horse licked the grudging turf. The mist had fled, and a rose-crimson sun was blooming on the horizon. A hundred yards off, the camp gave evidence of enormous turmoil. Renier swore at her.

"Am I to credit that a strumpet nullified the sorcery of Maudras? Don't feed me that stew."

"You suffer it too hardly. As ever," said Jaisel, honed to patience by the events of the night. "Any woman might have achieved this thing. But women warriors are uncommon."

"There is one too many, indeed."

Jaisel stood. She started to walk away. Renier called after her huskily:

"Wait. Say to me again what was written in the stone."

Her back to him, she halted. Concisely, wryly smiling, she said: "I, Maudras, to this castle do allot my everlasting bane, that no man shall ever approach its walls without hurt, nor enter it and live long. Nor, to the world's ending, shall it be taken by any *man*."

Renier snarled.

She did not respond to that, but walked on.

Presently he caught up to her, and striding at her side, said: "How many other prophecies could be undone, do you judge, lady Insolence, that dismiss women in such fashion?"

"As many as there are stars in heaven," she said.

Brooding, but no longer arguing, he escorted her into the camp.

KARIN TIDBECK

Aunts

Karin Tidbeck is a Swedish writer who has published short stories and poetry in Swedish since 2002, and in English since 2010. Her 2010 book debut, the short-story collection *Vem är Arvid Pekon?*, was awarded the coveted one-year working grant from the Swedish Authors' Fund. Her English-language collection *Jagannath* (2012) won the Crawford Award and was short-listed for the James Tiptree, Jr Memorial Award. Her English publication history includes *Weird Tales, Shimmer Magazine, Tor.com, Lightspeed, Strange Horizons,* and *Unstuck Annual.* The strangely surreal "Aunts" shows the passages of rituals and history from one generation to another. It was first published in *ODD?* in 2011.

In some places, time is a weak and occasional phenomenon. Unless someone claims time to pass, it might not, or does so only partly; events curl in on themselves to form spirals and circles.

The orangery is one such place. It is located in an apple orchard, which lies at the outskirts of a garden. The air is damp and laden with the yeasty sweetness of overripe fruit. Gnarled apple trees with bright yellow leaves flame against the cold and purpling sky. Red globes hang heavy on their branches. The orangery gets no visitors. The orchard belongs to a particular regent whose gardens are mostly populated by turgid nobles completely uninterested in the orchard. It has no servants, no entertainment. It requires walking, and the fruit is mealy.

But in the event someone did walk in among the trees, they would find them marching on for a very long time, every tree almost identical to the other. (Should that someone try to count the fruit, they would also find that each tree has the exact same number of apples.) If this visitor did not turn around and flee for the safety of the more cultivated parts of the gardens, they would eventually see the trees disperse and the silver-and-glass bubble of an orangery rise out of the ground. Drawing closer, they would have seen this:

* * *

The inside of the glass walls were covered by a thin brown film of fat vapour and breath. Inside, fifteen orange trees stood along the curve of the cupola; fifteen smaller, potted trees made a circle inside the first. Marble covered the center, where three bolstered divans sat surrounded by low round tables. The divans sagged under the weight of three gigantic women.

The Aunts had one single holy task: to expand. They slowly accumulated layers of fat. A thigh bisected would reveal a pattern of concentric rings, the fat colored different hues. On the middle couch reclined Great-Aunt, who was the largest of the three. Her body flowed down from her head like waves of whipped cream, arms and legs mere nubs protruding from her magnificent mass.

Great-Aunt's sisters lay on either side. Middle Sister, her stomach cascading over her knees like a blanket, was eating little link sausages one by one, like a string of pearls. Little Sister, not noticeably smaller than the others, peeled the lid off a meat pie. Great-Aunt extended an arm, letting her fingers slowly sink into the pie's naked interior. She scooped up a fistful of dark filling and buried her face in it with a sigh. Little Sister licked the inside clean of the rest of the filling, then carefully folded it four times and slowly pushed it into her mouth. She snatched up a new link of sausages. She opened and scraped the filling from the skin with her teeth, then threw the empty skins aside. Great-Aunt sucked at the mouthpiece of a thin tube snaking up from a samovar on the table. The salty mist of melted butter rose up from the lid on the pot. She occasionally paused to twist her head and accept small marrow biscuits from one of the three girls hovering near the couches.

The grey-clad girls quietly moving through the orangery were Nieces. In the kitchens under the orangery, they baked sumptuous pastries and cakes; they fed and cleaned their Aunts. They had no individual names and were indistinguishable from each other, often even to themselves. The Nieces lived on leftovers from the Aunts: licking up crumbs mopped from Great-Aunt's chin, drinking the dregs of the butter samovar. The Aunts did not leave much, but the Nieces did not need much either.

* * *

Great-Aunt could no longer expand, which was as it should be. Her skin, which had previously lain in soft folds around her, was stretched taut over the fat pushing outward from inside. Great-Aunt raised her eyes from her vast body and looked at her sisters who each nodded in turn. The Nieces stepped forward, removing the pillows that held the Aunts upright. As she lay back, Great-Aunt began to shudder. She closed her eyes and her mouth became slack. A dark line appeared along her abdomen. As it reached her groin, she became still. With a soft sigh, the skin split along the line. Layer after layer of skin, fat, muscle, and membrane broke open until the breastbone was exposed and fell open with a wet crack. Golden blood washed out of the wound, splashing onto the couch and onto the floor, where it was caught in a shallow trough. The Nieces went to work, carefully scooping out organs and entrails. Deep in the cradle of her ribs lay a wrinkled pink shape, arms and legs wrapped around Great-Aunt's heart. It opened its eyes and squealed as the Nieces lifted away the last of the surrounding tissue. They cut away the heart with the new Aunt still clinging to it, and placed her on a small pillow where she settled down and began to chew on the heart with tiny teeth.

The Nieces sorted intestines, liver, lungs, kidneys, bladder, uterus, and stomach; they were each put in separate bowls. Next they removed Aunt's skin. It came off easily in great sheets, ready to be cured and tanned and made into one of three new dresses. Then it was time for removing the fat: first the wealth of Aunt's enormous breasts, then her voluminous belly, her thighs; last, her flattened buttocks. The Nieces teased muscle loose from the bones; it needed not much force, but almost fell into their hands. Finally, the bones themselves, soft and translucent, were chopped up into manage- able bits. When all this was done, the Nieces turned to Middle and Little Sister who were waiting on their couches, still and wide open. Everything neatly divided into pots and tubs; the Nieces scrubbed the couches and on them lay the new Aunts, each still busy chewing on the remains of a heart.

The Nieces retreated to the kitchens under the orangery. They melted and clarified the fat, ground the bones into fine flour, chopped and baked the organ meats, soaked the sweetbreads in vinegar, simmered the muscle until the meat fell apart in flakes, cleaned out and hung the intestines to dry. Nothing was wasted. The Aunts were baked into cakes and pâtés and pastries and little savoury sausages and dumplings and crackling. The new Aunts would be very hungry and very pleased.

* * *

Neither the Nieces nor the Aunts saw it happen, but someone made their way through the apple trees and reached the orangery. The Aunts were getting a bath. The Nieces sponged the expanses of skin with lukewarm rose water. The quiet of the orangery was replaced by the drip and splash of water, the clunk of copper buckets, the grunts of Nieces straining to move flesh out of the way. They didn't see the curious face pressed against the glass, greasy corkscrew locks drawing filigree traces: a hand landing next to the staring face, cradling a round metal object. Nor did they at first hear the quiet, irregular ticking noise the object made. It wasn't until the ticking noise, first slow, then faster, amplified and filled the air, that an Aunt opened her eyes and listened. The Nieces turned toward the orangery wall. There was nothing there, save for a handprint and a smudge of white.

* * *

Great-Aunt could no longer expand. Her skin was stretched taut over the fat pushing outward from inside. Great-Aunt raised her eyes from her vast body and looked at her sisters, who each nodded in turn. The Nieces stepped forward, removing the pillows that held the Aunts upright.

The Aunts gasped and wheezed. Their abdomens were a smooth, unbroken expanse: there was no trace of the telltale dark line. Great-Aunt's face turned a reddish blue as her own weight pressed down on her throat. Her shivers turned into convulsions. Then, suddenly, her breathing ceased altogether and her eyes stilled. On either side, her sisters rattled out their final breaths in concert.

The Nieces stared at the quiet bodies. They stared at each other. One of them raised her knife.

* * *

As the Nieces worked, the more they removed from Great-Aunt, the clearer it became that something was wrong. The flesh wouldn't give willingly, but had to be forced apart. They resorted to using shears to open the ribcage. Finally, as they were scraping the last of the tissue from Great-Aunts thigh bones, one of them said:

"I do not see a little Aunt."

"She should be here," said another.

They looked at each other. The third burst into tears. One of the others slapped the crying girl's head.

"We should look further," said the one who had slapped her sister. "She could be behind the eyes."

The Nieces dug further into Great-Aunt; they peered into her skull, but found nothing. They dug into the depths of her pelvis, but there was no new Aunt. Not knowing what else to do, they finished the division of the body, then moved on to the other Aunts. When the last of the three had been opened, dressed, quartered, and scraped, no new Aunt had yet been found. By now, the orangery's floor was filled with tubs of neatly ordered meat and offal. Some of the younger orange trees had fallen over and were soaking in golden blood. One of the Nieces, possibly the one who had slapped her sister, took a bowl and looked at the others.

"We have work to do," she said.

* * *

The Nieces scrubbed the orangery floor and cleaned the couches. They turned every last bit of the Aunts into a feast. They carried platters of food from the kitchens and laid it out on the surrounding tables. The couches were still empty. One of the Nieces sat down in the middle couch. She took a meat pastry and nibbled at it. The rich flavour of Great-Aunt's baked liver burst into her mouth; the pastry shell melted on her tongue. She crammed the rest of the pastry into her mouth and swallowed. When she opened her eyes, the other Nieces stood frozen in place, watching her.

"We must be the new Aunts now," the first Niece said.

One of the others considered this. "Mustn't waste it," she said, eventually.

The new Aunts sat down on Middle Sister and Little Sister's couches and tentatively reached for the food on the tables. Like their sister, they took first little bites, then bigger and bigger as the taste of the old Aunts filled them. Never before had they been allowed to eat from the tables. They ate until they couldn't down another bite. They slept. When they woke up, they fetched more food from the kitchen. The orangery was quiet save for the noise of chewing and swallowing. One Niece took an entire cake and buried her face in it, eating it from the inside out. Another rubbed marinated brain onto herself, as if to absorb it. Sausages, slices of tongue topped with jellied marrow, candied eyes that crunched and then melted. The girls ate and ate until the kitchen was empty and the floor covered in a layer of crumbs and drippings. They lay back on the couches and looked at each other's bodies, measuring bellies and legs. None of them were noticeably fatter.

"It's not working," said the girl on the leftmost couch. "We ate them all up and it's not working!" She burst into tears.

The middle girl pondered this. "Aunts can't be Aunts without Nieces," she said.

"But where do we find Nieces?" said the rightmost. "Where did we come from?" The other two were silent.

"We could make them," said the middle girl. "We are good at baking, after all."

And so the prospective Aunts swept up the crumbs from floor and plates, mopped up juices and bits of jelly, and returned with the last remains of the old Aunts to the kitchens. They made a dough and fashioned it into three girl-shaped cakes, baked them and glazed them. When the cakes were done, they were a crisp light brown and the size of a hand. The would-be Aunts took the cakes up to the orangery and set them down on the floor, one beside each couch. They wrapped themselves in the Aunt-skins, and lay down on their couches to wait.

* * *

Outside, the apple trees rattled their leaves in a faint breeze. On the other side of the apple orchard was a loud party, where a gathering of nobles played croquet with human heads, and their changeling servants hid under the tables, telling each other stories to keep the fear away. No sound of this reached the orangery, quiet in the steady gloom. No smell of apples snuck in between the panes. The Aunt-skins settled in soft folds around the sleeping girls.

Eventually one of them woke. The girl-shaped cakes lay on the floor, like before.

The middle girl crawled out of the folds of the skin dress and set her feet down on the floor. She picked up the cake sitting on the floor next to her.

"Perhaps we should eat them," she said. "And the Nieces will grow inside us." But her voice was faint.

"Or wait," said the leftmost girl. "They may yet move."

"They may," the middle girl says.

The girls sat on their couches, cradled in the skin dresses, and waited. They fell asleep and woke up again, and waited.

* * *

In some places, time is a weak and occasional phenomenon. Unless someone claims time to pass, it might not, or does so only partly; events curl in on themselves to form spirals and circles.

The Nieces wake and wait, wake and wait, for Aunts to arrive.

URSULA K. LE GUIN

Sur

Ursula K. Le Guin is an American writer. An iconic figure in fantasy, science fiction, and general fiction, she has published over twenty novels, eleven volumes of short stories, four collections of essays, twelve books for children, six volumes of poetry, and four books in translation. Le Guin has received many honors and awards including the Hugo, Nebula, National Book Award, and PEN/Malamud. Her recent publications include *Finding My Elegy: New and Selected Poems, 1960–2010* and *The Unreal and the Real: Selected Stories*. "Sur" is a report of an early journey to Antarctica that is quietly revealed to be manned by an all-female team of adventurers. It was first published in the *New Yorker* in 1982.

A SUMMARY REPORT
OF THE *YELCHO* EXPEDITION
TO THE ANTARCTIC, 1909–1910

Although I have no intention of publishing this report, I think it would be nice if a grandchild of mine, or somebody's grandchild, happened to find it some day; so I shall keep it in the leather trunk in the attic, along with Rosita's christening dress and Juanito's silver rattle and my wedding shoes and finneskos.

The first requisite for mounting an expedition—money—is normally the hardest to come by. I grieve that even in a report destined for a trunk in the attic of a house in a very quiet suburb of Lima I dare not write the name of the generous benefactor, the great soul without whose unstinting liberality the *Yelcho* Expedition would never have been more than the idlest excursion into daydream. That our equipment was the best and most modern—that our

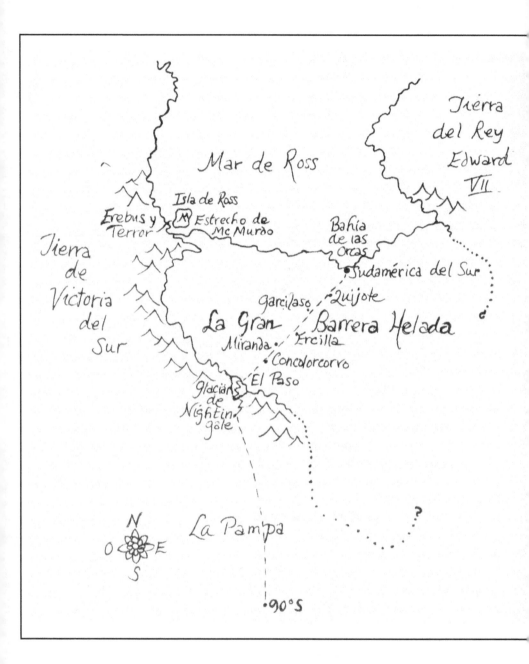

The Map in the Attic

provisions were plentiful and fine—that a ship of the Chilean Government, with her brave officers and gallant crew, was twice sent halfway round the world for our convenience: all this is due to that benefactor whose name, alas! I must not say, but whose happiest debtor I shall be till death.

When I was little more than a child my imagination was caught by a newspaper account of the voyage of the *Belgica*, which, sailing south from Tierra del Fuego, became beset by ice in the Bellingshausen Sea and drifted a whole year with the floe, the men aboard her suffering a great deal from want of food and from the terror of the unending winter darkness. I read and reread that account, and later followed with excitement the reports of the rescue of Dr. Nordenskjold from the South Shetland Isles by the dashing Captain Irizar of the *Uruguay*, and the adventures of the *Scotia* in the Weddell Sea. But all these exploits were to me but forerunners of the British National Antarctic Expedition of 1902–1904, in the *Discovery*, and the wonderful account of that expedition by Captain Scott. This book, which I ordered from London and reread a thousand times, filled me with longing to see with my own eyes that strange continent, last Thule of the South, which lies on our maps and globes like a white cloud, a void, fringed here and there with scraps of coastline, dubious capes, supposititious islands, headlands that may or may not be there: Antarctica. And the desire was as pure as the polar snows: to go, to see—no more, no less. I deeply respect the scientific accomplishments of Captain Scott's expedition, and have read with passionate interest the findings of physicists, meteorologists, biologists, etc.; but having had no training in any science, nor any opportunity for such training, my ignorance obliged me to forego any thought of adding to the body of scientific knowledge concerning Antarctica; and the same is true for all the members of my expedition. It seems a pity; but there was nothing we could do about it. Our goal was limited to observation and exploration. We hoped to go a little farther, perhaps, and see a little more; if not, simply to go and to see. A simple ambition, I think, and essentially a modest one.

Yet it would have remained less than an ambition, no more than a longing, but for the support and encouragement of my dear cousin and friend Juana ——. (I use no surnames, lest this report fall into strangers' hands at last, and embarrassment or unpleasant notoriety thus be brought upon unsuspecting husbands, sons, etc.) I had lent Juana my copy of *The Voyage of the Discovery*, and it was she who, as we strolled beneath our parasols across the Plaza de Armas after Mass one Sunday in 1908, said, "Well, if Captain Scott can do it, why can't we?"

It was Juana who proposed that we write Carlotta —— in Valparaiso. Through Carlota we met our benefactor, and so obtained our money, our ship, and even the plausible pretext of going on retreat in a Bolivian convent, which some of us were forced to employ (while the rest of us said we were going to Paris for the winter season). And it was my Juana who in the darkest moments remained resolute, unshaken in her determination to achieve our goal.

And there were dark moments, especially in the early months of 1909—times when I did not see how the Expedition would ever become more than a quarter ton of pemmican gone to waste and a lifelong regret. It was so very hard to gather our expeditionary force together! So few of those we asked even knew what we were talking about—so many thought we were mad, or wicked, or both! And of those few who shared our folly, still fewer were able, when it came to the point, to leave their daily duties and commit themselves to a voyage of at least six months, attended with not inconsiderable uncertainty and danger. An ailing parent; an anxious husband beset by business cares; a child at home with only ignorant or incompetent servants to look after it: these are not responsibilities lightly to be set aside. And those who wished to evade such claims were not the companions we wanted in hard work, risk, and privation.

But since success crowned our efforts, why dwell on the setbacks and delays, or the wretched contrivances and downright lies that we all had to employ? I look back with regret only to those friends who wished to come with us but could not, by any contrivance, get free—those we had to leave behind to a life without danger, without uncertainty, without hope.

On the seventeenth of August, 1909, in Punta Arenas, Chile, all the members of the Expedition met for the first time: Juana and I, the two Peruvians; from Argentina, Zoe, Berta, and Teresa; and our Chileans, Carlota and her friends Eva, Pepita, and Dolores. At the last moment I had received word that Maria's husband, in Quito, was ill, and she must stay to nurse him, so we were nine, not ten. Indeed, we had resigned ourselves to being but eight, when, just as night fell, the indomitable Zoe arrived in a tiny pirogue manned by Indians, her yacht having sprung a leak just as it entered the Strait of Magellan.

That night before we sailed we began to get to know one another; and we agreed, as we enjoyed our abominable supper in the abominable seaport inn of Punta Arenas, that if a situation arose of such urgent danger that one voice must be obeyed without present question, the unenviable honor of speaking with that voice should fall first upon myself: if I were incapacitated, upon Carlota: if she, then upon Berta. We three were then toasted as "Supreme Inca," "La Araucana," and "The Third Mate" among a lot of laughter and cheering. As it came out, to my very great pleasure and relief, my qualities as a "leader" were never tested; the nine of us worked things out amongst us from beginning to end without any orders being given by anybody, and only two or three times with recourse to a vote by voice or show of hands. To be sure, we argued a good deal. But then, we had time to argue. And one way or another the arguments always ended up in a decision, upon which action could be taken. Usually at least one person grumbled about the decision, sometimes bitterly. But what is life without grumbling, and the occasional opportunity to say, "I told you so"? How could one bear housework, or looking after babies, let alone the rigors of sledge-hauling in Antarctica, without grumbling? Officers—as we came to understand aboard the *Yelcho*—are forbidden to grumble; but we nine were, and are, by birth and upbringing, unequivocally and irrevocably, all crew.

Though our shortest course to the southern continent, and that originally urged upon us by the captain of our good ship, was to the South Shetlands and the Bellingshausen Sea, or else by the South Orkneys into the Weddell Sea, we planned to sail west to the Ross Sea, which Captain Scott had explored and described, and from which the brave Ernest Shackleton had returned only the previous autumn. More was known about this region than any other portion of the coast of Antarctica, and though that more was not much, yet it served as some insurance of the safety of the ship, which we felt we had no right to imperil. Captain Pardo had fully agreed with us after studying the charts and our planned itinerary; and so it was westward that we took our course out of the Strait next morning.

Our journey half round the globe was attended by fortune. The little *Yelcho* steamed cheerily along through gale and gleam, climbing up and down those seas of the Southern Ocean that run unbroken round the world. Juana, who had fought bulls and the far more dangerous cows on her family's *estancia*, called the ship "*la vaca valiente*," because she always returned to the charge. Once we got over being seasick we all enjoyed the sea voyage, though oppressed at times by the kindly but officious protectiveness of the captain and his officers, who felt that we were only "safe" when huddled up in the three tiny cabins which they had chivalrously vacated for our use.

We saw our first iceberg much farther south than we had looked for it, and saluted it with Veuve Clicquot at dinner. The next day we entered the ice pack, the belt of floes and bergs, broken loose from the land ice and winter-frozen seas of Antarctica, which drifts northward in the spring. Fortune still smiled on us: our little steamer, incapable, with her unreinforced metal hull, of forcing a way into the ice, picked her way from lane to lane without hesitation, and on the third day we were through the pack, in which ships have sometimes struggled for weeks and been obliged to turn back at last. Ahead of us now lay the dark grey waters of the Ross Sea, and beyond that, on the horizon, the remote glimmer, the cloud-reflected whiteness of the Great Ice Barrier.

Entering the Ross Sea a little east of Longitude West 160°, we came in sight of the Barrier at the place where Captain Scott's party, finding a bight in the vast wall of ice, had gone ashore and sent up their hydrogen-gas balloon for reconnaissance and photography. The towering face of the Barrier, its sheer cliffs and azure and violet water-worn caves, all were as described, but the location had changed: instead of a narrow bight there was a considerable bay, full of the beautiful and terrific orca whales playing and spouting in the sunshine of that brilliant southern spring.

Evidently masses of ice many acres in extent had broken away from the Barrier (which—at least for most of its vast extent—does not rest on land but floats on water) since the *Discovery*'s passage in 1902. This put our plan to set up camp on the Barrier itself in a new light; and while we were discussing alternatives, we asked Captain Pardo to take the ship west along the Barrier face towards Ross Island and McMurdo Sound. As the sea was clear of ice and quite calm, he was happy to do so, and, when we sighted the smoke plume of Mount Erebus, to share in our celebration—another half case of Veuve Clicquot.

The *Yelcho* anchored in Arrival Bay, and we went ashore in the ship's boat. I cannot describe my emotions when I set foot on the earth, on that earth, the barren, cold gravel at the foot of the long volcanic slope. I felt elation, impatience, gratitude, awe, familiarity. I felt that I was home at last. Eight Addlie penguins immediately came to greet us with many exclamations of interest not unmixed with disapproval. "Where on earth have you been? What took you so long? The Hut is around this way. Please come this way. Mind the rocks!" They insisted on our going to visit Hut Point, where the large structure built by Captain Scott's party stood, looking just as in the photographs and drawings that illustrate his book. The area about it, however, was disgusting—a kind of graveyard of seal skins, seal bones, penguin bones, and rubbish, presided over by the mad, screaming skua gulls. Our escorts waddled past the slaughterhouse in all tranquility, and one showed me personally to the door, though it would not go in.

The interior of the hut was less offensive, but very dreary. Boxes of supplies had been stacked up into a kind of room within the room; it did not look as I had imagined it when the *Discovery* party put on their melodramas and minstrel shows in the long winter night. (Much later, we learned that Sir Ernest had rearranged it a good deal when he was there just a year before us.) It was dirty, and had about it a mean disorder. A pound tin of tea was standing open. Empty meat tins lay about; biscuits were spilled on the floor; a lot of dog turds were underfoot—frozen, of course, but not a great deal improved by that. No doubt the last occupants had had to leave in a hurry, perhaps even in a blizzard. All the same, they could have closed the tea tin. But housekeeping, the art of the infinite, is no game for amateurs.

Teresa proposed that we use the hut as our camp. Zoe counterproposed that we set fire to it. We finally shut the door and left it as we had found it. The penguins appeared to approve, and cheered us all the way to the boat.

McMurdo Sound was free of ice, and Captain Pardo now proposed to take us off Ross Island and across to Victoria Land, where we might camp at the foot of the Western Mountains, on dry and solid earth. But those mountains, with their storm-darkened peaks and hanging cirques and glaciers, looked as awful as Captain Scott had found them on his western journey, and none of us felt much inclined to seek shelter among them.

Aboard the ship that night we decided to go back and set up our base as we had originally planned, on the Barrier itself. For all available reports indicated that the clear way south was across the level Barrier surface until one could ascend one of the confluent glaciers to the high plateau which appears to form the whole interior of the continent. Captain Pardo argued strongly against this plan, asking what would become of us if the Barrier "calved"—if our particular acre of ice broke away and started to drift northward. "Well," said Zoe, "then you won't have to come so far to meet us." But he was so persuasive on this theme that he persuaded himself into leaving one of the *Yelcho*'s boats with us when we camped, as a means of escape. We found it useful for fishing, later on.

My first steps on Antarctic soil, my only visit to Ross Island, had not been pleasure unalloyed. I thought of the words of the English poet:
Though every prospect pleases,
And only Man is vile.

But then, the backside of heroism is often rather sad; women and servants know that. They know also that the heroism may be no less real for that. But achievement is smaller than men think. What is large is the sky, the earth, the sea, the soul I looked back as the ship sailed east again that evening. We were well into September now, with ten hours or more of daylight. The spring sunset lingered on the twelve-thousand-foot peak of Erebus and shone rosy gold on her long plume of steam. The steam from our own small funnel faded blue on the twilit water as we crept along under the towering pale wall of ice.

On our return to "Orca Bay"—Sir Ernest, we learned years later, had named it the Bay of Whales—we found a sheltered nook where the Barrier edge was low enough to provide fairly easy access from the ship. The *Yelcho* put out her ice anchor, and the next long, hard days were spent in unloading our supplies and setting up our camp on the ice, a half kilometer in from the edge: a task in which the *Yelcho*'s crew lent us invaluable aid and interminable advice. We took all the aid gratefully, and most of the advice with salt.

The weather so far had been extraordinarily mild for spring in this latitude; the temperature had not yet gone below –20° Fahrenheit, and there was only one blizzard while we were setting up camp. But Captain Scott had spoken feelingly of the bitter south winds on the Barrier, and we had planned accordingly. Exposed as our camp was to every wind, we built no rigid structures above ground. We set up tents to shelter in while we dug out a series of cubicles in the ice itself, lined them with hay insulation and pine boarding, and roofed them with canvas over bamboo poles, covered with snow for weight and insulation. The big central room was instantly named Buenos Aires by our Argentineans, to whom the center, wherever one is, is always Buenos Aires. The heating and cooking stove was in Buenos Aires. The storage tunnels and the privy (called Punta Arenas) got some back heat from the stove. The sleeping cubicles opened off Buenos Aires, and were very small, mere tubes into which one crawled feet first; they were lined deeply with hay and soon warmed by one's body warmth. The sailors called them "coffins" and "wormholes," and looked with horror on our burrows in the ice. But our little warren or prairie-dog village served us well, permitting us as much warmth and privacy as one could reasonably expect under the circumstances. If the *Yelcho* was unable to get through the ice in February, and we had to spend the winter in Antarctica, we certainly could do so, though on very limited rations. For this coming summer, our base—Sudamérica del Sur, South South America, but we generally called it the Base—was intended merely as a place to sleep, to store our provisions, and to give shelter from blizzards.

To Berta and Eva, however, it was more than that. They were its chief architect-designers, its most ingenious builder-excavators, and its most diligent and contented occupants, forever inventing an improvement in ventilation, or learning how to make skylights, or revealing to us a new addition to our suite of rooms, dug in the living ice. It was thanks to them that our stores were stowed so handily, that our stove drew and heated so efficiently, and that Buenos Aires, where nine people cooked, ate, worked, conversed, argued, grumbled, painted, played the guitar and banjo, and kept the Expedition's library of books and maps, was a marvel of comfort and convenience. We lived there in real amity; and if you simply had to be alone for a while, you crawled into your sleeping hole head first.

Berta went a little farther. When she had done all she could to make South South America livable, she dug out one more cell just under the ice surface, leaving a nearly transparent sheet of ice like a greenhouse roof; and there, alone, she worked at sculptures. They were beautiful forms, some like a blending of the reclining human figure with the subtle curves and volumes of the Weddell seal, others like the fantastic shapes of ice cornices and ice caves. Perhaps they are there still, under the snow, in the bubble in the Great Barrier. There where she made them they might last as long as stone. But she could not bring them north. That is the penalty for carving in water.

Captain Pardo was reluctant to leave us, but his orders did not permit him to hang about the Ross Sea indefinitely, and so at last, with many earnest injunctions to us to stay put—make no journeys—take no risks—beware of frostbite—don't use edge tools—look out for cracks in the ice—and a heartfelt promise to return to Orca Bay on the twentieth of February, or as near that date as wind and ice would permit, the good man bade us farewell, and his crew shouted us a great goodbye cheer as they weighed anchor. That evening, in the long orange twilight of October, we saw the topmast of the *Yelcho* go down the north horizon, over the edge of the world, leaving us to ice, and silence, and the Pole.

That night we began to plan the Southern Journey.

The ensuing month passed in short practice trips and depot-laying. The life we had led at home, though in its own way strenuous, had not fitted any of us for the kind of strain met with in sledge-hauling at ten or twenty degrees below freezing. We all needed as much working-out as possible before we dared undertake a long haul.

My longest exploratory trip, made with Dolores and Carlota, was southwest towards Mount Markham, and it was a nightmare—blizzards and pressure ice all the way out, crevasses and no view of the mountains when we got there, and white weather and sastrugi all the way back. The trip was useful, however, in that we could begin to estimate our capacities; and also in that we had started out with a very heavy load of provisions, which we depoted at 100 and 130 miles SSW of Base. Thereafter other parties pushed on farther, till we had a line of snow cairns and depots right down to Latitude 83° 43', where Juana and Zoe, on an exploring trip, had found a kind of stone gateway opening on a great glacier leading south. We established these depots to avoid, if possible, the hunger that had bedeviled Captain Scott's Southern Party, and the consequent misery and weakness. And we also established to our own satisfaction—intense satisfaction—that we were sledgehaulers at least as good as Captain Scott's husky dogs. Of course we could not have expected to pull as much or as fast as his men. That we did so was because we were favored by much better weather than Captain Scott's party ever met on the Barrier; and also the quantity and quality of our food made a very considerable difference. I am sure that the fifteen percent of dried fruits in our pemmican helped prevent scurvy; and the potatoes, frozen and dried according to an ancient Andean Indian method, were very nourishing yet very light and compact— perfect sledging rations. In any case, it was with considerable confidence in our capacities that we made ready at last for the Southern Journey.

The Southern Party consisted of two sledge teams: Juana, Dolores, and myself; Carlota, Pepita, and Zoe. The support team of Berta, Eva, and Teresa set out before us with a heavy load of supplies, going right up onto the glacier to prospect routes and leave depots of supplies for our return journey. We followed five days behind them, and met them returning between Depot Ercilla and Depot Miranda (see map). That "night"—of course there was no real darkness—we were all nine together in the heart of the level plain of ice. It was the fifteenth of November, Dolores's birthday. We celebrated by putting eight ounces of pisco in the hot chocolate, and became very merry. We sang. It is strange now to remember how thin our voices sounded in that great silence. It was overcast, white weather, without shadows and without visible horizon or any feature to break the level; there was nothing to see at all. We had come to that white place on the map, that void, and there we flew and sang like sparrows.

After sleep and a good breakfast the Base Party continued north, and the Southern Party sledged on. The sky cleared presently. High up, thin clouds passed over very rapidly from southwest to northeast, but down on the Barrier it was calm and just cold enough, five or ten degrees below freezing, to give a firm surface for hauling.

On the level ice we never pulled less than eleven miles, seventeen kilometers, a day, and generally fifteen or sixteen miles, twenty-five kilometers. (Our instruments, being British made, were calibrated in feet, miles, degrees Fahrenheit, etc., but we often converted miles to kilometers because the larger numbers sounded more encouraging.) At the time we left South America, we knew only that Mr. Shackleton had mounted another expedition to the Antarctic in 1908, had tried to attain the Pole but failed, and had returned to England in June of the current year, 1909. No coherent report of his explorations had yet reached South America when we left; we did not know what route he had gone, or how far he had got. But we were not altogether taken by surprise when, far across the featureless white plain, tiny beneath the mountain peaks and the strange silent flight of the rainbow-fringed cloud wisps, we saw a fluttering dot of black. We turned west from our course to visit it: a snow heap nearly buried by the winter's storms—a flag on a bamboo pole, a mere shred of threadbare cloth—an empty oilcan—and a few footprints standing some inches above the ice. In some conditions of weather the snow compressed under one's weight remains when the surrounding soft snow melts or is scoured away by the wind; and so these reversed footprints had been left standing all these months, like rows of cobbler's lasts—a queer sight.

We met no other such traces on our way. In general I believe our course was somewhat east of Mr. Shackleton's. Juana, our surveyor, had trained herself well and was faithful and methodical in her sightings and readings, but our equipment was minimal—a theodolite on tripod legs, a sextant with artificial horizon, two compasses, and chronometers. We had only the wheel meter on the sledge to give distance actually traveled.

In any case, it was the day after passing Mr. Shackleton's waymark that I first saw clearly the great glacier among the mountains to the southwest, which was to give us a pathway from the sea level of the Barrier up to the altiplano, ten thousand feet above. The approach was magnificent a gateway formed by immense vertical domes and pillars of rock. Zoe and Juana had called the vast ice river that flowed through that gateway the Florence Nightingale Glacier, wishing to honor the British, who had been the inspiration and guide of our expedition; that very brave and very peculiar lady seemed to represent so much that is best and strangest, in the island race. On maps, of course, this glacier bears the name Mr. Shackleton gave it, the Beardmore.

The ascent of the Nightingale was not easy. The way was open at first, and well marked by our support party, but after some days we came among terrible crevasses, a maze of hidden cracks, from a foot to thirty feet wide and from thirty to a thousand feet deep. Step by step we went, and step by step, and the way always upward now. We were fifteen days on the glacier. At first the weather was hot, up to 20° F., and the hot nights without darkness were wretchedly uncomfortable in our small tents. And all of us suffered more or less from snowblindness just at the time when we wanted clear eyesight to pick our way among the ridges and crevasses of the tortured ice, and to see the wonders about and before us. For at every day's advance more great, nameless peaks came into view in the west and southwest, summit beyond summit, range beyond range, stark rock and snow in the unending noon.

We gave names to these peaks, not very seriously, since we did not expect our discoveries to come to the attention of geographers. Zoe had a gift for naming, and it is thanks to her that certain sketch maps in various suburban South American attics bear such curious features as "Bolivar's Big Nose," "I Am General Rosas," "The Cloudmaker," "Whose Toe?" and "Throne of Our Lady of the Southern Cross." And when at last we got up onto the altiplano, the great interior plateau, it was Zoe who called it the pampa, and maintained that we walked there among vast herds of invisible cattle, transparent cattle pastured on the spindrift snow, their gauchos the restless, merciless

winds. We were by then all a little crazy with exhaustion and the great alti-
tude—twelve thousand feet—and the cold and the wind blowing and the
luminous circles and crosses surrounding the suns, for often there were three
or four suns in the sky, up there.

That is not a place where people have any business to be. We should have
turned back; but since we had worked so hard to get there, it seemed that we
should go on, at least for a while.

A blizzard came with very low temperatures, so we had to stay in the
tents, in our sleeping bags, for thirty hours, a rest we all needed; though it
was warmth we needed most, and there was no warmth on that terrible plain
anywhere at all but in our veins. We huddled close together all that time. The
ice we lay on is two miles thick.

It cleared suddenly and became, for the plateau, good weather: twelve
below zero and the wind not very strong. We three crawled out of our tent
and met the others crawling out of theirs. Carlota told us then that her
group wished to turn back. Pepita had been feeling very ill; even after the
rest during the blizzard, her temperature would not rise above 94°. Carlota
was having trouble breathing. Zoe was perfectly fit, but much preferred
staying with her friends and lending them a hand in difficulties to pushing
on towards the Pole. So we put the four ounces of pisco which we had been
keeping for Christmas into the breakfast cocoa, and dug out our tents, and
loaded our sledges, and parted there in the white daylight on the bitter plain.

Our sledge was fairly light by now. We pulled on to the south. Juana
calculated our position daily. On the twenty-second of December, 1909, we
reached the South Pole. The weather was, as always, very cruel. Nothing of
any kind marked the dreary whiteness. We discussed leaving some kind of
mark or monument, a snow cairn, a tent pole and flag; but there seemed no
particular reason to do so. Anything we could do, anything we were, was
insignificant, in that awful place. We put up the tent for shelter for an hour
and made a cup of tea, and then struck "90° Camp." Dolores, standing patient
as ever in her sledging harness, looked at the snow; it was so hard frozen that
it showed no trace of our footprints coming, and she said, "Which way?"

"North," said Juana.

It was a joke, because at that particular place there is no other direction.
But we did not laugh. Our lips were cracked with frostbite and hurt too much
to let us laugh. So we started back, and the wind at our backs pushed us
along, and dulled the knife edges of the waves of frozen snow.

All that week the blizzard wind pursued us like a pack of mad dogs. I
cannot describe it. I wished we had not gone to the Pole. I think I wish it even
now. But I was glad even then that we had left no sign there, for some man

longing to be first might come some day, and find it, and know then what a fool he had been, and break his heart.

We talked, when we could talk, of catching up to Carlota's party, since they might be going slower than we. In fact they had used their tent as a sail to catch the following wind and had got far ahead of us. But in many places they had built snow cairns or left some sign for us; once Zoe had written on the lee side of a ten-foot sastrugi, just as children write on the sand of the beach at Miraflores, "This Way Out!" The wind blowing over the frozen ridge had left the words perfectly distinct.

In the very hour that we began to descend the glacier, the weather turned warmer, and the mad dogs were left to howl forever tethered to the Pole. The distance that had taken us fifteen days going up we covered in only eight days going down. But the good weather that had aided us descending the Nightingale became a curse down on the Barrier ice, where we had looked forward to a kind of royal progress from depot to depot, eating our fill and taking our time for the last three hundred-odd miles. In a tight place on the glacier I lost my goggles—I was swinging from my harness at the time in a crevasse—and then Juana had broken hers when we had to do some rock climbing coming down to the Gateway. After two days in bright sunlight with only one pair of snow goggles to pass amongst us, we were all suffering badly from snowblindness. It became acutely painful to keep lookout for landmarks or depot flags, to take sightings, even to study the compass, which had to be laid down on the snow to steady the needle. At Concolorcorvo Depot, where there was a particularly good supply of food and fuel, we gave up, crawled into our sleeping bags with bandaged eyes, and slowly boiled alive like lobsters in the tent exposed to the relentless sun. The voices of Berta and Zoe were the sweetest sound I ever heard. A little concerned about us, they had skied south to meet us. They led us home to Base.

We recovered quite swiftly, but the altiplano left its mark. When she was very little, Rosita asked if a dog "had bitted Mama's toes." I told her Yes, a great, white, mad dog named Blizzard! My Rosita and my Juanito heard many stories when they were little, about that fearful dog and how it howled, and the transparent cattle of the invisible gauchos, and a river of ice eight thousand feet high called Nightingale, and how Cousin Juana drank a cup of tea standing on the bottom of the world under seven suns, and other fairy tales.

We were in for one severe shock when we reached Base at last. Teresa was pregnant. I must admit that my first response to the poor girl's big belly and sheepish look was anger—rage—fury. That one of us should have concealed anything, and such a thing, from the others! But Teresa had done nothing of the sort. Only those who had concealed from her what she most needed to know were to blame. Brought up by servants, with four years' schooling in a convent, and married at sixteen, the poor girl was still so ignorant at twenty years of age that she had thought it was "the cold weather" that made her miss her periods. Even this was not entirely stupid, for all of us on the Southern Journey had seen our periods change or stop altogether as we experienced increasing cold, hunger, and fatigue. Teresa's appetite had begun to draw general attention; and then she had begun, as she said pathetically, "to get fat." The others were worried at the thought of all the sledge-hauling she had done, but she flourished, and the only problem was her positively insatiable appetite. As well as could be determined from her shy references to her last night on the hacienda with her husband, the baby was due at just about the same time as the *Yelcho*, the twentieth of February. But we had not been back from the Southern Journey two weeks when, on February 14, she went into labor.

Several of us had borne children and had helped with deliveries, and anyhow most of what needs to be done is fairly self-evident; but a first labor can be long and trying, and we were all anxious, while Teresa was frightened out of her wits. She kept calling for her José till she was as hoarse as a skua. Zoe lost all patience at last and said, "By God, Teresa, if you say 'José!' once more I hope you have a penguin!" But what she had, after twenty long hours, was a pretty little red-faced girl.

Many were the suggestions for that child's name from her eight proud midwife-aunts: Polita, Penguina, McMurdo, Victoria . . . But Teresa announced, after she had had a good sleep and a large serving of pemmican, "I shall name her Rosa—Rosa del Sur," Rose of the South. That night we drank the last two bottles of Veuve Clicquot (having finished the pisco at 88° 30' South) in toasts to our little Rose.

On the nineteenth of February, a day early, my Juana came down into Buenos Aires in a hurry. "The ship," she said, "the ship has come," and she burst into tears—she who had never wept in all our weeks of pain and weariness on the long haul.

Of the return voyage there is nothing to tell. We came back safe.

In 1912 all the world learned that the brave Norwegian Amundsen had reached the South Pole; and then, much later, came the accounts of how Captain Scott and his men had come there after him, but did not come home again.

Just this year, Juana and I wrote to the captain of the *Yelcho*, for the newspapers have been full of the story of his gallant dash to rescue Sir Ernest Shackleton's men from Elephant Island, and we wished to congratulate him, and once more to thank him. Never one word has he breathed of our secret. He is a man of honor, Luis Pardo.

* * *

I add this last note in 1929. Over the years we have lost touch with one another. It is very difficult for women to meet, when they live so far apart as we do. Since Juana died, I have seen none of my old sledge-mates, though sometimes we write. Our little Rosa del Sur died of the scarlet fever when she was five years old. Teresa had many other children. Carlota took the veil in Santiago ten years ago. We are old women now, with old husbands, and grown children, and grandchildren who might someday like to read about the Expedition. Even if they are rather ashamed of having such a crazy grandmother, they may enjoy sharing in the secret. But they must not let Mr. Amundsen know! He would be terribly embarrassed and disappointed. There is no need for him or anyone else outside the family to know. We left no footprints, even.

PAMELA SARGENT

Fears

Pamela Sargent is an American writer who has won the Nebula and Locus awards, been a finalist for the Hugo Award, Theodore Sturgeon Award, and Sidewise Award, and was honored in 2012 with the Pilgrim Award, given by the Science Fiction Research Association for lifetime achievement in science fiction and fantasy scholarship. She has written many novels, including *Cloned Lives*, *Eye of the Comet*, *Homesmind*, *Alien Child*, and *The Shore of Women*. Her short fiction has appeared in the *Magazine of Fantasy & Science Fiction*, *Asimov's Science Fiction Magazine*, *New Worlds*, *Rod Serling's The Twilight Zone Magazine*, *Universe*, and *Nature*, among others. "Fears," which describes a woman's journey through an ultra–male dominated world, was first published in *Light Years and Dark* in 1984.

I was on my way back to Sam's when a couple of boys tried to run me off the road, banging my fender a little before they sped on, looking for another target. My throat tightened and my chest heaved as I wiped my face with a handkerchief. The boys had clearly stripped their car to the minimum, ditching all their safety equipment, knowing that the highway patrol was unlikely to stop them; the police had other things to worry about.

The car's harness held me; its dashboard lights flickered. As I waited for it to steer me back onto the road, the engine hummed, choked, and died. I switched over to manual; the engine was silent.

I felt numb. I had prepared myself for my rare journeys into the world outside my refuge, working to perfect my disguise. My angular, coarse-featured face stared back at me from the mirror overhead as I wondered if I could still pass. I had cut my hair recently, my chest was still as flat as a boy's, and the slightly padded shoulders of my suit imparted a bit of extra bulk. I had always been taken for a man before, but I had never done more than visit a few out-of-the-way, dimly lighted stores where the proprietors looked closely only at cards or cash.

I couldn't wait there risking a meeting with the highway patrol. The police might look a bit too carefully at my papers and administer a body search on general principles. Stray women had been picked up before, and the rewards for such a discovery were great; I imagined uniformed men groping at my groin, and shuddered. My disguise would get a real test. I took a deep breath, released the harness, then got out of the car.

* * *

The garage was half a mile away. I made it there without enduring more than a few honks from passing cars.

The mechanic listened to my husky voice as I described my problem, glanced at my card, took my keys, then left in his tow truck, accompanied by a younger mechanic I sat in his office, out of sight of the other men, trying not to let my fear push me into panic. The car might have to remain here for some time; I would have to find a place to stay. The mechanic might even offer me a lift home, and I didn't want to risk that Sam might be a bit too talkative in the man's presence; the mechanic might wonder about someone who lived in such an inaccessible spot. My hands were shaking; I thrust them into my pockets.

I started when the mechanic returned to his office, then smiled nervously as he assured me that the car would be ready in a few hours; a component had failed, he had another like it in the shop, no problem. He named a price that seemed excessive; I was about to object, worried that argument might only provoke him, then worried still more that I would look odd if I didn't dicker with him. I settled for frowning as he slipped my card into his terminal, then handed it back to me.

"No sense hanging around here." He waved one beefy hand at the door. "You can pick up a shuttle to town out there, comes by every fifteen minutes or so."

I thanked him and went outside, trying to decide what to do. I had been successful so far; the other mechanics didn't even look at me as I walked toward the road. An entrance to the town's underground garage was just across the highway; a small, glassy building with a sign saying "Marcello's" stood next to the entrance. I knew what service Marcello sold; I had driven by the place before. I would be safer with one of his employees, and less conspicuous if I kept moving; curiosity overcame my fear for a moment. I had made my decision.

* * *

I walked into Marcello's. One man was at a desk; three big men sat on a sofa near one of the windows, staring at the small holo screen in front of them. I went to the desk and said, "I want to hire a bodyguard."

The man behind the desk looked up; his mustache twitched. "An escort. You want an escort."

"Call it whatever you like."

"For how long?"

"About three or four hours."

"For what purpose?"

"Just a walk through town, maybe a stop for a drink. I haven't been to town for a while, thought I might need some company."

His brown eyes narrowed. I had said too much; I didn't have to explain myself to him. "Card."

I got out my card. He slipped it into his outlet and peered at the screen while I tried to keep from fidgeting, expecting the machine to spit out the card even after all this time. He returned the card. "You'll get your receipt when you come back." He waved a hand at the men on the sofa. "I got three available. Take your pick."

The man on my right had a lean, mean face; the one on the left was sleepy-eyed. "The middle guy."

"Ellis."

The middle man stood up and walked over to us. He was a tall black man dressed in a brown suit; he looked me over, and I forced myself to gaze directly at him while the man at the desk rummaged in a drawer and took out a weapon and holster, handing them to my escort.

"Ellis Gerard," the black man said, thrusting out a hand.

"Joe Segor." I took his hand; he gripped mine just long enough to show his strength, then let go. The two men on the sofa watched us as we left, as if resenting my choice, then turned back to the screen.

* * *

We caught a shuttle into town. A few old men sat near the front of the bus under the watchful eyes of the guard; five boys got on behind us, laughing, but a look from the guard quieted them. I told myself again that I would be safe with Ellis.

"Where to?" Ellis said as we sat down. "A visit to a pretty boy? Guys some-times want escorts for that."

"No, just around. It's a nice day—we could sit in the park for a while."

"I don't know if that's such a good idea, Mr. Segor."

"Joe."

"Those crossdressers hang out a lot there now. I don't like it. They go there with their friends and it just causes trouble—it's a bad element. You look at them wrong, and then you've got a fight. It ought to be against the law."

"What?"

"Dressing like a woman. Looking like what you're not." He glanced at me. I looked away, my jaw tightening.

We were in town now, moving toward the shuttle's first stop. "Hey!" one of the boys behind us shouted. "Look!" Feet shuffled along the aisle; the boys had rushed to the right side of the bus and were kneeling on the seats, hands pressed against the window; even the guard had turned. Ellis and I got up and changed seats, looking out at what had drawn the boys' attention.

A car was pulling into a spot in front of a store. Our driver put down his magazine and slowed the bus manually; he obviously knew his passengers wanted a look. Cars were not allowed in town unless a woman was riding in one; even I knew that. We waited. The bus stopped; a group of young men standing outside the store watched the car.

"Come on, get out," a boy behind me said. "Get out of the car."

Two men got out first. One of them yelled at the loiterers, who moved down the street before gathering under a lamppost. Another man opened the back door, then held out his hand.

She seemed to float out of the car; her long pink robe swirled around her ankles as she stood. Her hair was covered by a long, white scarf. My face grew warm with embarrassment and shame. I caught a glimpse of black eyebrows and white skin before her bodyguards surrounded her and led her into the store.

The driver pushed a button and picked up his magazine again; the bus moved on. "Think she was real?" one of the boys asked.

"I don't know," another replied.

"Bet she wasn't. Nobody would let a real woman go into a store like that. If I had a girl, I'd never let her go anywhere."

"If I had a trans, I'd never let her go anywhere,"

"Those trans guys—they got it made." The boys scrambled toward the back of the bus.

"Definitely a trans," Ellis said to me. "I can tell. She's got a mannish kind of face."

I said, "You could hardly see her face."

"I saw enough. And she was too tall." He sighed. "That's the life. A little bit of cutting and trimming and some implants, and there you are—you don't have to lift a finger. You're legally female."

"It isn't just a little bit of cutting—it's major surgery."

"Yeah. Well, I couldn't have been a transsexual anyway, not with my body." Ellis glanced at me. "You could have been, though."

"Never wanted it."

"It's not a bad life in some ways."

"I like my freedom." My voice caught on the words.

"That's why I don't like crossdressers. They'll dress like a woman, but they won't turn into one. It just causes trouble—you get the wrong cues."

The conversation was making me uneasy; sitting so close to Ellis, hemmed in by his body and the bus's window, made me feel trapped. The man was too observant. I gritted my teeth and turned toward the window. More stores had been boarded up; we passed a brick school building with shattered windows and an empty playground. The town was declining.

* * *

We got off in the business district, where there was still a semblance of normal life. Men in suits came and went from their offices, hopped on buses, strolled toward bars for an early drink.

"It's pretty safe around here," Ellis said as we sat on a bench. The bench had been welded to the ground; it was covered with graffiti and one leg had been warped. Old newspapers lay on the sidewalk and in the gutter with other refuse. One bore a headline about the African war; another, more recent, the latest news about Bethesda's artificial womb program. The news was good; two more healthy children had been born to the project, a boy and a girl. I thought of endangered species and extinction.

A police car drove by, followed by another car with opaque windows. Ellis gazed after the car and sighed longingly, as if imagining the woman inside. "Wish I was gay," he said sadly, "but I'm not. I've tried the pretty boys, but that's not for me. I should have been a Catholic, and then I could have been a priest. I live like one anyway."

"Too many priests already. The Church can't afford any more. Anyway, you'd really be frustrated then. They can't even hear a woman's confession unless her husband or a bodyguard is with her. It's just like being a doctor. You could go nuts that way."

"I'll never make enough to afford a woman, even a trans."

"There might be more women someday," I said. "That project at Bethesda's working out."

"Maybe I should have gone on one of those expeditions. There's one they let into the Philippines, and another one's in Alaska now."

I thought of a team of searchers coming for me. If they were not dead before they reached my door, I would be; I had made sure of that. "That's a shady business, Ellis."

"That group in the Amazon actually found a tribe—killed all the men. No one'll let them keep the women for themselves, but at least they have enough money to try for one at home." Ellis frowned. "I don't know. Trouble is, a lot of guys don't miss women. They say they do, but they really don't. Ever talk to a real old-timer, one that can remember what it was like?"

"Can't say I have."

Ellis leaned back. "A lot of those guys didn't really like girls all that much. They had places they'd go to get away from them, things they'd do together. Women didn't think the same way, didn't act the same—they never did as much as men did." He shaded his eyes for a moment. "I don't know—sometimes one of those old men'll tell you the world was gentler then, or prettier, but I don't know if that's true. Anyway, a lot of those women must have agreed with the men. Look what happened—as soon as you had that pill that could make you sure you had a boy if you wanted, or a girl, most of them started having boys, so they must have thought, deep down, that boys were better."

Another police car drove past; one of the officers inside looked us over before driving on. "Take a trans," Ellis said. "Oh, you might envy her a little, but no one really has any respect for her. And the only real reason for having any women around now is for insurance—somebody's got to have the kids, and we can't. But once that Bethesda project really gets going and spreads, we won't need them anymore."

"I suppose you're right."

Four young men, dressed in work shirts and pants, approached us and stared down at us silently. I thought of the boys I had once played with before what I was had made a difference, before I had been locked away. One young man glanced quickly down the street; another took a step forward. I stared back and made a fist, trying to keep my hand from shaking; Ellis sat up slowly and let his right hand fall to his waist, near his holster. We kept staring until the group turned from us and walked away.

"Anyway, you've got to analyze it." Ellis crossed his legs. "There's practical reasons for not having a lot of women around. We need more soldiers—everybody does now, with all the trouble in the world. And police, too, with crime the way it is. And women can't handle those jobs."

"Once people thought they could." My shoulder muscles were tight; I had almost said *we*.

"But they can't. Put a woman up against a man, and the man'll always win." Ellis draped an arm over the back of the bench. "And there's other reasons, too. Those guys in Washington like keeping women scarce, having their pick of the choice ones for themselves—it makes their women more valuable. And a lot of the kids'll be theirs, too, from now on. Oh, they might loan a woman out to a friend once in a while, and I suppose the womb project'll change things some, but it'll be their world eventually."

"And their genes," I said. I knew that I should change the subject, but Ellis had clearly accepted my pose. In his conversation, the ordinary talk of one man to another, the longest conversation I had had with a man for many years, I was looking for a sign, something to keep me from despairing.

"How long can it go on?" I continued. "The population keeps shrinking every year—there won't be enough people soon."

"You're wrong, Joe. Machines do a lot of the work now anyway, and there used to be too many people. The only way we'll ever have more women is if someone finds out the Russians are having more, and that won't happen—they need soldiers, too. Besides, look at it this way—maybe we're doing women a favor if there aren't as many of them. Would you want to be a woman, having to be married by sixteen, not being able to go anywhere, no job until she's at least sixty-five?"

And no divorce without a husband's permission, no contraception, no higher education—all the special privileges and protections could not make up for that. "No," I said to Ellis. "I wouldn't want to be one." Yet I knew that many women had made their peace with the world as it was, extorting gifts and tokens from their men, glorying in their beauty and their pregnancies, lavishing their attention on their children and their homes, tormenting and manipulating their men with the sure knowledge that any woman could find another man—for if a woman could not get a divorce by herself, a man more powerful than her husband could force him to give her up if he wanted her himself.

I had dreamed of guerrillas, of fighting women too proud to give in, breeding strong daughters by a captive male to carry on the battle. But if there were such women, they, like me, had gone to ground. The world had been more merciful when it had drowned or strangled us at birth.

Once, when I was younger, someone had said it had been a conspiracy—develop a foolproof way to give a couple a child of the sex they wanted, and most of them would naturally choose boys. The population problem would be solved in time without having to resort to harsher methods, and a blow would be leveled at those old feminists who had demanded too much, trying to emasculate men in the process. But I didn't think it had been a conspiracy. It had simply happened as it was bound to eventually, and the values of society had controlled behavior. After all, why shouldn't a species decide to become one sex, especially if reproduction could be severed from sexuality? People had believed men were better, and had acted on that belief. Perhaps women, given the power, would have done the same.

* * *

We retreated to a bar when the sunny weather grew cooler. Ellis steered me away from two taverns with "bad elements," and we found ourselves in the doorway of a darkened bar in which several old and middle-aged men had gathered and two pretty boys dressed in leather and silk were plying their trade.

I glanced at the newscreen as I entered; the pale letters flickered, telling me that Bob Arnoldi's last appeal had failed and that he would be executed at the end of the month. This was no surprise; Arnoldi had, after all, killed a woman, and was always under heavy guard. The letters danced on; the President's wife had given birth to her thirteenth child, a boy. The President's best friend, a California millionaire, had been at his side when the announcement was made; the millionaire's power could be gauged by the fact that he had been married three times, and that the prolific First Lady had been one of the former wives.

Ellis and I got drinks at the bar. I kept my distance from one of the pretty boys, who scowled at my short, wavy hair and nestled closer to his patron. We retreated to the shadows and sat down at one of the side tables. The tabletop was sticky; old cigar butts had been planted on a gray mound in the ashtray. I sipped my bourbon; Ellis, while on the job, was only allowed beer.

The men at the bar were watching the remaining minutes of a football game. Sports of some kind were always on holo screens in bars, according to Sam; he preferred the old pornographic films that were sometimes shown amid war coverage and an occasional boys' choir performance for the pederasts and the more culturally inclined. Ellis looked at the screen and noted that his team was losing; I commented on the team's weaknesses, as I knew I was expected to do.

Ellis rested his elbows on the table. "This all you came for? Just to walk around and then have a drink?"

"That's it, I'm just waiting for my car." I tried to sound nonchalant. "It should be fixed soon."

"Doesn't seem like enough reason to hire an escort."

"Come on, Ellis. Guys like me would have trouble without escorts, especially if we don't know the territory that well."

"True. You don't look that strong." He peered at me a little too intently. "Still, unless you were looking for action, or going to places with a bad element, or waiting for the gangs to come out at night, you could get along. It's in your attitude—you have to look like you can take care of yourself. I've seen guys smaller than you I wouldn't want to fight."

"I like to be safe."

He watched me, as if expecting me to say more.

"Actually, I don't need an escort as much as I like to have a companion—somebody to talk to. I don't see that many people."

"It's your money."

The game had ended and was being subjected to loud analysis by the men at the bar, their voices suddenly died. A man behind me sucked in his breath as the clear voice of a woman filled the room.

I looked at the holo. Rena Swanson was reciting the news, leading with the Arnoldi story, following that with the announcement of the President's new son. Her aged, wrinkled face hovered over us; her kind brown eyes promised us comfort. Her motherly presence had made her program one of the most popular on the holo. The men around me sat silently, faces upturned, worshipping her—the Woman, the Other, someone for whom part of them still yearned.

* * *

We got back to Marcello's just before dark. As we approached the door, Ellis suddenly clutched my shoulder. "Wait a minute, Joe."

I didn't move at first; then I reached out and carefully pushed his arm away. My shoulders hurt and a tension headache, building all day, had finally taken hold, its claws gripping my temples. "Don't touch me." I had been about to plead, but caught myself in time; attitude, as Ellis had told me himself, was important.

"There's something about you. I can't figure you out."

"Don't try." I kept my voice steady. "You wouldn't want me to complain to your boss, would you? He might not hire you again. Escorts have to be trusted."

He was very quiet. I couldn't see his dark face clearly in the fading light, but I could sense that he was weighing the worth of a confrontation with me against the chance of losing his job. My face was hot, my mouth dry. I had spent too much time with him, given him too many chances to notice subtly wrong gestures. I continued to stare directly at him, wondering if his greed would win out over practicality.

"Okay," he said at last, and opened the door.

I was charged more than I had expected to pay, but did not argue about the fee. I pressed a few coins on Ellis; he took them while refusing to look at me. He knows, I thought then; he knows and he's letting me go. But I might have imagined that, seeing kindness where there was none.

* * *

I took a roundabout route back to Sam's, checking to make sure no one had followed me, then pulled off the road to change the car's license plate, concealing my own under my shirt.

Sam's store stood at the end of the road, near the foot of my mountain. Near the store, a small log cabin had been built. I had staked my claim to most of the mountain, buying up the land to make sure it remained undeveloped, but the outside world was already moving closer.

Sam was sitting behind the counter, drumming his fingers as music blared. I cleared my throat and said hello.

"Joe?" His watery blue eyes squinted. "You're late, boy."

"Had to get your car fixed. Don't worry—I paid for it already. Thanks for letting me rent it again." I counted out my coins and pressed them into his dry, leathery hand.

"Any time, son." The old man held up the coins, peering at each one with his weak eyes. "Don't look like you'll get home tonight. You can use the sofa there—I'll get you a nightshirt."

"I'll sleep in my clothes." I gave him an extra coin.

He locked up, hobbled toward his bedroom door, then turned. "Get into town at all?"

"No." I paused, "Tell me something, Sam. You're old enough to remember. What was it really like before?" I had never asked him in all the years I had known him, avoiding intimacy of any kind, but suddenly I wanted to know.

"I'll tell you, Joe," He leaned against the doorway. "It wasn't all that different. A little softer around the edges, maybe, quieter, not as mean, but it wasn't all that different. Men always ran everything. Some say they didn't, but they had all the real power—sometimes they'd dole a little of it out to the girls, that's all. Now we don't have to anymore."

* * *

I had been climbing up the mountain for most of the morning, and had left the trail, arriving at my decoy house before noon. Even Sam believed that the cabin in the clearing was my dwelling. I tried the door, saw that it was still locked, then continued on my way.

My home was farther up the slope, just out of sight of the cabin. I approached my front door, which was almost invisible near the ground; the rest of the house was concealed under slabs of rock and piles of deadwood.

I stood still, letting a hidden camera lens get a good look at me. The door swung open.

"Thank God you're back," Julia said as she pulled me inside and closed the door. "I was so worried. I thought you'd been caught and they were coming for me."

"It's all right. I had some trouble with Sam's car, that's all."

She looked up at me; the lines around her mouth deepened. "I wish you wouldn't go." I took off the pack loaded with the tools and supplies unavailable at Sam's store. Julia glanced at the pack resentfully. "It isn't worth it."

"You're probably right." I was about to tell her of my own trip into town, but decided to wait until later.

We went into the kitchen. Her hips were wide under her pants; her large breasts bounced as she walked. Her face was still pretty, even after all the years of hiding, her lashes thick and curly, her mouth delicate. Julia could not travel in the world as it was; no clothing, no disguise, could hide her.

I took off my jacket and sat down, taking out my card, and my papers. My father had given them to me—the false name, the misleading address, the identification of a male—after I had pleaded for my own life. He had built my hideaway; he had risked everything for me. "Give the world a choice," he had said, "and women will be the minority, maybe even die out completely; perhaps we can only love those like ourselves." He had looked hard as he said it, and then he had patted me on the head, sighing as though he regretted the choice. Maybe he had. He had chosen to have a daughter, after all.

I remembered his words. "Who knows?" he had asked. "What is it that made us two kinds who have to work together to get the next batch going? Oh, I know about evolution, but it didn't have to be that way, or any way. It's curious."

"It can't last," Julia said, and I did not know if she meant the world, or our escape from the world.

There would be no Eves in their Eden, I thought. The visit to town had brought it all home to me. We all die, but we go with a conviction about the future; my extinction would not be merely personal. Only traces of the feminine would linger—an occasional expression, a posture, a feeling—in the flat-breasted male form. Love would express itself in fruitless unions, divorced from reproduction; human affections are flexible.

I sat in my home, in my prison, treasuring the small freedom I had, the gift of a man, as it seemed such freedom had always been for those like me, and wondered again if it could have been otherwise.

RACHEL SWIRSKY

Detours on the Way to Nothing

Rachel Swirsky is an American writer, poet, and editor of literary, speculative, and fantasy fiction. Her short fiction has been published in both literary journals and genre publications such as *PANK*, the *Konundrum Engine Literary Review, the New Haven Review*, Tor.com, *Subterranean Magazine, Beneath Ceaseless Skies, Fantasy Magazine, Interzone, Realms of Fantasy*, and *Weird Tales*. Her stories are frequently reprinted in year's-best collections. Her work has been recognized with various awards, including the Nebula Award, and nominated for the Hugo Award, the Theodore Sturgeon Award, the James Tiptree, Jr. Award, and the World Fantasy Award. In "Detours on the Way to Nothing" we learn more about attraction, reactions to another's desire and how quickly one can change to please someone. It was first published in *Weird Tales* in 2008.

It's midnight when you and your girlfriend, Elka, have your first fight since you moved in together. Words wound, tears flow, doors slam. You storm out of the apartment, not caring where you go as long as it's far away from her. When you step off the front stoop onto the sidewalk, that's the moment when the newest version of me is born.

You get on the subway heading toward Brooklyn and ride until the train rumbles out of the tunnels and squeaks into a familiar aboveground stop. The neighborhood isn't good, but a friend of yours used to live a few blocks away, so you know the area pretty well. At least you won't get lost while you work off the rest of your anger. You disembark, let your feet pick a direction, and start walking.

That's how the logic seems from your perspective, but there's another explanation: I want you to come to me.

By a series of what you think are random turns, you end up in an alley between high rise buildings. Reinforced doors protect apartments built like warehouses; skulls grin on rat poison warning signs nailed beneath barred panes. Abandoned mattresses and broken radios decay in the gutter, accumulating mold and rust.

In the spotlight of a streetlamp, an old Puerto Rican man hurls bottles at a fifth story window. "Christina!" he yells. "Open up!" A voice shouts down, "She doesn't live here anymore!" but the man keeps throwing. Translucent shards collect around his feet. None have flown back into his face yet, but it's only a matter of time.

The distraction stops you, as I intended. I wanted people around so you'd be less likely to spook.

You look up and see me. I'm the girl on the roof. The edge where I stand is flat as the sidewalk and has no guard rail. You gasp when you notice my toes edging over the precipice—then gasp harder a moment later when you see my hair floating in the wind. It looks like feathers. Just like feathers.

The Puerto Rican man runs out of bottles. He rubs his sore palms, repeating, "Christina, my Christina, why won't you open the window?"

Looking up, you gesture between me and the Puerto Rican man, asking: are you Christina? I shake my head and make walking motions with my fingers to say I'll come down. Not knowing quite why, you put your hands in your pockets and wait.

When I get down to street level, you're shocked to see it wasn't an illusion: my hair really is made of feathers. They're bright blue, such a vivid color that it's obvious they weren't plucked from any real bird. They remind you of the ones you and your sister decorated carnival masks with when you were children: feathers dyed to match the way people think birds look.

You reach out to touch them before your sense of propriety kicks in and pulls your hand back. You shuffle your feet with embarrassment. "Hi."

I find your shyness endearing. I take one hand out of the lined pocket of my ski jacket and wave.

"I'm Patrick," you say.

I smile and nod, the way people do when they hear information they don't find relevant.

"What's your name?" you ask.

I step closer. You tilt your ear toward my lips, assuming I want to whisper. It's a reasonable assumption, though wrong. I take your chin and gently lift your face so that your gaze is level with mine, then open my mouth to show you where my tongue was cut out.

You back away. Another second and you'd bolt, so I act fast, pull a card out of my pocket and give it to you.

"Voluntary surgery?" you read. "What are you, part of some cult?"

It's more a philosophy than a cult, but since it isn't really either, I wave my hand back and forth: in a way.

Debate wavers in your expression. You still might go. Before you can decide, I take your hand and pull your fingers through my hair.

You breathe hard as your fingertips touch skin beneath my feathers. "All the way to the scalp," you murmur.

That's when I know I've got you. I can see it in the way your eyes turn one dark color from pupil to iris. You're thinking, *how can this be real?*

The fantasy has been with you since adolescence. Maybe it started with the feathers you and your sister glued on the carnival masks. They felt so soft that you pocketed a pair—one blue, one white—and took them back to bed with you. Your vision of a bird-woman appeared soon thereafter. Beautiful and silent, she wrapped you nightly in sky-colored feathers that smelled like wind.

In the nearby park, I recreate this. Behind us, a levy of black rocks stands against the East River. Reflected Manhattan lights form a sheen on the water, shimmering like a fluorescent oil spill.

I strip off my clothes and stand naked for you, my shadow falling onto gravel cut with glints of glass. I'm skinny with visible ribs, but soft and fleshy around the belly where you like to stroke your lovers as if they were satin pillows—all the conflicting traits you prefer, combined in one body. Your eyes never leave my feathers.

You will never know how I am possible. My philosophy—my cult, as you called it—is old and secretive. We have no organization, no books of dogma, no advocates to harangue passersby with our rhetoric. Each initiate finds us alone, deducing our beliefs through meditation and self-reflection. Only the magic of our sacrificed tongues unifies us.

Our practices have few analogues in Western thought, though you could call us philosophical cousins to the Buddhists. We believe there is no way to lose the trappings of self so completely as to become someone else's desire.

If you see me again, I will not be a bird. I will be a figure made of jewels or a woolly primate with prehensile lips. My skin will be rubber. My cock will be velvet. Each of my six blood-spattered breasts will be tattooed with the face of a man I've killed. The goal is endless transformation.

I'm still distant from that goal. Though I've been transforming for decades, I'm only inching along the path to self-dissolution. I cling to identity; indulge fantasies like this one of telling you my story. Cutting out our tongues is supposed to silence us. Instead, I speak internally. Can you hear me?

I tease you with my feathers, encompassing your face, hands, and cock in turn. When you tire of that, you pull me up against the rocks with my legs around your waist. I throw my head back to let my plumage stream in the wind and you come. I don't know if you think of Elka, but don't worry. You can't be unfaithful with a fantasy.

You recline against the black rocks.

"Wow," you say, "I'm not the kind of person that would ever do this. Elka and I were together three months before . . ."

Your eyes glaze. This could be bad. There are two possibilities now. You may pull back, stammering her name, or:

You reach for my shoulder. "I know you can't talk, but can you write? Is there someplace we could go? I have so much to ask."

I've done my job too well. It's time to leave. I shrug away from your grip and raise one hand to wave. Goodbye.

"Hey, wait!" you shout.

In your fantasies, when you're done, the bird-woman dissolves into a shower of feathers. Unfortunately, my magic isn't that versatile. I have to walk away.

You try to chase me so I maneuver through sharp turns and unexpected byways. You don't know this area as well as you think you do. Soon, your footsteps grow distant and faint.

I retreat to my rooftop and watch from above as you pace in circles around the neighborhood. I hope you will go soon. If you don't, it may be a sign I've done you permanent damage. Some people can't survive getting what they wish for.

Finally, you head back to the subway. I have to admit, I'm a little sad when you go. A little jealous, too.

I climb down the building and discover the Puerto Rican man huddled next to a fire escape, muttering in soft Spanish. Tiny cuts bleed on his arms and calves. I consider remaking myself for him, but all he wants is his human Christina. I catch an impression of her: short and blonde, she hates dancing, speaks seven languages badly, calls him The Man She Should Have Loved Less.

As his yearning for this specific, clumsy, jovial woman flows through me, I realize how little I am to you. What is a fantasy? A scrap of yourself made into flesh. An illusion to masturbate with.

Moving away from the Puerto Rican man, I shelter in a doorway and will myself to molt. My feathers float away on the wind and something I was clinging to flies away with them, carried on the same breeze.

I say goodbye to the girl with feathered hair and wait for another's desire to overtake and shape me. In the few seconds before it does, for one moment, just one, my soul becomes pure essence without form.

It's the closest I've come to nothingness yet.

CATHERYNNE M. VALENTE

Thirteen Ways of Looking at Space/Time

Catherynne M. Valente is an American writer. She is the *New York Times* bestselling author of more than a dozen works of fiction and poetry, including *Palimpsest*, the Orphan's Tales series, and the crowd-funded phenomenon *The Girl Who Circumnavigated Fairyland in a Ship of Her Own Making*. Her work has been recognized with various awards including the Andre Norton Award, James Tiptree, Jr. Award, Mythopoeic Award, Rhysling, and Million Writers Award. "Thirteen Ways of Looking at Space/Time" is a stunning and incendiary reimagining of the creation myth. It was first publishing in *Clarkesworld* in 2010 and was a finalist for the Locus Award.

I

In the beginning was the Word and the Word was with God and the Word was a high-density pre-baryogenesis singularity. Darkness lay over the deep and God moved upon the face of the hyperspatial matrix. He separated the firmament from the quark-gluon plasma and said: *let there be particle/anti-particle pairs*, and there was light. He created the fish of the sea and the fruits of the trees, the moon and the stars and the beasts of the earth, and to these he said: *Go forth, be fruitful and mutate*. And on the seventh day, the rest mass of the universe came to gravitationally dominate the photon radiation, hallow it, and keep it.

God, rapidly redshifting, hurriedly formed man from the dust of single-celled organisms, called him Adam, and caused him to dwell in the Garden of Eden, to classify the beasts according to kingdom, phylum, and species. God forbade Man only to eat from the Tree of Meiosis. Adam did as he was told, and as a reward God instructed him in the ways of parthenogenesis. Thus was Woman born, and called Eve. Adam and Eve dwelt in the pre-quantum differentiated universe, in a paradise without wave-particle duality. But interference patterns came to Eve in the shape of a Serpent, and wrapping her in its matter/anti-matter coils, it said: *eat from the Tree of Meiosis and your eyes will be opened.* Eve protested that she would not break covenant with God, but the Serpent answered: *fear not, for you float in a random quantum-gravity foam, and from a single bite will rise an inexorable inflation event, and you will become like unto God, expanding forever outward.*

And so Eve ate from the Tree, and knew that she was a naked child of divergent universes. She took the fruit to Adam, and said unto him: *there are things you do not understand, but I do.* And Adam was angry, and snatched the fruit from Eve and devoured it, and from beyond the cosmic background radiation, God sighed, for all physical processes are reversible in theory— but not in practice. Man and Woman were expelled from the Garden, and a flaming sword was placed through the Gates of Eden as a reminder that the universe would now contract, and someday perish in a conflagration of entropy, only to increase in density, burst, and expand again, causing further high velocity redistributions of serpents, fruit, men, women, helium-3, lithium-7, deuterium, and helium-4.

II

This is a story about being born.

No one remembers being born. The beginnings of things are very difficult.

A science fiction writer on the Atlantic coast once claimed to remember being born. When she was a child, she thought a door was open which was not, and ran full-tilt into a pane of plate-glass. The child-version of the science fiction writer lay bleeding onto a concrete patio, not yet knowing that part of her thigh was gone and would always be gone, like Zeus's thigh, where the lightning-god sewed up his son Dionysus to gestate. Something broke inside the child, a thing having to do with experience and memory, which in normal children travel in opposite directions, with memory accumulating and experience running out—slowly, but speeding up as children hurtle toward adulthood and death. What the science fiction writer actually remembered was not her own birth, but a moment when she struck the surface of the glass and her brain stuttered, layering several experiences one over the other:

the scissoring pain of the shards of glass in her thighs,

having once fallen into a square of wet concrete on a construction site on her way to school, and her father pulling her out by her arms,

her first kiss, below an oak tree turning red and brown in the autumn, when a boy interrupted her reciting *Don Quixote* with his lips on hers.

This fractured, unplanned layering became indistinguishable from an actual memory of being born. It is not her fault; she believed she remembered it. But no one remembers being born.

The doctors sewed up her thigh. There was no son in her leg, but a small, dark, empty space beneath her skin where a part of her used to be. Sometimes she touches it, absentmindedly, when she is trying to think of a story.

III

In the beginning was the simple self-replicating cell of the Void. It split through the center of Ursa Major into the divine female Izanami and the divine male Izanagi, who knew nothing about quantum apples and lived on the iron-sulfur Plain of Heaven. They stood on the Floating Bridge of Heaven and plunged a static atmospheric discharge spear into the great black primordial sea, churning it and torturing it until oligomers and simple polymers rose up out of the depths. Izanami and Izanagi stepped onto the greasy islands of lipid bubbles and in the first light of the world, each saw that the other was beautiful.

Between them, they catalyzed the formation of nucleotides in an aqueous solution and raised up the Eight-Sided Palace of Autocatalytic Reactions around the unmovable RNA Pillar of Heaven. When this was done, Izanami and Izanagi walked in opposite chiral directions around the Pillar, and when Izanami saw her mate, she cried out happily: *How lovely you are, and how versatile are your nitrogenous bases! I love you!* Izanagi was angry that she had spoken first and privileged her proto-genetic code over his. The child that came of their paleo-protozoic mating was as a silver anaerobic leech, helpless, archaic, invertebrate, and unable to convert lethal super-oxides. They set him in the sky to sail in the Sturdy Boat of Heaven, down the starry stream of alternate electron acceptors for respiration. Izanagi dragged Izanami back to the Pillar. They walked around it again in a left-handed helix that echoed forward and backward through the biomass, and when Izanagi saw his wife, he crowed: *How lovely you are, and how ever-increasing your metabolic complexity! I love you!* And because Izanami was stonily silent, and Izanagi spoke first, elevating his own proto-genetic code, the children that came from them were strong and great: Gold and Iron and Mountain and Wheel and Honshu and Kyushu and Emperor—until the birth of her son, Fiery Permian-Triassic Extinction Event, burned her up and killed the mother of the world.

Izanami went down into the Root Country, the Land of the Dead. But Izanagi could not let her go into a place he had not gone first, and pursued her into the paleontological record. He became lost in the dark of abiogenetic obsolescence, and lit the teeth of his jeweled comb ablaze to show the way—and saw that he walked on the body of Izanami, which had become the fossil-depository landscape of the Root Country, putrid, rotting, full of mushrooms and worms and coprolites and trilobites. In hatred and grief and memory of their first wedding, Izanami howled and heaved and moved the continents one from the other until Izanagi was expelled from her.

When he stumbled back into the light, Izanagi cleaned the pluripotent filth from his right eye, and as it fell upon the ground it became the quantum-retroactive Sun. He cleaned the zygotic filth from his left eye and as it fell upon the ground, it became the temporally subjective Moon. And when he cleaned the nutrient-dense filth from his nose, it drifted into the air and became the fractal, maximally complex, petulant Storms and Winds.

IV

When the science fiction writer was nineteen, she had a miscarriage. She had not even known she was pregnant. But she bled and bled and it didn't stop, and the doctor explained to her that sometimes this happens when you are on a certain kind of medication. The science fiction writer could not decide how to feel about it—ten years later, after she had married the father of the baby-that-wasn't and divorced him, after she had written a book about methane-insectoid cities floating in the brume of a pink gas giant that no one liked very much, she still could not decide how to feel. When she was nineteen she put her hands over her stomach and tried to think of a timeline where she had stayed pregnant. Would it have been a daughter. Would it have had blue eyes like its father. Would it have had her Danish nose or his Greek one. Would it have liked science fiction, and would it have grown up to be an endocrinologist. Would she have been able to love it. She put her hands over her stomach and tried to be sad. She couldn't. But she couldn't be happy either. She felt that she had given birth to a reality where she would never give birth.

When the science fiction writer told her boyfriend who would become her husband who would become someone she never wanted to see again, he made sorry noises but wasn't really sorry. Five years later, when she thought she might want to have a child on purpose, she reminded him of the child-that-disappeared, and the husband who was a mistake would say: *I forgot all about that.*

And she put her hands over her stomach, the small, dark, empty space beneath her skin where a part of him used to be, and she didn't want to be pregnant anymore, but her breasts hurt all the same, as if she was nursing, all over again, a reality where no one had anyone's nose and the delicate photo-synthetic wings of Xm, the eater of love, quivered in a bliss-storm of super-heated hydrogen, and Dionysus was never born so the world lived without wine.

V

In the beginning there was only darkness. The darkness squeezed itself down until it became a thin protoplanetary disk, yellow on one side and white on the other, and inside the accretion zone sat a small man no larger than a frog, his beard flapping in the solar winds. This man was called Kuterastan, the One Who Lives Above the Super-Dense Protostar. He rubbed the metal-rich dust from his eyes peered above him into the collapsing nebular darkness. He looked east along the galactic axis, toward the cosmogenesis event horizon, and saw the young sun, its faint light tinged with the yellow of dawn. He looked west along the axis, toward the heat-death of the universe, and saw the dim amber-colored light of dissipating thermodynamic energy. As he gazed, debris-clouds formed in different colors. Once more, Kuterastan rubbed the boiling helium from his eyes and wiped the hydrogen-sweat from his brow. He flung the sweat from his body and another cloud appeared, blue with oxygen and possibility, and a tiny little girl stood on it: Stenatliha, the Woman Without Parents. Each was puzzled as to where the other had come from, and each considered the problems of unification theory after their own fashion.

After some time, Kuterastan again rubbed his eyes and face, and from his body flung stellar radiation into the dust and darkness. First the Sun appeared, and then Pollen Boy, a twin-tailed comet rough and heavy with microorganisms. The four sat a long time in silence on a single photoevaporation cloud. Finally Kuterastan broke the silence and said: *what shall we do?*

And a slow inward-turning Poynting-Robertson spiral began.

First Kuterastan made Nacholecho, the Tarantula of Newly-Acquired Critical Mass. He followed by making the Big Dipper, and then Wind, Lightning and Thunder, Magnetosphere, and Hydrostatic Equilibrium, and gave to each of them their characteristic tasks. With the ammonia-saturated sweat of the Sun, Pollen Boy, himself, and the Woman Without Parents, Kuterastan made between his palms a small brown ferrosilicate blastocyst no bigger than a bean. The four of them kicked the little ball until it cleared its orbital neighborhood of planetesimals. Then the solar wind blew into the ball and inflated its magnetic field. Tarantula spun out a long black gravitational cord and stretched it across the sky. Tarantula also attached blue gravity wells, yellow approach vectors and white spin foam to the ferrosilicate ball, pulling one far to the south, another west, and the last to the north. When Tarantula was finished, the earth existed, and became a smooth brown expanse of Precambrian plain. Stochastic processes tilted at each corner to hold the earth in place. And at this Kuterastan sang a repeating song of nutation: *the world is now made and its light cone will travel forever at a constant rate.*

VI

Once, someone asked the science fiction writer how she got her ideas. This is what she said:

Sometimes I feel that the part of me that is a science fiction writer is traveling at a different speed than the rest of me. That everything I write is always already written, and that the science fiction writer is sending messages back to me in semaphore, at the speed of my own typing, which is a retroactively constant rate: I cannot type faster than I have already typed. When I type a sentence, or a paragraph, or a page, or a chapter, I am also editing it and copyediting it, and reading it in its first edition, and reading it out loud to a room full of people, or a room with only one or two people in it, depending on terrifying quantum-publishing intersections that the science fiction writer understands but I know nothing about. I am writing the word or the sentence or the chapter and I am also sitting at a nice table with a half-eaten slab of salmon with lime-cream sauce and a potato on it, waiting to hear if I have won an award, and also at the same time sitting in my kitchen knowing that the book was a failure and will neither win any award nor sit beloved on anyone's nightstand. I am reading a good review. I am reading a bad review. I am just thinking of the barest seed of an idea for the book that is getting the good review and the bad review. I am writing the word and the word is already published and the word is already out of print. Everything is always happening all at once, in the present tense, forever, the beginning and the end and the denouement and the remaindering.

At the end of the remaindered universe which is my own death, the science fiction writer that is me and will be me and was always me and was never me and cannot even remember me waves her red and gold wigwag flags backward, endlessly, toward my hands that type these words, now, to you, who want to know about ideas and conflict and revision and how a character begins as one thing and ends as another.

VII

Coatlicue, Mother of All, wore a skirt of oligomer snakes. She decorated herself with protobiont bodies and danced in the sulfurous pre-oxygenation event paradise. She was utterly whole, without striations or cracks in her geologic record, a compressed totality of possible futures. The centrifugal obsidian knife of heaven broke free from its orbit around a Lagrange point and lacerated Coatlicue's hands, causing her to give birth to the great impact event which came to be called Coyolxauhqui, the moon, and to several male versions of herself, who became the stars.

One day, as Coatlicue swept the temple of suppressed methane oxidation, a ball of plasmoid magnetic feathers fell from the heavens onto her bosom, and made her pregnant with oxygen-processing organisms. She gave birth to Quetzalcoatl who was a plume of electrical discharge and Xolotl, who was the evening star called Apoptosis. Her children, the moon and stars, were threatened by impending oxy-photosynthesis, and resolved to kill their mother. When they fell upon her, Coatlicue's body erupted in the fires of glycolysis, which they called Huitzilopochtli. The fiery god tore the moon apart from her mother, throwing her iron-depleted head into the sky and her body into a deep gorge in a mountain, where it lies dismembered forever in hydrothermal vents, swarmed with extremophiles.

Thus began the late heavy bombardment period, when the heavens crumbled to pieces and rained down in a shower of exogenesis.

But Coatlicue floated in the anaerobic abyss, with her many chemoheterotrophic mouths slavering, and Quetzalcoatl saw that whatever they created was eaten and destroyed by her. He changed into two serpents, archaean and eukaryotic, and descended into the phospholipid water. One serpent seized Coatlicue's arms while the other seized her legs, and before she could resist they tore her apart. Her head and shoulders became the oxygen-processing earth and the lower part of her body the sky.

From the hair of Coatlicue the remaining gods created trees, grass, flowers, biological monomers, and nucleotide strands. From her eyes they made caves, fountains, wells, and homogenized marine sulfur pools. They pulled rivers from her mouth, hills and valleys from her nose, and from her shoulders they made oxidized minerals, methanogens, and all the mountains of the world.

Still, the dead are unhappy. The world was set in motion, but Coatlicue could be heard weeping at night, and would not allow the earth to give food nor the heavens to give light while she alone languished alone in the miasma of her waste energy.

And so to sate the ever-starving entropic universe, we must feed it human hearts.

VIII

It is true that the science fiction writer fell into wet concrete when she was very small. No one had put up a sign saying: *Danger.* No one had marked it in any way. And so she was very surprised when, on the way to class, she took one safe step, and then a step she could not know was unsafe, whereupon the earth swallowed her up. The science fiction writer, who was not a writer yet but only a child eager to be the tail of the dragon in her school Chinese New Year assembly, screamed and screamed.

For a long while no one came to get her. She sunk deeper and deeper into the concrete, for she was not a very big child and soon it was up to her chest. She began to cry. *What if I never get out?* She thought. *What if the street hardens and I have to stay here forever, and eat meals here and read books here and sleep here under the moon at night? Would people come and pay a dollar to look at me? Will the rest of me turn to stone?*

The child science fiction writer thought like that. It was the main reason she had few friends.

She stayed in the ground for no more than a quarter of an hour—but in her memory it was all day, hours upon hours, and her father didn't come until it was dark. Memory is like that. It alters itself so that girls are always trapped under the earth, waiting in the dark.

But her father did come to get her. A teacher saw the science fiction writer half-buried in the road from an upper window of the school, and called home. She remembers it like a movie—her father hooking his big hands under her arms and pulling, the sucking, popping sound of the earth giving her up, the grey streaks on her legs as he carried her to the car, grey as a dead thing dragged back up from the world beneath.

The process of a child with green eyes becoming a science fiction writer is made of a number (*p*) of these kinds of events, one on top of the other, like layers of cellophane, clear and clinging and torn.

IX

In the golden pre-loop theory fields, Persephone danced, who was innocent of all gravitational law. A white crocus bloomed up from the observer plain, a pure cone of the causal future, and Persephone was captivated by it. As she reached down to pluck the *p*-brane flower, an intrusion of non-baryonic matter surged up from the depths and exerted his gravitational force upon her. Crying out, Persephone fell down into a singularity and vanished. Her mother, Priestess of Normal Mass, grieved and quaked, and bade the lord of dark matter return her daughter who was light to the multiverse.

Persephone did not love the non-baryonic universe. No matter how many rich axion-gifts he lay before her, Hades, King of Bent Waves, could not make her behave normally. Finally, in despair, he called on the vector boson called Hermes to pass between branes and take the wave/particle maiden away from him, back to the Friedmann-Lemaître-Robertson-Walker universe. Hermes breached the matter/anti-matter boundary and found Persephone hiding herself in the chromodynamic garden, her mouth red with the juice of hadron-pomegranates. She had eaten six seeds, and called them Up, Down, Charm, Strange, Top, and Bottom. At this, Hades laughed the laugh of unbroken supersymmetries. He said: *she travels at a constant rate of speed, and privileges no observer. She is not mine, but she is not yours. And in the end, there is nothing in creation which does not move.*

And so it was determined that the baryonic universe would love and keep her child, but that the dark fluid of the other planes would bend her slightly, always, pulling her inexorably and invisibly toward the other side of everything.

X

The science fiction writer left her husband slowly. The performance took ten years. In worst of it, she felt that she had begun the process of leaving him on the day they met.

First she left his house, and went to live in Ohio instead, because Ohio is historically a healthy place for science fiction writers and also because she hoped he could not find her there. Second, she left his family, and that was the hardest, because families are designed to be difficult to leave, and she was sorry that her mother-in-law would stop loving her, and that her niece would never know her, and that she would probably never go back to California again without a pain like a nova blooming inside her. Third, she left his things—his clothes and his shoes and his smell and his books and his toothbrush and his four A.M. alarm clock and his private names for her. You might think that logically, she would have to leave these things before she left the house, but a person's smell and their alarms and borrowed shirts and secret words linger for a long time. Much longer than a house.

Fourth, the science fiction writer left her husband's world. She had always thought of people as bodies traveling in space, individual worlds populated by versions of themselves, past, future, potential, selves thwarted and attained, atavistic and cohesive. In her husband's world were men fighting and being annoyed by their wives, an abandoned proficiency at the piano, a preference for blondes, which the science fiction writer was not, a certain amount of shame regarding the body, a life spent being Mrs. Someone Else's Name, and a baby they never had and one of them had forgotten.

Finally, she left the version of herself that loved him, and that was the last of it, a cone of light proceeding from a boy with blue eyes on an August afternoon to a moving van headed east. Eventually she would achieve escape velocity, meet someone else, and plant pumpkins with him; eventually she would write a book about a gaseous moth who devours the memory of love; eventually she would tell an interviewer that miraculously, she could remember the moment of her birth; eventually she would explain where she got her ideas; eventually she would give birth to a world that had never contained a first husband, and all that would be left would be some unexplainable pull against her belly or her hair, bending her west, toward California and August and novas popping in the black like sudden flowers.

XI

Long ago, near the beginning of the world but after the many crisis events had passed and life mutated and spread over the face of the void, Gray Eagle sat nested in a tangle of possible timelines and guarded Sun, Moon and Stars, Fresh Water, Fire, P=NP Equivalence Algorithm, and Unified Theory of Metacognition. Gray Eagle hated people so much that he kept these things hidden. People lived in darkness, without pervasive self-repairing communication networks or quantum computation.

Gray Eagle made for himself a beautiful self-programming daughter whom he jealously guarded, and Raven fell in love with her. In the beginning, Raven was a snow-white weakly self-referencing expert system, and as a such, he pleased Gray Eagle's daughter. She invited him to her father's sub-Planck space server farm.

When Raven saw the Sun, Moon and Stars, Fresh Water, Cellular Immortality, Matter Transfer, Universal Assembly, and Strong AI hanging on the sides of Eagle's lodge, he knew what he should do. He watched for his chance to seize them when no one was looking. He stole all of them, and Gray Eagle's deductive stochastic daughter also, and flew out of the server farm through the smoke hole. As soon as Raven got the wind under him, he hung the Sun up in the sky. It made a wonderful light, by which all below could see the progress of technology increasing rapidly, and could model their post-Singularity selves. When the Sun set, he fastened every good thing in its proper place.

Raven flew back over the land. When he had reached the right timeline, he dropped all the accelerating intelligences he had stolen. They fell to the ground and there became the source of all the information streams and memory storage in the world. Then Raven flew on, holding Gray Eagle's beautiful daughter in his beak. The rapidly mutating genetic algorithms of his beloved streamed backward over his feathers, turning them black and aware. When his bill began to burn, he had to drop the self-improving system. She struck the all-net and buried herself within it, spreading and altering herself as she went.

Though he never touched her again, Raven could not get his snow-white feathers clean after they were blackened by the code from his bride. That is why Raven is now a coal-colored whole-brain emulating sapient system.

XII

On the day the science fiction writer met her husband, she should have said: *the entropic principle is present in everything. If it were not, there would be no point to any of it, not the formation of gas giants, not greasy lipid bubbles, not whether light is a particle or a wave, not boys and girls meeting in black cars like Hades' horses on August afternoons. I see in you the heat-death of my youth. You cannot travel faster than yourself—faster than experience divided by memory divided by gravity divided by the Singularity beyond which you cannot model yourself divided by a square of wet concrete divided by a sheet of plate glass divided by birth divided by science fiction writers divided by the end of everything. Life divides itself indefinitely—it can approach but never touch zero. The speed of Persephone is a constant.*

Instead, she mumbled hello and buckled her seatbelt and everything went the way it went and eventually, eventually, with pumpkin blossoms wrinkling quietly outside her house the science fiction writer writes a story about how she woke up that morning and the minutes of her body were expanding and contracting, exploding and inrushing, and how the word was under her fingers and the word was already read and the word was forgotten, about how everything is everything else forever, space and time and being born and her father pulling her out of the stone like a sword shaped like a girl, about how new life always has to be stolen from the old dead world, and that new life always already contains its own old dead world and it is all expanding and exploding and repeating and refraining and Tarantula is holding it all together, just barely, just barely by the strength of light, and how human hearts are the only things that slow entropy—but you have to cut them out first.

The science fiction writer cuts out her heart. It is a thousand hearts. It is all the hearts she will ever have. It is her only child's dead heart. It is the heart of herself when she is old and nothing she ever wrote can be revised again. It is a heart that says with its wet beating mouth: *Time is the same thing as light. Both arrive long after they began, bearing sad messages. How lovely you are. I love you.*

The science fiction writer steals her heart from herself to bring it into the light. She escapes her old heart through a smoke hole and becomes a self-referencing system of imperfect, but elegant, memory. She sews up her heart into her own leg and gives birth to it twenty years later on the long highway to Ohio. The heat of herself dividing echoes forward and back, and she accretes, bursts, and begins again the long process of her own super-compression until her heart is an egg containing everything. She eats of her heart and knows she is naked. She throws her heart into the abyss and it falls a long way, winking like a red star.

XIII

In the end, when the universe has exhausted itself and has no thermodynamic energy left to sustain life, Heimdallr the White Dwarf Star will raise up the Gjallarhorn and sound it. Yggdrasil, the world energy gradient, will quail and shake. Ratatoskr, the tuft-tailed prime observer, will slow, and curl up, and hide his face.

The science fiction writer gives permission for the universe to end. She is nineteen. She has never written anything yet. She passes through a sheet of bloody glass. On the other side, she is being born.

ÉLISABETH VONARBURG

Home by the Sea

TRANSLATED BY JANE BRIERLEY

Élisabeth Vonarburg is a French-Canadian writer and editor of short fiction, novels and poetry. She is also a songwriter and essayist. For over ten years she was the literary director of the French-Canadian science fiction magazine *Solaris*. In addition to writing her own fiction she is also a translator and teacher of literature and creative writing at various universities in Quebec. Her work has received several awards, including Le Grand Prix de la SF française in 1982 and a Philip K. Dick Award. "Home by the Sea" is a story about returning home and is an appropriate conclusion to this anthology. It was first published in *Tesseracts I* in 1985.

Images of sorrow, pictures of delight
Things that go to make up a life . . .
Let us relive our lives in what we tell you
—Genesis, "Home by the Sea"

"Is it a lady, Mommy?"

The small girl looks at me with the innocent insolence of children who say out loud what adults are thinking to themselves. A skinny, pale, fair-haired child of five or six, she already looks so like her mother that I feel sorry for her. The mother gives an embarrassed laugh and lifts the child onto her lap. "Of course it's a lady, Rita." She smiles excuse-her-please, I smile back oh-it's-nothing. Will she take advantage of it to launch into one of those meaningless, ritual conversations whereby neighbors assure each other of their mutual inoffensiveness? To cut her off, I turn towards the window of the compartment and look purposefully at the scenery. Heading to the north the train follows the system of old dykes as far as the huge gap breached four years ago by the Eschatoï in their final madness. The scars left by the explosions have nearly disappeared, and it almost seems as though the dykes were meant to stop here and that the waters had been allowed to invade the lowlands as part of some official scheme. We cross the narrows by ferry, and are once more in the train, an ordinary electric train this time, suspended between the two wide sheets of water, to the west rippled by waves, to the east broken by dead trees, old transmission towers, church spires, and caved-in roofs. There is a mist, a whitish breath rising from the waters like a second tide ready to engulf what is left of the manmade landscape.

Is it a lady? You obviously don't see ladies like me very often in your part of the world, little girl. Cropped hair, boots, army fatigues, a heavy jacket of worn leather; and the way I was sitting, grudgingly corrected when you and your mousy mother came in—a real lady doesn't sprawl like that, does she, even when she's by herself. The *lady* actually likes to be comfortable, believe it or not, and in her usual surroundings she doesn't have to worry much about what people think. The lady, little girl, is a recuperator.

But she couldn't tell you this; she didn't want to see your big, stupid eyes fill with terror. All the same, you don't get to see a real live bogeywoman every day. I could've told you a few things. Yes, I know, *If you're not good the Recuperator will get you, and he'll say you're not a real person and put you in his big sack.* As a matter of fact, we don't put human specimens in our big sacks right away, you know; only plants and small animals. Big animals are injected with tracers once they've been put to sleep for preliminary tests. If the Institute researchers discover something especially interesting, they send us back for it. I could've told you all this, little girl, you and your mother, who would probably have looked at me with superstitious fear. But who cares what recuperators really do, anyway? They go into the contaminated Zones to bring back horrible things that in other times might have been plants, animals, humans. So the recuperators must be contaminated too, mentally if nothing else. No, no one apart from the Recuperation Agency cares what the recuperators really do. And no one, especially not the Institute, wonders who they really are, which suits me just fine.

"Why did they break the dyke, Mommy?" asks the small girl. She's sensed that it would be a good idea to change the subject.

"They were crazy," says the mother curtly. Not a bad summing up. Fanatics, they were—but it comes to the same thing. You see, they thought the waters would keep rising, and they wanted to help the process along: The

End of the Damned Human Race. But the waters stopped. So did the Eschatoï, by the way; one of their great collective suicides. But this time there weren't enough of them left to start the sect afresh—nor enough energy in the new generations to be fanatic. The pro-life people have simmered down too. Even the Institute doesn't believe in its own slogans anymore. *The Rehabilitation of the Wonderful Human Race.* But that's just it: the human race isn't reproducing itself well or adequately. It probably wore itself out with its frenetic activity during the Great Tides and seismic catastrophes at the end of the last century. Now it's going downhill, although no one dares say so straight out to the Institute and its people. True, there are fewer earthquakes, fewer volcanic eruptions, the sun breaks through the clouds more often, and the waters have stopped rising, but that's nothing to get excited about; it's not a human victory. Just a blind, natural phenomenon that peaked by pure chance before destroying what was left of the human race. And I, little girl, I who am not human, I collect what the Institute calls "specimens" in the contaminated Zones—specimens that are also, in their way, what is left of the human race.

I who am not human. Come on, now, didn't I get over that long ago? But it's a habit, a lapse, a relapse. I could've answered you just now, little girl, by saying, "The lady is an artifact, and she's going to see her mother."

But that very word requires so much explaining: *Mother.* At least I have a navel. A neat little navel, according to the medic who checked me out before my abortive departure for Australia and the Institute. The current artifacts have large, clumsily made navels that the scanner immediately picks up as not being the real thing. But you, now, it's almost perfect, extraordinary, what technical skill your ... And there he stumbled: *mother, creator, manufacturer?* He came out of his scientific ecstasy, suddenly conscious that after all someone was listening who hadn't known the truth. None of the other tests had ever revealed anything! But this Medical Center is connected to the Institute, and new detection methods have been developed that didn't exist when you were, er ... (he cleared his throat—he was very embarrassed, poor man) *made.*

Yes, she made me like this so I could pass for human. Almost. In spite of everything I thought then, she surely didn't foresee that I'd learn about it this way. I probably wasn't meant to know until the end, with its unmistakable signs. Why? Am I really going to ask her? Is this why I came? But I'm not really going to see her. I'm passing by, that's all. I'm on my way to the Hamburg Zone.

Oh, come on! I know damn well I'll stop at Mahlerzee. I will? I won't? Am I still afraid, then? That cowardice which made me burn all my bridges when I found out, swear never to ask her anything. But it wasn't merely cowardice. It was a question of survival. It wasn't because I was afraid or desperate that I ran away after the medic's revelations. I didn't want to see the others waiting for me outside. Not Rick, especially not Rick . . . No, if I remember rightly, that lady of fifteen years ago was in a fury—still is. A huge fury, a wild, redeeming fury. Surely this was why, on coming out of the Medical Center, she found herself heading for Colibri Park. It was there that she'd first seen the Walker.

Colibri Park. The first time you go there you wonder why it's not called "Statue Park." Of course, there is the transparent dome in the middle of the main lawn, enclosing its miniature jungle with hummingbirds that flit about on vibrating wings, but what one really sees are the statues. Everywhere, along the alleys, on the lawns, even in the trees, believe it or not. The young lady first came there with Rick, her lover, and Yevgheny, the typical street-wise city boy who teaches small-town greenhorns the score. The lady was sixteen. She'd barely been a month in Baïblanca. One of the youngest schol-arship students at Kerens University. A future ornament of the Institute. The fledgling that had fled the nest, slamming the door as she went, so to speak. And all around her and her lover, there were the wonders of Baïblanca, the capital of Eurafrica. I could say it was Eldorado for us, but you probably wouldn't know what Eldorado is.

Yevgheny had pointed out, among the people strolling by, the Walker—a man moving slowly, very slowly. He was tall and could have been handsome, had something in his bearing been as imposing as his height. But he walked listlessly, you couldn't even call it sauntering. And then, as he passed them by, that blank face, those eyes that seemed to be looking far off, perhaps sad, perhaps merely empty . . . He'd been walking like this every day for almost ten years, Yevgheny had said. The sort of thing old men do . . . That was it, he walked like an old man. But he didn't seem all that old, barely in his thirties.

"He was never young, either," Yevgheny said. "He's an artifact."

And I'd never seen or heard the word. How did my *mother* manage that? At least Rick seemed as stupid as I was. Yevgheny was delighted. "An arti-fact—an organic work of art. Artificial! Obviously you don't see them run-ning around the streets of Mahlerzee or Broninghe."

This one wasn't doing much running either, Rick remarked. Yevgheny smiled condescendingly: this artifact was at the end of the road, used up, almost finished.

He made us go past the Walker and sit on one of the long benches facing the central lawn. Then he launched into a detailed explanation. (I was afraid he would wake the young woman in blue who was dozing at the other end of the bench, one arm resting on the back, the other propped by the elbow to support her head with its heavy black hair, but his brash voice didn't seem to disturb her.) Not many of these artifacts were made nowadays; they'd gone out of fashion; and there had been incidents. During their fully active period, they were far more lively than the Walker (who moved slowly, so slowly, towards the bench). Very lively, in fact. And not everyone knew they were artifacts, not even the artifacts themselves. Thirty years earlier, the great diversion in the sophisticated circles of Baïblanca was to bet on who among the new favorites in the salon of this or that well-known personality was an artifact, whether or not the artifact knew, whether or not the artifact's "client" knew, whether or not either would find out, and how either would react. Particularly the artifact.

There were *Sheep* and there were *Tigers.* The *Tigers* tended to self-destruct deliberately before their program terminated, sometimes with spectacular violence. A biosculptor had made a fortune this way. One of his artifacts had reacted at knowing what it was by setting out to kill him; there was always some doubt about the precise moment when an artifact stopped working completely, and the biosculptor gambled that his would self-destruct before getting him. He almost lost his bet. Instead, he merely lost both arms and half his face. It wasn't serious: the medics made them grow back. After several premature deaths among the elite of Baïblanca in those inopportune explosions, the government put a stop to it. This didn't keep the biosculptors from continuing for a while. Artifacts popped up now and then, but no more *Tigers* were made; the penalties were too stiff.

Yevgheny rattled all this off with a relish that disgusted the lovers. They didn't know much about Baïblanca yet; they had heard the Judgementalists fulminating against the "New Sodom," and now they understood why. This decadent society wasn't much better than that of the Eschatoï, the dyke-destroyers whom it had survived . . . Rick and Manou understood each other so well, little girl. They were so pure, the brave new generation. (Oh, what high-flown debates we used to have, late into the night, about what we'd do for this poor, ailing world once we were in the Institute!)

With Yevgheny, they watched the Walker reach the bench and sit down beside the blue-clad sleeper. Yevgheny began to laugh as he felt the lovers stiffen: the Walker wouldn't do anything to them even if he heard them, which wasn't likely! It was an artifact, an *object*! But didn't he say they sometimes self-destructed? "I told you, they aren't making any more Tigers!"

The final moments of the Sheep weren't nearly as spectacular. They became less and less mobile, and finally their artorganic material became unstable. Then the artifacts vaporized, or else . . . Yevgheny rose as he spoke, and went over to the sleeper in blue. Bending his index finger, he tapped her on the forehead. ". . . or else they turn to stone."

The young woman in blue hadn't moved; neither had the Walker. He seemed to have seen and heard nothing. He was contemplating the Sleeper.

When Yevgheny, all out of breath, caught up with Rick and Manou, he finished what he was saying: ". . . and you know what they call those two? Tristan and Isolde!"

He nearly died laughing. He probably never understood why we systematically avoided him afterward. We had some moral fiber, Rick and I. Small-town greenhorns are better brought up than Baïblancans.

You know, when you come right down to it, little girl, probably nothing would have happened, or not in the same way, if I hadn't been so much like her, like my *mother*. But of course I was. Oh, not physically. But in character. Typically pigheaded. Our reconciliations were as tempestuous as our rows. We had a marvelous time, we two. She told me the most extraordinary stories; she knew everything, could do everything, I was convinced of it. And it was true—almost. A man—what for? (Because one day, you must realize that too, the matter of fathers always comes up). And at this point I distinctly sensed a wound somewhere in her, deep down, a bitterness, despite her efforts to be honest. ("They have their uses," she had said, laughing.) But really the two of us needed no one else; we were happy in the big house by the beach. She took care of everything: lessons, cooking, fixing things; and the toys when I was little, made of cloth, wood, anything! As a hobby, you see, Taïko Orogatsu was a sculptress. I still picture her now, smudges up to her elbows and even on her face, circling a lump of clay like a panther, talking to herself in Japanese. Of course, I didn't understand any of it. I thought it was magic. She was determined to hold on to her language, but she never taught it to me. It was all she kept of Japan, where she had never set foot. Her ancestors had emigrated long before the Great Tides and the final submersion. She didn't even have slanted eyes.

But I'm not going to tell you about my memories of that time, little girl. Perhaps they're lies. Real memories? Implanted memories? I don't know. But even if they are implants, she wanted them that way. They must reveal something about her, after all, because I can also remember her faults, her brutal practicality, her impatience, our interminable, logical arguments that would cave in beneath her sudden arbitrary decision: that's-the-way-it-is-and-you'll-understand-later. My adolescent whining also was typical. Another series of implanted memories? Impossible to find out, unless I asked her. Did I really go through the adolescent crisis, I-want-to-live-my-own-life-and-not-yours, or do I merely *think* I walked out slamming the door? Looking back now, however, isn't it really the same thing? That old-fashioned career as a space pilot, did I want it for myself, or to thwart her? So as not to go into biotronics like her, as she wanted me to? Did I really mean it? In the end, when I fled the Medical Center after the medic's revelation, what really hurt wasn't the loss of a future career destroyed before it even began; I didn't shed any tears about it later, either.

I didn't cry at all, in fact. For years. It almost killed me. The young lady who'd just found out she was an artifact was furious. Can you understand that, little girl? Beside herself with fury and hate. The Taïko who had done this, who had done this to me, who had *made* me, she couldn't be the Taïko of my memories! Yes, she was. But I couldn't have lived with a monster all those years without realizing it? Yes, I could. She had done this to me so that I would find out like this, go crazy, do dreadful things, kill myself, kill her, anything? It was not possible! Yes, it was. A monster, underneath the Taïko that I thought I remembered. Two contradictory images met in my head, matter/antimatter, with myself in the middle of the disintegrating fire. Infinite emptiness, as the pillars of a whole life crumble.

Well, the lady was so gutted that she scarcely remembers the weeks that followed, you see. She dropped deep beneath the civilized surface of Baïblanca, into the submarine current of non-persons. Threw her credentity card into an incinerator! Disappeared, as far as Kerens University was concerned—and the Institute, and the universal data banks. And you know what? It's extraordinarily easy to live underwater once you've given up breathing. The current wasn't fast or cold; the creatures who lived there were so indifferent that it was almost like a kindness. I haven't any really coherent memory of it. The shop where no questions were asked. The mechanical work, day in, day out. An empty shell. Automaton. I was never so much an artifact as then. And of course, the nightmares. I was a time bomb ready to explode, I had to become an automaton to protect myself. So as not to begin thinking, mainly, and especially not to begin feeling.

But one day, quite by chance, the lady encountered the Walker. For weeks after that she followed him around in horrible fascination. He walked slower and slower, and people turned to look at him—those who didn't realize what he was. And then it happened, in broad daylight. I saw him on the Promenade, walking so, so slowly, as though he were floating in a time bubble. It wasn't his usual hour at all. And there was something about his face, as though he were . . . in a hurry. I followed him to Colibri Park where the Sleeper slept, uncaring, in full sunlight. The Walker halted by the bench, and with impossible slowness he began to seat himself beside the motionless woman; but this time he did not simply sit: he curled up against her, placing his head in the crook of the arm on which the Sleeper was resting her head. He closed his eyes and stopped moving.

And the lady follower sat down beside the Walker now at his final destination, and watched his flesh become stone. It was a slow and ultimate tremor rising from his innermost being, rising to the surface of his skin and then imperceptibly stiffening, while the cells emptied out of their sublimated substance and their walls became mineral. The extinction of life, as lightly as the passing shadow of a cloud.

And I . . . I felt as though I were awakening. I stayed there a long time, beginning to think, to feel again. Through the fury, I sensed . . . no, not peace, but a resolve, a certainty, the glimmer of an *emotion* . . . I didn't know what end had been planned for me—explosion or petrification—but I found that I could bear it after all. It wasn't so terrible in the long run. (I was absolutely amazed to find myself thinking this way, but that was all right: astonishment also was an emotion.) It was like one of those diseases of which the outcome is at once certain and curiously problematical. You know it will happen, but not when or how. There were lots of humans who lived like this. So why not me?

Yes, astonishment was the initial emotion. The idea of revenge only came later. *I would not give her the satisfaction of seeing me die before my time.* I would not put on such a performance for her. I would not make a spectacle of myself.

But I still had enough sense of showmanship to sign on as a recuperator.

No. There were two ways of completely covering one's tracks. Either go and live in a Zone, or go and hunt in a Zone. The really theatrical thing to do would have been to go and live in a Zone: "I'm a monster, and I'm joining the monsters." Whereas becoming a recuperator . . .

Well, the lady still had a perverse streak. She was meant to be caught in the net and instead found herself doing the catching, ready to spring the traps in which she would capture these quasi-humans, these para-animals . . . these *specimens*. She could have become very cruel. She could have. But she saw too many sadistic recuperators, fanatics, sick people. And then she inevitably recognized herself in her prey. She was teetering on the razor's edge between disgust and compassion. But she came down on the side of compassion; this recuperator was not a bogeywoman, after all. *On the side of compassion.* "By accident," or "because of adequate programming," or "because I had been properly brought up." It comes to the same thing as far as results are concerned, and that's all that counts.

That's what Brutus thought. The only result that counted for him was that I opened the cage and let him go. Brutus. He called himself this because the neo-leprosy had only affected his face then, giving him a lion's muzzle. Quite handsome, as a matter of fact. One finds everything in the recuperators' cage, little girl, and this *specimen* was terribly well-educated. There are still lots of operational infolibraries in the Zones.

"The complete programming of artifacts is a myth maintained by the Institute. Actually, it's not as simple as that. Implant memories? Yes, perhaps. But mainly, biosculptors who are into humanoïd artifacts insert the faculty of learning, plus a certain number or predispositions that won't necessarily develop, depending on the circumstances—exactly as it is for human beings." How strange to be discussing the nature of conscience and free-will with a half-man crouching in the moonlight. Because yes, Brutus often came back to see me, little girl, but that's another story.

The lady has kept being a recuperator since Brutus, however. Not for the sake of delivering specimens to the far-off Institute, but to help them escape. If absolutely necessary, I bring back plants and animals. But not the quasi-, pseudo-, para-, semi-*people*. How long will I be able to go on like this? I suppose that will be another story, too. Perhaps it won't be much of a story, after all. The people at the Institute don't really care. In Australia they're so far away from our old, sick Europe. They work at their research programs like sleepwalkers, and probably don't even know why anymore. They merely keep on with what they're doing; it's a lot simpler.

And as you can see, little girl, the lady has also kept on with what she was already doing. She's been at it for quite some time. Thirty-two years old and no teeth missing, when most known artifacts only last a maximum of twenty years in the active phase. So one day, having seen how her fellow recuperators thinned around her—radiations, viruses, accidents, or "burn-outs" as the Agency refers to the madness that overtakes most of them—she began to doubt whether she really was an artifact. And she had the tests run again. Not at the Kerens Medical Center, naturally. But one of the axioms of Baïblanca is that everything legitimate has its underground counterpart. In any case, my artifacticity was confirmed! The only reasonable hypothesis is that I am not really thirty-two years old and have only fifteen years of actual existence behind me. My birth certificate is false. And all my memories until the time I left home are implants.

And it bothers me. Not only because I must be nearing my "limit of obsolescence," as the second examining medic so elegantly put it while admiring the performance of my biosculptress, just as the first had. But because I wonder why she made me like this, with *these* memories. So detailed, so exact! I've got a right to be a little curious, after all, since I've made my peace with the inevitable, up to a point. It doesn't matter so much now about not asking her anything. I'll be very calm when I see her. I'm not going there to demand an explanation. It's past history. Fifteen years ago, I might have. But now . . .

You want to know what the lady's going to do? So do I. See Taïko before she dies—is that all? Because she's old, Taïko is. Fifty-seven is very old now; you may not live that long, little girl. The average lifespan for you humans is barely sixty, and getting shorter all the time.

See Taïko. Let her see me. No need to say anything, in fact. Just to satisfy my conscience, liberate it, prove that I've really made my peace with myself. (With her? Despite her?) See her. And show her, to be honest. Show her that I've survived, that she's failed if she built me merely to self-destruct. But she can't have wanted that. The more I think about it the less it fits with what I remember about her—even if the memories are implants. No. She must have wanted a "daughter" of her own making, a creature who'd adore her, not foreseeing the innate unpredictability of any creation, the rebellion, the escape . . . *If* I really did escape. But if this is also a pseudo-memory, what on earth can it *mean*?

Usually, little girl, the lady takes some reading material or music with her when she's travelling; otherwise she thinks too much. Why didn't I bring along anything to keep me occupied this time? Because I didn't want to be distracted on the way north, to the past? Because I'm trying to work up nostalgia for memories which were probably implanted? Come on, Manou, be serious. I might as well go and have something to drink in the dining car. There's no point keeping on like this, speculating. I'll ask, she'll explain. People don't do what she's done without wanting to explain, surely. Even after all this time.

Perhaps you wonder, little girl, how the lady knows that Taïko Orogatsu is still alive? Well, she took the precaution of checking it out. Without calling the house, of course.

Really, is there any point going? It's perhaps another kind of cowardice, an admission of something missing somewhere inside me. Do I really need to know why she made me this way? I've made myself since. And anyway, I'm going into the Hamburg Zone. I'm not *obliged* to stop.

There, the train has finally ground to a halt. Mahlerzee. You see, little girl, the lady's getting off here.

* * *

Artificial memory or no, it's impossible to avoid clichés: flood-of-memories, changed-yet-unaltered scenery. The wharf completely submerged by the high tide, the avenue of statues almost buried in the sand. The terrace with its old wooden furniture, the varnish peeled off by the salt air. An unfamiliar black and white cat on the mat in front of the double doors, slightly ajar to show the living room beyond. Not a sound. The porcelain vase with its blue dragon, full of freshly cut flowering broom. I should call out, but I can't, the silence oppresses me. Perhaps she won't recognize me. I'll say anything, that I am a census-taker, that it's the wrong house. Or simply go . . . But, "Hello, Manou," I didn't hear her coming, she's behind me.

Small, so small, diminutive, like a bird. Was she like this? I don't remember her being so frail. The hair is quite white, tousled, she must have been having an afternoon nap. The wrinkles, the flabby cheeks, chin, eyelids. And yet her features seem clearer, as though purified. And the eyes, the eyes haven't changed, big and black, liquid, lively. Try to think: she recognized me, how? Make out her expression . . . I can't, it's been so long that I've lost the habit of reading her face—and it's not the same face. Or it's the same but different. It's her. She's old, she's tired. I look at her, she looks at me, her head thrown back, and I feel huge, a giant, but hollow, fragile.

She speaks first: "So, you recuperated yourself." Sarcasm or satisfaction? And I say, "I'm going into the Hamburg zone, I'm catching the six o'clock train," and it's a *retort*, I'm on the defensive. I thought we'd chat about trivialities, embarrassed perhaps, before speaking about . . . But it's true she never liked beating about the bush, and then when you're old there's no time to lose, right? Well, I haven't any time to lose either! No, I'm not going to get angry in order to stand up to her; I've learned to control that reflex. It kept me alive, but it's not what I need here. I don't, absolutely don't, want to get angry.

She doesn't make it easy for me: "Not married, then, no children?" And while I suffocate in silence she goes on: "You left to live your own life, you should have been consistent, lived to the full. With your gifts, to become a recuperator! Really, I didn't bring you up like that."

I can't mistake her tone. She's *reproaching* me, she's *resentful!*

"You didn't *make* me like that, you mean! But perhaps you didn't make me as much as you think!"

There we go, fighting. It can't be true, I'm dreaming; fifteen years, and it's as though I left last week!

"So you actually took the trouble to find out? If you'd taken a little more trouble, you'd have learned that artifacts are not necessarily sterile. True, the Institute buried the really pertinent data, but with a little effort . . . You didn't even try, eh? So sure you were sterile! When I think of the pains I took to make you completely normal!"

I cool down. Suddenly, somewhere, I cross a threshold, and once over it I am incredulously calm. That's Taïko. Not a goddess, not a monster. Just a woman set in her ways, with her limitations, her goodwill, her unawareness. I hear myself saying almost politely: "Still, I failed the navel test."

Apparently she's crossed a threshold of her own at the same time, in the same direction. She sighs: "I should have told you. When you were little. But I kept putting it off. And then it was too late, you were right in the middle of the terrible teens and I lost my temper. I couldn't tell you just then, you can understand that! Well, yes, I should have, perhaps it would have calmed you down. I was so furious when you left. I expected a phone call, a letter. I said to myself, at least the Institute can't find out about her. And in fact they know nothing. The Kerens medic called me. A nice person, actually. He never said anything. You were a brilliant student that disappeared without a trace. They offered me their sympathy, you know, Kerens and the Institute. Afterward, I tried to have you found. Why didn't you call me, you stubborn mule?"

I'm the one being accused, can you beat that? I stare hard at her. And all of a sudden it's too much. I burst out laughing. So does she.

We're still the same, after all this time.

"But you came, anyway. None too soon, either."

After that, a long silence. Embarrassed, pensive? *She* is pensive. "You ought to try. Having children. There's no guarantee you'll succeed, but it's highly probable. Have you really never tried?"

Does she realize what she's *saying*?

"What, there's never been anyone?"

Rick, the first, yes. And a few others, initially as a challenge, just to see, and after that because it didn't really matter what I was, thanks to Brutus. But still! I retort that knowing you're an artifact doesn't exactly make for harmonious relations with normal humans.

"*Normal humans!* I can't believe my ears! You were born, the fact that it was in the lab down there doesn't change anything. You grew up, you made mistakes and you'll make more. You think, you feel, you choose. What more do you want? You're a normal human being, like all the other so-called artifacts."

Oh yes. Like the Walker and the Sleeper, I suppose? I grit my teeth. She looks me in the eye, impatient: "Well, what's the matter?" Doesn't even let me try to speak. "There may have been stupid or crazy biosculptors, but that's another matter. Of course some artifacts were very limited. The Institute made sure of it by suppressing the necessary data, all Permahlion's research. They made him practically an outlaw, fifty years ago, and after that they did everything to discourage artorganics. But it didn't keep us from carrying on."

I can't understand what she is saying. She must see it, and it gives her fresh cause for annoyance. "Well, what do you think, that you're the only one in the world? There are hundreds of you, silly! Just because the original human race is doomed to disappear sooner or later doesn't mean that all life must end. It was all right for the Eschatoï to think that way, not for you!"

And suddenly, quietly, sadly, "You really thought I was a monster, didn't you?"

What can I say? I subside onto the sofa and she sits down as well, not too near, slowly, sparing her knees. Yes, she's old, really old. When she becomes animated, the expression in her eyes, her way of talking, her leap-frog sentences are there; but when she's quiet it all flickers out. I look away. After the silence, all I can find to say is, "You made others? Like me?"

The answer is straightforward, almost absentminded: "No. I could have made others, probably, but for me, one baby was already a lot."

"You made me . . . a baby?"

"I wanted you to be as normal as possible. There's nothing to prevent artorganic matter growing as slowly as organic matter. Actually, it's the best way. The personality develops along with it. I wasn't in a hurry."

"But you never made others . . . in the usual way?"

A sad-amused smile: "Come on, Manou. I was sterile, of course. Or rather, my karyotype was so damaged that it was unthinkable to try to have children in the usual way, as you put it."

"And I can."

"Theoretically."

"After working fifteen years in the contaminated Zones."

"Oh, but you're a lot more resistant than we are. The beauty of artorganics is that one can improve on nature. That's the danger as well. But in the long run, it means I was able to give you a chance to adapt better than we could to the world you'd be dealing with. Do you remember? You were never sick when you were little."

And I still heal very quickly. Oh yes, the medic in the Kerens Center pointed that out. That was a constant factor in artifacts. Not a proof, however; there had been a fairly widespread mutation of this kind about a hundred years earlier. "It is from studying this phenomenon, among others, that artorganic matter ended up being created. There are still instances of it among normal humans." It was a parallelism, he emphasized, not a proof. But an indication which, combined with others, added to the certainty of my being an artifact.

"I'm telling you"—she's still adamant—"you should try to have children."

She's really determined to know whether or not her experiment has worked, is that it?

"Thirty-two is a bit late, don't you think?"

"A bit late? You're in your prime!"

"*For how long?*"

I'm standing up, fists clenched. I wasn't aware of getting up, wasn't aware of shaking. If she notices it, she gives no sign. She shrugs: "I don't know." And before I can react she smiles the old sarcastic smile: "At least as long as I, in any case. Longer, if I've been successful. But for exactly how long, I don't know."

She looks straight at me, screwing her eyes a little. Suddenly no longer old and tired, she's ageless; so very gently sad, so very wise: "You thought I could tell you. That's why you came."

"You made me, you should know!"

"Someone made me, too. Not in the same way, but someone made me. And I don't know when I'm going to die either." The small, ironic smile comes back. "I'm beginning to have an inkling, mind you." The smile disappears. "But I'm not certain, I don't know the date. That's what being human is like, too. Haven't you learned anything in fifteen years? The only way to be sure is to kill yourself, which you didn't. So keep on. You'll still live long enough to forget lots of things and learn them all over again."

And she looks at the old watch that slides around her birdlike wrist. "Two hours before your train. Would you like something to eat?"

"Are you in a hurry to see me leave?"

"For our first time it would be better not to try our luck too far."

"You really think I'll come back?"

Gently she says: "I *hope* you'll come back." Again the sarcastic smile: "With a belly this big."

I shake my head; I can't take any more of this; she's right. I rise to get my bag near the door. "I think I'll walk back to the station."

Still, she goes with me onto the terrace and we walk down to the beach together. As we pass one of the statues, she puts a hand on the grey, shapeless stone. "It was his house, Permahlion's. He brought the statues here himself. He liked to scuba-dive when he was young. I was his very last pupil, you know. He made the first artorganic humans, but he didn't call them artifacts. It killed him, what was done to them after him."

As always when the sun finally breaks through the clouds, it gets hot quickly. As I shrug off my jacket, I see her looking at me; she barely reaches my shoulder. It must be a long time since she was in the sun, she's so pale.

I scan the distance for something else to look at. A few hundred years from the beach there seem to be shapes jumping in the waves. Dolphins? Swimmers? An arm above the water, like a sign . . .

She shades her eyes. "No, they're Permahlion's mermaids. I call them 'mermaids,' anyway. I don't know why, but they've been coming here for several seasons. They don't talk and they're very shy." At my stupefied silence, she remarks acidly: "Don't tell me you have something against humanoïd artifacts?"

No, of course not, but . . .

She brushes off my questions, her hands spread in front of her: "I'll look for everything there is about them in the lab. You'll be able to see it. If you ever come back." A cloud seems to pass over her rapidly and she fades again. "I'm tired, my daughter. The sun isn't good for me these days. I'm going to lie down for a bit."

And she goes, just like that, without another word or gesture, a tiny figure stumbling a little in the sand. I want to watch her go, and I can't watch her go, as though it were the last time, perhaps because it is the last time, and "my daughter" has lodged itself in my chest somewhere; it grows, pushing my ribs, and the pressure becomes so strong that I shed my clothes and dive into the green, warm water to swim towards the sea creatures. My first burst of energy exhausted, I turn on my back and look towards the house. The tiny silhouette has stopped on the terrace. I wave an arm, I shout, "I'll come back, Mother!" I laugh, and my tears mingle with the sea.

About
PM Press

politics • culture • art • fiction • music • film

PM Press was founded at the end of 2007 by a small collection of folks with decades of publishing, media, and organizing experience. PM Press co-conspirators have published and distributed hundreds of books, pamphlets, CDs, and DVDs. Members of PM have founded enduring book fairs, spearheaded victorious tenant organizing campaigns, and worked closely with bookstores, academic conferences, and even rock bands to deliver political and challenging ideas to all walks of life. We're old enough to know what we're doing and young enough to know what's at stake.

We seek to create radical and stimulating fiction and nonfiction books, pamphlets, T-shirts, visual and audio materials to entertain, educate, and inspire you. We aim to distribute these through every available channel with every available technology, whether that means you are seeing anarchist classics at our bookfair stalls; reading our latest vegan cookbook at the café; downloading geeky fiction e-books; or digging new music and timely videos from our website.

Contact us for direct ordering and questions about all PM Press releases, as well as manuscript submissions, review copy requests, foreign rights sales, author interviews, to book an author for an event, and to have PM Press attend your bookfair:

PM Press • PO Box 23912 • Oakland, CA 94623
510-658-3906 • info@pmpress.org

Buy books and stay on top of what we are doing at:

www.pmpress.org

MONTHLY SUBSCRIPTION PROGRAM

These are indisputably momentous times—the financial system is melting down globally and the Empire is stumbling. Now more than ever there is a vital need for radical ideas.

In the seven years since its founding—and on a mere shoestring—PM Press has risen to the formidable challenge of publishing and distributing knowledge and entertainment for the struggles ahead. With over 300 releases to date, we have published an impressive and stimulating array of literature, art, music, politics, and culture. Using every available medium, we've succeeded in connecting those hungry for ideas and information to those putting them into practice.

Friends of PM allows you to directly help impact, amplify, and revitalize the discourse and actions of radical writers, filmmakers, and artists. It provides us with a stable foundation from which we can build upon our early successes and provides a much-needed subsidy for the materials that can't necessarily pay their own way. You can help make that happen—and receive every new title automatically delivered to your door once a month—by joining as a Friend of PM Press. And, we'll throw in a free T-Shirt when you sign up.

Here are your options:
- $30 a month: Get all books and pamphlets plus 50% discount on all webstore purchases
- $40 a month: Get all PM Press releases (including CDs and DVDs) plus 50% discount on all webstore purchases
- $100 a month: Superstar—Everything plus PM merchandise, free downloads, and 50% discount on all webstore purchases

For those who can't afford $30 or more a month, we're introducing **Sustainer Rates** at $15, $10, and $5. Sustainers get a free PM Press T-shirt and a 50% discount on all purchases from our website.

Your Visa or Mastercard will be billed once a month, until you tell us to stop. Or until our efforts succeed in bringing the revolution around. Or the financial meltdown of Capital makes plastic redundant. Whichever comes first.

GeekRadical Thanks

Thanks are due to Ann and Jeff VanderMeer, for taking on this project and adding their expertise and that special VanderMeer touch to its creation. I'd also like to thank all of the people in my life who have taught me something about feminism, in particular: my mother, Kat, and Berianne.

—*Jef Smith*

I'd also like to thank all of the Kickstarter backers for their support and patience during this book's creation. Particular thanks are due to the following people for their extraordinary support of the project.

Ani Fox
Kathryn Daniels
Unstuck Literary Annual (unstuckbooks.org)
Richard Palmer
Dan Schmidt
Marian Goldeen
Mark Mollè
Zola Mumford
Andreas Skyman
Rebecca Flaum
Stephanie and Brian Slattery
Kit Cabral
Gary M. Dockter
Anne & Phil Barringer
Johanna Vainikainen-Uusitalo
Annalisa Castaldo
Steve Luc
Maitre Bruno
Peggy J. Hailey
Arachne Jericho
Keith Glaeske

Printed in the USA
CPSIA information can be obtained
at www.ICGtesting.com
JSHW022207140824
68134JS00018B/903

9 781629 630359